Lilith looked at her over her shoulder, all sparkle and wickedness, and grinned so widely that perforce Celia produced a watery little smile in response.

'Well, if you don't care, then I do! No stupid boy shall upset my Celia. So, you do not know where he lives? That is no difficulty! We shall set old Hawks to seek out his address. She has her ways, the old besom, and shall set herself to it. Go and tell her, now, you hear me? His name is Lackland. *Lackland*. There cannot be many in London of such a name, who are surgeons! Hawks will find his father's house soon enough, I promise you. Go on, now—go and *tell* her!'

And Lilith stamped her foot and frowned, and wearily Celia rose to her feet and went. She knew better than to gainsay her mother when she was in such a mood of contrasting anger and softness, gaiety and rage as she was this morning. Celia had seen it all before. Her mother was always so when she found some new man to follow at her heels——

For the rest of the day Celia worked very hard at not thinking about her mother's interest in Jo Lackland, and worked even harder at not thinking about how she felt hers

Also by Claire Rayner in Sphere:

THE PERFORMERS BOOK I: GOWER STREET
THE PERFORMERS BOOK III: PADDINGTON GREEN
THE POPPY CHRONICLES VOL I: JUBILEE
THE POPPY CHRONICLES VOL II: FLANDERS
THE POPPY CHRONICLES VOL III: FLAPPER
REPRISE
MADDIE
CLINICAL JUDGEMENTS

CLAIRE RAYNER

The Haymarket

Book II of
THE PERFORMERS

SPHERE BOOKS LIMITED

A *Sphere* Book

First published in Great Britain by
Cassell & Co Ltd 1974
Corgi edition 1975
This edition published by Sphere Books Ltd 1991

Printed and bound in Great Britain by
Cox & Wyman Ltd, Reading

ISBN 0 7474 0741 X

Sphere Books Ltd
A Division of
Macdonald & Co (Publishers) Ltd
Orbit House
1 New Fetter Lane
London EC4A 1AR
A member of Maxwell Macmillan Pergamon Publishing Corporation

For Edwin Harper
(Unalarming, after all!)

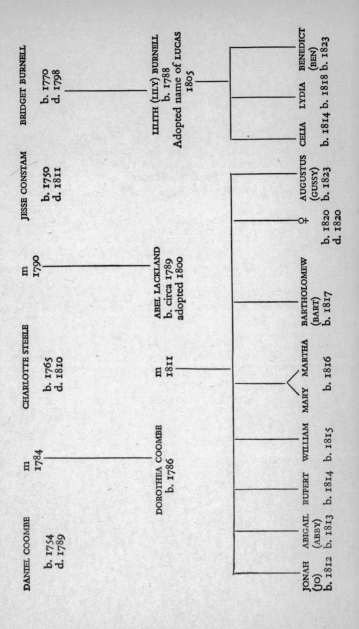

THE HAYMARKET

He could not quite make up his mind as to whether he should sit well forward in his box in order that he might the more easily observe the auditorium sweeping so elegantly away into the smoky glitter of the high balconies, or whether he should sit further back so that his view into the stage wings remained unimpeded. And although he was loth to admit it, even to himself, there was the question of simple prudence to be taken into account. To be here at all, and on such a night, was a defiance of his father that was quite breathtaking in its impudence. To compound it further by being observed by some member of the audience who might be acquainted with his father, and who might mention in passing that he had been so observed, would be less than politic. It had been hot-headed enough to have told Edward where he was going——

Not, he assured himself, as he arranged the little gilt chair towards the back of the box, and disposed his long legs on it with what comfort he might, not that it matters one whit to me what he says! He shall learn, indeed he shall learn, that I am not to be treated like some schoolroom chit. Let him give his orders and his demands to Rupert and William, to the girls, to Bart and little Gussie. He may have joy of their obedience. For my part, I care not what he does——

But there was, after all, a certain stylishness to be found in sitting there in such a way that no more than the gleam of his white piqué waistcoat—an elegant and exceedingly fashionable single-breasted waistcoat, to boot—should be observed from the body of the house. He fell to imagining the glances that would be cast at the stage box by fashionable ladies sitting in the stalls below him, and tried to thrust his father and his anger to the back of his mind.

But not with much success. While one part of him played the young-man-about-town who sat in the stage box at the Haymarket Theatre every night of his life, if he so chose, with one slimly trousered leg thrown with stylish laziness over the other, and perusing the playbill with a bored expression on his face, another part of him shrank deep inside, a prey to all the fears of not quite seventeen years old.

Suppose he were to beat him? Abel had never in all his life beaten any of his children; he had always been too remote and altogether too chill a figure for so human an action; yet Jonah knew of the power of his father's temper. He had seen him once attack a footman who had turned a patient away from the door with abusive language, and had cringed against the wall of the staircase, an unobserved seven-year-old terrified half out of his wits as the servant had been beaten to almost insensible bloodiness before dragging himself away whimpering and shaking, leaving Abel white-faced and rigid with rage in the hallway. Small Jonah had fled up the stairs to the comfort of his mother's boudoir that night, and had kept an even greater distance from his large and alarming father thereafter; and now, for all his apparent insouciance he remembered the sight of his father's fury and shook a little. *Suppose* he were to beat him?

Well, if he did attempt it, he might find he got more than he bargained for. Jonah stretched his legs out before him, and looked approvingly at their length, at the well-muscled thighs and calves the snug cloth so clearly delineated, and reminded himself that he was nigh as tall as his father now, and lighter on his feet, no doubt, and younger——

But that didn't help. Jonah bleakly surveyed the picture of his father that rose in his mind's eye, the long lean body, the squared shoulders, the legs as muscled and hard as his own. For a man of so many years as thirty-nine Jonah had to admit Abel carried himself remarkably well.

Well, if it came to a fight, so it did. It would settle matters one way or the other. That was all he wanted; an end to this disagreement between them.

For a moment Jonah tried to imagine a different situation, one in which a young man newly left school could tell his father that he had no wish to be a surgeon but asked no more of life than to be allowed to make his way in the world by means of his pen, and would enjoy his father's approval of his ambition, his admiration of the poems and polemics, essays and stories that his talented son displayed to him, all culminating in an agreement to permit him—nay, *encourage* him—to follow his vocation. But imagination shivered and balked at so impossible a picture, and Jonah was again in the stage box at the Haymarket Theatre, a very young and very worried rebel.

Celia, standing on the prompt side in the shadow of the wing flats, had noticed him as soon as he entered his box. Quite apart from the fact that the auditorium was still very thin of people, for it wanted half an hour yet to the start of the play and it was unusual for the occupant of the stage box to be so early (for fashion decreed a noisy late entrance for those rich enough to afford the most expensive seat in the house) he was noticeable because of his good looks; and although Celia, unlike silly Lydia, was not particularly interested in mere good looks (for heaven knew she saw enough handsome people hanging about the theatre and her mother) she was not totally immune to them. Now, because she was bored, and because she did not want to think about the scene that had just passed between herself and her mother—indeed, she would *not* think about it—she fell to watching the young man.

Certainly he was pleasant to look at. His hair was dark and curly, gleaming warmly in the bright gaslight that illumined his box, and most fashionably cut with curls on his forehead and a pair of creditably thick side whiskers. His eyes were wide and light-coloured—that much she could tell, though the precise colour was not discernible at this distance—and he was tall and clearly well-made under the fashionable evening suit that he wore. No stays were needed to produce that narrow waist, of that she was sure; he moved too easily to be corseted. And there was something about the set of his neck that showed his shoulders were not all modern padding. She guessed him to be perhaps two or at most three years her senior (in which she was not far wrong, for she was more than midway between her fourteenth and fifteenth birthdays) but trying to ape one much older.

She wanted to giggle as he moved his chair forwards, and peered down at the auditorium, and then hitched himself back, before trying out various postures, eventually settling to a rather stiff pose of would-be casual elegance. There was something very endearing about his unsureness of himself; she who had seen so many real men of the town, had grown up knowing how truly sophisticated men moved, talked, behaved, found this fresh young man on the far side of the vast stage a person to whom she could warm. She too knew what it was like to feel the need to put on a pose for others' benefit. She too knew the loneliness of sitting in solitude, and pretending to be someone quite other.

She watched his face for a while, as he sat there staring into the middle distance, and wished with a sharp curiosity that quite startled her that she knew what thoughts they were that chased such expressions across his face. He looked by turn angry and alarmed and stubborn and then alarmed again, and she moved forwards a little in order to see him better, all the time staring at him, and, as she always did, unconsciously imitating what she saw.

Jonah was now rehearsing a conversation with his mother inside his head, in which he would tell her that though he knew how deeply it would grieve her the time had come for him to leave Gower Street for good and all; and though he wished, deeply, that he had no need to ask her aid he would, he feared, have to seek some financial support from her if it were within her grasp to provide it. And he suddenly became aware of the figure on the other side of the stage as it moved into a pool of light thrown from the gas jet high above.

He saw a girl, tall and rather square-shouldered, with long dark hair lying on her shoulders unfashionably straight though thick and glossy, and wearing a rather old-fashioned and childish white muslin gown. But it was not her clothes he noticed so much as her face, for she was grimacing quite ferociously at him, alternately frowning and then raising her eyebrows. He blinked and set his head on one side in puzzlement, and immediately she followed suit, and at once he flushed a dull and angry red. The child was *imitating* him; she was standing there in the wings of the theatre, and staring at him and imitating him quite unashamedly.

Suddenly he could hear his mother's soft voice inside his head again, but now saying fondly, 'My darling little boy, you should not tell me lies, you know! You have so open and expressive a countenance, my own, that all you think is writ large upon it!' and he reddened even more deeply as he wondered how long she had been observing him and what she had read upon his face.

The girl on the other side of the stage was looking at him now with her upper lip caught between her teeth and an expression of ludicrous anxiety on her face, and this time it was she who blushed. He could see the tide of colour move up her white face even at this distance and it pleased him to see it, pleased him to see her discomfiture. She deserved it for being so shocking ill-mannered. Were she his sister he would tell her how to mend her ways, he told himself, just as he told Abby when it was needful (he ignored the fact that the spirited Abby gave him back as good as she got) but now he merely looked superciliously at her and dropped his eyes to his playbill. He would not give her the gratification, chit as she was, of knowing that he cared at all about her ill manners.

But when he raised his eyes again, with great casualness, he was a little surprised to find how piqued he was that she had disappeared.

Dorothea stood in the dining-room, gazing at the table with its load of shining crystal and silver, its heavy white linen and yellow wax candles, and tried to concentrate on what Jeffcoate was saying.

'Cook regrets the accident with the salmon, ma'am, but ventures to say you will not find it amiss when it comes to table, since she has dressed it with cucumbers, and will send it second to the turbot. With your permission, ma'am, I believe it best to serve it at the sideboard, rather than *à la russe*. I doubt then the Master will be aware of any mishap.'

'No,' Dorothea said vaguely, not in the least concerned whether or not Abel would be aware of the broken state of the salmon, knowing as she did that he rarely noticed any such mundane matters as the food he ate. 'No, I daresay you are right——'

'And the roast turkey, ma'am, and the roast leg of mutton for the removes, with six entrées, you will recall. The casserole of rice with *purée* of game, the salmi of young partridges *à l'espagnole*, the *vol-au-vent* of chicken with truffles, the——'

'Yes, Jeffcoate,' Dorothea said edgily as his voice began to penetrate her consciousness, overlaying her desperate anxiety with a sense of nausea at the relish with which he enunciated each dish. 'I am sure you have arranged all to a perfection, and I am indeed appreciative of your efforts. I would not have left so much to you had I not been—had not Master Jonah—if it had not occurred that—Oh, Jeffcoate, do, please, go and see again whether he has returned! I would not have him disturb this evening for all the world, and I am so alarmed that he might have come to some mischief——'

Jeffcoate looked at her with a faint expression of mingled pity and disgust on his face; that a lady should so demean herself to speak to her servants so! But the pity won at the sight of her wide and pale eyes pleading in the narrow pinched face.

'Indeed, ma'am, I knew of your concern, and spoke again to Edward about him not ten minutes ago. I am sure he has come to no harm, for Edward now tells me he put on all his best fig—his evening clothes, ma'am, and took the entire contents of his cashbox, and said if he was asked for we was to tell his father that he had gone to the theatre for the evening, and would dine in a chophouse, for he had no mind to discuss such matters as his father chose——' He coughed then. 'I took it upon myself, ma'am, not to deliver the message to Mr Lackland, thinking you would rather I spoke to you of it first——'

Dorothea had closed her eyes in anguish but now she opened them, and spoke with all the dignity she could muster. 'Thank you, Jeffcoate. You did well, indeed. I do thank you, indeed I do. Oh, the *wretched* boy——' Her pale face took on a tinge of pink, and she stamped her foot in a sudden petulance. 'How *could* he treat me so? He must know I will suffer as much as he at such a display of—oh, well, thank you, Jeffcoate, I need not disturb you further, I think, until dinner is served—though if it ever gets so far, once his father discovers his absence, does not bear considering and—oh, do go *away*, Jeffcoate. You must see that my nerves are sorely irritated just at present!'

And Jeffcoate withdrew to tell the cook and the footman and the extra servants hired for the evening of the situation that was brewing above stairs (and to tell it with great glee, for none enjoyed discomfiture of their employers more than the servants in the Lackland household) leaving Dorothea in a state of wretched misery as she stood undecided and almost sick with alarm in her candle-lit dining-room.

Abby found her there a few minutes before seven o'clock, when she came down ready dressed for dinner. She stood at the door for a moment and looked at her mother standing there beside the table, picking mechanically at the tines of one of the forks, and pitied her deeply, though feeling the usual wave of irritation rising in her.

That Mama should be so lily-livered! She created her problems with Papa, indeed she did, and if only she could be made to see it, how much happier they would all be. If she would but stand up to his anger the way Abby herself did, then he would soften to her, surely, as he always did when Abby behaved so, and life would be much pleasanter. But she knew her mother to be long past the stage of changing her behaviour, and now she crossed the room and put her arm about her mother's thin shoulders and hugged her briefly.

'Now, Mama, there is no sense in standing here and quaking! To be sure, Papa will be greatly put out by Jonah's silliness—to pick such a night to take himself off in one of his sulks—the boy has not the wit he was born with! But standing here bemoaning it will not help. We must decide what we shall tell Papa, and how we shall contrive to——'

'Oh, Abby, what shall we do?' Dorothea looked up at her daughter, who despite her mere sixteen years stood almost half a head taller than herself, and her eyes were pink and damp. 'When your Papa discovers that he has—where he has gone—oh, Abby, if he had sought about for the very worst thing he could do, he could not have found a greater insult!'

'Wherever he has gone, Mama, it matters not a whit. All that need concern us is that he is not here and——'

'He told Edward he has gone to the theatre!' Dorothea almost wailed it. 'And though Jeffcoate told me they will not tell your father, you know what servants are! And if—when he hears that——'

'Oh.' Abby's face sobered, and she stood very still for a moment, looking at her mother with both hands held consideringly to her mouth in one of her most characteristic poses. 'Oh dear! That was indeed more than usually foolish of him, if that were possible.'

She sighed sharply then, and moved purposefully, rearranging the lace at the neck of her mother's gown, and gently leading her away from the table.

'Well! There is still no sense in our standing here debating. Gone he is, perhaps, but I shall see to it that neither Edward nor Jeffcoate speak to Papa of it tonight. Now, Mama, go to the drawing-room, please, and await your guests there. I shall speak to Jeffcoate—and do not look like that at me, Mama! Come! We shall contrive. I always have, have I not?'

Dorothea stood still and looked up at her daughter, and then smiled a little thinly. 'Yes. You always have, indeed. But there, you are not as I am, are you? You are more of a person for whom he can easily show regard——'

Abby flushed a little at that, and a little more firmly again put her hand on her mother's shoulder, and urged her towards the door. 'Well, that is as may be,' she said, a little roughly, for she was suddenly shy. 'But he has a deep regard for you as well, Mama, and for Jonah also, although I know you doubt it. It is just that——'

'Indeed, I know!' Dorothea was standing with her hand on the door-knob now, and she lifted her chin a little. 'Indeed, I know. No man could have a wife who cared more deeply for his welfare, nor could any wife be so happy in her state as I! But it was ever the case that a man's daughter can be more beguiling to him than his wife—or his son——' Her moment of pride shivered then, and melted. 'You will speak to the servants, Abby? And—when Papa asks about Jonah you will——'

'Not to fret yourself, Mama! We shall contrive,' Abby said gently, and Dorothea nodded, and turned and went tremulously upstairs to her drawing-room.

2

He had quite forgotten his situation. He had forgotten everything but the enchantment of the moment. There before him, so close beside him on the stage that if he reached out his hand he could touch them, the actors moved, and spoke, and moved again, unfolding their story of misunderstandings and wilful maidens and wicked younger sons with smooth eloquence, and all for him. The painted scenery had melted into reality under the golden gaslights, the painted actors had completed their sea-change from grimacing strutting dolls to creatures of total reality so that they *were* Lords and Ladies and cheeky maids and artful grooms, and he knew them all intimately, and loved them all dearly, and they in return capered and bowed and spoke to him, and for him, and only him. He could not recall ever knowing such pleasure in all his life, and he laughed and clapped and cried aloud, and threw himself into his joy with total abandonment.

Especially did he love her, the splendid quicksilver creature in the blue dress, the girl with the sparkling narrow green eyes and curls that bounced so enticingly on her slender neck as, light as a puff of wind, she flitted about the stage, especially did he respond to her with applause and laughter, and once or twice almost with tears.

When she had first come on, slipping into the centre of the stage as though it were the only place she could possibly be, to the greeting of a great roar of delight from the packed auditorium, he had been a little startled. Her eyes, with black lines painted so heavily about them, the incredible scarlet of her mouth, the impossible rosiness of her cheeks, all combined to make him feel, just for a moment, that he was asleep, that none of this was real, that at any second he would wake in his narrow white bed in the long dormitory of Mr Loudoun's school in Islington.

But then she moved and spoke, and it was all real again, more than real, for it was now as though reality were the dream, and the only thing that mattered, that could ever matter, was the action going forward on the stage. Would the naughty lady in the blue dress beguile her harsh father, would she avoid the unwanted elderly husband, would she find her lover, would the scheming maid spoil all, would the tangle never be put right?

The curtain swished, and thudded heavily against the wooden boards of the stage, and the audience roared and screamed and stamped, and the girl in blue was skipping forward and curtseying deeply, over and over again, as flowers came up to meet her out of the dark auditorium, and still she dipped and smiled her brilliant smile, and still Jonah sat and stared at her, unwilling to let it all go. He knew it was all over, knew the enchantment had to end, but he did not wish to relinquish it ever.

But when the curtain at last stayed closed, no longer parting in response to the cries of the audience, and the gaily dressed and painted throng below him began to move unwillingly out of the theatre, he stirred himself, and stretched a little, and then stood, doubtful and filled again with that slightly sick anxiety that had been part of him this past six days, ever since he had come home from school for the last time.

Now what? He had made his gesture. He had refused to be at home for this dinner about which his father was so determined; worse still, he had gone to the theatre—and told them at home he was doing so. The bravado that had kept him buoyant thus far began to deflate, now that the adventure was so very nearly over and the time had come to return and face his father and admit that yes, he *had* done the one thing his father hated above all; he *had* gone to a theatre. The anxiety in him thickened and clotted and became actual fear.

He moved out of his box, his overcoat over his arm, to stand bareheaded in the throng of top-hatted men and elegant women moving along the narrow passageway outside. He had no money in his pocket, he was thinking mournfully. Every penny he had had left of his term's allowance had gone on the price of the box. He could not even go to a chophouse for a meal, and he was suddenly very aware of the thrust of hunger in his young belly.

'I think, my dear Lady Margaret, that you will find him in the greenroom before us,' a voice came flutingly out of the chattering crowd that was pushing past him. 'You know he can never abide to be outpaced by anyone——'

The greenroom. Jonah brightened a little. He had been to very few theatres, heaven knew, and only on those few occasions during the past three years or so when he and fellow choice spirits from school had sneaked away for a night of truancy at a pantomime, so he had never visited a greenroom. But he knew of them. He knew that for some fortunate members of the audience there was this chance to meet the actors and talk to them, and gossip and drink and——

He let himself be moved by the crowd then, allowed himself to be swept along. He was no longer a schoolboy, after all, but a man grown, and one who was to be a poet, no matter what his father said about the study of surgery. Why should he not go to the greenroom as well as anyone else in this noisy, glittering, sweating crowd?

James Caspar knew at once that something was wrong.

He had been looking forward with mixed feelings towards this dinner, ever since the day three weeks ago when Abel had made one of his rare visits to the shop in Piccadilly, and told him in his usual dry fashion that there were business matters to discuss, matters which would involve his son Jonah and the governors of the hospital as well as himself, and that the best way to arrange such talks was to hold a meeting at Gower Street.

'Eat your dinner with us, Caspar, and we shall talk more easy and with smallest waste of time. Seven o'clock. We shall be looking for you.'

That the 'business matters' would have something to do with an even earlier visit Abel had made to the Piccadilly shop, some three months earlier, James was fairly certain. His employer was not one given to being over-generous with information, but he had not hidden the way his interest had been kindled by the conversation they had had that day.

James had been sitting hunched over his desk on that June morning, his apothecary's brass scales set up before him, working yet again on his attempt to devise a truly accurate measure for Decoction of Dried Whole Ox Kidney. This favoured ingredient of many of the medicines he prescribed for obstruction of breathing, wheezing in croup, runnings of the nose due to the season of the year and similar afflictions, he had first learned of from old Josiah Witney, who had himself learned of it from his master, a man much given to the use of country remedies. At first James had been a little doubtful of its value, for the use of animal parts seemed to him a most repugnant and old-fashioned form of apothecary's care; but the material had proved itself too effective to dismiss so easily. And on that morning he had been cock-a-hoop when Abel had arrived, bringing the smell of fresh air and the horse-busy streets into the powdery, aromatic stuffiness of the shop.

He had looked up at Abel and with his narrow face uncharacteristically flushed had said impulsively, 'It has been staring me in the face these many months, and I never saw it, fool that I am! The way to do it is to mix the decoction with the base, do you see, in standard amounts, and then measure that in scruples. I can add what I will thereafter, and still have an even distribution of the kidney in each pill!'

'Which pill?' Abel had asked a little absently, shrugging off his heavy-caped coat, and moving across the room to start looking through the ledgers, nowadays his only purpose in coming into the shop, for though he was the owner of the establishment he had long been content to leave its day-to-day running largely in James's careful hands. 'Is this yet another of Caspar's mixtures to add to the battery of medications upon our shelves?'

James had hardened his jaw a little at the note of dismissal in the other's tone. 'I seek such standard mixtures not so much to glorify my name, sir, as to make more economic use of the skills I have!' he had snapped, and Abel had looked up, a little startled, and then smiled thinly.

'I am sorry if I offend you, Caspar!' he had said. 'Indeed I am—but I am somewhat out of touch with my old trade, as you well realize. Tell me, do, of the problem you have solved. It must indeed have been a most knotty one that you show such gratification at its resolution.'

'I have been seeking a way to standardize the use of ox kidney,' James said, a little sulkily at first but then more eagerly as his interest overcame his chagrin. 'You will recall its usefulness in many cases, but I have been limited in my application of it for I could find no way to hold the dose stable while I stored it, and to make a fresh decoction each time it is required——' He shook his head. 'It is hardly practical

20

for ordinary purposes. For this reason I have found myself using it too often for the richer of our patients who will gladly pay for my time but neglecting it for the ordinary sort. And that is hardly the best practice of the skill of an apothecary——'

Abel had raised his eyebrows at that, and James had gone on, tumbling over his words a little. 'And apart from this, there is the question of other costs. A fresh decoction each time is most wasteful of the substance itself, for it rapidly deteriorates. But now I have this method, I believe I can make a standard pill that will have an excellent effect and be able to keep it about us and sell at a reasonable price.'

He had left his scales to bring to Abel a small box, and held it out to him, and Abel had taken one of the pink-tinted globules it contained between his thumb and forefinger and turned it, staring at it with his eyes a little narrowed as he thought.

'They are an uncommon colour,' he said after a moment and James blushed a little.

'So often these breathing pills are required for the treatment of children,' he said, 'so I amused myself seeking a way to make them more interesting. The base I use is tragacanth, of course, but I dip 'em in sugar boiled with cochineal. 'Twill mask the bitterness of the kidney and the ipecac. I made a basic mixture, do you see, Mr Lackland, one grain of the kidney, and one grain each of opium and ipecacuanha in each pill. A child could take but one to relieve an affliction of his lungs while an adult could have two or even three. Neither would come to harm.'

Abel had sat in silence for a while, still turning the sugared pill between his fingertips, and then said sharply, 'I believe there are no other apothecaries using ox kidney?'

James had laughed at that. 'Why no, Mr Lackland, you know how hard they mocked at Mr Witney for it, and I have long since learned to keep my mouth shut in my fellows' company, for they would mock yet. But they can laugh as much as they please, for my part. While the medicine has an effect, I will use it——' He hesitated then. 'I have found another use for it that may interest you. You will recall Mr Holmere the lawyer's clerk of Lyon's Inn? For all he lives so far from the shop, he honours me by calling me always when he has need of an apothecary——'

Abel had nodded. 'He has an ulcer of the stomach, as I recall. There is little to be done for him, except to rest him and bleed him when the attacks are on him.'

'Lately he has been vomiting blood,' James said. 'And has become very thin, for he cannot eat without the food setting fire to his belly. So I made for him a pill—for he would not have a mixture, finding it difficult to bear the bottle about with him, and preferring a medicine he can take quietly when he is in court or about his affairs—and it has been of great use to him. He says his symptoms have much abated, and I have tried the same pill on others, and they too say it is of value——'

Abel cocked his head encouragingly, never taking his eyes from ames's face. 'And what is in this pill of yours?'

'Mag. Carb. Pond. for its aid against the acid in his constitution, but I added to it a grain of opium as well as a grain of the kidney, together with some peppermint. It makes a big pill, to be sure, but it can be chewed like a sugar plum for it does not taste too ill, and it stops the bleeding within the stomach and that is its prime value.'

'A useful remedy,' said Abel slowly, 'and one that you can prepare at a good low cost?'

James had gone back to his desk, taking his sugary pink pills with him. 'It could be lower yet, no doubt, were I able to obtain my supplies for making them in greater amounts. However——'

Abel had gone on with his study of the ledgers, but clearly he was abstracted, and very soon had closed them with a snap. 'I will try some of your pills at the dispensary, Caspar. Supply me with several boxes, for I have patients who display such symptoms as your Mr Holmere— we shall try their efficacy for the people of Seven Dials.'

And James had been more than content to agree, and had worked late that night and indeed every night that week to prepare the pills, wishing, not for the first time, that there was some way to lessen the effort needed for laborious massing of the base, the addition of the drugs, the further labour of cutting, weighing, rolling, dipping, counting, packing——

And then, three weeks ago, Abel had returned with his brusque invitation, and deeply interested and curious though James had been, he soon shrugged off his ponderings, for that was the only practical thing to do. Abel Lackland was not one to say a word before he was ready, so there was small point in giving any thought to it. Instead he thought about Abigail—and felt the old familiar wrench inside, and ached with it.

Ever since he had seen her for the first time on her emergence from the schoolroom on her fifteenth birthday, over a year ago now, it had been like this. Wanting her, that tall neat young woman with the quiet rather plain face and the square sensible hands. He had told himself, over and over, that she was a child half his age, and his employer's daughter to boot (and, he shrewdly suspected, a favourite child at that, for Abel had talked of her sometimes with a gentle note in his voice, whereas he spoke rarely of Jonah, and then sharply, and even less often of the handful of younger children still in schoolroom and nursery). But it had made no difference. He could not see her as a child, only as a young woman, a quiet, warm and wise young woman who had the ability to make his belly constrict with a sharp tug of need for her by no more than a turn of her head, a faint smile that lifted the corners of her wide mouth, a friendly quirk of one eyebrow when she caught his eye. He could not remove her from his mind.

Not, he had thought a little wryly, that he had been given much chance to do so. Dorothea had brought Abigail to the shop on that day they had first met, saying that as she was now to leave the schoolroom behind and go a little into society with her mother she could be permitted to choose and use some of the more innocuous of the complexion washes the shop had to offer.

Thereafter, Abigail had come many times without Dorothea, sending her maid off on some errand or other and sitting with James in his office behind the shop, and talking to him gravely about the business of an apothecary, asking him how it was he worked for her father instead of himself, for was he not an apothecary in his own right? And James had explained a little of his history, though telling her nothing of his sudden descent into poverty in his youth, of the early orphanhood that had fixed him so unwillingly close to her father's side (for there was much of deep personal pride in James Caspar, however little of it he showed in his quiet mien and controlled behaviour) only telling her how he had come as second apprentice to old Josiah Witney when her father Abel had been senior apprentice but also a student of surgery, how with Josiah's increasing ill health and Abel's increasing preoccupation with his dispensary in Tavistock Street he had become more and more the person upon whom the shop depended.

23

'And since old Mr Witney died two years ago, Miss Lackland, and your father has used some of his inheritance from him to turn the dispensary into a hospital, why, I have been needed here more than ever.'

'I wish you would call me Abby,' she had said, and smiled at him so that for a moment his belly had contracted in that sick familiar way and he had wanted very much to put out his hand and touch her, and had reddened and then stammered a little.

'Indeed, Miss—Abigail, you honour me. I—it is kind in you to take such an interest in my work.'

'Oh, pooh!' she had said, and laughed suddenly, and her rather plain square face had wrinkled into real prettiness. 'I have no illusions about my grandeur, Mr Caspar. And may I call you James? *Mr Caspar* sounds very stiff and unkind in my ears—as I say, I have no illusions. My Papa has told me of his youth. Do you know of it, James?'

'A little.'

'You are embarrassed? Yes, I think you are! Why should you be? Papa has no shame that he was a gutter boy, with no name of his own, nor I any shame in being his daughter. Indeed, James, I am very proud of my Papa. It is not many men can lift themselves as he has done, is it not so?'

James had smiled then, looking down at her face framed in its fashionable bonnet. 'Indeed it is not. I am not embarrassed, I can assure you. I hold a high regard for your father's abilities, Miss La—Abigail. I—when I first met him, I held him in such esteem it was barely this side of idolatry.' But that was before he changed, became the hard-etched, sharp-tongued creature he now is, he had thought, and immediately pushed the thought away as unfit to be put into words for this warm delightful daughter of his. Though how such a man could have such a daughter. . . . He had given her a tight little smile then. 'He is—well, he is not an easy man to make a friendship with——'

She nodded then in quick comprehension. 'I know, James, but you must not mind him. He has a temper of which many are afraid, though I am not, and is too easy thrown into a fit of the blue devils, but I believe he has good cause. He has never told me of all his life but I understand there have been unhappinesses to it that have made him so. Mama knows of them, but will not tell me, so——' she shrugged

24

lightly, 'so we must perforce be kind, and coax away his blue devils, and be proud of him, must we not?'

He had smiled again, and said nothing, finding it a good deal less easy than she did to forgive his employer's sharp tongue and sometimes cruel anger, any more than he could easily forget his harshness, his frequent imperious disregard of the rights and needs of any but himself. Abel Lackland was very much a product of his background, in James Caspar's eyes, and the tide of resentment that he felt against his employer ran deeply inside him. But looking at Abigail James had smiled. He could understand full well how it was she could make Abel less angry, could soothe his 'blue devils' for she, he was sure, could soothe anyone with that calm good sense of hers, that warmth and generosity that he recognized in her.

Watching her now across the drawing-room as she stood close beside her father talking earnestly to him he knew something was wrong, and tried to guess what it might be. Dorothea was watching too; she was standing a little away from him, flanked by Sir John Kutner and his dreary stick of a wife, and apparently listening to the rumblings the old man was producing, nodding a little now and then, but never taking her eyes from her husband and daughter.

In the window embrasure old Hunnisett was standing very straight and still, clearly ill at ease in his employer's drawing-room, and James allowed a little quirk of humour to lift his face. After all these years to be as much in awe of Abel as he was—it was absurd. Hunnisett, who had been old Jesse Constam's chief clerk and had known Abel since his gutter days, should, of all of them, be most comfortable with him, yet was in truth the most likely to worry. But there, that was his character, and James smiled reassuringly at the old man as he caught his eye, and Hunnisett nodded stiffly back.

Jeffcoate at the door announced sonorously, 'Mr and Mrs Daniel Cloudesly and Miss Cloudesly!' and the room rustled a little, and then Dorothea moved forwards to greet the last of her expected guests but casting a look of anxiety at Abel as she went.

There was a little more movement as the newcomers moved into the centre of the drawing-room, and the groups shivered and broke and reformed, though old Hunnisett remained by the window, neatly framed by the yellow velvet drapes and muslin curtains.

Abel was talking now to Daniel Cloudesly, a thin tall man with an almost totally bald head which gleamed fatly in the light of the oil lamps, and Dorothea was looking more animated as she talked with his stout little wife, for Maria Cloudesly was one of her few friends, the woman with whom she felt more comfortable than any other.

James, watching them all and still aware of the feeling of something being very wrong, lifted his head a little and managed to catch Abby's eye. She was standing talking to Sir John, and she gave him the ghost of an acknowledgement, and then with a smoothness that would have done credit to a hostess twice her age transferred Sir John to Hunnisett, and moved softly across the room to James's side.

'What's amiss?' he asked quietly, and she looked up at him with a faint smile on her face.

'You have a most observant eye, James,' she murmured. 'What should be amiss?'

'Apothecaries are taught to observe, Miss Abigail. And I know you too well now not to know when you are exercised in your mind——'

She put her hand out and touched his lightly. 'Thank you, James, I—I am so very glad you are here——' and looking down at her he was startled, for her face was suddenly pink, and at his glance she took her hand away hastily and went on a little breathlessly: 'You are quite right, of course. There is something amiss—that wretched Jonah! I could wring his neck. I know he has cause for anger, but to do this——'

'You do not explain yourself too well, Miss Abigail,' he said softly, still watching her face, and wondering, right at the back of his mind, just what that moment of confusion in so usually calm and sensible a girl could have signified. 'What has your brother done?'

'Pah!' She made a soft yet angry little sound. 'He knew tonight was planned expressly so that Papa should put to you and to Hunnisett and the Governors his new plan, and that he was deeply a part of it, and yet in some fit of childish pique he has chosen to go out and about his own ploys. I——' she swallowed. 'To make it worse, he has gone to a theatre, and I believe you know how Papa feels on *that* head!'

'I don't believe I do,' James said. 'Is he in opposition to them? I do not generally talk of religious matters with Mr Lackland, but I did not have the impression that he was one of the new evangelists.'

'Oh, no! It is not a *religious* matter, though some may think it is. No, he has his own reasons for it, no doubt, though he has never told us. Whatever they are, he will not countenance any of us ever visiting a theatre. We may go to music concerts, and have been to Astley's, you know, to see circuses and the like, but to the theatre—he just will not permit it. And now Jonah has told the servants that is where he is, knowing full well that they will make full use of the knowledge, and I know he did it expressly to anger Papa further. I have no patience with him. None at all! The house has been full of nothing but arguments and sulks and more arguments since he came home from school, not a se'ennight ago, and for my part I would——'

Jeffcoate, at the door, announced dinner and the room rustled again, and James stepped back to let the procession to the dining-room form, watching Abel's face as he led Lady Kutner out. It was grim and very tight, and James sighed softly as he took his place at the end of the line with Miss Cloudesly on his arm. Tonight promised to be one of the least agreeable he was likely to spend.

3

The room was hot and noisy and very smoky, but that did not bother him at all. He had discovered against one wall a table on which were several mutton pies, and bread and cheese and cold beef and jugs of porter, and hungry as he was he simply helped himself. Though no one offered him the food and drink no one stopped him from taking it either, so he turned to with a will. Once his hunger was assuaged, he told himself, he would move further into the crowd, and see if he could find that enchanting creature in the blue dress, and talk with her. She was someone he would very much like to know——

'Are you enjoying our supper?'

He started, and then coughed, for a piece of the pie he had been eating had stuck in his throat, and as his eyes began to stream and he choked harder the girl beside him laughed softly and thumped him hard upon his back to dislodge the crumb. It was a hearty blow and had the desired effect, and he wiped his eyes and swallowed the remnants of his mouthful of pie, and turned to see who it was who had so startled him.

And then went scarlet, for it was the girl who had been staring at him across the stage. She looked a little different now, and he realized after a moment that she had twisted her thick hair into a rope and pinned it on top of her head, and this somehow made her look smaller, and more fragile—for there were a few wisps escaping from the knot to lie on her slender neck—and yet a little older than he had at first thought her. Her eyes were a very dark grey and so heavily lashed that they looked like smudges on her white skin.

'I am sorry,' he said stiffly. 'I did not know that this was your supper. I had thought it was—' he waved one hand to take in the crowded room. 'I had thought it was entertainment for the guests who come after the play.'

She looked over her shoulder and stared round, and then back at him. 'Guests, you call them? I do not! Guests are those a person bids to visit and offers victuals to, not these—these—pah! I have no time for them!'

'Then what are you doing here?' he asked and let a faint sneer creep into his voice. 'I did not see you perform upon the stage tonight, although to be sure I did observe you mopping and mowing away to yourself at the side——'

She reddened. 'I wish to make my amends for that,' she said, and sounded suddenly gruff. 'I—indeed, I meant no harm. But I—I observed you, and I have this—this unfortunate ability to reproduce that which I see others do. It happens with speech, too, and I am often embarrassed by it. If I speak to one who comes from Scotland or from Wales or others that speak different, they come to think I mock them for immediately, willy-nilly, I speak as they do. I cannot help it. Mama is just the same, though she has control of it as I have not. As for why I am here—well, because of Mama. She is a player.'

'Oh?' He cocked his head to one side, immediately interested. 'Which is she?' He cast his mind back over the performance he had seen, and tried to visualize which of the women might have been this strange child's mother.

'She is over there——' the girl said, jerking her head at the thickest part of the crowd. 'You will see her, no doubt, soon enough. All do who come here after the play.' She stopped then, and bit her upper lip and said abruptly, 'You are no longer angry with me for my—for watching you?'

For a moment he remembered the sight of her grimacing away there at the side of the stage, and wanted to turn his back on her, the ill-mannered creature that she was, but then he saw her face and the curiously pleading expression on it softened him, and made him smile a little ungraciously, but at least smile.

'Well, it is no great matter, I suppose,' he said gruffly. 'As one who suffers from younger sisters and brothers, I dare say I have fared worse at a child's hands. And at least you——'

'I am not a child!' she flared. 'No more than are you! I dare say you have no more than two years advantage of me! I shall be sixteen in two months' time!'

He looked surprised at that. 'Sixteen? I had not thought you so old. My sister is such an age and she put off her schoolroom dresses long since!'

Again that flush rose in her thick white skin, and she looked away from him. 'Aye. I dare say. But she has not a mother such as mine, who—ah, what does it matter to you, anyway?'

He was feeling more comfortable with her now, more in command, and leaned back lazily against the wall and looked down at her, smiling a little. She glanced up and caught his eye and looked confused, and smiled, and then reddened again.

'Perhaps it does not matter, but I am interested. You have the advantage of me, after all, for you stood and watched me for—how long? I do not know! Now it is my turn! So, who are you? What is your name?'

'Celia.'

'Celia? An unusual name: I cannot think of any girl I ever heard of called that.'

She shrugged. 'It is one of my mother's whims that we be named for whatever part she is playing at the time—she was in *As You Like It* for me and *The Rivals* for Lydia and *Much Ado About Nothing* for Benedict. I think it a foolish fancy, for my part, but——'

'Foolish? Not at all foolish!' He was standing more upright now, and looking much more interested. 'I think it a most poetical idea, and——'

'Poetical? Are you a poetical sort of person, then?' There was a faint sneering edge to her voice, and he looked at her with his eyebrows raised.

'Why? Should a person not be poetical?'

She shrugged. 'If that is the way their fancy takes them. For my part, I have met too many poets and most of them are exceeding boring.' She looked at him a little sideways. 'I had thought you looked more—more *busy* than the poets I know.'

It was his turn to redden then. 'Well, I am not a poet, precisely,' he said, and suddenly looked his age. 'Although I care very much for it. I mean, I have written poetry—but other things as well. Essays, and polemics, you know, and——'

She nodded. 'Oh, I know. There are many such who spend their time here at the Haymarket. So much time, I cannot for the life of me

30

see when it is they write their poetry and polemics and whatever it all is. Always mooning over Mama as they are, it is——'

He cocked his head to one side again in what she began to realize was a characteristic way with him. 'You speak of your mother in such terms that—do you not care for her?'

There was a short silence and then Celia said gruffly, 'Care for her? Indeed I care greatly for her. When she will let me do so.'

With an impulse that surprised him he put out one hand and set it on hers, curling his fingers round their warmth, and she looked up at him, surprised, but did not take her hand away.

'Does she alarm you? Does she try so hard to set her will upon you that you cannot—cannot be yourself, and love her as you would wish? Is that what you mean?'

He could not have explained the sudden sense of closeness he had felt rise in him at the bleak little sound in her voice. He knew, too well he knew, what it was to care for a person who would not let you care back as you would have wished. He knew the sense of loneliness that could overcome you when every attempt to talk of personal matters became a sour argument. He knew what it was like to ache for a father who would not, could not, did not look at you with anything in his eyes but blankness.

She was looking at him strangely, her eyes wide, and after a moment she smiled a little. 'You speak as one who knows a lot about loving!' she said, trying to be light. 'For my part I make no special claims to such understanding. I just——' she shrugged. 'I just am as I am.'

Still he held her warm fingers clasped in his, but now he held them a little tighter. 'I know,' he said. 'My father is just such a one. He is so with all but my sister. He treats my mother so——' His face darkened. 'I know how it is with such a parent,' he said again, and now let go her hand.

There was an awkward silence, and then she said with a little laugh, 'La, sir, for one that was to discover all about me, I know much more about you! Item!' She touched her forefingers together to begin counting. 'You have a sister of sixteen, and many other brothers and sisters beside, you have a father and a mother, you are a poet and—indeed, I know all but your name! There you are a step ahead of me.'

He smiled. 'Jonah,' he said. 'My friends call me Jo, however, and I prefer it.'

'Oho, so we are friends, are we?' she sounded mocking now, standing smiling a little crookedly at him. 'Well, so be it! You have eaten my supper, after all, and——'

He grinned then. 'So I shall have to repay it, shall I not?' And then, remembering his empty pocket, added hastily, 'But not now. Perhaps I shall come again here, and bring with me a supper fit to repay you for my mutton pie and pint of porter! For I promise you, that is all I have had, so——'

'Celia!'

They both looked round, a little startled, and Jonah felt the colour in his face recede and then rise again, and knew he was gaping like a fish, and could do nothing about it.

The room had largely emptied during their conversation, and there were just themselves and three other people apart from the two or three servants desultorily clearing away costumes and tidying dressing-tables; a tall thin man with a narrow face and hair that though cut to a fashionable length clung closely to his head in such a way that his skull looked pointed; a much younger one with very heavy shoulders, a sulky face and a great deal of fair fuzzy hair which he wore *en brosse* between collar points so high that he could hardly turn his head, and standing between them looking very diminutive and delicate, the enchanting actress in the blue dress.

She had changed from her stage costume but was still wearing blue, an evening dress of taffeta with lace frothing at the low neck from which her shoulders rose as soft and pink as sugar icing. Her hair, dark curls with flowers woven into them, was piled on her head enchantingly, and her eyes, long and green and narrow, glittered at him so that he felt almost giddy.

But for all his bedazzlement he could see her clearly; could see the slight crêpiness of the skin on that sugar icing throat, the radiation of faint lines that met at the corners of those glittering eyes, the dimpled creases that ran from each side of that delectable little mouth to the nose; yet he did not see these signs as anything but extra dimensions of enchantment. He thought her the most beautiful woman he had ever seen in his life.

She looked at him for a long moment, a hint of puzzlement on her face, and then said flutingly, 'Dear Celia! It does not become you so, silly child!' and put out her hand to Celia's head. She stood there,

32

turning her fingers in the glossy hair, but still looking sideways at Jonah, and then she tugged lightly, and pulled out the pins, and Celia's thick hair came tumbling girlishly about her shoulders. Celia said nothing, and did nothing; just stood with a look of mulishness upon her face, her gaze fixed on the floor.

'There! That is much better! Is it not, m'lord?' and she turned and looked up at the tall man with the thin pointed head, and laughed, and he laughed too, a high-pitched and silly laugh, it seemed to Jonah, who was still standing and staring open-mouthed.

'Celia, dear heart, I think, you know, you should not be here so late! You should have been at home and in your bed long since. But there, it seems you have met a friend?' She turned her head to one side, and looked brightly at the silent girl. 'Please to present me, my dear!'

'This is my Mama,' Celia said after a moment, and her voice was quite flat.

Jonah blinked, and looked at Celia and then back at the other. 'Your—Mama? But you did not say—I mean—but you are—cannot be so much more of an age than Celia, ma'am! I cannot—I mean—your pardon, ma'am!'

She produced a trill of laughter that flustered him even more. 'Such a charmer! With a tongue as ready with compliments as that you will bid fair to cut out half the gallants on the Town, will he not, Gerald?' The fair young man scowled and opened his mouth to speak, but without turning her head she lifted her hand peremptorily and he scowled even more deeply and subsided. 'My dear boy, there is no pardon to beg, I promise you! Celia is but a child of course, but even so—oh, indeed you're a charmer! And I believe, you know, that you meant it in all truth—were not offering idle compliments. Tell me, did you not know who I was!'

'Indeed, truly, no, ma'am,' Jonah stammered. 'I—you must forgive me, ma'am. I rarely attend the theatre and to tell the truth this is the first time I have ever been here—I mean to this theatre—and the first time I have seen you play, so——'

'First time you have seen Mistress Lucas play, boy?' the tall thin man said, and his speech was pitched as shrill as his laughter had been. 'Good God, now, where have you been these past years? Locked in a dame school? Indeed, though, boy, I envy you, damned if I don't. To

33

see the divine Lilith Lucas for the first time—that such a revelation could be mine again! That each succeeding view is greater than the first, there is of course no denying, but——'

'Hush, Richard,' Lilith said, but almost absently, for she was staring at Jonah still, with that same slightly puzzled look upon her face. 'You have never been here before, dear boy? Now that is strange. I thought I knew your face——'

'Er—no, ma'am. I—I have indeed been away at school ,of course, and I trust that that is no shame—' and he shot a sharp look of dislike at the thin man. 'But I am unable to visit the theatre as much as I would choose, though I have a great liking for the—dramatic art. But I am not able—it is difficult—my father—' he stopped, confused, and scarlet-faced again, subsided, and Lilith laughed softly.

'Well , never mind, dear boy! There is no need for explanations! Celia, you did not tell me your friend's name.'

Celia had not moved, except to raise her eyes to watch Jonah's face, and now without shifting her gaze at al she said dully, 'His name is Jonah. His friends call him Jo. He has a mother and a father and several brothers and sisters.'

Lilith nodded, smiling that brilliant smile still, but she shot a sharp glance at her daughter, and then looked back at Jonah.

'And what other name do you have? I hardly know you well enough yet to call you so familiarly, however *close* a friend may be to my daughter,' she said lightly.

'Lackland, ma'am. My name is Jonah Lackland,' he said a little breathlessly, and then stopped in puzzlement for her face had become suddenly quite still, and then she nodded very slowly.

'Lackland. Jonah Lackland,' she repeated. And then smiled very widely. 'Well, now, tell me more of yourself. You have a father and a mother and sisters and brothers? Well, so have many, so have many. But t ell me of these relations of yours. Your father, now. He would be a—surgeon, perhaps?' and she put her head on one side.

'Why, yes, ma'am,' Jonah said woodenly, feeling as though someone had thrown a bucket of cold water at him. 'Do you know him?' He had a sudden mad vision of this lovely woman talking to his father, their heads close together, she telling him—he whitened.

'Know him?' she laughed with great gaiety, throwing her head back and opening her mouth very wide so that he could see her pink tongue and sharp little white teeth. 'Know him? But who does not know of Mr Abel Lackland? Was there not a time when he was surgeon to this very theatre? Aye, and Covent Garden too, and others.'

His brows snapped into a frown. 'Surgeon to—oh, no, ma'am. You must be mistaken. My father has such a horror of the theatre—he will not permit us to attend, ever! It cannot be the same one! He has, I am sure, never set foot in such a place as——'

'Never set foot? He's set more than his foot in such a place!' He blinked, for her voice had slipped into a roughness that was quite new. 'He's seen as many plays as you've had hot dinners, you can be bound!' And she looked at him sharply, at his puzzled face and again, bewilderingly, changed and became soft and sweet once more, the moment of raucousness quite gone. 'After all, perhaps there *is* another surgeon in London called Abel Lackland!' she said. 'Your papa is no doubt someone quite other!' She laughed again then, a much softer bubbly little laugh. 'So, your papa, whoever he may be, has a horror of the theatre, has he? Forbids you come? Well, well, well! My boy, my young Mr Lackland, let me tell you that you may come here at *any* time—any time at all! You have disobeyed him once—no, don't redden up so, you were right to do so, for the man who forbids so well grown a son the normal pleasures of his young manhood does not deserve filial obedience! So disobey him again as often as you would, and you shall be welcomed here, shall he not, Celia? Now you promise me, young Jonah Lackland, young Mister Jo? You will come to see me —see us again? You shall not stay away and listen childlike to your father?'

She was standing closer to him now, her head tilted so that she could look up at him, for he was much taller than she, and he grinned widely and bent and took her hand in his, and kissed it, a little awkwardly, but kissed it all the same, and she laughed that trill of accomplished laughter again, and patted his cheek, and nodded, and then swept past him, the two men at her heels.

'Do not forget, now. I shall be looking for you,' she said, glancing back at him over her shoulder as she reached the door. 'Come to see us again soon!' and then she was gone, leaving a sharp silence behind her.

'Well, don't stand there like a great ninny!' Celia's voice pulled him back from his reverie, and he turned and looked down at her, and smiled hugely.

'I did not expect that such a—so lovely a lady could be your mother', he said. 'It seems so——'

'Aye,' she said, and her voice had a hard edge to it. 'So they all say, and Mama is not averse to letting them say it.' She pulled pettishly at her white muslin skirt. 'Now you see why—oh, go away, you great mooncalf! You are no better than all the others, after all!'

He stared at her, his face tightening into a frown. 'All the others? I do not understand you.'

'I do not understand you!' she mimicked him viciously, and turned and flung herself at the door to hold it open. 'No doubt you don't, for you are like them, a stupid great—great—*poet*—with no eyes in your head to see nor ears to hear. Go away, do, and leave me to what you have left of my supper! I am tired of talking to you!'

He raised his eyebrows at that, and bowed a little stiffly, and turned to pick up his overcoat from the chair upon which he had laid it.

'Very well. I shall bid you goodnight. I shall return, however, despite your—well, I must pay my debts and return the food I have eaten tonight. Goodnight to you, ma'am.'

And then he was outside in the dark corridor, thick with the smell of glue size and dust and limelight, the door flung closed behind him leaving him to grope his way out to the stage-door and t he rumbustious noise and activity of the Haymarket beyond, a bewildered and now very tired young man.

But not too tired to walk home to Gower Street with the picture of Lilith Lucas before his eyes all the way, and the sound of her voice in his ears. Somewhere behind that glittering vision he was aware of another figure standing, a dour girl in white muslin with her hair upon her shoulders, but he ignored that. With Lilith Lucas to fill his mind's eye and his mind's ear, what time had he for a silly child like Celia?

4

Abel sat crumbling a piece of bread between his thumb and forefinger, and let Sir John's voice drone on, giving up any attempt to listen to him. The old man was talking about his experiences with Moore at Corunna in '09 and Wellington at Waterloo in '15 and could rumble on happily enough with no need of an attentive audience.

He stared down the table at Dorothea, who was sitting upright and pale with her head inclined to one side as she listened to Lady Kutner. She caught his eye, and at once that expression that so enraged him appeared on it; half apologetic, half pleading. Irritably he snapped his gaze away. If only she would not do it; she was his wife, God damn it, not some puppy dog whining for favours! And if only he could control his own responses to her! He knew perfectly well that it was because of his irritability that she reacted so, knew that it was her reaction that fed his feelings, and yet felt powerless to break the miserable spiral.

Abby was sitting leaning forwards across the table to say something to Caspar and her face looked like that of an eager woman, not a girl, and her green taffeta dress clung to her ribs and pushed up her breasts to a soft roundness. She looked so much older suddenly that he felt a small constriction in his chest. He did not like the idea of his Abby growing older, did not like the way Caspar was smiling at her, his rather dour face somehow looking younger than it usually did.

But it must have been a trick of the bright candlelight, for Abby, leaning back again, had caught his eye on her and smiled that conspiratorial smile of hers, the corners of her mouth downturned, her brows raised so that her face had the familiar look of his wicked child, and Abel raised his own eyebrows in response, and glanced again at

Caspar; and he now looked as he always did, a quiet, freckled, reddish sort of man in his early thirties, inturned and self-sufficient.

Jeffcoate at his shoulder offered him roast partridge, and he shook his head impatiently and the man moved on to heap Sir John's plate—Sir John encouraging him while losing not one word of his tedious narrative about Wellington's strategy at Quatre Bras—and Abel gave up trying to prevent his mind sliding into the channel it was determined to follow.

Jonah. He should have been sitting there half-way along the table between Cloudesly and Hunnisett. He should have been sitting with his square shoulders outlined against the dark panelling of the dining-room wall, his dark head bent attentively to one of his neighbours, being part of Abel's plan for this evening. And instead he was—God knew where.

Abel moved sharply in his chair, and down the table Abby noticed and looked worriedly at him, but his head was bent, watching his own fingers on the tablecloth still kneading the bread, and she sighed. Had she been inside his head she could not have known more certainly what he was thinking, she told herself. Poor Papa——

Why is it? Abel was asking himself, why is it the boy always balks me so? Why has it always been so—so *sharp* between us? It was not my fault, God knew. I cared for the boy, worried a great deal about his welfare, planned for him, wanted good and only good for him, and yet——

Behind him the dining-room clock softly chimed the hour, and it was as though it were a hair trigger to his memory. He was standing again in Dorothea's bedchamber with the clock on her mantel over the flickering coals chiming the hour, and he was looking down at them both, she flushed and damp, but her face triumphant, clutching the infant—awkwardly, for was he not her firstborn?—and the infant red-faced, crumpled and stained still with his mother's blood lying wrapped in a towel in her arms and screaming hugely and lustily.

He felt it again, the sudden surge of amazement and a sort of wild joy and felt it overwhelmed with an equally sudden anger. There had lain the baby, his boy, the boy he had got on this damp and crooning little woman, lying screaming in the midst of warmth and security and comfort. He had looked up and round the room, at the heavy velvet window drapes and bed curtains, the fringed chaise-longue beside the fire, the red Turkey carpet with the chairs and little tables set so neatly on it, the servant moving from press to table with baby clothes in her arms, and had looked back at the infant, and hated him. To lie there and be rich in so much, when the man who had begot him had started his own infancy in some corner of the Seven Dials slums with only a helpless abandoned girl to care for him, and no father to see or be interested—how dared that infant lie there and scream and have a father?

He had known it to be confused and foolish thinking, had known himself overcome with irrationality, but he had not been able to control it, for all afternoon while Dorothea had moaned and wailed and grunted ineffectually—for even in giving birth she was a pallid stupid creature, he had told himself scornfully and then been ashamed of the thought—he had remembered the woman whose child this ought to have been, the woman who should have been thrusting his boy out of her body into the open air, and hated everyone and everything because it wasn't her. And hated himself most of all.

And then, seeing the child, the confusion and the anger and the misery of lost happiness had been too strong for the underlying joy that could have been so splendid, too strong for the concern and protectiveness and pride that had also lain deep within him, and when Dorothea had said timidly, 'He is a beautiful baby, is he not, dear Abel? Are you pleased with him? Are you happy? What shall you call him?' he had looked blankly at the child, and shrugged his shoulders and said harshly, 'You may call him what you wish. He is your child.'

And then added, almost to himself, 'You may call him Jonah for aught of me. He'll bring——' and swallowed the rest of the sentence, for he was going to say, 'he'll bring me no more joy than you have——' but that was cruelly unjust, and even in his misery he knew it.

And Dorothea, poor hopeful loving Dorothea had taken that as his wish, and christened the boy Jonah.

Jonah. His very name had hung over his father like a reproach all his life, had come between their attempts to talk, to be as a father and son should be. All through his baby years, his growing years, his schoolboy years it had gone on, with Abel making odd awkward little sorties towards the boy, not knowing how he alarmed the child, and the boy shrinking away back to the protection of his doting mother.

Over and over again it had happened, driving a wedge ever wider between not only the boy and his father, but the parents too. They had never been close, God knew, but now——

Not that he had not tried to make his marriage work. Over and over again, he would tell himself how cruel he was, for Dorothea loved him so deeply, and tried so hard, and he would see the anguish on her face, and come again to her, and she would open her arms to him, glad, unquestioning and totally loving, and he would try to love her. And over and over again it happened, that vision of another woman's face rising before his eyes, another woman's body; while it was Dorothea who twined her pale arms and legs about him, strained close to him in whimpering adoration, had gasped and panted beneath his desperate longing thrusting, i t had been *her* body he had longed for, *her* he had needed——

So Abigail's birth had swiftly followed Jonah's, and glad he had been of her, for she was a little girl, and therefore easy and uncomplicated to love; indeed he had poured so much of his feeling into the fat solemn baby who would sit on his knee when her nurse put her there and stare and stare at him, and then quite suddenly produce that toothless adoring grin, that he had had little interest in the children who followed her. Rupert and William and then the twins (pallid sickly little things they had been, and hard to rear; he had seen little of them until they were nigh a year old) and then Barty, and the child who had been dead at her birth and lastly Augustus—definitely last, for he was five years old now, and not since his birth had Abel made any further attempts to love Dorothea, for after so many years, he knew, as surely she did, that the time had gone for trying——

'Papa?'

Startled, he looked up, and found them all sitting looking at him, even Sir John beside him quiet now, replete with food and the telling of his tales, and he blinked and nodded at Abby who was looking at him expectantly. She turned her head immediately to look pointedly at her mother, and he followed her gaze, and at once Dorothea stood up and glanced at the ladies, and they all rose to their feet in a flurry of taffeta skirts so that the candles on the table danced and flickered.

'We shall not expect you in the drawing-room for some time, I believe, gentlemen,' Dorothea said carefully, as Abel had told her she must when planning this evening some three weeks ago, and he nodded and stood up, and the other men followed suit, standing there waiting until the women had all left the room.

Abby left last, and looked back over her shoulder at her father, and made a little admonitory movement of her head; and for the first time that evening he smiled slightly and she smiled too and went, closing the door softly behind her.

There was a sense of relaxation in the room as the men resettled themselves, closing up along the table so that they were all clustered at Abel's end, and refilling their glasses from the decanter of port that Jeffcoate had set before Abel as soon as the cloth was drawn. Sir John Kutner lit a cigarillo, saying gruffly that he trusted his host would forgive an old soldier for adopting a Spanish custom from his years spent in that most barbaric of countries during the late wars and- Abel nodded a little abstractedly and coughed to clear his throat before speaking.

'Gentlemen, I trust you will forgive me if I cease now to be the polite host, and set at once about the matter of business I would discuss with you all. As I told you when I arranged this evening, I have plans that I would set before you——'

He coughed again, and frowned slightly, and then said, 'We are not as complete a party as I would have wished. As I told you, Sir John, Mr Cloudesly, it had been my intention that my eldest son should be present here tonight, since the matter concerns him. However, he is—indisposed——'

James, watching him carefully, felt a twinge of sympathy. He could well understand the boy's difficulty in his relationship with his father, for Abel was an autocratic, self-willed man and not one to be gainsaid in his ideas, yet now, looking at the long face with its deepset green eyes and the harsh clefts that were cut so deeply between the nose and mouth and above the narrow black eyebrows, he felt an unexpected stab of pity. Abel was not simply angered because one of his plans had been set aside; he was hurt.

'But we must go on despite his absence. I must speak for him. So, briefly, gentlemen——'

Abel paused, and then looked up and let his glance run round them all, silent retiring Hunnisett, the well-fed City men, the watchful Caspar, and he smiled suddenly. 'There are some who would think I have run mad to talk to you as I am about to do, for you are all businessmen, are you not, and though you have the—the welfare of your fellow men at heart, no doubt, care first and foremost for the sensible ordering of your business affairs?'

James stirred a little and said softly, '*Your* business affairs, Mr Lackland.'

'Eh? What's that?'

'I said, *your* business affairs. You must remember, sir, that while I am indeed one who thinks largely in terms of profit and loss, I do so on your behalf. I gain no more from my efforts to run a business as a business should be run than a salary. It is you who reap the benefits of any—success I may have.'

'Aye, I know that!' Abel said sharply. 'You need not remind me of it! It is as true of Hunnisett as of you—although it is my wife's inheritance that he has care of, rather than mine——'

'You are very punctilious, Lackland,' Cloudesly said, and laughed. 'My wife too has the enjoyment of a respectable inheritance, but I do not disown it!'

'I prefer to be punctilious,' Abel said a little stiffly. 'I have never had any wish to make any use of my wife's fortune that did not meet with her approval. As Mr Hunnisett will tell you, she is present at every discussion of the management of her affairs that becomes necessary——' Hunnisett bobbed his head in agreement, 'and she has given her full consent to the matter I wish to put to you tonight.'

'Well, let's have it, Lackland, let's have it!' Sir John said. 'For my part I have dined well, and will be at risk of falling fast to sleep if we do not reach a point soon——'

Abel smiled thinly, and nodded. 'Well, then, gentlemen. I am to ask of you more charitable use of money, Sir John, Mr Cloudesly, in your capacity as trustees to the dispensary and hospital. I——'

'Now, Lackland, Lackland, not again!' Sir John grunted, and put down his cigarillo. 'Not a week has passed this six months but you have wanted a new something—linen, or beds or instruments or food for in-patients and suchlike. We have in this past five years come on at such a pace that it takes all our income to run as we should. If you are seeking more capital investment, it cannot be done! To sell such sources of income as we have had to to raise more money to enlarge the place cost us enough last year. To do so again would be——'

'Be patient, be patient, Sir John!' Abel said. 'Hear me out! The plan

I have will demand a capital outlay, yes, but could bring in an income too, in due course——'

'Hmmph! Well, it had better be a good return, or I for one wash my hands of the running of Tavistock Street, and so I tell you!' Sir John said. 'For we are running on a shoestring now, with you so set on giving these patients of yours so much of the best in food and care and clean linen—they fare better than a respectable working man——'

'I insist that they have no more than they need,' Abel said shortly, 'but we will not start again on that tack, if you please, Sir John, not tonight. No, my plan is quite other and I believe it will serve all our interests. It is, simply, this. We do, at present make up such medicaments as we need at Tavistock Street for the use of both in-patients and daily patients as and when we need them—a costly operation. Now, I have, in James here, an apothecary of good experience, as well as in Hunnisett a man who is very knowing in the buying and selling of spices—and therefore of other commodities. I have, in addition, at the warehouse at Wapping Wall, a goodly space in which to set up a manufactory——'

'A manufactory?' Cloudesly was frowning. 'What sort of manufactory? Are you entering in competition with such as I?'

'Good God, no!' Abel said impatiently. 'I am no engineer, nor have any interest in engineering matters. It is a manufactory for medicines I wish to set in motion——'

'A manufactory for *medicines*?' James sat up sharply. 'I had not gone so far as that in my thinking——'

Cloudesly shot a sharp look at James over the edge of his glass, and then turned to Abel. 'You have discussed this matter with Caspar before bringing us to this meeting, Lackland?'

'Not precisely discussed,' Abel said. 'But I will not hide from any of you the fact that it was the work of Mr Caspar that put into my head the idea that I am about to set before you. He has devised some standard pills that I have tried at Tavistock Street, and found to be most efficacious.' He turned to James. 'Further, Caspar, there have been times in the past, have there not, when you have talked of your impatience with handrolling methods of pill-making, and said you had ideas that could be used to mechanize the time-honoured ways of the craft. Is that not so?'

'Aye,' James said slowly. 'I have thought so, and indeed, I have made some drawings that I believe I could translate into a practical reality, given space and time and materials with which to build.'

'But what is the point of all this as far as we are concerned, Lackland?' Kutner asked gruffly, and suddenly yawned. 'That was a damned fine dinner, man! Let us not ruin it with unnecessary talk now——'

Abel's lips thinned a little, but he controlled his impatience and said carefully, 'The usual manner of the apothecary's trade, Sir John, is to make each man's medicine for him alone, according to the dictates of his condition. There are some standard mixtures, of course, but they are few. Yet often the same mixtures are made again and again, for different patients. Now, why should I—or any surgeon come to that—instruct a new receipt each time when ten out of twelve of the patients who come to me may need just one essential mixture or pill? Caspar has devised two pills which I believe could be of very wide application, not only to the poor of Seven Dials and Covent Garden who come to me for free care, but to the more prosperous sort of citizens. Why should we not devise more medicines of our own, manufacture them in ready dosages, and sell what we can to those who come to the shop in Piccadilly?'

'And to other shops perhaps, those which do not have the services of an apothecary at all times—' James said slowly.

Abel looked at him sharply. 'That is yet another possibility,' he agreed. 'Clearly, you think upon my lines, Caspar. I so far had considered only that the hospital should buy the mixtures at cost, and the shop should sell at a large profit. Thus one will set off the cost of the other, and the manufactory will survive to make its own profits——'

Cloudesly leaned forwards. 'Let me understand you, Lackland. You will set up a manufactory using your own premises and the services of your own men, sell your mixtures to the hospital——'

'It will be cheaper than the present method of buying in our materials piecemeal and employing a dispenser there,' Abel said.

'Aye, maybe. But where do such profits go as emerge from this venture? It sounds as though it will be *your* shop and *your* manufactory that will benefit the most——'

Abel became very still, and his voice hardened. 'Have you forgotten, Cloudesly, that it is the profits of the shop and the Constam spice

44

warehouse that founded Tavistock Street? That much of its income still derives from these sources? And that I deliberately arranged that there should be two trustees to whom I must apply always for the moneys for the running of the hospital, in order that I might avoid any such imputation as——'

'Indeed, Lackland, indeed, you are right,' Sir John said soothingly. 'Come, Cloudesly, your wits must be softened by the excellence of your dinner here tonight. This plan of Lackland's will gain the hospital much, I can see that. A large part of our costs is in medicines and if it is possible for these to be made cheaper, why, we shall all benefit, the hospital most of all——'

'Aye, but *can* they be made cheaper?' Cloudesly retorted. 'I see no difference in making medicines at Tavistock Street with our own people than in making them at Wapping Wall and transporting them——'

'To buy in vast quantities, as I believe I can buy the materials that you would require, makes it possible for me to make excellent savings on costs,' Hunnisett spoke very precisely and then, as all eyes turned to him, developed a sallow flush, and went on rather more hurriedly. 'I have, at Mr Lackland's instructions, investigated the market for the commonest of the ingredients you should require. I believe I can effect savings in the area of twenty per cent at present prices.'

'Twenty—come, Hunnisett, it cannot be so high!' Sir John said.

'Indeed, sir, it can.' The little man blinked and bobbed his head. 'The trade of the apothecary is one sore beset with rogues, I find. And I have my sources of reliable supply which will not seek to cheat me. I am, I venture to say, well-known in my trade.'

'You can take his word for it, gentlemen,' Abel said. 'Hunnisett has run the affairs of the spice business upon which my wife's family's fortunes were set these twenty-five years and more. He knows what he is about. And Caspar——'

Abel turned his head. 'I have much faith in Caspar. He is a man of good understanding of his craft, and will, I have no doubt, find ways in which to save great costs in the handling of these medicines.'

James, who had been sitting with his eyes slightly narrowed and his arms folded looked up sharply at the sound of his name, and smiled faintly.

'I am gratified by your faith in me, sir. However——' he hesitated, and his pale face looked a little strained suddenly. 'I would not wish in this company to appear in any way a grasping man, but you will no doubt agree that much of the labour involved in this matter will devolve upon my shoulders?'

'I know it will,' Abel said, 'and I had thought I had made that clear enough to the present company.'

'It is clear enough to me,' Cloudesly said sharply. 'You need have no fear that your contribution to such a scheme, were it to go forward, would be unnoticed.'

James looked even more uncomfortable, but went on stubbornly, 'I would not have you think, sir, that it is the glory of recognition of my efforts that I am concerned about. Pleasant though it may be to have one's abilities recognized, I find myself more concerned with the business aspects of the matter. In short, gentlemen, I would wish to be assured that although I will work for the shop in shop time in preparing these pills and this machinery, the fruits of my skill will be available to me. There will no doubt be patents to be taken out, and——'

Abel had been frowning heavily, but now his face cleared. 'Oh, patents! If that is all that concerns you, Caspar, you may rest quiet. You may settle patents, if there are any, in your own name. And welcome. I had not thought upon that side of it! I am concerned only that my medicines should be made and extra moneys be available to Tavistock Street. The details of such City matters hold no interest for me——'

'Then you are not the man I took you for,' Cloudesly grunted and he threw a sharp sideways glance at James. 'In these times of progress— and God knows, some new and devilish machine is thrown to the world on every day of the week, including God's own Sunday!— it is a wise man who looks forward and holds to what he can. That Caspar should wish to hold in his own hands any patents for machinery that he might develop is understandable enough—but that you should toss them aside so easily is not so comprehensible to a man of my kidney.'

Abel shrugged. 'I am not concerned with such matters,' he said again. 'I have enough to fill my mind with in dealing with my patients and Tavistock Street. You will be content to do this work, Caspar, if you hold the rights to the patents?'

'Yes,' James said simply, and Abel nodded.

'Then so be it—if you will agree in return to demand no further remuneration than that you already receive.'

James hesitated for a moment, thinking a little wryly of his thin pockets, but very aware of the weight of disapproval coming at him from Cloudesly said again, 'Yes'; and now Cloudesly threw him a look of clear disdain, and James reddened, knowing full well the City man thought him a complete flat. But he recovered fast enough for he felt, obscurely, that he had made some small stand against his employer's larger, stronger and altogether more admirable personality in gaining the promise of the patents (though in truth he rather doubted that any value would ever accrue from them for he could not imagine any but Abel being interested in his machinery), and he was content enough. And the work would be interesting indeed and that, he felt, would not be inconsiderable recompense for his labours.

He let the talk roll over his head as his mind slipped away to the design of a machine for cutting equal weight pills from a large mass of prepared material, and remained thus abstracted until Abel's voice rose again above the general talk.

'You will see, gentlemen, why I wanted to have my son here with us tonight? If James is to be set to considering ways of making a manufactory succeed for this purpose, he will need a reliable and intelligent man at his side. My son, while young, is no fool at his books, so his schoolmasters tell me, and it was my intention to set him to apprenticeship to James, for this part of his career, and when the manufactory is well upon its way, to set him to the training of a surgeon. Although when my own training fell into the pattern of first apothecary and then surgeon I thought it tedious, I know now it is an excellent experience for the man who would be a truly good practitioner. My knowledge of drugs has avoided, on occasion, the need for intervention with the knife, and my understanding of surgery has saved many for whom medicines would have been but a short road to the grave. This is why I offer my son the same opportunities. However, he is not here with us tonight, and I must discuss the matter with him separately. The point now, gentlemen, is to ask you if you are all willing that this plan be put into operation, and to ask you, Sir John, Mr Cloudesly, to release sufficient moneys to make the scheme practicable. We will need considerable sums to make the first purchases at low prices possible, for we must buy in great bulk—and we will need moneys to equip the manufactory. For my part, neither the shop nor the warehouse has such capital sums available, for as you know all profits that can be are put to the hospital funds forthwith, and we run all our affairs from quarter to quarter with little leeway.'

He smiled a little crookedly then. 'In order to protect myself from the boredom and irritation of having the handling of the hospital's money affairs I suspect I created for myself more difficulties than I foresaw. However, no man can prophesy all events. I did not think that the hospital would grow as fast as it has——'

'You've prodded us, and pushed, and fought hard enough for two to have grown to twice the size,' Sir John said, and then laughed. 'Come, man, I've a great respect for you. You have done more for the people of those stinking slums of yours than——'

'Well, I think we will not speak of it now, Sir John,' Abel said shortly. 'So, it is agreed?'

'Well——' Cloudesly said after a moment, 'Sir John?' The other man nodded. 'Well, then, I can say that we shall give it fair consideration. It sounds a hopeful enough plan, though for my part I shall require more information. Hunnisett, tomorrow, if you will, come to me at my counting house in Somers Town, and I will discuss with you the sums you need for your buying. Then, we will arrange to see the site of the proposed manufactory—and reach our final decision——'

Abel sat back in his chair, well satisfied. With the two hospital governors and Hunnisett deep in discussion, and James equally deep in thought on his ideas for making medicines more quickly, his plan seemed fairly set to succeed. It would make it possible, he told himself, to treat more patients more quickly at Tavistock Street, and could perhaps bring in sufficient profit eventually for us to buy another house, more room, where I could operate on more patients, even have pupils——

Deliberately, he pulled his mind away from that. The pupil he most wanted was yet to be persuaded of the wisdom of the plan his father had made for his future. Somehow he would have to find a way so to persuade the stiff-necked young fool, a way to wean him from this romantic nonsense that filled his head. Somehow.

5

Jonah had, for one wild moment when he woke up and memory of last night's escapade filled him with sick anxiety, considered sending down a message that he was ill and not fit to come to table.

But he dismissed that thought almost as soon as it came to him. For one thing, announcing ill health might well bring his father to investigate, and discovery of Jonah's mendacity would create an even more fearful rage in him; and for another, there was no point in delaying the confrontation any longer. The whole point of last night's rebellion had been to make it clear to his father that he would, no matter what happened, he *would* make his own choice of career. It had been a gesture of great defiance, of immense courage, Jonah told himself as he sat and let the junior footman shave him (a new mark of his status as a man which he much enjoyed) and to hide away from his father now in skulking childish fear would undo all his good work.

If, he thought then with considerable gloom, if it had been good work. In the cool light of this September morning he could not be quite as sure as he had been when he had gone to bed.

He dressed carefully; not because he wished to present to the world the most fashionable appearance of which he was capable, as he usually did (for he was very much a young man of fashion, in which he was encouraged by his adoring mother, who delighted in giving him extra money to spend on his wardrobe) but because he wanted to please his father. Although as a rule Abel did not pay much attention to clothes, he had been known to scowl at some of Jonah's wilder flights of sartorial fancy, and today, Jonah told himself wisely, he would avoid upsetting him on this score; enough that he would be upset by Jonah's intransigence in the more important matter.

So, he chose dull grey cloth trousers cut not too tight, and wore them with plain leather shoes (even to please his father he would not wear boots in the daytime—not at his age; such a fashion was for the established boring older man, and none other, in his estimation) and a plain shirt and a collar with only moderately high points. His cravat was a simple white one, tied very plain, and his coat modest in its waisting and its shoulder padding. Surveying himself in the pier glass between the two long windows of his bedroom he told himself he looked the very epitome of the sensible young man, perfectly capable of running his own life with wisdom.

But as he went softly down the stairs, moving past the white panelling and the elegant landscapes in their handsome gilt frames, he quaked within. Two floors below him the hallway floor gleamed with the soap and water gloss that had been scrubbed upon its black and white squared tiles by a tired scrawny servant girl at the crack of dawn and the thin autumnal sunshine laid its delicate pattern of fanlight tracery on the section behind the front door. He looked longingly at that uncompromisingly solid front door and thought of the busy streets beyond, and then sighed softly.

Jeffcoate, coming out of the drawing-room wearing his morning work-jacket of buff and yellow stripes, and wrapped in a heavy baize apron, grinned leeringly at him over his tray of silver and said with mock deference, 'Your father's been in the breakfast parlour this past fifteen minutes, Master Jonah, and rare quiet he is, even for him. I'd walk gentle if I was you.'

'Thank you,' Jonah said, his head high, and started down the next red carpeted flight. And stopped and turned his head to look anxiously at the older man. It was difficult to be dignified with one who had known him since his infancy and who had helped him through more childish escapades than he cared to remember. 'Jeffcoate—did you— did Edward tell m'father what—I mean, I told him last night that——'

Jeffcoate grinned even more widely, and turned to carry his burden towards the back stairs. 'No we did not tell your Pa, nor shall we! And it's your sister you have to thank for that. She's a rare good friend to you, is young Miss Abigail, and deserves better at your hands than she gets, you wicked young varmint. Get away with you to your victuals, now, or you'll have him set off in one of his takings and then not even Miss Abby'll get you out of his reach——'

'Thanks, Jeffy,' Jonah said and smiled his wide smile and the old man laughed and went on his way back to the kitchen. He would not have admitted it to many, but it was the children of the house who kept him in his post, rather than any concern he had for his employers. Dorothea he despised; she was so vacillating and so easy to cheat that there was little pleasure to be found or skill needed in obtaining the butler's usual perquisites of money gained from selling wine at the back door, and money taken from Cook as his percentage of her food sales at the same door; and Abel he feared. But the children, especially Miss Abby and the little one, small Gussy—for them he would put up with much. And even young Jonah, for all his airs and graces, had something about him that engaged the affections.

Jonah himself had reached the breakfast parlour, which lay at the back of the house at the street level, and looked out over the narrow walled garden, now glowing with masses of Michaelmas daisies and late geraniums. His mother, sitting tidily behind her coffee-pot, looked up nervously as he came in and he smiled at her as insouciantly as he could and at once her own face relaxed and softened and she smiled back at him.

Abel, at the other end of the table, observed the exchange and felt his own face harden. Why could not the boy look at his father like that? But then he felt Abby's eye upon him, saw the warning look in it, and relaxed a little himself. She had talked to him long and earnestly both last night and again this morning, when they had been alone at the table for ten minutes before Dorothea's arrival, and he had assured her that he had listened to what she had to say, and would act accordingly.

'Jo is a good boy, Papa,' she had said. 'Yes, indeed he is, so do not bend your brows upon me in so sharp a manner, for I am not one to be thrown into a quake by your scowls! He is—but he is stubborn, and has a mind of his own, and surely in all truth you would not have him otherwise?'

'You meddle too much in what does not concern you, Miss,' Abel had said a little sourly.

'No, I do not,' Abby had said firmly. 'For it is much my affair, and indeed everyone else's in this house when you and Jo are set against each other. We all suffer, for you are two men cut of the same piece of cloth and——'

'Men!' Abel had snorted. 'If he thinks himself a man yet he thinks more than——'

'Man he is,' Abby had retorted. 'As you were at his age, I have no doubt. And he knows his own mind as you did too. You cannot *force* him to do as you would wish—but he is like you in other ways too, so it is possible that you can bend him to your own wishes if——'

Abel had moved restlessly in his chair, and pushed away his plate, the cold beef upon it still untouched.

'Good God, girl, you make me sound a very ogre! Bend him to my wishes, indeed—it is not my wishes I have in mind, so much as his good! I offer him the chance to learn my skills, the chance that to get for myself I had to suffer such—well, never mind! Enough to say that I offer him a gift, not a punishment! And he behaves as though——'

'Well, Papa, so it may be,' Abby had said pacifically. 'Whatever it is you mean and whatever it is he comprehends of your meaning it is all too apparent that you do not see the same events through the same eyes. Nor ever will unless one or both of you bends a little! And I am asking you, Papa, to be the one that bends, for truly, I cannot bear to see you so angered as you have been since Jo came home, nor can I gain any pleasure from seeing my brother so cast down in his spirits. All that I ask of you is that you stop *telling* him what you would have him do, and help him find reasons for wishing it for himself. It is the only sensible way, in all conscience!'

There had been a short silence then, and she had sat looking at him, her chocolate cup held between her two hands, staring at him over the rim of it with her eyes wide and calm and he had looked up at her and then grunted.

'Well, you could have some sense in what you say. For my part, the boy exhausts me with his—well, I will say no more on that head,' as Abby raised her brows at him. 'Very well. I shall try to find reasons to *persuade* him rather than command him. That is what you mean, I take it?'

'That is precisely what I mean,' Abby had said, and stood up as the door opened. 'Good morning, Mama. It is a lovely morning, is it not? Shall I bring you some meat, or——'

'No thank you, my dear,' Dorothea had said, looking worriedly at Abel. 'I will take only a little bread and butter, I believe. Good morning, Abel,' and there was a faint questioning in her voice.

'Good morning,' Abel had said, and nodded at her, and at once she went to the table and poured for him a cup of the bitter black brew of coffee that he so oddly liked at his breakfast, and the three of them lapsed into silence, only Abby seeming composed as she ate her own cold meat with a hearty appetite.

And now Jonah stood hovering a little beside the table and Abby smiled at him and said, 'Sit you down, Jo, and I shall bring you some food. Now, shall it be the beef or the ham? Mama, you are sure you have had sufficient? Indeed, you eat so little the winds will blow you quite away one day!'

She talked on gently and inconsequentially as she loaded a plate for Jonah, and fetched more chocolate for her mother and herself, and gradually the atmosphere relaxed, until the two women were discussing an expedition to buy new clothes for the baby, small Gussy, and the men were sitting in comparative peacefulness over their own plates.

'He does not know,' Jonah was telling himself. 'He truly does not know, and I must confess I am glad of it after all, for it would have helped little. But now what? Does this quietness mean he will agree to my rejection of his choice for me? Or is it but the lull before the storm——'

Abel for his part was thinking too, but to what seemed to him to be better purpose than he had for some time, and he smiled wryly as he realized that it had been Abby's sensible speech that had made this possible. She was right, of course. There was no point in forcing the boy to any course of action. He must wish for it with as much strength as he had himself, all those years ago.

Memory came pleating itself about him then; a memory of the sight of a dead girl, hugely pregnant, lying deep in her newly opened grave, in the gleam of a shaded lanthorn, and looking helpless and sad and infinitely young; of the brilliantly lit and over-filled basement in Old Windmill Street where he had helped first old James Wilson, and then Charles Bell, and learned his anatomy; of the bleak dark wards at Guy's Hospital, of the long hours of his youth spent poring over books and cadavers and books again, and felt once more the old and never-changing enthusiasm rise in him. It could still come, that bursting of deep pleasure in the work that lay ready for his hands, could still rise hotly in him as he went striding up Tavistock Street towards his dispensary. If the boy could once feel that, or even a shadow of it, he would know why it was his father had made the plans he had.

'Jonah,' he said now abruptly, standing up. 'There is much that I have to tell you of the matters discussed at dinner last night——'

Jonah whitened a little and then set his jaw and raised his chin defiantly to look his father in the eye. Now it would come. But Abel went on without a pause.

'—but it is in my mind first that you have been given little opportunity to understand the matters with which I would concern you. In short, it is high time that you saw something of the work I do, and where I do it, so that you might see for yourself what it is I am preparing for you—No,' he raised his hand as Jonah opened his mouth to speak, 'I am not entering into any discussion at this point. I wish only to show you, to exhibit to you, matters that it is necessary for you to understand. I shall be leaving for Tavistock Street immediately, so please to be ready to accompany me. I believe it is a chilly morning, for all the deceptiveness of the bright sunshine. I suggest you wear a heavy coat. Good morning, Dorothea, Abby. I shall eat my dinner at home tonight,' and he nodded curtly and was gone.

'There he goes again!' Jonah burst out, jumping to his feet and staring wrathfully at the door his father had closed so purposefully behind him. 'He will not understand no matter what I say! Not that he permits me the chance to say anything! I shall not be a surgeon, I shall *not* and that is all that——'

'Oh, Jonah, please do go with him! He is being more kind than any father could be expected to be, after your disobedience of last night!' Dorothea said breathlessly. 'You know he could have beaten you for so wickedly flouting him, and none would have said him wrong, not even I, and I am far too partial in matters to do with you! You cannot be so churlish as to refuse! He wishes only to show you, no more, and for my part it seems but fair that you should agree to it.'

'Of course Mama is right, Jo,' Abby said, and leaned back in her chair to stare up at him consideringly. 'And even you in your irritation must admit it to be so. You are stamping your foot and throwing yourself about into postures of such rage, and after all you know nothing of what it is that you are objecting to! Papa is not saying you shall not be a poet, if it so pleases you to be! You may write your poetry until you are quite worn out, and none will object, for you have your free hours as have we all! He asks merely that you set your mind to selecting the career of your future, and in seeing the practice of his own profession as suitable for you he is acting only as a careful father should! If you refuse now to allow him to show you what it is he offers then indeed you are being stupidly stubborn.' Her eyes dropped then. 'As stubborn as Papa himself too often is,' she finished, and her voice was silky.

And Jonah, staring at both his mother and sister, felt himself beaten. Well, if they wished to delay it, so they might. Nothing would change his mind, and that was all about it. If his father wished to display his hateful dispensary to his son's gaze, that was his affair. He would go and look and repeat his decision. He would not be a surgeon.

Sitting at her breakfast table in her enchantingly pretty blue and silver boudoir in North Audley Street, Lilith Lucas ate transparently thin bread and butter and drank her chocolate from a porcelain cup, and thought about the evening before. That boy; that very tall and handsome boy, so absurdly like his father before him! It was her own private angel of chance that had driven him to her greenroom last night, she told herself with some glee and giggled softly into her chocolate cup. No one could behave to Lilith Lucas as that boy had behaved to her, all those years ago; not and get away with it. It might take time for the wheels to turn full circle, but turn they did, and their revolution had brought to her hand the opportunity to repay in good measure the insults Abel had hurled at her that long ago day.

It is not that I *care* at all, she told herself. If I ever did! It makes no matter to me what he thinks or feels or does! He was as gaping a fool as any of them——

She shook her head sharply to dispel a sudden vision of the tall grave twelve-year-old boy who had sat on her little truckle bed in an Old Compton Street basement and watched her with his eyes full of warmth and approval, in a way that had made her feel warm and happy too. *That* had been too long ago to matter. Far too long ago. What mattered now was the opportunity to amuse herself—and life was full of ennui just now—while paying off an old score.

And so she thought, and smiled to herself, and thought again. And then rang the bell that lay beside her right hand.

It was Lydia who came running to put her head around the door, and Lilith frowned. 'Where is Hawks?' she demanded petulantly. 'Am

I to have no part of the day to call my own? I will *not* have you brats come squawking to me at this hour of the day, and well you know it! Hawks!' and she raised her voice to call sharply yet again, 'Hawks, goddamn you, where are you?'

'She is giving Ben his breakfast,' Lydia said equably, unperturbed by her mother's shrill anger. She was a neat child, round-faced and curly-haired and small for her ten years, with sharp black eyes that missed not a movement within their gaze, and an air of being prematurely knowing that sat ill on so young a face. 'She told me to come to see what it was you wanted *now* and you'd have to wait, for she was sore beset with that brat——'

'Oh, hold your tongue,' Lilith said and pushed the table away pettishly. 'So where is Celia? It is Celia I want anyway. Go tell her.'

'She's still abed,' Lydia said. 'She was awake late last night. I heard her.' The child nodded sagely. 'I heard her, for she woke me when she came to bed, slamming about as she was and I heard the Watch cry four o'clock, and she lay there crying long after. I told her to be hushed, for she was waking me, but she just lay there and sniffed, silly thing. Why is Celia so silly, Mama? She is, for she——'

'Hold your tongue!' Lilith said again, irritably. 'And go tell her I want her. She may come in her bedgown—and tell her I'm waiting, and if she keeps me waiting long I shall wring her neck, and so I warn her—go *on*, now——'

Celia was scowling when she came into the boudoir ten minutes later, wrapped in an old silk peignoir of her mother's, and with her eyes puffy and a little red-rimmed.

'Lyddy said you wanted me,' she said sulkily and stood there in the doorway hugging herself with her shoulders a little bowed and staring at her mother under her straight brows.

'La, look at you!' Lilith said, and sounded suddenly good-humoured. 'To be so young, yet look so drab as you do—I'd have been ashamed at your age! What's this Lydia says about you crying last night? What have you to cry about, tell me? You've a better life than I ever had, with food to your belly and clothes to your back——'

'So you have told me before,' Celia said, her voice still thick with sleep and sullenness. 'Lyddy said you wanted me. Was it to tell me yet again how ill I look?'

Lilith laughed then, and held her arms out towards her daughter.

She was sitting on her blue brocade chaise-longue, her silvery wrapper barely covering her long slender legs, her hair tumbled prettily on her shoulders, and she looked quite enchanting.

'Oh, there, you silly baby, come to your Mama then, and don't look so sulky at me! You *make* me say these cruel things to you when you come to me with such a look upon your face! Now come here and we shall be comfortable together as we were when you were little and not so saucy a madam as you have become—now, come along!'

And in spite of herself, Celia did, pulled as she always was by her mother's beauty and sparkling gaiety when she was minded to show it, and by all the memories of the past years when Celia had been little and Lilith so loving, playing with her for all the world as though she were a doll, and a dearly beloved one at that.

If only it could always have been so, if only Mama could be again as she had been before that day when Celia had come to her weeping and bewildered, her shift and drawers all blood spattered, and shaking with alarm at the strangeness of it all. Her mother had looked at her, at the state of her muslin dress, and her face had hardened suddenly and she had said shrilly, 'Get out of my sight, you dreadful creature—out of my sight, to come to my drawing-room in such a state! You make me puke——' And Celia had fled, in tears of terror, bewildered by the blood and by her mother's sudden cold rage, and Hawks had gathered her into her bony old arms and told her shortly that she was a woman now and to mind her ways, and showed her how to set herself to rights. But Hawks had refused to talk of her mother's anger and had just shrugged her shoulders and hooded her eyes in the way she did when she was questioned and disliked it, and it had never again been the same with Mama——

But now she sat there on her chaise-longue and held out her arms, and as though she were a child again Celia crept into them, and rested her head upon that pink and white softness, and closed her eyes, knowing it meant nothing and that her mother was about to ask something of her that would be disagreeable, and yet being glad of it, for it was better than never being able so to rest her head.

'You shall not fret yourself so, my pretty,' Lilith crooned. 'You shall tell me what it is that made you weep, and Mama shall put it right!' There was a silence and then she went on softly: 'Was it that young man who so distressed you? Did he speak ill to you? You looked black enough at him last night when I was speaking to him——'

Celia closed her eyes and shrank a little inside herself, but still lay there against her mother. The boy last night? Of course it was not the fault of the boy last night! And yet of course it *was* he that had made her weep away the long dark hours of the night and made her sleep so ill and wake so miserable and heavy this morning. It was he inasmuch as Lilith had seen him, and he had seen Lilith. And whether that was his fault, or her mother's fault, Celia, tired and miserable as she was, did not know. All she knew was that she had seen a boy and liked him, and spoke to him and liked him more, and then—and then what? Then Lilith had spoken to him and all had been immediately different.

'Well, he shall not make my little Celia so sad!' Lilith said after a moment, and moved briskly so that Celia had to sit up, and Lilith swung her legs down and off the chaise-longue, almost pushing Celia to the end of it, and began to walk about the room in the way she had when she was excited about something. Celia sat and watched her, dully, trying not to think of anything at all.

'I shall tell you what we shall do, my Celia,' Lilith was saying, as she flitted about her room, touching the gilt and china ornaments on the little tables and running her fingers over the heavy sea-blue velvet drapes that framed the windows. 'We shall punish the wretch for making my Celia sad. You shall write to him and bid him come to see you again, and then we shall contrive a way to make him sorry he——'

'I do not know where he lives,' Celia said with a sudden sharpness. She had not the least desire to see that boy again, she told herself, nor to see him looking at Mama. 'I do not know, nor do I care one whit whether he——'

Lilith looked at her over her shoulder, all sparkle and wickedness, and grinned so widely that perforce Celia produced a watery little smile in response.

'Well, if you don't care, then I do! No stupid boy shall upset my Celia. So, you do not know where he lives? That is no difficulty! We shall set old Hawks to seek out his address. She has her ways, the old besom, and shall set herself to it. Go and tell her, now, you hear me? His name is Lackland. *Lackland.* There cannot be many in London of such a name, who are surgeons! Hawks will find his father's house soon enough, I promise you. Go on, now—go and *tell* her!'

And Lilith stamped her foot and frowned, and wearily Celia rose to her feet and went. She knew better than to gainsay her mother when she was in such a mood of contrasting anger and softness, gaiety and rage as she was this morning. Celia had seen it all before. Her mother was always so when she found some new man to follow at her heels——

For the rest of the day Celia worked very hard at not thinking about her mother's interest in Jo Lackland, and worked even harder at not thinking about how she felt herself.

6

They had walked in silence to the end of Gower Street, and across Bedford Square to Charlotte Street debouching at last into the noise and rush of Oxford Street. The elegant houses they passed, with their neat front doors crowned with the fragile plaster shells and tracery of their fanlights and their froth of iron-lace balconies marched away on each side of them in a constant procession, and still neither of them spoke.

To those who passed them—and there were a few men of their own class, dressed like them in heavy caped overcoats and beaver hats, as well as many servants scrubbing front steps and burnishing the link rings and boot-scrapers and brass work that adorned the housefronts—they were an agreeable sight. Each was tall and upright, each walked with a long and easy stride that was so perfectly matched that they almost appeared to be marching, and each was of undoubted good looks.

The little tweeny scrubbing the steps some six houses from their own had looked up yearningly as they passed, for she thought them the handsomest men she had ever seen, and could not decide which had the better looks—the older stern one, or the younger soulful-looking one. And with the two of them so alike, she had told herself, returning to the whitestone that so hurt her red and swollen hands, how could any choose? She envied the unknown Dorothea for her fortune in being wife to one and mother to the other, and sighed and scrubbed her step harder than ever.

In Oxford Street Abel paused for a moment and stood looking along its length at the fashionable shops where apprentices were starting the day by taking down the shutters that protected the precious plate-glass windows and hanging out the merchandise for passers-by to see and touch and haggle over, at the carts and heavier drays pulled by tired sweating horses bringing produce and goods from the western villages into the great hungry maw of the city lying smokily to the east, and grunted.

'It is my custom to walk all the way, Jonah. I find it less fatiguing than seeking one of these scoundrelly hacks who shake one's bones to jelly, they drive so ill. The way I choose goes through streets and alleys you know little of, but it is necessary that you should if you are to comprehend what it is I have to show you. But I warn you, it looks ill and smells worse. And the people who live here take it very amiss if those dressed as you and I show any disgust. You understand me? We shall walk this way and be safe enough, for I am known in these parts and enjoy a certain—respect. You shall share in that as long as you do not let any hint of dismay show on your face. You understand me?'

Jonah frowned irritably. 'Of course, sir. I am not one given to sneering, I promise you. I may regard myself as—as a man of fashion in some small way, but I do not lack manners, I trust!'

Abel laughed suddenly, with a glint of real amusement in his eyes which made Jonah blink.

'I have no doubt, my young man of fashion, that you would not sneer. I spoke only because you have a very speaking countenance. I ask you simply to control it.'

And he raised his stick imperiously and plunged into the traffic in the mire of the roadway, so that one horse reared and its driver cursed and another had to dodge so fast that he almost locked his wheels with a handcart, and Jonah had perforce to follow his father through the swearing, shouting mêlée into the tangle of tiny streets and alleyways that lay between the respectable richness of Oxford Street and the narrow thoroughfare of Tavistock Street, pressed hard up against the northern flank of the Strand.

That such places existed he had always known, for he was a child of London and had been reared too close to these warrens not to have heard of them. But he knew of them only in the abstract, just as he knew of the deserts of Arabia and the jungles of Africa; exotic places he had been told of but had never seen. These slums partook of the same remote strangeness to him now. His nurses had warned him of the evil men who lurked in the Dials and Bermudas and Porridge Island, those rookeries teeming with thieves and pimps and whores and thrust so hard against the river that they bade fair to fall in, as warning tales to make him obedient. He had imagined them as being intensely frightening, and gloriously romantic in consequence. What he had never imagined, could never have visualized in his own comfortable home, was the sheer misery that met his eyes and the stench that greeted his nose as he picked his way after his father's erect and striding figure over the greasy cobbles and reeking gutters.

There were children everywhere, scrawny pallid whey-faced creatures with faces lined like those of old men, bearing expressions of preternatural knowingness that made his throat tighten with embarrassment. Their legs were sticklike, the flesh of their thighs lying in dry dead folds above knees that looked swollen in their boniness, and their bellies protruded with pitiful arrogance from their rags.

Looking over his shoulder Abel saw the look on the boy's face, and slackened his pace. 'That is the face of hunger, my boy,' he said with rare gentleness, as he put his stick kindly enough behind his son's back to urge him forwards more rapidly. 'And these you see are the so-called fortunate ones, for they have survived. For each of these there are some two or three below ground, I promise you. The women here breed like flies, for all their poverty, so there is a never-ending flow of these starving objects to replace those who so mercifully die.'

He looked sideways again at his son and then said abruptly: 'I was once such a one.'

Jonah turned his head to look at the face a little above his own, and tried to see in its harsh lines and the set of the mouth a grey-faced child with lack-lustre eyes and flaking skin, tried to see him as one of the starving empty-eyed creatures sitting on doorsteps and leaning against the slimy walls they were hurrying past, and quite failed.

'One of these, Papa?' he said, and essayed a smile. 'You are bamming me, are you not? You had a—a strange childhood, that much I know, for Mama has told me you have not a family of your own beyond herself and us, and told me a little of your history, besides, but I cannot imagine——'

'No,' Abel said sourly, 'I dare say you cannot. But so it is.' And again he lengthened his stride so that Jonah had to hurry faster to keep up with him.

And it was as well that they moved so fast, for that helped him to control the waves of nausea the smells around him sent heaving in his chest. His nose was not an unduly delicate one, for he had spent five years at school, sharing a dormitory with thirty healthy boys, none of whom were overfond of washing nor overshy about their physical functions. They had shared chamber-pots and laughed raucously at each other's farts and belches, and sneered at any schoolfellow that showed offence, and he had been as coarse as any of them; but this— this was something quite different. For it was not just the heavy reek of human excreta, the sour weight of unwashed human flesh that filled the air, but a thick sweetish odour that was almost palpable in its power.

'You dislike the smell?' Abel said abruptly, and Jonah nodded, afraid to open his mouth, quite sure that it was only the clenching of his lips and teeth that kept his nausea at bay.

'It is the odour of putrefaction,' Abel said calmly. 'Death is a common experience in these parts, and to bury a body is a costly business. So they keep their dead until they can find the money to get them set decently aground, or until they can find some helper to assist them deal with the matter at the edge of the river or in any corner they can find. They are great fools, of course, for if they went to Charles Bell at Windmill Street or Joshua Brooks in Blenheim Street they would do more than take their corpses off their hands; they would pay them good money besides. But these people are superstitious and put more of a value on the bodies of their dead than on the needs of the living flesh. For every body sold to the anatomists, there are ten or more left here to stink.'

'The anatomists?' Jonah managed, concentrating his mind on his father's words in an effort to ignore the urgent messages assaulting his other senses.

'Aye, the anatomists. Those who teach medical students their business—and teach such apothecaries' apprentices as have a mind to apply for the membership of the Royal College of Surgeons as well as enter for the examinations of their own Society.' He snorted then. 'Times have changed since my own apprenticeship. Then I had to scramble for such education as I could get from my master, and good a man as old Josiah Witney was, a fair scramble I found it, between keeping his shop and casting his accounts. Today the Society lays down such rules of training that the veriest laziest fool can get himself qualified. And now they have added midwifery this past year, they will set fair to regard themselves the complete hand at the profession. Yet without the study of anatomy! How can a man ever be a midwife of any skill or understanding at all if he has never set his knife to a corpse? It makes no sense to me, Act of Parliament or no Act of Parliament!'

Jonah blenched even more, if that were possible, and stumbled a little as he followed his father, still hurrying southwards, through the narrow winding alleys. His imagination was a powerful one, had plagued his infancy and childhood with the vividness of the dreams and nightmares it threw up, and hearing his father talk so calmly now of setting knives to corpses was making his flesh creep with horror and sending tiny rivulets of sweat snaking down his body beneath his clothes.

'Papa—' he essayed, and swallowed, and tried again. 'Papa, I could not, I do assure you, I could not possibly make a study of the sort that— that you did. I have vast respect for you, sir, and for your learning and for the work you have done, but to ask of me the same ability to— to handle human flesh as you have done—indeed, it is not possible, Papa!'

Abel glanced over his shoulder at Jonah's white and pleading face and again felt the wave of irritation rise in him; why was the boy so *stubborn*? Why could he not understand the beauty that lay beneath each human skin, the elegant and so deeply satisfying organization of the parts, the splendour of the sinuous arteries all fitting so perfectly into their appointed places? And then he sighed sharply and reminded himself of the purpose of this journey; the boy was to see for himself what it was all about, and to discover his own joy in the work that had to be done. So he merely grunted, and hurried on, with Jonah as close behind him as he could safely get.

Tavistock Street came as a considerable relief to Jonah, for it was wider and cleaner than the alleys. It ran parallel with the Strand, and the back of the huge building that was the English Opera House loomed over its eastern end. He looked up at the building for a moment and opened his mouth to say something of it to his father, and then thought again. To speak to him of theatres, even opera houses, would be hardly politic.

Alongside the Opera House ran a row of houses which had a look that was both dilapidated and new. He said as much to Abel, who grunted again.

'Aye, they were ill-built, these houses. They made a great to-do about widening the Strand some eight years ago, and ripped this street apart, but the houses ran down so fast I was able to get one cheap enough for the dispensary when I wanted it. But already it is falling into disorder—the builders were ill craftsmen, and so we spend more than we should of our money to keep the fabric in good heart. I would rather we spent it on people as on bricks and mortar—but without the bricks and mortar, what can we do for the patients? It is a never-ending battle.'

They picked their way through the crowded street, and now Jonah became aware of a sort of excitement in the air, a certain movement among the crowds who hitherto had watched their progress with dead eyes and no apparent interest. But the people clustered in Tavistock Street turned their heads to look, and fell away before them, while others pressed closer. It was an odd sensation, like walking through a field of corn, he thought with a sudden access of poeticism, with people instead of high golden heavy-headed stems opening a path before them and closing it behind them. And very active corn it was, he told himself, as the press of the crowd came between him and Abel, forcing him back and separating them by several yards.

'Good day to you, yer honour! Is yer honour in good 'ealth this lovely mornin' then? Will yer honour do a little business with a poor man this mornin' as 'as need of a few pennies to bless 'isself with? I got some of the real stuff, yer honour, none o' yer rubbish, the real stuff——'

A little thin man so wrapped in rags that no vestige of his shape could be seen was pressing hard against Jonah and he pulled away, wrinkling his nose at the smell of him, and looked down at the sharp-eyed little face that was peering up at him from a thicket of dirty reddish coloured whiskers.

'The real thing, yer honour,' the man wheezed again, and dropped his voice. 'Lotion of the 'orn of the fabled rhino, yer honour, and there's no girl alive as'll resist yer wi' some of this inside 'er, as well you may 'ave 'eard!' The old man held up one claw of a hand, clutching a dark green glass bottle, and thrust it invitingly under Jonah's nose, making him rear back in even greater distaste. 'Come on, yer honour, a nothin' to you—just a shillin' in me 'and, and this little bottle's in yours and none'll know as where you——'

Abel, well ahead by now and pushing purposefully through the crowds became aware of Jonah's absence from his rear and turned his head, and from his vantage-point—being a head taller than the accompanying mob—saw the little man clinging to Jonah's side; and he let out a roar of rage. The little man looked up and saw Abel for the first time and immediately his eyes narrowed, and he turned and melted away into the crowd before Abel could push through the mob to reach Jonah's side.

'By God, I thought I was rid of that one!' Jonah looked at his father and was startled at the rage that was hardening his face to planes that looked carved from solid wood. 'I tell you, I'll——' he stopped and looked round at the crowd, and shouted at the top of his voice. 'If I hear that any of you have sold your medicines to him or any like him, I'll turn you from the doors, and so I tell you! I'll not have the likes of that gutter rat anywhere near my dispensary, nor any of my patients. So if any of you here think you are going to gain aught but medical care from me, you can be about your business! You hear me, all of you? We'll give you care for your ills at the dispensary, and medicine for those that need it, but if I hear of any selling what they get free from me, I'll kill them with my own hands and toss them into Windmill Street with the topped ones! Do you all hear me?'

Jonah stood and stared, quite stunned by the effect his father was having. The crowd which had been heaving and pushing was standing quite still now staring at Abel, women with heads covered in greasy old shawls despite the thin warmth of the September sunshine, ragged children, barefoot and some bare-arsed besides, with only a dirty grey shift across their scrawny flanks, and men with shoulders hunched and eyes peering narrowly from beneath matted hair, all quite silent. And Abel stood there glaring around at them and all that could be heard now that he stopped shouting was the rumble of wheeled traffic from the Strand behind them, and the shriek of some seabirds that had come flying upriver from the chill of the mud-flats of Essex.

'You hear me?' Abel said again, less loudly now, and there was a movement through the crowd, a bobbing shifting sway, and Abel nodded curtly and turned, jerking his head at Jonah to follow him, and now the crowd parted before them with no pushing at all on their part, and opened a path that led directly to one of the houses.

As they walked briskly up the worn steps towards the closed yellow door Jonah said quietly, 'What was all that? I did not understand——'

Abel thrust at the door with his stick, and immediately it opened, and he walked in, nodding brusquely to the little maidservant who stood bobbing behind it, and Jonah followed him.

'There are rogues who buy my patients' medicines from them, and then sell it, purporting it to be some sort of love potion. And there are fools that believe it—young men of fashion who come to the Garden after the tails—the whores—and think to improve their performance and their pleasures with such rubbishes. I give medicines for the cure of the belly-ache of the sick and they try to use it for the firing of the bellies of fools. I have no patience with them——' and now he turned and looked at Jonah with one lip slightly raised in a sneer. 'Nor with those who think it clever to frequent these streets in the clothes of a dandy. Such as they deserve all that the cheats can do to them. You were mistaken for one of them—Give your coat to Betty here, and we'll be about our business.'

Sullenly Jonah peeled off his coat with the aid of the little maid, who had to stand on tiptoes to reach him, and followed his father along the narrow dark hall, his heart sinking again. Bad enough the journey through the alleys; if those pushing stinking dirty people outside were the ones that he was now to see being patients, the morning would be an even worse ordeal than he had supposed.

Abel led the way into a big room at the rear of the house, one that was bright with the sunshine pouring in through unexpectedly wide windows, but cold and exceedingly airy, for the panes were set wide to the day outside, so much so that Jonah shivered slightly.

But Abel seemed unaware of the temperature of the room, and was shrugging on an old black coat of antiquated cut. As he pulled its greenish stiffness across his wide shoulders he caught Jonah's eye, and said shortly, 'Do not look so disgusted! I wear this with pride. This was the coat I wore to my first operation with Astley Cooper and I have worn it for every operation I have done since. You would not expect it to look otherwise, would you? Well, girl, let's about it, let's about it! Go and fetch Nancy at once! Looking at the street outside there's work and enough to keep me here till gone tomorrow——'

The little maid scuttled away, and Abel turned to a bench that ran beneath the windows, leaving Jonah time to look about him. Not that he liked what he saw. The room was bleak and spare and ugly to a degree, with a floor of scrubbed bare boards and walls painted a heavy green below and a plain yellow above, in a manner Jonah had only seen before in his schoolroom at Mr Loudoun's. It seemed quite out of place here, in what was patently an ordinary house.

In the middle of the room there was a bare board bed, with a rough sacking blanket thrown across it, and on the far side was a tall desk big enough for two men to stand at. Facing this was a long table on which were ranged so fearsome a display of instruments that Jonah turned his eyes away, and then, fascinated as a rabbit is fascinated by a stoat, turned his gaze back to look at the knives and scissors, the saws and chisels and other pieces of ominous metalware that lay there, mute yet threatening. After that conversation with his father on their journey here he could visualize all too easily how such objects were meant to be used, and could not decide which sickened him more; the thought of their being used on dead flesh, or on the living flesh of a feeling person. Either way, the whole idea of surgery was revolting to him.

He opened his mouth to say as much to his father's back, bent over the rows of bottles and jars set higgledy-piggledy on the bench, and then closed it as the door opened and a tall and well-fleshed woman, with her hair tied up in a housemaid's white cap and wearing a lavender print dress covered with a voluminous white apron, came bustling in, rolling up her sleeves to reveal heavy muscular arms as she did so.

'Good morning to you, sir! I'm sorry not to have been ready at the door for you, but there's one above that I'm sore beset about, and couldn't leave for the moment——'

She looked up then, her sleeves set to her satisfaction, and for the first time saw Jonah standing there with his hands set in his pockets in a pose of attempted insouciance, but with an expression of strained caution on his face. She stood there and stared at him, and slowly a smile moved across her face, lifting the heavy red-veined cheeks into round apples of real delight.

'Well, Master Lackland! Oh, none other but Master Lackland! Oh, Mr Abel, but he is so much your son it is almost laughable! To see him standing there—why, it is like seeing you, as you were, in the days of my trouble all those years ago—' She slid her eyes sideways to look at Abel, who had turned and was looking at her, and she smiled even more widely so that her pale blue eyes almost disappeared into her rotund face, and said softly, 'Not that there could ever be one who looked to me as *you* did then——'

68

'Well, enough of that, Nancy! I've told you before, there's no sense in turning over all the past. There's now and tomorrow to think about and——'

'Aye, so you always say, Mr Abel.' She moved across the room to stand in front of Jonah, her hands on her hips, and her head on one side, appraising him quite shamelessly. 'But for my part, my gratitude runs too deep to be silent, and I must tell all that will hear me of what I owe to you. 'Twas your father, my boy, who made it possible for me to be standing here and looking at you, for without him I'd ha' died at the age of thirteen more than twenty years ago. I've said it ever since that all men in this wicked world are sinners, set to make the lives of poor women a hell and a burden, all, that is, except your father who is no less than a saint on earth, and to be——'

'Nancy, hold your tongue!' Abel said, but there was no real anger in his voice, and Jonah looked curiously at him, and was startled at the expression he saw on his face. On any other man it would have been embarrassment, but since he had never seen his father display any hint of such an emotion, it seemed incredible to Jonah that it could be such an experience that moved him now. 'Away with you, woman, and get the patients, for there's a street full out there, and more to come besides, I've no doubt, for the weather for all its brightness is getting treacherous cold and they'll be falling prey to it and in need of us.'

'Well, they can wait a little longer, while I take my time to look at the boy, Mr Abel! You'd not deprive me of that! Do you know, my lad, I've not seen you since—oh, it must be a dozen years or so—do you remember?'

'Remember?' Jonah frowned and shook his head. 'You must forgive me, ma'am, but I think you are in error. I have not been here before in all my life and——'

She shook her head impatiently. 'Not here, boy, not here. At Lucy's. Your good father brought you there to see her when she was ill and fit to die and had set her heart on a sight of you, and Mr Abel bent himself to her will—for who does not bend to Lucy's will?—and took you there, and I saw you then, as pretty a baby as ever I set eyes upon, with your curls and your——'

'Lucy?' Jonah frowned even more deeply and then said again—more uncertainly, 'Lucy—that sounds a—I believe—a house of great light?

With many vast pictures on the walls, and a great woman in a bed in a room so hot I could scarce breathe?——'

'He does remember! You see, Mr Abel? He remembers!' Nancy cried delightedly. 'Aye, Lucy's——'

'Nancy, will you be about the morning's business, *now*!' Abel's voice came more sharply across the room and now she looked at him, and nodded, and some of the pleasure slipped from her face but she still looked friendly and sketched a wink at Jonah as she turned to go.

'We'll talk again later, boy, when your father is less beset. Mr Abel, there's one above that I am concerned for—she's been labouring these past eight hours or more, and I fear for her, poor creature. Will you go above to see her while I set the first patient ready for you in here? Young Jonah can remain here while you are gone—there's Mary or Nellie there to give you aught you need, or shall I come with you?'

'No,' Abel said, and moved to the door. 'I can manage with either of the others. Send in all the children first, now, for I want no squalling to drive us mad all through the morning. I'll be soon back——' and he went, leaving Nancy with her hand on the door.

'Before you go,' Jonah said urgently, suddenly unwilling to be left in this big cold airy room with its ugly instruments and ominous flat couch, 'tell me more about our last meeting—I remember so little. Just Lucy's name, and—who is Lucy? And did she die of her illness?'

'Lucy die?' Nancy threw back her head and laughed hugely. '"Twould take more than a mere illness to kill our Lucy! No, she's as hale as ever she was, but vaster if that were possible—and will she be sick with rage when I tell her Mr Abel brought you here! She'll demand he take you to see her, see if she doesn't! Oh, you'll see her again soon enough, or my name's not Nancy Barbett!'

'It will be a remarkable woman who can command my father to do aught,' Jonah ventured and looked carefully at the woman, for he was now in no doubt that she was not one that would willingly listen to any hint of criticism of Abel. He was not at home now, talking to the servants.

'Lucy *is* a remarkable woman,' Nancy said, and now turned more definitely, 'as you will see for yourself, I promise you! She is your father's oldest friend in all this world, after all, and one he loves most dearly. Bar one, that is——' and then she was gone, leaving Jonah frowning at the closed door and for the first time that morning more interested in what he was discovering than in his own feelings. How could his father's oldest friend be one whose name he had never heard mentioned at home, and one he had himself visited only once in his most distant infancy? And what on earth had Nancy's mysterious 'bar one——' meant? It was more intriguing than he would have thought possible.

7

In the event, Abby went alone to buy the new clothes for Gussy. Dorothea, in her anxiety and confusion about her son (for she was worrying herself a great deal about how they would be faring together, and fearing the worst for her beloved Jonah) had quite forgotten, until her friend arrived in a flurry of pink silk and breathlessness to call for her, that she had promised Maria Cloudesly that she would accompany her to a luncheon of the London Ladies' Society for the Rescue of the Children of the Profligate Poor. Since this was a Society in which Dorothea was held in some esteem (more by virtue of her status as daughter of the late founder, Mrs Charlotte Constam, than because of her own industriousness or influence in the Society's work) she could not escape attendance, and went off apologizing profusely to Abby for so sadly disordering her plans, and needing considerable soothing from her daughter as she climbed into the carriage.

But Abby, a little guiltily, was glad it had fallen out so. Dorothea was far from being a restrictive parent (and indeed the two females enjoyed a degree of friendship that many girls of Abby's acquaintance envied) and made no objections at all when Abby suggested visiting the Witney shop in Piccadilly whenever they went out upon shopping expeditions. Even so, Abby preferred that her mother should not know just how often she made these visits, and just how important they were to her. Dorothea might be far more aware of her son's feelings and reactions than her daughter's, but even she could hardly fail to notice Abby's growing partiality for James Caspar if it were paraded too clearly before her eyes.

And Abby had for some time now been more than a little concerned about her feelings for James. She had hardly been aware of what was happening at first. She had found James a warm good friend, she had admired his good sense, and wise speech, and appreciated his acceptance of her as an equal rather than as a child of much fewer years than his own, and it had come almost as a shock to realize that what she felt for him was more, much more, than mere friendship. But so it was, and it had been such a foolish thing that had opened her eyes to her feelings, an everyday, common-or-garden sort of thing, and in the years to come she was often to marvel at it, and think of how little it could take to point a person's life in a totally different direction.

It had been a blustery spring-like morning, with a faint scent of distant flowers in the air blowing into the dust of Piccadilly from the fringes of Hyde Park. They had been standing at the door of the shop, she bidding him farewell for she had been there half the morning and it was high time she returned to Gower Street; but he had seemed to be in no hurry to part with her, and they had stood there laughing as the insolent young wind whipped at her skirts and sent the ribbons of her bonnet tossing around her face and ruffled his red hair into absurd and rather childlike curls.

The street was, as always, full of people. Fashionable people strolling and staring at the shop fronts, country people up for a day at the markets trotting and gawping at the fashionable, and shrewd traders keeping a close eye on them all and displaying the most seductive of their wares at their shopdoors for everybody's delectation, rich or poor.

Quite suddenly, in the middle of some nonsense she was saying, James had put out his hand and set it on her wrist, and stared over her shoulder and she turned her head to follow his gaze to see, standing on the edge of the road with the hooves and wheels of the rattling traffic terrifyingly near to him, a man of somewhat past middle age though not yet old enough to be regarded as really elderly. He had both hands to his face, and was swaying a little, shaking his head in obvious distress, and suddenly James moved forwards with startling speed and set his hands firmly on the man's shoulders, pulling him back so that he fell against his chest—and just in time, for clearly he had been about to lose his balance and pitch forward into the road. The old man still held his hands clasped tightly to his face, and as Abby reached the pair of them, for it had taken a moment for her to realize what had happened, James turned him, exerting a firm but kindly enough pressure on his shoulders, and led him towards the safety of the shop doorway, out of the whipping of the wind which was still tossing up great clouds of dust.

The old man's hat, a tall and clearly costly beaver of elegant make, had blown from his head and Abby darted to pick it up from the mud of the gutter (to the undoubted chagrin of a street urchin who had seen it go and had hoped to get such rich pickings for himself) and then followed James and his companion into the shop.

She found the old man sitting on a chair, his head back and resting on James's chest, while James leaned over him and with infinite gentleness took the eyelid of the right eye between his fingertips and raised it. The old man whimpered, and Abby blinked in sympathy, for she knew how painful could be grit in the eye. The old man was clearly suffering much distress, for his cheeks were streaked with tears, and his nose was running so piteously that she found herself thinking of little Gussy, and the way his nose ran when he wept.

'There!' James had said after a moment and leaned over the old man to tuck his handkerchief into his grasp. ''Tis out, sir. No harm done, I'll be bound! But it was big enough a piece of stuff to do damage, and it is no surprise it hurt you so! I shall bring you soothing oil to bathe your eye, if you will wait a moment,' and he went away to the back of the shop, leaving the old man wiping away at his now reddened lids.

'Well, there was my good fortune, I must say,' he said a little tremulously as he peered up at Abby and essayed a smile. 'To find so kindly a gentleman and one able to deal with my discomfort so prompt and careful.' He turned his head as though to look about the shop, blinking a little to clear his gaze, and then shook it and said to Abby, 'Forgive me if I seem foolish, but I can see but little at the best of times, for I have a cataract of the left eye, and with an unwanted object afflicting t'other, I am in sorry case—there *is* someone there, is there not?' And again he peered in Abby's direction.

'Indeed, yes, sir,' Abby said, and moved forwards. 'And I have here your hat which blew from your head as the object flew into your eye. I am happy to return it to you—it is not too muddied, and I have brushed off what I may.'

'Why, thank you, ma'am,' the old man said, and managed a watery smile. 'And could you tell me where I am and to whom I am indebted for such help? I can assure you I was much afraid when I felt my eye pierced, for I am purblind enough, Heaven knows, and the fear of total darkness is always with me.'

74

'This is the apothecary's establishment, sir,' Abby said. 'It bears the name Witney above the door although the owner is Mr Abel Lackland, the surgeon, and the man who cares for it Mr James Caspar. It was he who came to your help.' And she was a little startled at the note of pride she detected in her own voice; and stood still in her surprise at herself as James came hurrying back with a small blue glass vessel in his hand.

As James bent over the old man and bathed his eye, murmuring to him gently as he worked, Abby watched him and carefully explored the new feelings that were rising in her. And realized with a faint sense of shock that the sight of that narrow, red-headed figure, the sound of that gentle, controlled voice, was very dear indeed to her.

It was as though she had not quite seen him before today, as though observing him tend so lovingly to the minor mishap of a speck of grit in an old man's eye was to see him clearly for the first time. And when James had completed his task and stood back to let the old man straighten his dress and adjust his muddy hat on his sparse grey hair, he looked up at her and smiled, and she felt a strange lurch within her, and smiled at him; and though she did not know it her smile was so brilliant, so filled with warmth and approval, that it made James, in his turn, become aware of his own feelings in a new and startlingly agreeable way. And he reddened and turned back to his unexpected patient in some confusion.

There had been a little fussing as James sent for a jarvey to convey him to his home in the City—'Near Lombard Street, my boy, Lombard Street, no doubt you know it? 'Tis where I and my family have our business, d'you see,' the old man had chattered—and saw him on his way after accepting his card but refusing any payment, for as James said, ' 'Twas merely an accident. I will gladly serve you again if any future need arise, but there is no cause for us to make a pother over so minor a matter now!'

And after he had gone, they had said no more about it at all, and he had handed her to her carriage as he always did and she had bade him farewell with her usual friendly smile, and no more. But she knew, from that time on, that her feelings for James Caspar were far stronger than those of a young woman for a friend, that they had a much higher status indeed; and with her usual calm good sense had given much thought to what should be done about it.

That she should marry James was a decision that she reached quite early in her cogitations. The fact that James said no word nor made any gesture of particular affection towards her made no whit of difference. She knew perfectly well that he could not, in his position as her father's employee, and guessed shrewdly that despite his treatment of her as an equal he was sorely aware of the age difference between them.

But she knew equally well that her feelings were reciprocated. She knew when that tightening of the throat overcame him, knew when his belly seemed to lurch beneath his ribs, knew how much he wanted to touch her, for did she not experience the same sensations, the same needs, the same longings? They did not need to speak to each other of such things, she told herself: they knew, and that was enough.

But, of course, one day they would have to speak of them, and when that time came it would have to be Abby who would tell James of the regard she had for him, Abby who would have to encourage him and soothe his inevitable doubts, Abby who would have to give him the strength to face the problems with her family that would undoubtedly ensue. In their relative positions, this was inevitable.

But this knowledge did not worry her at all. For as long as she could remember she had held in her family the position of counsellor and particular friend to all. Her older brother had started it when they were both still in the nursery by seeking her protection against his father, her father had compounded it by seeking her companionship in preference to all others in the Gower Street house, her mother had underlined it by leaning on her quite shamelessly.

The two younger boys had followed the same pattern, and wrote politely enough to their parents each week from school but urgently to their sister Abby when Mr Loudoun pressed too hard upon them, or when they wanted some extra money or comestibles sent to them in Islington. The quiet and pallid twelve-year-old twins, Mary and Martha, chose her as their only confidante outside each other (for they were happy enough in their absorption with themselves for most of the time) and the little ones—eleven-year-old Bart, soon to join his older brothers in Islington, and of course the baby Gussy—adored her and told her of all their troubles.

Her role as the calm centre of her complex family was one she had always accepted, seeing it as inevitable to her position as oldest daughter of the house. And in a curious way she enjoyed it. Certainly she preferred being herself to being one of the silly vapid girls who proliferated among her acquaintance and who thought of nothing but frills and foolish novels.

As soon as her mother had gone she went collectedly to the nursery to discuss Gussy's clothing needs with his nurse, and having listed them and measured the squirming, laughing, squealing Gussy (for as the youngest and patently the last entry to the nursery, his nurse adored him and spoiled him quite outrageously), then went to her room to put on her lace-edged shoulder cape and small straw bonnet with the mulberry feathers.

Looking for a moment in the tall glass in her dressing-room she tried to see herself as James might see her, setting her head on one side to regard the green and white taffeta gown with its lace ruffles, the white kid gloves and the neat black slippers; but all she could see was herself as she always looked.

For an uncharacteristic moment she faltered, and wondered if perhaps James did *not* regard her as in any way desirable, for in her own eyes she was far from pretty, and even began to wonder whether she was perhaps deluding herself in believing him to bear affection towards her; and then smiled at her own foolishness. James cared for her as she did for him, and to concern herself with such nonsense as prettiness was quite absurd.

She dismissed her maid in Piccadilly, sending her to buy ribbons, an errand which she knew would occupy the girl for a contented hour or more, and went quietly into the shop to stand just inside the door for a moment before making her way through to the back where she knew James would be.

Young Peter, the fourteen-year-old who served as errand boy and unarticled apprentice and general assistant to the busy James, was polishing the brass strip that edged the long mahogany counter and looked up and bobbed his head and moved as though to call James, but she shook her head at him and stood quietly looking about the shop and breathing in its ambience.

She had come to love this peaceful haven of mahogany and cool dark panelled walls, the tall glass jars of scarlet and indigo and emerald liquids throwing bars of vivid colour from their place in the window on to the polished black boards of the floor; the japanned tin boxes with their painted labels—ipecacuanha and quassia chips, cinnamon and

77

pennyroyal, digitalis and magnesium salts—and the smaller white stone jars with their neater lettering—syrup of squills, and oil of camphor, cascara sagrada and oil of cloves. Above all she loved the smells of the place. Some of the odours were soft and beguiling, caressing her nose with gentleness and coaxing her to travel further in search of them. That was the orange-flower water and vanilla pods, the rose water and parma violets that James used in the complexion washes. Then there were the thicker warmer smells that brought back cosy memories of winter nights in the nursery, lying snug in bed with a tight chest and a stuffed head, full of the warmth of Nurse's hot milk and the rich scent of the cloves and cinnamon and ginger with which she had laced it. And then the mysterious and exciting bite of wintergreen and turpentine and spirits of salts—it was all becoming more and more dear to her, sharing in some way in her regard for James. It was as though this place were in physical fact a part of James, instead of simply the place where he spent his time, as though it shared his personality as much as he shared its, for his clothes always smelled a little of the shop.

She shook herself slightly at such fancies, and smiled at Peter and went quietly through the shop towards James's office at the back as the door opened again and a couple of women came in. Peter bobbed at them, and scurried to fetch James—for only in very specially busy circumstances was he allowed to deal with customers—and James came out to greet them, his eyes crinkling with great pleasure when he saw Abby.

He touched her gently on the shoulder in welcome as he passed her, and she smiled at him and went composedly into the office to sit down in the old chair which had been Josiah Witney's and which was now so sadly worn (and which James would not hear of discarding) to wait for him.

Anyone seeing her there with her gloved hands clasped neatly upon her lap, her ankles politely crossed and her shoulders straight would not have guessed for one moment that she was shaking a little inside, but so it was. For she had decided that although it would be many long months—perhaps even years—before any approach could be made to her father on their behalf, she was not prepared to be mute any longer about her affections, nor to let James continue to have to suffer his emotions in silence. They needed to be honest and direct with each other, she told herself, if their mutual regard was to grow as it should.

A longer silence would carry the danger of distorting their friendship, and she would not wish that for the world.

But despite her candour in most matters, she could not bring herself to admit the real cause of her decision. She needed to hear James admit his care for her in so many words, just as she needed to tell him of hers. Just like one of the silly frippery girls she really rather despised, she wanted to speak to her beloved of love.

For a long time now Jonah had been concentrating his mind on one matter only; the necessity to control the sense of nausea that filled him and the need to prevent himself from leaping to his feet and escaping from this putrid hateful room with its putrid hateful people, into the clean air outside.

He had watched them from the stool his father had set for him at the head of the couch, these ragged starving creatures, watched them display their sores to his father, listened to them describe to him with all too vivid imagery the sensations they knew, had stared with horror at the wasted bodies of the infants and children that were displayed to their joint gaze.

He did not know what it was that distressed him most; the patient suffering of these people who followed each other in bewildering numbers to sit upon the couch, or the impassivity with which his father listened to their accounts of their ills. Abel listened and looked, touched and examined, gave terse orders to the dispenser (a young man with a prematurely bald head and a perpetually worried look upon his face, who had come to stand beside the long bottle-and-jar-cluttered bench to make up the medicines ordered for the patients) and equally terse instructions to Nancy, who stood at the end of the couch and applied lotions and unguents and bandages; and never once did any expression cross his face. Even when the sores displayed to him were of so vast and fungating a nature that the very bones showed pearly grey beneath the ravaged flesh, and the stench that arose made Jonah's mouth turn dry with the horror of it, Abel looked the same.

After a little while Jonah had become aware of rage rising in him. How could such things exist in God's world? How could it be that people, human creatures like himself, should suffer such terrible things? How could any man of any heart observe such misery and not be moved to tears of anguish? And Jonah had looked at his father and hated him for his lack of concern and love; until he saw that Nancy too bore the same look of passive acceptance on her face, and saw that the young dispenser too could look upon these hatefulnesses and show no response—and he realized, albeit dimly, that these faces did not bespeak a lack of concern so much as a vast control.

But as the morning wore on, and the horrors followed each other with sickening regularity his rage became blunted, and then thickened and shifted, until he realized he was directing it not at the huge nothingness of Providence but at the people themselves. How dared they suffer so, and show their sufferings to him? What right had they to be as they were? They were an affront to nature as well as to him, and he hated them for it.

And then he found bewilderment rise in him, for had he not had an excellent education, was he not aware of the greatness and goodness of the God who loved them all, and held the world in His special regard? To hate one's fellow men instead of the sins they committed was a sin in itself, so Mr Loudoun had taught him through all his schooldays, and till now Jonah had believed him right. But this . . . this parade of men and women and children who had so obviously been abandoned by their God—and everyone else besides—filled him with a great confusion. A confusion which was the more compounded because of his struggling awareness of what his father was doing in giving them care. It was as though his father had taken on some of the attributes of God, a creature who was to be loved because that was what he existed for, a creature who was to be feared for his immense power, and a creature who was to be hated for his impersonal injustices.

Altogether, Jonah was a miserable young man, uneasy in body and mind, and deeply fatigued by the welter of feeling that these new and confusing sights and smells and sounds created in him.

Abel looked at him from time to time as the morning wore on and wondered what effect was being worked upon the boy. He recognized the horror and the bewilderment, for he had seen these often enough on the faces of medical students. All of them suffered in this way when they were first exposed to the realities of their trade. Most of them responded to it all by developing a carapace of coarseness behind which they hid their lacerated feelings until they healed—or died altogether. Knowing some of his colleagues as he did, Abel suspected that for many of them feeling was long since moribund. Like Astley Cooper whose immense pride in his speed and prowess carried him from operation to operation apparently untouched by the screaming agony of the people upon whom he practised those famous sweeps of knife and incredibly swift manipulations of agonised muscle and joint and bone.

But was there more to Jonah's reaction than the natural revulsion of healthy youth faced with the realities of disease? Was there, he wondered, the anger, the pity and the wonder that had so filled his own boy's mind on a cold night long ago in St Giles's Churchyard when, with Finch, the resurrection man, he had dug up his first body to sell to the anatomists? He remembered the pallid look of that long dead corpse and thought with gratitude of the way she had in her dead dumbness opened to him the door of his career. Were these people having the same effect on Jonah? If they were, then surely the boy would not be able to prevent himself from the study of his father's profession. Abel knew this as certainly as he knew he breathed.

Sometimes, as he cast a glance at the boy, he thought he saw the rage he so wanted to see on that smooth young face, but then he doubted it, for the trouble with Jonah's face was that it was too mobile, too expressive, and reactions chased each other across it with such speed that even the most devoted of observers could be misled; and Abel had little time to devote to observing his son, for the pressure of work from his outside patients was, as usual, immense.

At twelve o'clock he sent Nancy to the front door to tell the people outside—who still stood there in clusters, pushing and shoving each other aside as they tried to reach the door, that no more outdoor patients would be seen until after four of the afternoon and they must take themselves off till then.

'They'll not go, of course,' he told Jonah, as he washed his hands in the bowl held ready for him by the silent dispenser. 'For they never do. Each day I see more and more and each day more and more of them come. The tide of disease, Jonah, is one that never turns, and for each man I send away from here with some small help for his ills—though not enough, for what will cure most of these is meat to their bellies and a dry roof to their head—there come ten more. Do you see why I am so set that you should be apprentice to James, which is my wish, to learn the business of an apothecary and then to me to learn your surgery? There is *work* to be done, boy, such work to be done that no

81

man who calls himself a man can turn away from it! And it can only be done by such as have been properly taught to do it. You speak to me of poetry—how can I give ears to such talk when every day I come here and see such things as this? Your sister told me that you would not understand until I showed you for yourself—so here you are, to see for yourself. Now tell me, am I so harsh a man to seek to teach you the care of these people?'

Jonah sat and stared at his father, and opened his mouth to speak, and then closed it again and mutely shook his head. For a moment Abel's brows snapped together. Was Jonah displaying his lunatic stubbornness again? After so rare a display of tenderness on his own part—and he had been well aware of the conciliatory note that had been in his voice—he could not have borne that. But then he looked again, and saw the dumb misery in Jonah's expression, saw the way his eyes glittered with what might have been unshed tears, and he too closed his mouth and turned away to dry his hands with unusual thoroughness, temporarily shamed by his own emotions, and filled with a curious shyness he would not have believed himself capable of knowing.

Nancy came bustling back into the room, shouting, 'Betty!' over her shoulder at the top of her voice, and the little maid followed her, scuttling shyly past Abel and Jonah to begin busily clearing up the mess of dirty bandages and discarded charpie that lay upon the floor.

'Well, Mr Abel, you'll be rare busy come four o'clock, for they're pressing thick upon the door, fit to bust it in. You'd best leave by way of the Strand door, I'm thinking, if you don't want them mobbing you. After you've gone I'll deal with such as seem simple enough, and try to ease the load upon you that way. But come to the girl above stairs before you go, if you please, for I've looked to her again, and I tell you, she's not like to last much longer, poor creature. If her child's not set crossways to her, then——' she grimaced suddenly, and said more softly. 'You'd best to look yourself, Mr Abel, for you know how I am when I see such girls. I cannot but remember——'

Abel nodded and moved to the door, and looked back at Jonah over his shoulder as he paused there. Should he take the boy with him to see the patients above stairs? Their state, while not so revolting to look upon as that of the street patients—for Nancy washed and barbered and kept in clean linen all she nursed here in Tavistock Street—was still a parlous one, for if they were not sick almost to death they would not qualify for a place in one of his precious beds. Had the boy had enough to start him on the way he should go? Abel wondered briefly. Or would his intention be further created and then strengthened by the sight of the suffering that Abel knew awaited his eyes in the crowded rooms above?

He was never to know how close he had come to winning his battle for his son's future. He was never to know that inside the boy sitting very still and a little slumped upon the tall stool by the head of the couch, with the little maid clearing away the mess beneath his feet, were the glimmerings of a compassion born of the anger his father had looked for so eagerly in him. Had those glimmerings been left alone it could indeed have been that they would grow and strengthen and become like the flame that filled Abel's belly with a constant burning need to work among the sick.

But Abel made the wrong decision, and in so doing, ensured that the emotion and concern he had kindled in his son that morning should be finally and thoroughly doused.

'Before I set upon my visits to the private patients I must treat, for it is they who pay our keep, I must see the inpatients,' he said and his voice had its customary harsh note. 'Come with me. As soon as we have done, you shall be on your way back to Gower Street to ponder on all you have seen.'

8

'Please, Hawks,' Celia said again. 'It is rare enough I ask you for such favours. I am not like Lyddy and Ben—I do not plague you with a million things! But do just this for me, will you? I would be indeed so grateful——'

'Miss Celia, I've told you and I've told you, when yer Ma sets her mind upon a thing, set it is. She'd have my clothes ripped from my back and my eyes scratched out as soon as look at me if I went to her and told her I'd failed in so easy a task! And it'd make no nevermind anyway—after she'd flailed me for not doing her bidding she'd find another as would, for she always does, does she not? and then you'd be worser off than ever on account of you wouldn't have old Hawks about to ease yer way for you——'

She put down the heavy goose iron with which she was smoothing the flounces of one of Lilith's blue dresses, and stretched her back a little, curving her neck tautly in an attempt to ease her tired aching muscles. Looking at her from her seat beside the hot fire in the dark basement kitchen Celia thought sourly that Hawks was quite the ugliest and most hateful woman she had ever seen. And then bit the thought back, for it would be wrong to think ill of someone while begging for a favour.

'You do not have to say you have failed, dear Hawksy,' she said, and her voice now was soft and cajoling. 'Just say you found him, but that—that he's gone away to University and will not be back this six months! That would be a capital tale! She would be put out, I dare say, but she will forget it, and then I'll be left in peace.'

'You 'aven't told me why it matters so much to you, Miss Beg-a-favour.' Hawks picked up the iron again, and shot a malicious glance at Celia from under her heavy brows. 'What should it concern you that yer Ma wants to see the boy again? You've never objected before to her fly-b'nights. Are you getting an attack of the moralities, that you care so now? Why should you be plaguin' old Hawks to tell wicked lies for you? You can't expect me to take aught you say serious when you're so close with your words.'

'Oh, damn you——' Celia muttered under her breath, and swung her legs down from the curled up position she had taken in the big armchair. And then said louder, 'Damn you! If you'll not do as I ask, you'll not, and I know better than to think you'll do it even if I did try to—if I could explain. You'll pick at my thoughts and feelings till they're white and dead as a bone, and then go tittle-tattling to Mama, and make great mock of me!'

'I do no such thing!' Hawks said indignantly. 'I does my duty, and none can say I don't. 'Tis my duty to keep care of you three young limbs o' Satan, and to tell yer Ma when you goes astray. A fair one I'd be to keep it all to myself when you goes misbehavin'! What sort of rearing would that be for the children of Mistress Lucas! And her so lovely and so clever besides——'

'Oh, you're as bad as the rest of them!' Celia said, and her voice was high and tight with tears now. 'Besotted with her! She's not such an angel, God damn you! She's naught but a woman like many others, and the way you worship her, all you idiots, makes me sick. You hear me? It makes me sick!'

'You're a wicked evil girl to talk so of your dear Ma!' Hawks cried, and slapped the iron heavily on to the table, standing with arms akimbo to glare at the girl. ' 'Twould serve you fair if I went above stairs the moment she comes back from the theatre and told her every word you said! And wouldn't you get a beating, and wouldn't you deserve it ——'

'You see?' Celia shouted, and thrust her head forwards to glare at the maddening woman on the other side of the table. 'You see? Tattle-tale, tattle-tale! That's all you ever do! We trust you, stupid fools that we are, me and Lyddy and even poor Ben, and you go and pour your hateful poison into her ears and——'

'Hoity toity miss!' Hawks said, and laughed suddenly and raucously. 'Such airs as you give yerself! I knows why it is you want me to tell yer Ma such wicked lies! I'm not so green as I'm cabbage looking, and I've seen you mooning all day about the place! Lovesick, that's what you are! Sick with love of this boy, and fit to bust for fear he'll not look at you when yer Ma's standing by! *And* nor will he, for yer Ma's worth ten of you! She's as beautiful and as spirited and as clever a lady as ever drew breath and you—you're a silly shadow beside her! Never think that keeping this lad away from yer Ma'll make the least difference to you, on account it won't. If he's once seen her, he'll have no eyes for such as you, you can be bound!'

'Oh, may you rot in hell, you horrible old besom!' Celia roared, and turned and made for the door. 'I hate you, and I don't care what you do! You can't hurt me! Not so much as I can hurt *you*, anyway. I know the tricks you get up to, you evil creature, and if you say aught of me to Mama I'll tell her! And then where will you be, you ugly old fool? Out on the street, that's where——' and she shot out of the door and slammed it behind her, but for all the noise she made she couldn't drown out the sound of Hawks's mocking laughter as it followed her down the dim stone-flagged passage and up the back stairs that led to the hallway above.

'How dare she be so?' Celia raged within herself, trying to choke back the tears of fury that filled her throat. 'How dare she? I hate her, I hate her, I hate her!' But who it was she hated or why she hated she couldn't be quite sure, so miserably bewildered was she. Did she hate her mother for being as she was, so magnetic and beautiful a creature that none could help falling fast into admiration of her, least of all an impressionable poetic boy? Or did she hate Hawks for being unhelpful, or for being so shrewd as to recognize why Celia had wanted her to flout her mother's instructions about finding Jonah and giving him a message? She could not tell and suddenly felt she was too weary to care.

She found Lydia in the bedroom they shared, sitting at the dressing-table and pinning her curly hair into different styles, tying it up with the contents of Celia's ribbon box and, relieved to have someone on whom to vent her feelings, Celia cuffed her and snatched the ribbons from her grubby hands and sent her bawling furiously out of the door to go downstairs to Hawks with her complaints.

'And tell her what you like!' Celia shouted after her. 'For I don't care! I'll not be here to listen to her ravings, anyway, for I'm going to the theatre tonight, and all of you can rot, for all I care!'

And she seized her cloak (for once not caring that it was so childish

86

and old fashioned a garment for one of her mature years) and went stamping down to the front door and out into North Audley Street.

Long before she had traversed the leafiness of Grosvenor Square (ignoring the disdainful glances of those who clearly disapproved of a girl being out without a chaperone at so late an hour of the afternoon) and had made her way through Grosvenor Street to the spanking new elegancies of Regent Street, she had calmed down.

She had ever been thus; up in her high trees at one moment, burning with passion, and deep down in the depths of despair the next. How much of this temperament she had inherited from her father she did not know. Her mother had told her that he had been a man of high position in society, not to speak of vast wealth, but bedevilled by a maggot in his brain that swept him from mood to mood so bewilderingly (according to Lilith) that he had become a dead bore, and she had abandoned him long before Celia's birth.

'And the foolish man died for me!' Lilith had trilled, when telling eleven-year-old Celia the tale. ' 'Twas said he drowned accidental in his own ornamental lake—which had been made special for him by Capability Brown, for he was a man of great fashion, your father—but, there, I knew better! He loved me to a degree that was plain foolish in one of his position.'

Remembering this now, Celia shivered a little, and drew her cloak closer about her shoulders against the chill of the darkening autumn afternoon. Was there such a maggot in her own brain? She was too easily swept from one state to another, she told herself mournfully, and mayhap she too would be found one day floating face down in a pond somewhere——

But not for love, she told herself stoutly then, and managed to walk almost as far as Regent Circus before she finally had to give up the effort to convince herself of the facts. For there was no doubt that she had been struck in a very strange manner by the face and form and conversation of Jonah Lackland. It was no use to tell herself, as she had done a hundred times since last night, that it was foolish in the extreme to fall into such a trance about a person she had seen but for a few minutes, and talked to for very little longer. The facts could not be gainsaid; his face filled her memory's eye as his voice filled her memory's ear, and she was making herself very miserable indeed about him.

She had wondered whether her partiality was fed by the fact that her mother had displayed so great an interest in the young man; she was no fool, Celia, and was well aware, even if she were not able to put it easily into words, of the complexity of the feelings she entertained for her mother. She hated and loved her in virtually equal parts, each emotion constantly striving to overcome the other, and was as fascinated by her, as besotted by her, as heartbroken by her, as anyone else who came into her orbit.

She had wondered if her feeling for Jonah was in truth an expression of her jealousy of her mother—for this emotion too moved in her breast, and she was able to recognize it for what it was—but had decided that while this made her feelings more painful, it did not have any part in the creation of them.

As she moved now into the muddy roadway, to avoid walking under the tall iron columns of the Quadrant (for footpads and rogues of all sorts were known to hang about in the subfusc shadows of that stately pile) she told herself not for the first time since that fateful meeting only twenty-four hours ago (could it be such a short period?) that she was a fool, but there it was; the young man had made a painfully indelible impression on her with his narrow green eyes and thick dark hair and handsome white face, and there was nothing she could do to alter that. She had seen him and for better or ill she was obsessed with him, and that was all there was to it.

She crossed Regent Circus, hurrying now, for the light was fast failing and the crowds were beginning to gather. The fashionably dressed strollers of Mayfair and Grosvenor Square had given way to the clusters of doubtful characters who hung about in the purlieus of the Haymarket, and the buildings dwindled from the high-storeyed elegancies of Regent Street to the dingy, shabby and undoubtedly ill-smelling muddle of rotting structures that lined Coventry Street and the Haymarket.

There was more light here, however, for the few linkmen of rich Mayfair were replaced by a multitude of lighted shop windows, cookshops and ribbon shops, wineshops and gin parlours and itinerant sellers bearing smoking flares strapped to their makeshift stalls.

The air smelled of food and drink, of smoke and dirt and above all of humanity, and Celia breathed it in deeply as she went on her way along the Haymarket towards the theatre where her mother had held sway these sixteen years or more. She let optimism lift her spirits a little. Maybe Jonah would ignore her mother's summons; maybe he would return, but on his own behalf and to seek out Celia rather than Lilith—but at that absurd idea she had to grimace, and recognize the lunacy that had gripped her. Such a thing could never happen, and it was quite ridiculous to pretend otherwise.

Even as Celia's cloaked figure disappeared into the hubbub and smoky lights of the Haymarket, the hackney-carriage bearing Abby and her maid went clattering through the mud past the entry to the street, on its way to Leicester Square and St Martin's Lane before turning north to make its way to Gower Street.

Abby sat quietly in her corner, her back quite straight against the dusty squabs, staring out of the murky window at the streets lurching past and trying to keep her thoughts in order. In the opposite corner her maid sat with her head drooped on her chest, fast asleep, and for a moment Abby felt shame. To keep the poor girl out of the house so long, and to have sent her to a common cookshop for her midday meal had been very selfish, especially when she had herself sat so cosily in James's office with a pie brought by Peter from Mr Jackson's splendid food emporium further along Piccadilly and drinking—rather guiltily —from James's mug of heavy porter, and being very very happy.

It seemed incredible that the day had gone so far on its way before she realized the time, but so it had been. James had stirred and looked at his pocket-watch and cursed softly.

'Dear heart,' he had said. 'It is gone five o'clock, and you have been here since eleven this morning. I have done no work, and your Mama, I have no doubt, will be beside herself with anxiety. I hate to part with you, my love, but——'

Abby had giggled then, in a very uncharacteristic fashion.

'She will but assume that I have had much difficulty in finding the clothes I came to seek for Gussy. Not until I tell her that I return empty-handed will she be at all suspicious. But I shall not fret, and nor should you, for I can tell her that I left them in the shop for further work to be done, and return tomorrow and do the buying very swiftly. Believe me, it is not necessary to spend half a day to make one or two purchases as do most of the ladies of our acquaintance. They do but do it because

89

they are so sore beset by ennui, poor creatures. But you, dear James—is the work you have not done today of great import? Shall I return tomorrow to help you with it that you may not be in arrears with your tasks?'

James had laughed softly and took her upturned face tenderly between his two hands.

'You, my little love? I know you to be a capable person, and one better equipped with brains than almost any man I know, myself included, but how could you do the work of an apothecary? You have no training, after all! No, do not worry yourself. I shall remain here tonight and soon catch myself once the shutters are up and Peter is gone away home to Hoxton.'

She had smiled at that. 'I would not be so sure that I am not capable of your work, to a small degree,' she said perkily. 'Have I not sat here time after time, these many months, and watched you and listened to you, and stored all in my memory? A woman has little enough to fill her head with in these days of fuss about fashion. There is ample room in my life for stronger meat.' She had paused then and looked more closely at him, and said, a little awkwardly, and in a tone quite unlike her usual confident one, 'James, you do not think too ill of me? I was very brazen, I know, but as I told you, I could not foresee that you would ever—because of our circumstances—I could not wait longer, and—oh, James, are you *very* shocked by my unmaidenly behaviour?'

In answer, he had bent his head and kissed her, very gently at first, and then with an increasing passion to which she had responded whole-heartedly, throwing her arms about his neck and opening her mouth eagerly to his importunities. And then both had raised their heads a little breathlessly, and laughed softly.

'Unmaidenly or brazen or whatever you call it, I love it in you, as I love all there is about you. I care not a whit for proper behaviour—at least not now when I am with you——' He had grimaced then, and pulled back a little to look down at her with a slightly rueful expression on his face. 'How I shall be when you are gone from here tonight, of course, is any man's guess. My own is that I shall be so beset by anxiety and doubts and such feelings of wickedness in leading so young and delicate a lady as yourself astray——'

'Oh, pooh!' she had said, recovering some of her normal aplomb. 'If anyone has led anyone anywhere, it has been I who led you. As for fretting yourself about our ages—dear James, have we not discussed that over and over again, all through these long hours? Did you not admit to me that you share my feelings, and that you want to be with me as much as I yearn to be always with you? You will not change your mind?'

'As if I could,' he said eagerly, and seized her again, and began to kiss her with increasing urgency, but she pushed him gently away, and set her hands upon his shoulders, and looked into his eyes very directly.

'Then let us hear no more of this anxiety about our ages, or our stations in life, or aught else that matters so little. We shall be wed— I do not know when, but we *shall* be, for that is the way it is meant to be and I shall contrive. I always have, and I shall again—dear James! I do love you so distractedly I bid fair to make a complete cake of myself!'

And again they had clung to each other and kissed, and only separated at the call of the clock striking the half hour from St James's Church hard by. He had seen her to the street, collecting the yawning maid from the front of the shop as they went through, and called a hackney for them, and handed her in with such punctiliousness and gentleness that tears had stung her eyes. She had clung to his hand for a long moment before unwillingly leaning back so that the door could be closed, and the driver could turn his vehicle to go swaying back along the darkening streets to home. Home and parents.

She stirred again in her dark corner, and tried to think about how she would approach her parents. Of her mother's reactions she had no fears whatsoever. She knew full well how romantic a nature lurked beneath Dorothea's pale shrinking exterior; Abby had but to tell her of her consuming passion for James, she was quite sure, and her mother would agree whole-heartedly to her match. But her mother's partisanship would be of little value when it came to handling her father. Abby knew that as sure as she knew the sun would rise next day.

She closed her eyes for a moment, and into her dark vision swam a picture of Abel with his mouth snapped shut and his eyes opaque and secret as they usually were, and saw the way they would soften and even smile at the sight of her, and wished, for the first time in her life, that she was not so beloved.

To be loved as she was by her father had long been the source of her private strength; she had gloried in it, had deeply valued her ability to soften his mood and change his direction and lift his angers in a way no one else in the household could. She had never found anything but deep personal pleasure in her role as his favourite (though sometimes some twinge of guilt when she saw her mother's yearning expression when she looked at her remote and chilly husband) and now—now she knew that this very love that she had so enjoyed stood between her and the only love she would ever again want to enjoy.

She could imagine all too well what her father's reaction would be to any suggestion of a liaison between herself and James. He would dismiss it on the grounds of James's age, and almost certainly on the grounds of his lack of status, but above all because he would not willingly part with her.

For a moment black despair rose in her, and she could see no way out of her dilemma. She had told James of her love, had broken down his pitiful attempts at pretence until he had seized her hands in his and poured out in breathless eloquent phrases the adoration he felt for her (and her lips curved delightedly as she remembered those words, and the look on his face, and the touch of his hands)—and now what was to happen? Was all that day's sharing of joy, of confidence, of deepest personal secrets, to be not only wasted, but to become a weapon that would turn against them? If Abel put all blocks in their way, would not the memory of this blissful afternoon be always agony?

But she refused to think of any such pessimistic notions. 'I shall contrive,' she whispered into the darkness as the hackney went rattling over the cobbles of Bedford Square and thence to the smoother surface of Gower Street. 'I shall contrive. I always have, have I not?——'

But even so, she was not totally convinced as she stepped down in a flurry of taffeta frills, her sleepy maid lumbering along behind her, to seek out her mother and tell her some tale that would satisfy her regarding her daughter's long absence from home.

9

Jonah no longer felt sick. He no longer felt anything, it seemed to him. He was just one vast numb nothing, aware of what was reaching him through his eyes and his ears and his nose, but locked away from real knowledge of it.

They had climbed the stairs, his father in the lead and he bringing up the rear after Nancy, to the long narrow rooms above where the patients lay. Some of them were in wooden-framed beds with clean linen and heavy grey blankets piled upon them, but others lay upon straw mattresses on the floor, set between the beds.

Abel had seen the look of amazement on his son's face, and said shortly: 'For our patients, having a bed at all may well be a remarkable experience. You must remember that you are one of this city's fortunates, in that you have not only a bed of your own, but a chamber of your own besides. For most of the people in these streets and alleys such luxury is unimaginable. They sleep four and five together on a heap of straw and rags ten and more to a room. So lying upon a mattress on the floor because there are not enough beds to supply for all is no hardship, for the mattresses are stout and clean and well provided with linen.'

Jonah had opened his mouth to speak, but closed it again, for at the sight of Abel many of the patients had set up a calling and a crying that made it difficult to hear anything else.

Abel sighed sharply, and moved to the far end of the room to start a progress from man to man, inspecting wounds and bandages, looking at mouths and tongues and inside eyelids, and giving Nancy curt instructions which she acknowledged with a nod.

Jonah stood at the door, and watched and listened and felt the numbness creeping into him, and was grateful for it. He had suffered so many blows this morning, so many attacks upon his sensibilities that he felt his nerves were stretched to screaming point. He could no more have gone nearer than he was to the patients, he told himself, than he could open his arms and grow wings to fly out of the window. And if only he could have done that.

But when they left this room to enter the women's room on the floor above, he found he could indeed be stretched further; a great deal further. For it was there that the final completion of his numbness overtook him.

The room was much the same in appearance as the one below, but felt quite different. The men below, sick and in pain as they were, had still exuded a sort of vitality, a sense of potential health, but here the very air was filled with fatigue and hopelessness. The women lying on the narrow mattresses looked more pale, had darker purplish shadows beneath their deepset lacklustre eyes, were more still, or more restless, than the men below had been.

It was Nancy who explained it to him, for his father had gone directly into the room to start examining a woman in the far corner. She lingered at the door for a moment and said softly: 'Women suffers more than do men, young Master Jonah, and it's right and proper you should know it. God made us, poor cows that we are, to be burdened with the lusts of men and with their children, and we pays for it over and again with a mortification of our flesh as no man can ever suffer. You take heed, my lad, and when the time comes for you to take a girl to yourself, you remember what you sees here, and make her life as good a one as you can, for she will suffer hell for you and your children one day——'

He watched her cross the room in a swish of her print dress and her scrubbed calico apron, and wondered briefly about her history, for she seemed to know so much, to have so special a relationship with his father, that there must be much in her past of special interest to him. But that thought was banished when his father looked up and with a jerk of his head beckoned him nearer.

He walked into the room and past the women lying in rows on each side of it with his face flaming with embarrassment, and his eyes fixed straight ahead. It was not the fact that some of them were lying with their shifts so disarrayed that their pathetic breasts could be seen that disturbed him; it was more that their state of illness and poverty was the affront, something to be hidden from.

'This girl came here to us yesterday, Jonah,' his father said in a low voice. 'She is perhaps fourteen. No more. Look at her——'

Unwillingly Jonah dropped his gaze and looked. And saw a thin-faced girl lying with her eyes partly closed, so that a rim of white showed horribly beneath her lids, and a face so pallid that it looked muddy, with deep shadows filling the temples and the hollows of the cheeks. Her lips were parted laxly to show rotting teeth beneath and were edged with yellowish crusting. She was breathing shallowly, so shallowly that her body hardly seemed to be moving at all; but even if her chest had been positively heaving it would have been difficult to see it, for her whole figure was dominated by the vast dome of her belly.

It rose from her pathetic shape so unexpectedly and so absurdly as to seem to be no part of her. It was a smooth yet vertiginous curve running down to her thighs below and her ribs above, much as a mountainside drops sheer to the plain, and Jonah swallowed as he looked and tried to imagine the infant that he knew was lying there beneath the stretched and straining flesh, and could not.

'The child is locked fast across the outlet,' Abel said, and sat down on the edge of the bed to push the clothes away from the belly and to run his hands across it. 'You see? Here—this is the way the backbone lies——' and he sketched with his forefinger a line which ran in a parabola from groin to groin, across the smudge of reddish hair between them. Again Jonah felt his face flame, and was angry with himself because of it. He was no prude, God knew; in his years at Mr Loudoun's school he had learned much from the ribald whispered conversations with the other boys in the darkness of the dormitory after the lights were blown out; but this exhibition of a girl's body was somehow such an intrusion upon her, was so pathetic in its inability to raise any response in him that he was filled with an enormous shame.

'—and here lies the head——' Abel was saying, his hand spread wide across the left side of the curving belly. 'Here, give me your hand—come along boy, give me your hand!' His voice sharpened as Jonah shrank back, and almost without his own volition he found he had put out his hand and his father took it and set it firmly against the girl's body.

It felt chill and waxen under his touch, and he felt the skin of his shoulders shrink and curl, felt the hair on the back of his neck move against his skin, and then, gratefully, the numbness finally overtook him. His father made him spread his fingers widely, and unresistingly Jonah let him do as he would, and found that the tip of his thumb and the tip of his forefinger were set against something very hard beneath the surface.

'Flick your thumb, so——' Abel said, pressing on the knuckle, and obediently Jonah did so. At once he felt the hardness yield beneath his touch and experienced a small shock as he felt a return bounce on the other side against his finger-tip.

'Exactly right—excellent!' His father said. 'That is the head you have there—the action you are performing is called ballottement. It enables us to feel the infant's precise position in the womb. We are fortunate here that our patients have no absurd notions of modesty. When I must make these examinations upon women of the better classes, I must grope under a blanket like a thief. Here I can use my eyes as well as my hands, and thank God for it. If I could not do so, and learn so, the modest wives of rich cits would suffer more damage than they do. Now, feel here, and here—you recognize it? Those are the limbs of the baby—and set here as they are each side of the navel makes it even more clear that the child is in a transverse lie. I must try to turn it if it is to be born safely——'

At that moment Jonah pulled back his hand as sharply as if it had been burnt, feeling his pulses beat thickly in his throat as he did so. It was as though he had suffered some deep pain so strong was his reaction and he stared at the great belly with his eyes wide and fixed.

'What ails you, boy?' Abel said sharply.

'It—it moved.' Jonah almost whispered it, and from behind him Nancy let out a sharp crack of laughter.

'Why should it not move?' she said, her voice cutting roughly across the quietness of the room. 'Babes are living creatures, after all! 'What else would you have them do?'

Abel was standing up now, and he set one knee upon the bed and put his hands to the belly, one each side and with his head bent forwards and his eyes closed, began pressing and pushing on each side alternately. It was almost as though he were kneading the belly, like dough, but it was quite clear to Jonah that he was attempting to shift the child within the womb, and he shut his eyes to block out the sight.

And snapped them open again as there was a choking hoarse cry from the bed.

The girl had moved, was now lying with her back arched so high that it seemed that she was lying upon the bed only on her head and her heels. Her face was suffused with a dull and ugly bluish red, and her lips were drawn back in a grimace which displayed her blackened teeth, tight clenched within them. Her eyes were wide open now, but rolled so far back that she had the blank look of a piece of church statuary. Even as Jonah stared at her a shudder seemed to run through her, and her body jerked sharply, and then again and yet again, and her face went even bluer and a heavy froth appeared at the corners of her mouth.

Jonah stood and watched in horror, as both Nancy and Abel moved swiftly to the head of the bed to try and hold the girl's body still, but it went on and on, that sick jerking and shuddering, and the sounds that were coming from her, thick and strangled, were horrible to hear. Jonah could feel more than hear the silence in the room around him, a watchful knowing silence, as though every person there were holding her breath and straining towards the corner bed where still that swollen yet scrawny body jerked and shuddered.

And then it ended as sharply as it had begun, with one final huge jerk that bade fair to lift the girl clean off the bed. For one seemingly eternal moment Nancy and Abel held her, and then she collapsed into almost nothingness, as the muscles let go their straining tension, and the sounds stopped coming.

For another long moment they stood there staring down at a now perfectly still body, its face blotched and wet, the eyes still open but no longer turned upwards, just staring dumbly at eternity.

'God damn it all to hell and back,' Nancy said, her voice clear and loud and expressionless. 'She's dead, God damn it, God damn it, God damn it——' and for all the flatness in her tone, the distress came through as clear as a church bell tolling for a funeral.

Jonah heard another voice then, and it seemed to come from miles away, and then he realized it was his own. He had been staring at the swollen belly, and the words had come out almost automatically.

'It moved again,' he said. 'See? It's moving again——'

Abel turned his head to look, and saw the ripples of movement

97

passing across the taut skin, and immediately moved down the bed, and bent to set his head against the skin, his ear pressed hard against it, and his face screwed up with the effort of listening.

'I'm not sure——' he muttered after a second. 'There is too much water there—I cannot be sure—yes, there it goes again! It is still alive, and we must—Nancy a sheet, two sheets, as fast as you can——'

He was standing up now, and reaching into his breast-pocket to pull out a small leather case. As Jonah watched, unable to move his eyes from the whole scene, dearly as he longed to, Abel opened the pack and again Jonah saw knives and chisels, needles and forceps, only on a much smaller scale than those he had seen downstairs.

'No time to get the better pieces,' Abel was talking almost to himself, 'but this is sharp enough, and we need not fret ourselves about the loss of blood—Nancy, be fast, woman, be fast—now, set one at the side here, to catch—aye, that is it. And be ready with t'other—now——'

He was holding in one hand a long curved tortoiseshell-handled knife, and as Jonah watched with sick fascination he flicked the blade out, and locked it with a twist of one thumb. And then set his hand to the dead belly before him, and took a deep breath.

It seemed to Jonah that time began to run down. Slowly, infinitely slowly, the knife came down, sparkling a little in the light of the mid-day sun coming through the window, slowly it touched the skin, and then with exquisite delicacy described a gentle curve from the protruding navel, perched absurdly on the very crest of the mountain, down to the pitiful red curliness of the sparse hair at the foot of it.

As it moved across the yellowish skin it seemed to Jonah to cease being a knife, and to become instead a slender and lovely ship, cutting its elegant way across a creamy ocean, moving in a perfect line, and opening out behind it a wake that grinned widely and then spread itself pinkly into an ever-growing triangle.

It reached the hair line, and rose out of its ocean bed, to move back through the air to the beginning of its journey again, and now it seemed to the staring Jonah as though it were a great bird of such length and thinness that it needed no wings to fly over the deep cleft valley— no, not valley, gorge—below.

Again the knife descended, again became a ship, but one that sailed lower in its seas now, and then, quite sharply, the simile overtook him with real horror for behind the knife rose water, shooting high at first, and then slowly yet plentifully welling up and out, pink and then more deeply stained red, falling down the sides of the mountain that was the ship's sailing place in a steady flood until the bedding on each side was stained and soaked.

He wanted to close his eyes, for they felt hot and sandy, and he realized he had not blinked for a long time, and tried to pull his lids down to remove from his vision that now gaping hole in the human body that lay so sickeningly still before him. Had the girl moved, had she screamed with pain, made some sign of being aware of what was happening he could have borne it better, but to see this happening to so very dead a body was—he retched suddenly, feeling his chest tighten and heave under his shirt, and his throat sting with the pain of it.

But neither his father nor Nancy seemed to have any awareness of his presence, for now Abel had dropped his knife, and had thrust one hand into the gaping abyss before him, was groping about with his eyes almost closed as he concentrated on what he could feel.

And then, with a jerk, he moved his elbow, pulled his hand upwards, brought the other down to meet it and pulled again, and the hand emerged clutching a pair of very small wrinkled feet, and still pulling.

Again time slowed down for Jonah, as he saw the feet emerge and then the legs, small legs that looked incredibly ancient, so wrinkled and twisted were they. Then came the buttocks and Abel turned the child so that Jonah could see the male genitals, looking huge and swollen below the scraggy thighs, and then the abdomen so domed it looked almost like a miniature of the belly from which it was emerging, and crowning it a great bluish twisted glistening rope, instead of the protuberance that had been the navel on the girl's belly.

The head came then, and seeing it upside down as he was it seemed to Jonah to be an infinitely wise, infinitely old face, a face that had seen a million decades of human absurdity parade before it, a face that had seen all human wisdom for the foolishness it was, and all human foolishness for the inspiration it could be. The eyes were closed and the whole mask was covered with a thick yellowish waxen material behind which the skin shone a sickly blue-white.

The child dangled there from Abel's clutching hand, for what seemed an eternity, the arms drooping so that they swung free above the head, and there was no movement anywhere in that small body. Abel dropped it then, across the leg of the dead girl on the bed, so that it lay with its head lower than its heels, and he crooked his smallest finger and put it into the baby's mouth with a sharp scooping action. Still the baby did not move, and with a soft curse, Abel picked it up, and bent his head towards it.

For one mad second it seemed to Jonah that he was kissing that streaked and moistly blue face, for he had clamped his lips about the baby's mouth and nose, but then he realized that Abel was blowing in an attempt to move the collapsed little chest.

It was at this point that the control of his own body came back to him, and he was at last able to move. And he did what he had been wanting to do ever since this day had begun. He turned and lurched towards the door, pushed his way through it and down the stairs to the front door, and seized that to pull it open and let himself out into the noisy street beyond.

Once there he stood and clutched the railings beside the steps for a moment, as black lines and dots began to dance before his eyes, and he heard a great roaring in his ears. And then he bent over and began to vomit, hugely and horribly, and yet with a sense of enormous relief.

10

Lucy was sitting in the kitchen of her house in Panton Street, her bandaged leg up on a stool before her, her vast body somewhat inadequately clothed in a paisley wrapper and holding a bowlful of bread soaked in hot porter to her mouth with both hands.

Standing in the doorway and looking at her, at the familiar comfort of the old room with its huge fire and snugly shuttered windows, its heavy scrubbed wooden table and cushioned chairs, Abel felt the first moment of pleasure he had known in a fortnight. In a world full of problems and perturbation Lucy remained as she always had been, the solid centre of such comfort as there was in his life.

She looked up and saw him and at once put her bowl of slops down on her lap, held out her arms to him, and grinned her great toothless grin.

'And high time, too, you young varmint!' she said equably, and her voice, so thick and cracked and so dear in its familiarity washed over him like a benison. 'Not 'ide nor 'air 'ave I seen of my likely lad this past three weeks. I ought to 'it yer for treatin' yer Lucy so cavalier! Come and give us a kiss then——' and Abel grinned at her and went and submitted to a hug from those elephantine arms, letting her, as she always did, bury his head in her vast bosom until he thought he would choke for want of air, and then sat himself down on the edge of the stool on which she was resting her foot.

'How is it, then?' he asked, touching the heavy bandage, and she leaned over and slapped his hand lightly and said, 'You keep yer meddlin' 'ands orf, young man. Nancy did it fer me not 'alf an hour gone, and that's good enough for me——' and he smiled up at her, and dropped his hand to sit staring into the leaping flames of the fire and listen to the hiss of the kettle that swung above it on its chain.

She leaned back in her chair and looked down at him, and tried to see inside his head but, as ever, failed. In all the years she had known him, this beloved likely lad of hers, he had been one able to keep his own counsel. She knew only of what he was willing to let her know, and she had learned to be happy enough to settle for that. She knew quite well that, secret a man as he was, she was the person in all the world who knew him best of all, the person he loved most—well, almost most, she amended with a twinge of irritation—and she could ask little more.

Looking at him now as the firelight played on his hair, lifting out the deep-reddish tones of it and quite disguising the flecks of white that now adorned its thick curliness, at the shape of his face so grimly honed to lines of sharpness by the years, she tried to remember the boy she had known.

She saw again the burly figure of Jesse Constam at her door, with a little scrawny rat of a dirt-bespattered child half hidden in the skirts of his coat; saw again that pale little body sitting hunched in terror in the strangeness of a bath of hot water, remembered how he had squealed and leaped as she had scrubbed him on that long ago night, and she let out a soft little snort of laughter.

He looked up at her and raised his eyebrows gently. 'So? Is life so good, Lucy, that you must laugh at it?'

'I laughs for many reasons, and it's none o' yer concern,' she said with mock sharpness and he grinned again and said, 'So? Well, let be. How is business then? Enough to satisfy even you, you wicked old heap of rubbish?'

She snorted again at that. 'Business? How could it be other than good? Did ever you hear of a house like mine being out of favour? As long as men are the wicked evil creatures they are, and girls are as soft and obligin' as they are, Lucy'll make a livin', never you fear.'

'I don't fear,' he said. 'And I've told you, anyway, that as long as I live you have no need to fret yourself about——'

'We'll have none of that!' she said, and stirred awkwardly in her chair. 'I could buy and sell you thirty times over, I'll be bound, so don't you go comin' the great benefactor to me! Save it all for yer precious dispensary——'

'Aye,' he said, and turned his head to stare again into the fire. 'Aye, that's true enough. But you know my intention, so I shall say no more.'

They lapsed again into companionable silence, Lucy sitting with her head resting on the back of her chair, and her sharp gaze never leaving Abel's face, and Abel sitting staring abstractedly into the fire; until she could stand it no longer.

'You'd best tell me what's besettin' you so. Not that I doesn't know a bit about it, on account of Nancy. You know as well as yer knows yer breathes as she comes and tells me of all that 'appens around you, for I'd throw 'er out o' doors if she did not, so mind you don't go railin' at 'er. And she told me she'd seen yer oldest boy——'

His shoulders seemed to tighten under her gaze, and she put out one meaty hand and touched his shoulder with real gentleness. 'You can tell me, boy. This is Lucy, remember? I'm as good as the other 'alf of you, and you've nought to fear in talkin' to me. It'll be as secret as if you talked to yerself, and you'll feel the good of it. Whenever did Lucy let you down?'

His shoulders relaxed a little, and he said harshly, 'He's gone. Abby was wrong, though I cannot blame her for that. Her idea was right, but I think I—expected too much. He's away from school now, I told you. Had some maggot in his brain that he would be a poet and a writer of what he called polemics—such rubbishy ideas. I wished him to enter my own profession. Was that so strange? And it would all have fallen so pat, damn his eyes! I need a new apprentice to Caspar as I never have before, and who better than my own son? None of the others is fit yet, so what am I to do? Cast around among my acquaintance for some son of theirs, who won't have half the wits that Jonah has? It's all so—ah, he makes me puke!'

'Where is he?' she said softly, and he looked up at her, and his eyes were as full of misery as anger.

'Where is he?' she said again, a little louder, and now Abel got up and began restlessly to prowl about the room.

'God damn his stinking soul to hell and back, I don't know!' he roared. 'He walked out of the dispensary two weeks since and not a sound nor sign of him has there been since! His mother's drooping about like some half-sick cow, his sister's in such a glower as—pah! The house is not fit to live in, all for a whining stupid—stupid—poet!' And he almost spat his disgust.

She laughed suddenly. 'He's your son, no doubt about that! Nancy told me as 'ow 'e's yer spittin' image, and now 'e goes and be'aves just as did you! No one's goin' to tell 'im 'ow to run his life, nor what career 'e should foller, no more'n you was willin' to be told! You should be glad of it, Abel, not jumpin' around like some scalded cat!'

'If that's all you have to say, then you can hold your tongue!' he said shortly, and stood beside the table, his head down and glaring at her under his brows. 'And I'll be about my business and leave you to stew in your own curiosity,' but he made no move to leave.

She sighed gustily, and moving with creaking heaviness hauled herself from her chair to go padding round the table to stand beside him.

'Abel Lackland, you was ever the most stubborn creature as drew breath in this wicked world, and that's no lie. I knows why you came 'ere to see old Lucy. You wants me to find out where 'e is, ain't that it? Yer knows no one knows more about what goes on in the 'ole of London than does old Lucy, and yer wants me to tell yer 'ow the boy is, and make sure 'e comes to no 'arm——'

'I do not give a tinker's curse what happens to him!' Abel said loudly. 'If he's minded to follow his own mad path so be it! 'Tis his life to make or mar. I've done my best for him, and I wash my hands of so stupid a creature——'

'But you wants to know as 'ow 'e's fit and in no danger. It's natural enough. 'Is mother must be in a rare takin' and——'

'His mother!' Abel said and his voice was filled with a vast scorn. 'His mother! 'Tis at her door I lay much of the blame for his mulishness, for all you may choose to recognize of likenesses between us—though how you can know aught of the boy when you've seen him but once in his life is more than I can—well, I say it is his *mother* that must bear the brunt of this. All his life she has coddled him, and fussed him, and treated him as if he were made of finest porcelain and not common clay like the rest of us, and pandered to his vanity and foolishness and mooned over his nonsensical poetasting, for all the world like a green girl rather than a respectable matron and the mother of a brood of offspring! I sent him to as good a school as any I knew of, which though harsh did me naught but good, and would have for him, and yet she has softened his brain to such a mawkishness that——'

''Old 'ard, 'old 'ard!' Lucy said sharply. 'I've no great love for your Dorothea, nor never 'ave done, though I got a lot o' pity for 'er. To take you on when you felt as you did about that Li——'

He turned then, and drew himself up very straight and his face hardened so that even she drew back in a moment of fear, and he said in a voice so soft that she could hardly hear him, and yet with such steel in it that it seemed to cut right through her ears, 'You shall not mention that matter.'

'Oh, all right, all right! I was just sayin'—well, I don't 'old no coat for yer Dorothea, but you got no call to set about 'er with such a tongue lashin' as that. Your fight with your boy is yours, not 'ers, and you've no call to go——'

'Oh, do not talk any more of it! All I want of you is that you should enquire for me. You understand me? I want no alerting of him, no suggestion that I have any intention of digging him out of whatever hole it is into which he is crept. Just knowledge that I might set the household's mind to rest, and then set about more important matters than Master Jonah's stupidity! You comprehend me, now, Lucy? I want no hue and cry, nor——'

It was her turn now to draw herself up straight and with a great dignity in her voice, that even in the midst of his anger and distress made his lips quirk a little, she said, 'Did I ever set any cats among any pigeons except when I'd a mind to? You mind your business and I'll mind mine! I dare say I'll know all that's to be known in a matter of hours, but you come again to me this day se'nnight, and I'll tell aught that's to be told. Now get away with you. I'm weary enough, and the night above stairs to be got through before I'll see my bed. Be on your way, you wickedness, and give yer old Lucy a kiss afore you go, and tell 'er as 'ow you'll always come to 'er when you feels the need——'

And she threw her arms around him and kissed him lustily and then clung to him for one eager moment before stepping back and grinning her great ugly loving beam at him.

'Poor girl, yer dead Ma, dear Abel. I'd like to thank 'er, indeed I would, for the gift of 'er son as she gave me in dyin' as she did. For you're more than son to me, and that's all about it——' and then, with a gruffness that ill disguised her embarrassment at such a descent into emotion, she pushed him away towards the door, and said, 'Get aht of it now, fer Gawd's sake. Seen enough o' you tonight to last a week or more. Get goin' now——'

And so he did, leaving her house with a small sense of achievement and even of relief. He knew perfectly well that Lucy would find out all he needed to know of his son, that she would see to it that whatever company the boy had fallen in with he would come to no harm, for she was a powerful person in the gutters and byways of London, and none would dare gainsay her.

But it had been hard to come to her, even she who knew all his weaknesses and foibles as well as he knew them himself, hard to come and have to admit his failure with his own son. But he had done it, and felt the good of it.

'Just as she said I would,' he thought wryly, and turned out of Panton Street to start the long familiar walk back to his home in Gower Street. Successful man though he now was, he had never lost the habit of his starving London childhood, this ability to cover long distances threading through the alleys at great speed in his silent loping gait. He would be home in under half an hour.

Lucy, for her part, went creaking her way up her red Turkey carpeted staircase, as the maid below lit the candles in the lustre chandeliers so that the black-and-white tiled hall with its spindly gold furniture and luscious tumbling painted nudes in their gilt frames leapt into glittering radiance, and sighed heavily. Not because she had any doubt she would find her Abel's boy for him, but because of what had happened to her 'likely l ad'.

All the time she dressed, grumbling at her maid as she climbed into her hated stays and poured herself into the yellow cloth-of-gold chiffon and painted her old raddled face and filled her frizzed out old hair with gold and silver plumes so that she looked as splendid as befitted the proprietor of the most famous brothel in all the Haymarket district, she thought of him.

That his miserable experience of life in the slums of the Dials in his baby and childhood years should have marked him in some way was inevitable; but it was a tragedy that his good fortune thereafter had not softened the streak of selfish cruelty in him.

'All the love 'e has 'e pours into those stinkin' patients of 'is,' she told herself mournfully, as she leaned forwards to apply a heart-shaped patch to her chin (old-fashioned now, but what cared Lucy for fashion? All her adult existence she had worn patches, and she was not about to change her ways at her time of life) 'and p'r'aps a little for me. And that daughter of 'is. I'd dearly like to see 'er——'

But that was unlikely and it was proper that it should be so, she thought as she made her way to her elegant salon, with its crimson and purple hangings and overheated, overscented atmosphere. He had brought the baby Jonah to see her when she had the pneumonia that dreadful winter of 1813 and 1814, when the snow had fallen so relentlessly and the Thames had froze so hard that they had set up stalls and booths upon the ice and had a Frost Fair, and she had been fit to die. But both of them knew that that was a special case, and was not to be repeated, and that certainly there could be no question of bringing a gently reared girl of respectable background, as was Abigail, to visit a house such as Lucy's.

But knowing this still she sighed her gusty sigh again. It would give her such pleasure to see her Abel's children, even if they did have so insipid a mother (and her lip curled as she thought of Dorothea and the tales she had heard of her timidity and her meek stubbornness over the years); if Abel was in her eyes the son she had never borne, his children equally gave her the status of grandmother, she thought, and then laughed aloud as she went stumping about the room, inspecting the girls who sat about languorously on sofas and loveseats, stuffing themselves with sweetmeats. She, Lucy, a grandmother! Such airs to give herself! She mut be getting soft in the head!

Abby sat between her parents at the long dining-table, composedly eating her way through poached cod in oyster sauce, her face serene and quiet; but she was cogitating very hard.

In all the excitement and anger and anguish of Jonah's disappearance there had been no opportunity to speak to either of her parents about her situation with James Caspar, and she was content that that should be so. After careful consideration she had decided that it would be most politic to keep her tongue between her teeth, even as far as her mother was concerned, for some time yet. So she had gone quietly on her way, pretending even to herself that nothing of mark had happened in her private life at all.

And it had not been difficult, for Jonah's absence from his home that first night had created a most miserable situation that quite over-shadowed all others. It had been Dorothea who had discovered at gone twelve o'clock that he had not returned home, and she had been so distressed that she had gone to her husband's bedside (for he slept in the small dressing-room beside her chamber; both had long since given up any attempt at pretending to their household that they lived in connubial bliss) and woken him.

His rage had been terrible to behold. He had been angered enough by Jonah's precipitate departure from Tavistock Street, yet had come home fully prepared to say nothing of it to the boy, but to be mag-nanimous. When he had discovered that Jonah had not returned to Gower Street and he would therefore have no chance to exercise that magnanimity his fury had been monumental. And when he was waked at midnight to be told that still the truant was absent, the whole house-hold quaked at his display of temper.

Abby herself had been struck with a great sense of guilt. Had it not been her suggestion that Papa should take Jonah to see the work of the dispensary? Had it not clearly been some aspect of the affairs of that house that had sent him hugger-mugger away? Her remorse filled her with heaviness and twisted her face into uncharacteristic anxiety, and in reacting so she added, all unbeknownst, to Abel's wrath.

He saw the distress upon that square face that he loved so well, and his fury against his son rose even higher. He knew quite well that Abby's distress came because she saw herself as the prime cause of her brother's defection, and shifted his concern for her to his son's back, thus giving himself even greater cause to hate the boy.

For hate him he did, he had told himself, hate him he did, and from here on always would. And I am a man with a great gift for hating, he had thought sombrely, remembering for one brief and agonizing second the face of the woman he had hated heartily this past seventeen years, and then pushing the memory away.

On the following day it had been Abby, sitting in the schoolroom, who had received the message from Jonah, and enormous indeed had been her relief at finding out that her brother was apparently well and safe.

The sour-faced woman, in a black bombazine gown and an uncompromisingly funereal bonnet quite untrimmed with feathers or anything else, had stood before her and flatly refused to answer any questions.

'I was instructed, ma'am, to bring this 'ere note to you, and to take away such objects as you might give me after you 'ad read of it. I can't tell yer nothin' more.'

'But who are you?' Abby had said, looking from the note in her hand to the woman. 'What is your name? Where do you come from?'

'I'm sure I can't say, ma'am,' the woman had said woodenly, staring over Abby's head at the wall beyond, and no more than that *would* she say. Abby had looked again at the note and considered.

'Dearest Abby,' Jonah had written. 'I trust you as I never have before, and I cannot say more than that, as I know you will appreciate. I beseech you to treat me with the consideration due to a brother who has suffered as have I at your father's hands (I cannot bring myself to regard him longer as my own parent) and to give the bearer of this missive such of my clothes and effects as it is possible for you easily to set your hands upon. I most particularly would ask for my green velvet smallclothes and the brown merino coat and my second best leather shoes as well as the best ones, and the stocks that lie in the red leather box situated on the shelf at the top of my closet. Should you be able to also set my linen shirts in the portmanteau you will prepare, and such of my other linen as you, in your wisdom, consider both essential to me and capable of being borne by my messenger you will oblige your ever-loving brother, Jonah Lackland. Post scriptum. I am sure I need not tell you that I throw myself upon your mercy in this matter, and that it would do me grave hurt if you reveal anything of me to your father. He wishes me no good, and would not comprehend my emotions ,regarding me as one altogether beset by my sensibilities; and indeed so I may be, and not ashamed of it. To my mother I send my dearest love and greatest regret. I would not cause her, or you, dear sister, any pain could I avoid it, but your father has made it quite impossibl e for me to behave in any way other than this. Again I ask your help and guidance as only a brother can. J.L.'

She thought carefully, and then told the woman to wait in the schoolroom where she could be alone, for the governess had taken the other children for their daily walk around Bedford Square, and gone to Jonah's room to pack a portmanteau for him. She had worked methodically and speedily, and at the last moment added pocket handkerchiefs and several of the books that had lain upon his desk, and then carried the bag back to the schoolroom.

The woman had put out her hand for it, but Abby had said crisply, 'Not yet, if you please. I shall write a letter which I beg you will deliver to the same hands as those that will receive the portmanteau from you. Please to wait.'

She wrote swiftly in her neat sloping hand.

'Dear Brother. It is of course a matter of great regret to me that you feel unable to accept your father's roof and care for you. I am fully persuaded that despite his occasional sternness of mien he holds nothing but the deepest regard for you. His distress at your absence was considerable, and I must assure you that though his behaviour indeed bespoke great rage, it was clear to me that this was but masking his true concern. However, it is much apparent that no amount of cajoling on my part is like to bring you here to Gower Street to seek any reconciliation with him. Instead, I do beseech you to write a letter to Mama at every opportunity that presents itself to you. She is bereft in your absence, for you must know that you have always held a most special place in her regard, and without you her heart is clean cut in half. I tell you this not in any attempt to bring you back to live in Gower Street, for if your mind is set upon a separate establishment, so be it; I say it simply that you may be persuaded to consider the feelings of your Mama, and indeed, of your most affectionate sister, Abigail Lackland.'

Despite Jonah's request that she should not speak of his message to her, she did, of course, tell Dorothea that her son was well, and that she had at present no cause to fear for his well-being.

Dorothea had been lying on her chaise-longue in her bedroom with the curtains closed against the dull afternoon and the coals piled high in the grate, for she was sorely afflicted with the headache. But at Abigail's words she had lifted herself on one elbow and stared at her daughter with eyes wide and glittering.

'Abby! Thank God! Oh, where is he? Let me go to him at once, the poor boy, he must be so——'

'I am sorry, Mama,' Abby had said, gently pushing Dorothea's head back on the cushions. 'His messenger would not say where he was, and I did not know her. So I could not deduce anything about his whereabouts from her visit. But I sent by her a letter begging him to write to you regularly, and you need have no fear, Mama, but that he will. He may be a heedless headstrong boy, but he does not lack any concern for you. Just wait a few days, Mama, and I have no doubt but that you will have a letter from him.'

'You should have set one of the servants to follow the messenger, whoever she was,' Dorothea had turned her head fretfully upon the yellow cushions, against which her complexion looked more than ever muddy and sallow. 'He may be in great distress, Abby! He may lack food and warmth and——'

'I think not, Mama,' Abby had said coolly, smoothing her mother's forehead as though she were a baby needing to be settled to sleep. 'For his letter was more concerned with obtaining possession of his clothes than anything else. Had he been hungry, I have no doubt that he would have returned home before this, for you must know, Mama, that headstrong though he may be Jonah is not one to suffer unnecessary privation. I think we may depend upon it that he is in some comfort wherever he may be. After all, he made many friends when at school, and there must be many households in London where he would be a welcome enough guest.'

Now, sitting at the table over dinner a full two weeks later, Abby looked consideringly at both her parents in turn. Dorothea, though still pallid and somewhat thinner, for she had quite refused to eat until she had heard from her beloved Jonah (which fortunately she did within a week of his departure, a letter arriving by hand in the middle of the afternoon, clearly so despatched so that it might not be intercepted by his father) looked more composed. Her one concern now was that Jonah would reveal to her his whereabouts so that she might visit him.

Abby knew this, and smiled a little twistedly to herself. It would be some time, she suspected, before Jonah would risk imparting to his mother his present address in London.

She looked then at her father, sitting as he so often did these days with his food but half eaten before him and his eyes fixed unseeingly on the piece of bread he was kneading between the fingers of his right hand. She looked, considered, looked again, and then setting down her knife and fork neatly upon her plate leaned forwards.

'Papa!' she said, and her voice was low but very clear. 'There is a matter of business I would discuss with you.'

He looked up at that, and stared at her with his brows raised a little, and his mouth down turned in that affectionate half-smile he reserved for her alone.

'Business?' he said. 'Now, what matter of business could you have to discuss with me? I know you to be a young woman of great wit and sense, but in matters of *business*——' he shook his head.

'It is about the matter of your need for an apprentice to Mr Caspar, Papa,' she said, and at once the half-smile disappeared from his face and his brows clamped down heavily.

'I believe we shall not talk of that,' he said stiffly.

'I believe we shall, Papa! The matter must be settled one way or the other. And I have a plan that might seem at first to be—surprising—but which I am persuaded has all to commend it. If you will but hear me out.'

He looked at her consideringly, and then pushed his plate away from him, and folded his hands on the table before him.

'Well?' he said, looking at her quite unsmilingly. 'I know, none better, that if you have made up your mind to speak of something speak you will, no matter what my wishes. So let me hear it and be done.'

She took a deep breath. 'Well, Papa, I know that it is your wish that Mr Caspar should expand the business to start a manufactory to pack your medicines and pills and the like in larger quantities, both for the dispensary and for the shop, and any other shops beside that choose to patronize the service you will offer——'

'How do you know that?' He sounded genuinely startled.

'Because I keep my ears open, and my wits about me,' she said, a trifle impatiently. 'Come, Papa, you know you have discussed it here many times with your trustees from Tavistock Street, and with Hunnisett! I may be sitting quiet over my needlework, but I am not quite stupid! Now, Papa, it is quite understandable that your scheme should demand the whole-hearted efforts of other persons, not yet involved in the affairs of the shop. I appreciate that it was no more than natural that your eye should fall as it did in seeking that person—no, Papa, hear me out! You *shall* not stop me, even if my mention of my brother shall anger you, until I have explained my plan to you. As I said, it was natural that you should want one of your own family to be incorporated into the new matter. Well, as it has fallen out, it cannot be Jonah—*no*, Papa, please to be silent until I have completed!—and of course it will be a year or even more before Rupert and then William shall be of an age to be of value to you. And you cannot wait so long. So, to my plan, Papa.'

And now she stopped, and took another deep breath, looking sideways at his face, now closed and very watchful as he stared at her.

'If your son was of an age, why should not your daughter, who is to be sure almost a year younger, but none the worse for that, be considered to be of value to you? I know it is not customary for females to be set apprentice to the apothecary's trade, but what care you or I for custom? We do what we will, Papa, and always have, and care nothing for the opinions of fools and outsiders——' she knew a note of wheedling was creeping into her voice; and sternly controlled it. This decision must be made on the basis of good sense, not childish cajoling.

'Why not, Papa? Who better can you trust than I to see to it that all is done as you wish? Who has more sense than I? I say that in no spirit of self-aggrandisement but merely to repeat back to you words that I have heard you say many times, and I know your judgement to be sound! Consider, Papa, the many virtues of such an arrangement! You will have a member of your own family dealing with your affairs, you solve what is clearly a problem of considerable size in your eyes at this time, and you give me something for which I have yearned ever since I left the schoolroom. Some activity of real *worth*. Mere female I may be, Papa, but that does not mean I have only the tedious preoccupations of other persons of my sex and age! I am indeed heartily bored by the foolishness of the girls I must consort with, as Mama will tell you——'

Abby turned her head and looked at her mother for the first time since she had begun her dissertation, and was a little startled at the expression on that pale pinched face.

Had she thought about it she would have expected to see surprise at least, and perhaps disapproval; what she saw was a strange mixture of knowingness and—could it be agreement? She pulled her eyes away, and returned her attention to her father.

'It would please me vastly, Papa, to be occupied in some manner that would give my existence a real purpose. I am happy enough here at home with Mama, and concerning myself with matters of the household,' she added hastily, suddenly realizing how unkind her words might sound to her mother. 'But this is a new world now, Papa, a most exciting and interesting world! Since the end of the French Wars, the country and affairs have moved apace, have they not? And females are of more import today than they have ever been! Think of Mrs Fry and all she is doing for the poor wretches of Newgate! Why should not your daughter be as she is, and work for the sick under the shelter of your eye? Indeed, Papa, I should like it above all things, and only consider the benefits that would accrue to you and to the shop and to the dispensary in due course, for you cannot much longer delay your new scheme, and where are you to find a suitable apprentice if you do not choose me?'

She stopped more because she was breathless than for any other reason, and then sat staring at her father, her head tilted on one side and her face now quite closed and still, the animation that had filled it quite under control again.

He looked back at her for a long moment in silence, and then said uncertainly: 'It would be most irregular, Abby! I do not even know whether as a female you would be acceptable to the Society of Apothecaries! To my knowledge no such question has ever been mooted. I—indeed, you have thrown me quite upon my heels!'

She smiled at that. 'Have I, Papa?' she said softly. 'I feel *that* to be a most considerable achievement, for few are as steady as you! As for the Society—pooh! Even I have heard of un-articled apprentices! Is not Peter such an one? Why should not I be? We can worry later about the matter of admission to the Society. It may not be needed, besides, for have you not James, Mr Caspar, who is a Fellow? As long as he is part of the establishment, it makes no matter at all whether I be admitted or no!'

For one sick moment she wondered whether he had noticed her slip of the tongue in using James's first name, but that seemed to have passed above his head in a cloud, for he was sitting hunched in his place, his eyes staring unseeingly at the cloth before him.

They sat so for what seemed to Abby, quite quaking within for all her calm exterior, to be an eternity and then he raised his head and looked at her, and very slowly a smile curved his lips, and then crept up his face till his whole countenance was alight with merriment. And he threw back his head and laughed with the first real note of pleasure that she could remember hearing since she had left her childhood behind.

'Abby, my dear child, I do believe you have hit upon a capital notion! Indeed, why *should* we concern ourselves with what is usually done, or what people might think of such an arrangement? Why *should* your considerable wisdom and good sense be frittered away on kitchen affairs? You shall not waste your substance so! Oh, Abby, my dear girl, you are such a daughter as a man might dream of, and worth a dozen of that scoundrel brother of yours! You shall work in the shop, and help Caspar, and free him in due course to concentrate his mind upon the affairs of the manufactory! A capital notion, a capital notion!'

And they sat and beamed at each other in vast good humour, neither in the least aware of Dorothea's silent figure at the end of the table, nor of the expression of sudden cunning that had crept into those pale blue eyes.

12

That Lilith was deeply aware of the effect she was having was quite clear to Celia.

She was sitting on the long table at the back of her mother's dressing-room, her legs hunched up under her muslin dress and her expression sulky beneath the heavy wings of hair that lay on each side of her face and half hid it, making herself look as awkward and ugly as she could.

She knew it was absurd, that such a posture made Jonah even more unlikely to be aware of her in the way she wished him to be, and her mother even more likely to crow at her with her eyes, but still she did it, with a mulish and melancholy satisfaction.

And as she sat there she watched her mother at the mirror and Jonah's bemused face beyond, and let the pain of it gnaw at her like a classic fox at her vitals.

He was standing behind the mirror so that he could lean forwards and eagerly hand to Lilith whatever colour it was he thought her ready for; and she primped and played among her paint pots and brushes and hares' feet like a wicked child, sometimes disdaining his offering, and searching among the clutter for something different, only to pick up again the one he had offered and, crestfallen, had set down, then to sparkle up at him under her lashes as if to say, 'Amn't I cruel? And don't you adore me for it?' making him beam besottedly back at her, his entire soul throbbing for all the world to see in that mobile expressive face of his.

That he could be such a fool! Celia raged within. Cannot he see that she is using him, that she is playing with him like some foolish toy, and that she does it only to distress me?

For Celia was by now quite sure that her mother's determination to seek out Jonah had been born of her other determination to keep her daughter as a child. When he had arrived at the door of the green-room at the Haymarket Theatre that evening four weeks ago, his face white and drawn, and stood there looking about him for Lilith, letting his eyes pass quite unrecognizingly over her own face, she had known that she had lost. Hawks had obeyed her mother's behest and found the boy, and he had come running.

She had felt her lips curl with sick disgust as she had looked at him, and he had looked uncomprehendingly back. But sick and angry or not, she had felt a great lurching excitement within her at the sight of that long lean body and the dark head set so neatly upon the strong yet elegantly slender throat, the narrow green eyes in that white face. That he should be so disturbingly, achingly beautiful; that she should be so disturbingly, achingly responsive to him—it was a cruel wicked twist of Providence to bring before her so deeply desirable a person, and to make him oblivious of all but her mother.

It was as though, she had thought sombrely, Providence had for obscure reasons of its own decided that she, Celia, was born to suffer, and had in ice-cold malice quite deliberately devised a scheme that would involve her complex feelings for her mother as well as her powerful feelings for this boy.

On that night when he had arrived at the theatre she had heard her mother's voice cry liltingly above the general hubbub of the room, 'Why, to be sure, is that not young Mr Lackland at the door? Are you come to visit me, my boy, together with all the elegants of the town? Indeed, you are more gallant than any of them!——' and Celia had fled the greenroom, sick and raging and close to tears.

She had sat in the wings of the vast stage, curled up on a heap of old sacks with one of them about her shoulders to keep off the chill draught that came whistling through the flats, and flapped the border curtains hanging high above her in the flies with an eerie susuration, staring into the dimness so barely-lit by one small hissing gas jet and pondering.

She sat there for so long that not until the doorman came seeking her to deliver her mother's peremptory command that she come immediately to the carriage, for they were to return home at once, had she realized that the night had crossed from one day to the other, and that it was past one in the morning. And she still remembered the sick shock she had felt when, on climbing into the carriage, yawning and gritty-eyed for want of sleep, she had near fallen over the long legs of Jonah Lackland, who was ensconced in the corner opposite her mother.

She had peered at him in the fitful light thrown by the linkboy's smoky torch, her body half in and half out of the carriage, and said stupidly, 'You? What are you doing here?' and he had said nothing, sitting staring at her mute and whitefaced in the dimness, but Lilith had said sharply, 'He is to stay in North Audley Street. Do, Celia, cease your gaping and get *in*. It is late and I have need of the comfort of my home.'

They had gone rattling noisily over the cobbles, past the last of the street drabs taking drunken customers to their foul dens, and the slinking figures of late roisterers, past the rattling carts coming in on their way to Covent Garden with their loads of country fruits and vegetables, and said not a word to each other.

Nor had any word been later said about Jonah's taking up of residence in North Audley Street. He had been given a room at the top of the house, a full floor away from her mother's, but that had made no difference to Celia. She knew he had been brought in as her mother's 'friend' as had so many before him, and that in due course all pretence would be allowed to dwindle away and he would share her bed-chamber——

The thought of that had so hurt and sickened her that for the first two weeks of his stay she had assiduously avoided him, just as she had her mother. She spent long hours sitting in her bedroom, ignoring Lydia's chatter, ostensibly reading novels but in truth brooding over the evils that were being done to her, and refusing to talk to anyone, except in the most essential of monosyllables.

And so it was she had not heard of the truth of the reason for Jonah's new status as a permanent guest in the house. On that first night in the theatre he had told Lilith in stumbling awkward words a little of what he had seen that day in his father's dispensary, something of the horrors he had felt, and said almost piteously, 'I cannot bear to see him again. He is to me, now, some—some monster of a creature, and to know I am of the same flesh is—is——' and he had started to shake, and his face had glistened with sweat. With a rare gentleness in one of so ebullient a nature she had sent all the other people in the greenroom packing, had set him down upon her own sofa, and wrapped him in her shawl and plied him with brandy until his teeth stopped their chattering and the sense of nausea left him for the first time since the morning, and a little colour came to his face.

He had looked up at her after a while, and tried to struggle to his feet, embarrassed, but she had pushed him back and laughed at him, and told him not to be such a flat as to think it mattered to her that he had been so unmanned by his experiences.

'It is no matter of surprise to me that your father is so hard a man in your eyes. Forget him! You have come to Lilith Lucas for succour and that shall you have, dear boy. I shall not turn you away, but bring you to my house and there you shall live as one of my own—as my dear friend. And you shall be my good friend, shall you not?' and she had leaned forwards and kissed his forehead as light as a bird's wing, and he had gone scarlet with a curious mixture of delight and shame, and she had laughed again, that lovely trilling laugh that he was coming to know as part of her.

She had stroked his brow then with one white hand, sitting looking at him a little abstractedly and after a while said abruptly, 'Your father —did you tell him you were coming to me?'

'Tell him? Indeed, ma'am, I told him nothing! I left his—his dispensary and was so put about that I must confess I cast up my accounts there and then in the street. But I said no word to him about where I would go, for to be sure I did not know! I walked about the streets thinking, and—and trying to see a way to contrive my future and then I found myself here in the Haymarket and remembered you, and how you had said—and I felt—well, ma'am, I came.'

'And glad I am that you did!' she had said, and smiled down at him so sweetly he felt his heart would burst with pleasure at the sight of her. 'For who else should a boy in distress come to than Lilith Lucas? You never shall regret it, my lad. And even when your dear Papa does discover where you are——' her lips had curved then into a secret little smile, and she had hooded her eyes, but he had not noticed this, for he had started up at her words, and cried, 'No, ma'am! Oh, indeed, ma'am, he must not know I am here, for his view of the theatre is such that— and I would not, in any case, have any conversation with him, nor have him know aught of me, and——'

'Do hush yourself, dear boy, do hush! You are safe with me. Or will be once you stop calling me "ma'am" in that stiff fashion. Amn't I now your good friend? You shall call me Lilith, as do all my friends—now say it—go on, young Jonah Lackland, let me hear my name upon your lips.'

And, blushing, he had muttered 'Lilith' and liked to say it, and she had smiled at him and again kissed his forehead and then set about righting herself for the street—a time-consuming task indeed—humming a little below her breath, and throwing occasional questions at him, which he answered with an eager guilelessness that made her smile. He was never to know how much he revealed to her that night of the situation in his family's household at Gower Street.

But Celia knew none of this, and for two weeks she sat at home and avoided the new member of the household as though he were the plague or the devil himself, and would not talk to anyone, not even Hawks (who could have told her precisely how it had come about that Jonah was now living with them, for there was nothing that she did not know of her mistress's life or secrets) and would not go to the theatre in the evenings.

Instead she filled her mind with her obsession with Jonah, and her growing hate for her mother, which for the first time in her life bade fair to outdo the strength of her adoration of her.

And so it could have gone on, with the two young people circulating separately, never having any communication, and Celia eating out her heart in silence, had not on one bitter cold afternoon—for it had snowed unseasonably soon this year, a full inch and a half coming in these early October days to cloak the roofs of London with soot-streaked sugar icing, and burying the cobbles in a slushy slippery morass in which horses and people slithered and fell and were chilled to the bone—Lilith had had to go to her mantua-makers.

This was a ritual to which she always gave her whole-hearted attention, and generally no one was ever allowed to accompany her; but Celia, watching from her bedroom window to see Hawks take Lydia and a squealing joyous Ben to play in the snow in Hyde Park with all the other children from miles about, had observed her mother being handed into her carriage by an attentive Jonah, and had immediately dropped the curtain and closed her eyes in misery. She could not decide which distressed her most; seeing Jonah accepted by Lilith in so familiar a fashion that he could share this most intimate of expeditions, or the fact that although she had pleaded often with her mother to take her on such visits—for she had a keen interest in matters of fashion in clothes—it had been this interloping boy who had been given the privilege.

She had stood there in her icy room for a while, miserable and becoming steadily more chilled—for fires were not lit in bedchambers until gone six of the evening—and let her loneliness and misery wash over her. To be quite alone in the house as she was with no one to care aught about her; it was cruel and wicked and yet all she could expect, for had not Providence decided in its cruel malice to heap more and more suffering upon her head?

And then with a momentary return of her more usual common sense she had pulled her thin woollen shawl about her shoulders and told herself she could as well be cosy in the drawing-room, where a fire was sure to be lit for her mother had been sitting there all morning, as stay here and be chilled half to death.

She had gone right into the big gold-and-white drawing-room on the first floor of the house and was crouching gratefully before the fire stirring up the embers with the long steel poker before she realized that she had quite misread the situation. She heard a movement behind and turned her head with a start to see, standing quite near her, the tall shape of Jonah.

He seemed to loom above her like some giant, as she crouched there in the hearth, feeling the new-stirred flames warming her half-turned shoulder and her cheek, and for one mad moment she wanted to complete her turn and throw herself at his feet and cry, 'Love me! Love me! She is hard and cruel and you will suffer so if you love her! Love me, Jonah, love me!'

He, for his part, saw a face lit by the uneven flames to a soft prettiness that was something he had not seen in her before. He had been aware on their first meeting of the strength of character in her, of a face that could light with humour, and that could, above all, bend itself into wickedly easy mimicry of all it saw, but he had not seen the heaviness of the thick dark lashes or the greyness of the eyes, with their oddly darker ring around the iris, nor had he noticed the softness of the down-drooping mouth.

Looking at her now he liked what he saw and despite himself (for he had intended to tease this silly child about the obvious way she had sulked since his arrival in her mother's house) he smiled at her, a warm and quite spontaneous smile that crinkled his green eyes very charmingly, and displayed his strong white teeth to great advantage.

She had crouched there staring up at him for a long moment, wanting quite desperately to smile back, but she controlled that ignoble impulse—for that was how she saw it—and scowled and scrambled a little awkwardly to her feet.

'What do you do skulking about here like some damned thief?' she said, and knew her voice sounded shrill and was ashamed of it. 'I saw you go in the carriage with Mama!'

His smile faded and he said shortly, 'Then you saw quite wrong, did you not? I did but do the polite thing and hand her to her carriage! In case the matter had escaped your observation the weather is fit to kill, and the roads disgusting with their dirt. No gentleman could fail to escort a lady in such conditions—and I trust I know how to behave with a lady!'

She sniffed at that. 'Aye, I dare say you do—*poet* that you are——'

'There is no need to be so disparaging about my—about the work I wish to do with my life!' he had snapped, and his face suffused a little, and his brows came down in a frown, and immediately she felt better, as though it were now she who were the big strong one and looming above him. So she had smiled, not a wide and warm one as his had been but a tight and mocking grimace.

'La, have I insulted you, then? You must forgive me, sir, for I am one made of very ordinary clay, and quite below the great imaginings of the poets of this world. Console yourself with that thought, and seek such comfort as you may from my mother. She, I have no doubt, will appreciate your work!'

He looked at her, standing there very straight-backed in front of him, her feet spread wide and her arms akimbo, the light from the fire lighting her shape with a soft nimbus, and set his head on one side, displaying his puzzlement.

'Celia, why is it that you are so set against me?' he asked abruptly. 'What have I done to you that you should treat me so shrewish? You have swept about the house like some queen of wrath whenever you have seen me, and generally kept so far away that you would think I had the cholera! Yet surely it is I, if any, that should be distant with *you*, for you cannot but recall that you were—well, not to put too fine a gloss upon it, you were shocking ill-mannered that night, to imitate me so cruelly as you did! Now, if I hold no grudge, why should you? Come, cannot we be friends? I am to live in this house, your Mama says, for some time yet, and I would I could do so in amity with all its occupants!'

And he held out his hand in so frank and friendly a manner that she felt her belly soften and churn with the desire to respond as warmly.

But she stood there scowling still, her lower lip thrust out, and stared at him with her eyes as hard as pebbles. She would *not* be charmed out of her distress. Had he not come here only at her mother's behest? Was he not merely laying butter to her paws in order to make his stay at her mother's side more pleasant? She almost spat at him in her re-doubled rage, but produced only a sharp and bitter, 'No!'

He looked dumbfounded at that, and uncertainly he let his hand fall, and stared at her, his face creased with genuine surprise, a surprise too strong to be overcome by the anger that would have been a natural reaction to so chilling a rebuff.

'Why?' he said with great wonderment in his voice. '*Why?* I ask again, what have I done to you that you should bear so strong an anger against me? I do not comprehend you——'

It was more than any woman could have borne, and was certainly too much for a girl as young and raw in the ways of men and women as was Celia.

'What have you done? What have you done, you foolish—foolish *object*?'

She heard her voice rising more and more shrill, and now felt no shame at all, only the enormous satisfaction of at last giving vent to all the words that had burned their way into her mind all through these long weeks.

'You ask me that? I will tell you, then! You have behaved like any one of those fops and idiots of the town who hang about my Mama for no better reason than that she crooks her finger and lifts her chin to them! You have become as have all the other fools and been so beguiled by her, and so flattered by her, that you have given back to her even greater flattery and beguilement and filled her with so inflated an opinion of herself as a woman that she has no thought for aught but herself and her fops! She has not time for me or Lyddy or even Ben, who is but a baby and needs a mother's care, but what do you or those other limping useless pieces of rubbish that call themselves her friends care for that? You mop and mow at her feet like some savage heathen worshipping its God, and she is as icy cold and careless in her heart as any such idol, I promise you, but you do not care, you do not see the truth, and when one appears that sees in you a person—a person of worth and—and interest, at one look from those lying eyes of hers you are gone, flung away in some mad dream of her devising, and seeing no more of other people about you than a—a cow sees of the mouse it stamps upon in a field! She has but to lift her finger and beckon you and you leave home and family and come to live here in her house and—and—ah, faugh, you sicken me! You *sicken me*——'

And now she realized to her horror that tears were running down her cheeks, and her shoulders were shaking with the intensity of her emotion as she struggled to express the desperate jealousy of both her mother and of him and the agony of the years of growing up and wanting and aching for her mother's concern while being used, as she so painfully knew, but as an audience, and hating, hating, hating ever more greatly even while she loved.

Her voice strangled itself deep in her throat and she had put up her hands to cover her face and bent her head and stood there, the fire hot at her back, letting the luxury of her tears wash over her.

He had stood quite stunned at first but then, quite unthinkingly, he stepped forwards and put his hands upon her shoulders, and she, just as instinctively, swayed a little forwards, and they stood there in the curious greenish-white light thrown through the windows from the snow-covered roofs on the other side of the street, as still and silent as two carved creatures in the mocking impersonal emptiness of the gold-and-white room.

But then a small shuddering gulp had escaped her and she moved a little as though to pull away from him, but he held her closer and stroked her hair and soothed her with soft whispers, just as he had often done for small Gussy at home when he was in one of his tantrums, and gradually her sobs had eased and then stopped. She let her hands go from her face and wiped her wet cheeks with the back of one of them in a most touchingly awkward manner, and he looked down at her stained cheeks and red-rimmed eyes, and slightly running nose, and smiled at her with all the tenderness he would have felt for a bedraggled half-drowned kitten or a woebegone puppy. And quite without his own volition, he bent his head and kissed her cheek gently.

And then, as much to her amazement as his, he found himself clutched in her arms and her face turned up to his, and her mouth clasped hot and fast on his own, her lips parted and her tongue pointed and eager between his teeth. She was no longer a half-drowned kitten or a woebegone puppy, or even a child recovering from a tantrum, but a woman of enormous warmth and need as she clung to him, and he, with all the inevitableness of his own young body, responded to her with an equal strength.

They separated as suddenly as they had embraced and both stepped back with an almost military precision and stood staring at each other, he with his face rather red from the impact of all this emotion, and she quite pale and composed.

'You must forgive me,' she said at length, and her voice now was hard and controlled, and heavily veneered with politeness. 'I do not know what overcame me. I have slept but little of late, and perhaps—if you will excuse me, I shall return to my room and——'

'It is I who should apologize,' he said stiffly. 'I meant but to comfort you in your distress and—my—my animal instincts appear to have overcome me. You will, I trust, forgive me. I will, of course, make all arrangements to leave the house immediately, for I would not intrude further on your family's hospitality after so——' he swallowed, 'so ill an exhibition. I again crave your pardon.'

'You cannot go!' She said it with a sudden anxiety that startled him. 'It was as much my fault as yours, for I had no right to lose my—indeed, the blame is fully mine. And if you leave, Mama will be so sore set about that—after all, it is entirely at her invitation that you are here, and——'

'That is not so.' He said it almost impatiently. 'Your Mama has been most discreet in her kindness to me, if she has let you think she summoned me to be her guest. I did in fact come to her for help in—in a family situation which I could no longer tolerate. In short, I left my father's home and had no one else to turn to, and came to your Mama, and she in her goodness offered me her home to use as my own. And now I have behaved so ill that it is clear that I cannot stay longer and——'

It was now her turn to look startled, and she stood and stared at him with her mouth half open. But as the import of what he was saying reached her her whole face was lifted by a smile, and she moved towards him impulsively and put her hand on his sleeve.

'Oh, Jo, please to forgive me! I did not know this! I thought that you were here because she had—well never mind that! Please to forgive me that shocking exhibition? Will you? Pretend it never happened, and talk to me as though we were friends, and think no more of it than you would if—oh, please Jo, do not go!'

He looked down at her, his brow creased a little.

'You are a very mercurial person, Miss Celia,' he said uncertainly, and neither of them seemed to notice the new form of address he had used. It was as though both had tacitly acknowledged the change in their status, to that of almost equals rather than of adult and child, which was the way in which Jonah had hitherto seen her, and the way in which she had perforce seen herself in relation to him. 'One moment flown into alt, and the next——'

She had smiled at that, a sparkling joyous smile that had quite erased the last traces of tearfulness from her face, and pulled on his sleeve to make him sit down beside her on the sofa.

'Say it is but due to my inheritance,' she had said gaily. 'And pay no heed to my moods. I am a child of the theatre after all, Jonah, and you would not expect me to behave as a linen mercer's dutiful daughter, now, would you? Now please tell me—how was it you ran away from home? That is the most romantic thing imaginable, and one to which I have often given much consideration! Please to tell me all! And we will say nothing of this afternoon's talk to my Mama——' and her face had creased suddenly at that, and she had said uncertainly, looking up into his face: 'I have not misunderstood, Jo? You are not, as I had believed, besotted with her, and thrown into a quake by her? We can be friends?'

'I admire your Mama greatly,' he had said a little stiffly. 'And I am filled with gratitude that she should give me a home here and arrange, as she has promised to, that my work shall be considered by the theatre for performance. She is giving me the career I most long for and I cannot but feel great warmth for her. But as to besotted—come, Miss Celia, I am no foolish child given to swoons or nonsenses of that nature!'

And he tried to look as serious as he could, and tried even harder to bury under the surface of his mind an uneasy conviction that he lied, for it was true—was it not?—that in Lilith's presence he felt quite different, quite unable to think clearly, or to feel anything but a formless helpless delight.

She had sighed softly at his side, and he had felt her body relax, and she had said softly, 'Then let us talk of other things. Of all you would do with your life, and what you have done hitherto, and of your family, and all there is to tell. For I will not hide from you, Jo, that I find you a most interesting person, and one I would dearly like to count among my friends.'

She had smiled at him then and added ingenuously, 'To be sure, I have no friends at all, for I do not go to any school and there are none of the theatre of my age, so to have one to whom I can unburden my thoughts and who will do as much with me will be a rare luxury——'

And so they had sat all through the dwindling afternoon, talking and silent by turns, he curiously comfortable in her company, and she deeply uncomfortable, but in a most delicious and agreeable manner. All that she had felt about this handsome boy when she had first seen him across the smokily brilliant stage of the Haymarket that evening all those weeks ago was confirmed and strengthened that afternoon. He was beyond any shadow of a doubt the most splendid person she had ever met, and she fell quite hopelessly and helplessly further than ever into a passion for him. And yet managed so to disguise her feelings that he could sit comfortable and easy by her side.

For two weeks thereafter she had drifted through life in a dream of delight, going again to the theatre in the evenings with her mother, for now Jonah did so too, and she was happy to be, happy just to exist.

None of which had escaped her mother's eye, she now realized, sitting there hunched in gawky ugliness on the long table at the back of her mother's dressing-room and watching Jonah, a most foolish grin upon his face, handing her paint pots and brushes. Lilith knew what effect she was having, and was creating it deliberately. All the old familiar misery came creeping back into Celia as she watched, raged and suffered within.

13

Abby was supremely happy. Each day she was carried to the shop in Piccadilly by her father's coachman, arriving promptly at eleven in the morning (for despite her desire to commence the working day at the same time as the shop opened its shutters, both her father and James Caspar had been adamant that this was neither proper nor necessary) and settled herself, fine cambric apron over her morning gown and a pair of linen sleeves set neatly from wrists to elbows, at the tall desk in the back office, there to bring the day book up to the mark and deal with all such clerical matters as needed attention.

James had averred within a week of the new arrangement taking force that he did not know how he had managed hitherto, for she was so neat in her ways, not to say finicky in her careful entering of figures in her elegant sloping hand, and so swift with her understanding. She had, furthermore, what amounted to a positive genius for comprehending money.

She had quietly pointed out to her father and James that their method of accounting for the costs of their materials, and assessing the prices they should charge, was one all to likely to result in a small but steady loss of legitimate profits for the establishment, and although Abel at first had regarded this suggestion of hers with an indulgent eye, he had been not a little taken aback to discover upon further investigation that she was quite right.

' 'Twas a method of costings used by Josiah Witney before me, and I never thought to make any question of it,' he had said, looking at the neat rows of figures she had presented to him and James's gaze. 'Indeed, Abby, I had no notion that that milk-and-water governess of yours taught you to cipher so well! She should perhaps, be set to teach the boys their numbers, for Mr Loudoun has ill enough success with either of them——'

'Oh, it was nothing taught to me by Miss Ingoldsby,' Abby had said, a little flustered by his praise, but trying not to show it. 'I devised this for myself, for figures, you know, fall into patterns by their own volition. I find they speak to me so clear that it is a matter of some surprise to me that others do not hear it! But I am glad you like my method, Papa. Shall I set it to work for the future, then? And you, too, Mr Caspar, you approve?'

She had looked up demurely at James under her lashes, making him sweat a little as he tried to continue to display his usual calm mien. 'You have no objection to my wishing to make changes so soon after becoming your—apprentice?'

And her tiny pause before the word made his expression go wooden with the effort of maintaining his composure, and she had curled up within with pleasure at the sight of that dear face so put about. Oh, it was sheer delight to be so near him, to share these secret glances, these unspoken jokes, the whole delicious private language of two people deep in love.

In one way her presence in the shop, and her swiftness in learning the work that was to be done with books and accounts, acted against her interests, as she said to James with mock melancholy a month after she had commenced her new tasks.

'I should be stupid, dear James, and one much in need of example and precept and correction, for that way I would keep you by my side,' she said, and put up one hand to touch his cheek, for he was leaning over her shoulder looking at the ledger. 'I declare I see less of you now than in the days when I was but a visitor here. Now, because I am here, you are able to go rushing off to Wapping at every opportunity.'

'And if I did not have to do so, do you suppose your Papa would have agreed to this quite outrageous arrangement?' he said fondly, looking down at her with his whole face alight with his pleasure in her company. 'And do you suppose I would love you so well if you were a nincompoop like other females? Indeed, do you not realize, Miss Abby, that it is not so much your person which throws me into such a state of admiration, as your brain? The perfections of your figure are undoubted with its splendid shapeliness and grace, but it is the shapeliness and grace of your *accounting* that quite oversets my reason——'

And they both laughed at his carefully wrought joke, and settled to talk of the development of the new manufactory—which was coming on apace, and hoped to produce its first batches of medicines and drugs for both the dispensary and the Piccadilly shop soon after the turn of the year—with great absorption. Other lovers might talk to each other in romantic imaginings, or exchange absurd and over-flowery compliments, but Abby and her James talked of business matters, of the prices of tree barks and roots and seeds, the iniquities of the masters and crews of the Indiamen which brought their supplies, and of possible ways to make pills without the individual labour of rolling them by hand.

Such conversation was to them all the food that their love needed, and it throve indeed on such victuals, for as the weeks pleated into months they grew ever closer together, ever more dependent on each other for happiness, a happiness that glowed within them even during the long hours when he was sweating amid the machinery slowly growing under his direction at Wapping, and she sat with her head bent over her ledgers at Piccadilly.

At home in Gower Street in the evenings when she arrived there at seven o'clock—for it was agreed she should leave the shop before the shutters were set up at nine—life was not quite so happy. But this did not perturb Abby unduly for her home had never been a particu-larly joyous one and the new shadow cast by Jonah's absence added only a little to the prevailing atmosphere, as far as she was concerned, cocooned as she was in her own serene contentment.

But even in her private happiness she could not fail to be affected by her mother's situation. Dorothea looked more fragile than ever, in sad contrast to her daughter's blooming and rather solid young healthiness, yet Abel appeared not to notice this in the least. But Abby did, and enquired solicitously of her Mama, at frequent intervals, how she did, and how she spent her time. In the days when Abby herself had been continually at home and perforce often in her mother's company, she had not concerned herself overmuch with her mother's health, but now she worried a good deal about it.

All that she managed to discover was that her mother spent no more time than she had been used to do when Abby was at home in the nursery and schoolroom. Mother of a large brood though she was, and affectionate and dutiful a parent though she might appear, it was clear to Abby—indeed it always had been—that all the maternal love of which Dorothea was capable had been ignited and then expended in Jonah, her first born.

She had developed a kind of dependent affection for her eldest daughter and was deeply aware of her duty to her other children, the numerous result of her tedious loveless pregnancies, but without Jonah there to watch over and worry about, and admire and yearn over, motherhood was for Dorothea an empty shell.

So it was that she spent her daily hour in the schoolroom with Mary and Martha and Barty and the requisite hour each afternoon with Gussy in the nursery, but found in these contacts with her younger children little pleasure.

The twins were so silent a pair, so absorbed in each other, and so self-reliant that they had little need of her, and could give her nothing but the politeness due from well-bred children to their Mama. Any affection they might have to spare they gave to Miss Ingoldsby, the silent little mouse of a governess who, for all her lack of presence, had a shrewd brain and was teaching her charges a great respect for their own minds, just as she had taught their sister before them.

As for Bart—he was all boy, involved with rumbustious games, and messy activities, forever inky and noisy, and yearning only for the day, still two years off, when he could go away to school with his admired older brothers Rupert and William. His mother tried to hug and love him, but succeeded only in shrinking from his exuberance, a fact which he well recognized, and which made him remote with her.

Even her youngest born, Gussy, could give her little pleasure, for his nurse adored and cosetted him to such a degree that he loved her above all others, and treated his mother with the sort of suspicious shyness more due to an acidulous maiden aunt than to a parent. Which made Dorothea guiltily but gladly leave him to his nurse's arms so that she could return to her boudoir to sit and fret and worry about her beloved Jonah.

This much Abby knew. However, what she did not discover was the new practice into which Dorothea had slipped almost as soon as Abby had taken up her new duties at the shop.

Each day she would drive out, instructing the coachman as she climbed into the carriage to take her to Hyde Park, and as regularly she called upon him as they turned into Piccadilly to stop and set her down to shop.

He would drive on to the park to return two or three hours or more later (and glad enough he was to have the chance to foregather with his friends at the noisy coachmen's rest near Tyburn Gate instead of driving insipidly about the park with his even more insipid passenger) there to pick up his employer's wife and convey her back to Gower Street.

He knew not how she spent the intervening time, and cared less. Had he thought of the matter at all, which was unlikely, he would have said his mistress did as she said she did—shopped among the bazaars.

But what she did in fact was much less inspiriting. She simply strolled up and down the northern pavements of Piccadilly, ostensibly interested in the shops and their well-displayed wares, but in fact never taking her attention from the front of the Josiah Witney establishment across the traffic-curdled street.

The first time she had done it she had remembered, momentarily, the occasion long ago when she had come to this selfsame spot, a palpitating girl head over ears in love, to seek out her beloved Abel; but that was not a thought to be pursued, and she thrust it away from her immediately. For she was now in search of another beloved, and it was he to whom she gave all her thoughts.

For Dorothea had developed a conviction, a conviction so strong it could only be considered an obsession. Ever since the evening when Abby had propounded to her father and mother her plan to become an apprentice apothecary, Dorothea had been seized of the notion that this was no more than a blind for something else. In her own absorption with her son, it did not occur to Dorothea that other people could be less interested in Jonah than she was, and when she recognized, as she did, that Abby had some other purpose than the one she professed in seeking to be her father's apprentice, she assumed at once that the other purpose (so well hid by Abby but so apparent to her mother, for wasn't Dorothea one who had all her life had to dissemble her true feelings, and as such one most peculiarly fitted to recognize such dissembling in others?) involved Jonah.

He was to come to visit his sister at the shop, Dorothea had decided. That was how it was to be. He was in need of money, of course, poor boy, and in his refusal to approach his father, and his unwillingness to distress his Mama (for that was how fond Dorothea interpreted his flat refusal to tell her of his address) what other course was open to him but an approach to his sister? And she, clever minx—for Dorothea knew her daughter well enough to have a healthy respect for her sharp wits— had devised this scheme for both meeting Jonah, and for finding money to give him. For where else, argued Dorothea to herself, could Abby find money for her brother, but from the coffers at the shop? It was altogether just such a plan as the romantic Dorothea would herself once have devised, and she applauded it.

It was as the result of all this careful reasoning that Dorothea acted as she did. The day would come, she told herself optimistically, when she would see her dear Jonah approach the shop, when she would recognize his beloved handsome figure across that busy street and would be able to hurry across and greet him there and beg him to tell her of his situation, and make plans to visit him regularly. She was sure, poor, frantic, yearning, aching Dorothea, sure that he would not be able to refuse her personally expressed request, the request she could not send to him in a letter, because of his steadfast refusal to reveal his address.

Had Abby been less wrapped up in her own affairs it is possible that on one of those interminable afternoons when Dorothea walked up and down, up and down, through the icy muddy slush of the pavements of Piccadilly she would have seen and recognized her, for normally she had a lively curiosity about what went on around her and would have spent some time happily enough watching the street crowds go by, had she not had her James to think about. But she had, so when other shopkeepers stood at their doors filling the cold air with wafts of steaming breath and looking proprietorially about them (and hardly noticing the quietly veiled little woman who walked there every day, for she was indeed so very nondescript), when other people from other establishments went along the street in search of refreshment or some private purchase, Abby sat happily in the back office poring over her books, and eating the hot pies and drinking the milk fresh from the cow at Tyburn Gate brought to her by young Peter, oblivious of the busy street outside. And of her mother's new obsession.

That Abel should be equally unaware of Dorothea's behaviour was not so surprising. He did not normally pay her much attention anyway; and although he had been aware of her distress in the early days after Jonah's departure, he had now quite dismissed that spark of rare concern for his wife which had invested his thoughts and had, in part, spurred him to seek Lucy's aid in finding out where his son had gone to ground.

For Lucy had failed him. He had gone again to visit her a week later, as she had bade him, and great had been his chagrin when she told him shortly that she 'knew naught of the boy'. He had been surprised too, for Lucy's boast that she knew all that happened in the Town, knew every person of consequence, and that she had her fingers in every dubious pie cooked up in those sour back streets and alleys was no idle one. She did know all—and yet had failed to discover Jonah's whereabouts.

When he had said he was surprised, she had turned on him with the anger of a virago, which had quite set him back on his heels.

'Surprised, are you?' she had almost snarled it. 'If you think you can do better then go set about the streets yourself! You go asking the bully boys questions, an' see what sort of answers you'll get, you with yer jumped up fancy swell ways! If I 'aven't found out, it's on account there's naught to be found. 'E's left the town, an' that's all about it, for if 'e were 'ere, I'd have smoked 'im out, and if 'e'd been 'armed I'd 'ave found that out too. I'm tellin' you as 'e's not about the Town, and you mun settle for that, you 'ear me? Leave the boy be. 'E's chosen to shed yer for reasons of 'is own, and gone about 'is business. So you go about yours and tell yer lady wife to set 'er 'eart to 'er other sprigs. She's enough of 'em, in all conscience!'

He had gone away angry, but curiously comforted. He had wanted to know where the boy was because he was a man who wanted to know everything and took ill to being out of control of any aspect of his life, and it was infuriating to find his own son had moved so easily out of his sphere of influence. But at least the boy had come to no harm. Lucy had said so, and he believed her, for she had never lied to him about anything, and he had no reason to doubt her. If she said Jonah had come to no harm that much must be so. It was indeed likely that he had left the Town, and with his usual practicality Abel pushed his son away from the forefront of his mind. He was a past episode, to be forgotten. He had rejected his father, and his father would return that in kind.

But Lucy was able to forget less easily. To have lied to her likely lad, to have been asked by him for information that he wanted and to fail him—that had been hard. But she had had to do it, she had decided.

She had of course discovered almost within a day and a night where Jonah was. He had been seen by too many of her clients in the green-room at the Haymarket, there had been too much ribald gossip about 'Mistress Lucas's pretty new boy' for her not to know. Indeed, she had not had to seek the information at all; it had come to her as naturally as the sun rose in the morning. But what to do with the information; that had been her problem. She had had near a week in which to ponder, and ponder hard she had, sitting there in her frowsty kitchen.

She had not been able to talk even to Nancy about it, for although that hard-headed and practical woman was now her closest friend—indeed, the only woman friend in any true sense that Lucy had ever had and as attached to Abel as herself—this was not something to be discussed with her. How could she? Nancy did not remember the way Abel had been all those years ago when first he had lost the only girl he had ever loved, and then suffered the agony of finding her again.

Lucy, during those half dozen days, remembered and remembered and remembered with intense clarity the way Abel had looked then, how he had ached and yearned and suffered for Lilith Lucas, and how bitter and agonizing had been the end of it all. And now his son had fallen into the same trap. That hellborn bitch—for Lucy could not think of her in any other way—had set her greedy claws first into the father and now into the son, and Lucy was the only person who knew of it.

Apart from the bitch herself, she had reminded herself with a sudden chill. Did she know who 'her pretty boy' was? Was she, through the boy, again going to make Abel unhappy as she had almost a score of years ago? Well, if she was, the news of it would have to come from her, not from Lucy. Lucy was not going to be the one to tell Abel. Let him rest as happy as he could a little longer——

So she had lied to her beloved likely lad, and hated herself for it.

While Abel, for his part, turned his mind away from his domestic affairs to other matters. And he had, indeed, much to occupy his mind.

The growth of the new manufactory produced few problems, for with Abby so well ensconced in Piccadilly James Caspar was free to do sterling work at Wapping, and Abel had good reason to be well content with the way matters were going there.

Even Cloudesly and Sir John Kutner, cautious though they were, had announced themselves pleased enough with the way plans were going forward, and allowed themselves to be well content with the use being made of the moneys they had released—albeit reluctantly—from the dispensary funds.

Abel's worries were elsewhere; in Tavistock Street to be precise. From the day he had opened his dispensary doors sixteen years before he had been busy, God knew. The sick and the halt had come to him in their tens and then their hundreds from the very first, pouring out of their hovels and their gutters wrapped in their rags and their diseases and their hunger to debouch on to Tavistock Street.

In the beginning it had been to Endell Street they had come, for that had been where he had opened his first establishment, and remembering those two small crowded basement rooms as he sometimes did he found it in him to marvel at the fact that he had problems now. Then he had treated only the outpatients, anointing sores and ulcers with his caustic salves, putting soothing drops into eyes reddened and half destroyed by the pox, instilling cleansing tinctures into ears pouring greenish reeking pus, and dosing and clystering and pilling wherever he thought it might do some small good. A very few of his patients he had been able to treat as a surgeon should, when they would permit him (and many did, thinking the agony worth it for the chance to get blind oblivious drunk on the brandy he provided as a way to ease the pain of his knife), and on these he would cut for the stone or the wen and would try to repair the horrendous injuries they did themselves in fights with rusty knives and broken gin bottles.

Most of those in need of surgery, however, he had to send across the river to his old mentor at Guy's, Sir Astley Cooper, or to the ever open doors of St Thomas's hospital further along the street from Guy's. And that had angered him, had filled him with a sour-tasting frustration, especially when the patients he had had to turn from his doors were women in the last stages of childbirth. He had wanted above all to help them and still did, wanted always to exercise the skill of his hands in extricating from their maternal prisons these infants of the Dials. He felt a special care for these babies, and he could not have explained for the life of him why it should be he felt so strongly for the art of the man midwife—an art much sneered at by some of his colleagues among the apothecaries and certainly by most of those he knew at the Royal College of Surgeons. Perhaps it was because of his first sight of a dead body, a young and pregnant body, gleaming in the lamplight long ago in St Giles's Churchyard; perhaps it had been that night in the greenroom at the Haymarket Theatre when he had saved the life of Nancy by delivering her dead infant (thus to make her his devoted servant and eventually his chief nurse); perhaps it had been because he had himself been an infant of these stinking Dials. He did not know, and it did not really matter. He wanted to care for these women and their babies, and in Endell Street that had not been possible.

It had taken him five years to get away from there to the bigger better house in Tavistock Street where he could care for inpatients as well as street ones, and he remembered still the glow he had felt when he had first seen those two big rooms on the upper floors set ready with straw pallets and rough grey blankets, waiting for their first occupants. 'Now,' he had told himself, 'now, the people of the Dials have *their* hospital, like the people of Southwark. *Now* I can care for them properly——'

But that had been gone ten years ago, and now he was in many ways in the same situation as in Endell Street. Overcrowded, unable to work as well as he would have wished, desperate for space, space, space, anywhere to put the hordes of greyfaced, diseased and dying people who came each day to stand patiently and with eternal tired hope at his steps, letting themselves be turned away because there was no room within for them. It was all *wrong* that it should be so, it was a sin of the greatest possible magnitude that every ill person should not be as of a right entitled to a surgeon's care and a bed to die in decently; so he would rage within himself.

But, wisely, he kept such thoughts to himself, for people would think him run mad if he suggested that a bed in a hospital was a man's right. To be half-starved and ill and to die in the gutter was the only right that a man could claim, when he lived in the Dials. To give such people medicine and care, as did Abel Lackland and his trustees, could be construed as an act of simple Christian piety and charity. To suggest that the poor had a right to such acts would be little short of heresy, and certainly would smack of total lunacy.

Yet such were his feelings, and daily he fretted against the limitations of the small house in Tavistock Street, daily he felt those frustrations rise ever higher as patients he believed he could have saved died for want of a bed, and the food and shelter that bed provided, as women brought him dead babies, and stood before him blank-faced, uncomprehending, too hungry and ill themselves to grieve as they should. He needed more space, a bigger hospital, with beds for hundreds. The new manufactory promised they could give better dispensing care to the street patients, at lower cost, but would that do anything to help the people who needed to be inside the hospital? Would that do anything to help those who needed the attentions of the knife? Grimly he would tighten his jaw, and ill-temperedly would snap at Nancy (who paid no attention whatsoever, serenely continuing her work; she knew her Mr Abel well enough) and did what work he could as best he could.

And then in January of 1829 he was shown a possible way to find the better bigger hospital he needed and the money (or part of it at least) with which to build it.

The snow was thick in the London streets that winter. The Thames was half blocked with ice under a lowering grey sky, and the air crackled with the chill as people died in their hundreds in the thick clustered rookeries of the Bermudas and Porridge Island, Clare Market and the Dials. Abel, arriving at Tavistock Street one day wrapped in a heavy grey cloth coat of close fitting cut and with a black fur collar in which he could hide his frozen face, his ears glowing under his curly brimmed beaver hat, found a man who was patently not a Dials resident standing on his steps.

He was most fashionably dressed, a round man with a tip-tilted nose that was quite cherry red, and which peeped out above his high cravat like a child's. He peered at Abel with very bright round black eyes and said in a rather high-pitched tone, 'Mr Lackland? Glad to see you here, sir. Been waiting for you this past half hour, sir, and fit to freeze to the pavement, with your woman within refusing to let me in, for she says she lets in none she does not know. A strange keeper of your door, sir, a strange keeper in such chill weather! Well, let be, let be. My name, sir, is Gandy Deering, at your service, and I have a matter of important business to discuss with you. May we go in before I die of the cold altogether?'

14

The big front room was tolerably warm, for Nancy had set sticks and coals to the fireplace, and put a vast kettle above the flames to fill the air with its steamy comfort.

As she helped Abel to remove his coat, leaving the other man to the little maid's attentions, she muttered in his ear, 'I would not let him in, Mr Abel, till you came, for I feared he might be up to no good. I've seen him around here these many days, a'measuring of the street and the 'ouses, and altogether be'avin' most sinister. I don't like the looks of 'im, and I'd be careful if I was you. 'E could be up to anythin'——'

Abel grunted and nodded. He knew quite well what it was that alarmed Nancy. It had been some years now since he had had time to go regularly to the Great Windmill Street school of anatomy, where his friend Charles Bell taught the students who flocked to his fame (for ever since the Battle of Waterloo, at which he had attended Wellington's injured soldiers and made breathtakingly beautiful and exceedingly accurate anatomical drawings, Bell had been a name of great importance in London medical circles), but that did not mean he had lost interest in the subject.

Far from it, for he had arranged in the basement of his Tavistock Street house a small anatomy room of his own. Only Nancy knew of it, and only Nancy, apart from he, had a key, for there was much anxiety among the common people about the activities of the anatomists; had it once got out that some of the patients who died in Abel's beds stood a chance of ending up in his basement being explored with a knife the goodwill the people of the surrounding slums felt for him could change to ugly frightened rage overnight.

So when there was a death in one of the upstairs beds and none to claim the body, Nancy and Abel would quietly bear away the corpse and set it in the basement and, weather permitting, Abel would keep it long enough to dissect it and make his notes and his own careful drawings before removing on a dark night the somewhat noisome remains at last to the quietness of St Giles; there was always a newly open grave or two in that overgrown and crowded patch of grey earth able to take an extra and unknown and unwanted body.

But Nancy did not at all enjoy this aspect of the work she did for Abel, and it said much for her affection for him and her still burning gratitude towards him that she bore with the task and the secret at all. Always she was hung about with the fear that the law would discover this side of their work, and always did she fear that there would be trouble. News of the doings of Burke and Hare in remote Edinburgh last November had rapidly filtered south, and half London was talking of the Irish resurrectionists who had found it simpler and swifter to despatch people to make their own corpses than to dig up those created by more normal means, to supply the egregious Dr Knox with his anatomical specimens. Should the taint of such activities touch Abel—Nancy would shiver at the thought. Not for nothing had the sellers of Jemmy Catnach's penny ballads hawked them so assiduously about the streets, five miles each side of the Monmouth Street shop where they were printed. They had managed to fill many far more sophisticated minds than Nancy's with the resurrectionist terrors. And well did Abel know it.

He smiled a little now, seeing her look so sharply and edgily at the man standing warming his hands at the fire. 'You need not concern yourself, Nancy,' he said, and advanced towards his guest. 'I think you have no cause for alarm,' and she shot a sideways glance at him, and went sniffing away to tell the crowds at the door they would have to wait a while yet, for Mr Lackland had other matters to concern himself with this morning apart from their stinking carcases.

'You must forgive her, Mr—Deering, I think you said?—for her caution. The way of a surgeon working in such a part of London is not easy,' Abel said. 'Now sir, you say you have business to discuss with me? I must tell you that if it concerns my interests in the spice trade you must go to the counting house in Eastcheap, for it is there that Hunnisett deals with such affairs, and if it is to do with the shop in Piccadilly then you——'

The round-faced man turned from the fire to stand with his back to it, flicking up his coat tails to warm his not inconsiderable buttocks. He looked at Abel with his eyebrows a little raised, and his head on one side.

'It is not of spice I wish to talk to you, Mr Lackland, nor yet of shopkeeping matters,' he said, and his voice was now not quite so high-pitched, but still had a slightly womanish ring to it. 'I did not know, in fact, that you were such a man of substance, sir! I took you for a surgeon only. I know you have consulting rooms for your private patients in Leicester Place, as well as your charitable affairs here, but a spice man to boot! You must be warm, sir, very warm——'

'I think we will not discuss my private affairs,' Abel said stiffly. 'And I have many patients waiting upon me, as you will have observed outside. Perhaps you will come sharply to the point, Mr—Deering?'

'You do not know my name, Mr Lackland?' The other man looked quite unruffled. 'Well, to be sure, why should you, since your interests are so many and yet so far from mine. I, sir, am an architect. You may have heard of me by my patronymic—John Gandy? No? Oh, well. It was possible, for until a twelvemonth ago, when I came into the estate of my good friend Henry Deering at Missenden, so was I called. Well, sir, to my point. I am, as I say, an architect of some note, and it will not have escaped your notice that despite that at this present time money is hard to come by, much building is going on about these parts.'

'Indeed, sir, I have noticed,' Abel said dryly. 'For how could any man fail to do so? With the dirt and noise occasioned a man would have to be blind, halt and mad to miss observation of it. The Strand is hardly the street I remember from one day to the next—indeed, since the Exeter Exchange went, I have been hard put to it sometimes to know where I was——'

'Precisely so!' Mr Deering nodded his head fatly and with great satisfaction. 'It is a great improvement we are wreaking, is it not? I take much pride and pleasure in the work we are doing.'

'Well, no doubt,' Abel said, and looked pointedly out of the window at the crowd waiting outside for him. 'But I cannot see that this is a matter for my attention.'

'Ah, we come to a point, sir, we come to a point! These alterations and improvements are not ended, far from it, indeed! We have at present a great plan afoot to carry further the improvements we started at the splendours of Waterloo Bridge. It is the plan, sir, to erect a new Hall, of which I am honoured to be appointed architect and chief supervisor.'

'So?' Abel was rapidly becoming irritated by the pomposity of this self-important little man, and was not afraid to show it. But Mr Deering seemed quite unaware of his irritation and went on, swaying a little on his heels, his hands still clasped beneath his coat tails.

'It will be such an edifice as the King himself would be proud to call his own, if all goes ahead as I have planned it. It will not be an easy building to create, for I have at best but a narrow frontage to the Strand, but create it I shall, and it will have proportions of the most classical——'

Abel's patience finally snapped. 'Well, sir, I have no doubt that this is all a matter of great importance to you. For my part, I find it of no more moment than the progress of a cockroach across my floor. If you will be so good as to take your leave, sir, I will about my day's work, for unlike you, I do not find myself in the happy situation of having naught to do, and the whole day in which to do it. Good morning to you——' And he crossed the room to the door and snapped it open.

But Deering stood still in place, and smiled at Abel with what was clearly meant to be a conciliatory smile, although there was a hardness and glitter about his eyes which made it clear that his self-esteem had been not a little buffeted.

'Indeed, Mr Lackland, you will find that this matter concerns you far more than the activities of cockroaches, since you are intimately involved with this plan, inasmuch as you stand in the way of it.'

'I—what?' Abel said, and frowned sharply. 'You may do as you damned please, sir, as long as you depart my house and give me leave to set about my business!'

Deering shook his head, almost regretfully. 'Ah, there you are wrong, Mr Lackland, there you are wrong. I cannot do as I please as long as you are setting about your business. Your business here in Tavistock Street, that is. You see, Mr Lackland, not to put too fine a point upon it, we need the land upon which this house stands. We wish to pull it down and replace it with the new Hall. The properties on both sides of you have fallen in with these plans, and I am here today to ask you to follow the suit of your neighbours.'

There was a long silence and then, very carefully, Abel closed the door.

'You wish to take this house from me? Be damned to you, sir, if you do! Have you seen out there? Have you? Come here, Mr Deering, and cast your eyes outside——' and he marched across the room, grasped the smaller man by the elbow in a cruel grip and positively hustled him to the window. 'Look out there, sir, and tell me what damned good your precious classical Hall would be to them? Hey, sir? What about them? Take this house from me, and where are we to put ourselves?'

Deering stared down at the people outside, his lip lifting a little in distaste at the sight and he pulled his elbow away from Abel's grip and felt in his pocket for his snuffbox.

'Indeed, Mr Lackland, I take your point that you make use of these premises in a way you consider laudable, though for my part, I cannot see you do any good in ministering to such riff-raff as this! Feed 'em, dose 'em, and all you do is make more of 'em, for they breed like the vermin they are, and are beyond the reach of any good sense. Do not these same creatures of yours keep coming back and back despite all your efforts? I'll be sure that they do! These creatures are irredeemable, sir, and you should by now know it, for what good has your care of 'em done? What satisfaction you may get from such work is past my comprehension! The work *we* are doing here on the Strand, and for that matter in many other parts of the Town, is more good for these creatures than your efforts, for we at least are destroying the rookeries and the warrens where they huddle! We need to get this sort of sickness out of our great city, sir, and let it destroy itself in a natural manner, and not encourage the growth of this canker on the body politic——'

'I need no Malthusian lecture from you, nor any parading of your money-grubbing views, sir!' Abel said, and his voice was very hard and thin. 'You come here to take my dispensary from me, and I am telling you that you shall not! And do not think that in dealing with me you deal with the sort of weak and helpless persons that my neighbours are. Where a harness maker and a widow woman may be put out of doors by such as you, I am not to be so mishandled! I have my friends, as powerful as yours, and so I tell you! For every counting-house-minded creature such as you, there is a good and honest man who will see that the charitable work we do here is of value and who will defend me! So go to perdition, and take your damned hall with you!'

And again Abel seized the door and dragged it open to stand there staring venomously at the little fat man beside the window.

But the little man did not move. He stood with his hands set in his pockets, and a narrow smile upon his face.

'Indeed, Mr Lackland, they told me, those who know you, that you are a fiery man, and one not given to accepting any balk in your way, but I had not taken you for a complete fool! It is your affair if you prefer to spend your time on such as these——' and he jerked his head over his shoulder—'instead of with your private practice or your manifold business affairs! But I am surprised to discover you *are* a businessman, since you did not think it worth asking me what I proposed to pay for the property!'

'I am not interested in your money, Goddamn it!' Abel roared. 'Has that quite escaped you? Have I been talking to my own ears? I am interested in the provision of a decent dispensary and hospital for my patients, and nothing more! I care for the work I do, not the fiscal reward it gives me. So will you be so good as to be about your business and let me set about that work!'

Gandy Deering set his head on one side, and looked consideringly at Abel. 'I see, sir. Suppose then, I were not to offer you money for this house, but instead another property of equal size and value? Would that satisfy you? For I tell you, with no mincing about it, that I am determined to have this property, come hell come Devil, and we may as well find some way to deal amicably as not. I am not a man to wilt under a few insults, Mr Lackland, no more than are you. So let us waste no more of each other's time but discuss honestly—what do you want to be persuaded to leave this house and take your patients with you before the first of June next?'

15

From his seat on the precarious wooden platform half-way up the huge elm tree, Jonah could see her quite clearly. She moved upon the ice for all the world like a fragment of it, her blue pelisse with the white swan's-down edging alternately reflecting in the glistening surface as she moved into the brightly lit areas and merging with it in the shadows under the trees. She was wearing a blue bonnet, exactly matching her dress and pelisse and repeating the swan's-down trim, and with that and the drift of muff in which her hands were snugly enclosed the total effect of elf-like enchantment was complete.

As she skated, she looked up trustingly from time to time into the face of the man beside her, who was holding her waist with one very proprietorial arm, and Jonah felt his teeth clench as he watched. He could not see the loveliness of the snow-encrusted ice with the fairy lights glittering in the surrounding trees, nor the scarlet and golden glow of the vast bonfire which lit the side of the grotto; nor was he aware of the many other skaters swooping and lifting themselves about the blue-grey surface under the blackness of the midwinter sky. All he saw was she, and all he wanted was to be down there beside her, not up here like a useless clod.

But she had laughed at him, very prettily and with much warmth, yet laughed all the same when he had tried to lead her out to the melody so busily produced by the blue-fingered musicians sitting on the bank; and struggling to be sprightly despite the manifest discomfort, for he was little more than a novice on ice skates and the first time he had tried he had fallen twice, ignominiously, once actually having to clutch at her for support. Even her children were better skaters than he, he had thought miserably, watching six-year-old Ben go careering across the surface with his small face under his tasselled cap scarlet with exertion and pleasure, hand in hand with an equally adept Lyddy.

Celia had recognized his irritation and despite the fact that she was, as ever, more irritated than he by the way that he could be so put down by her mother, chose to forego her own skating (although she loved the sport and was very skilful at it) to sit beside him on the tree platform.

'Are you sorry now that we came?' she said looking sharply at him from under her brown bonnet, and sitting with her chin tucked deeply into the collar of her green merino cape, for it was bitter cold this February night and the temperature was only tolerable for those who were heated by their physical exertions on the ice. 'You thought it a capital idea when Mama first broached it, after all! You said you could not imagine anything more delightful than a jaunt to Cremorne in winter, did you not? I heard you myself! So why do you sit here now glowering like Hawks on washday?'

'Celia, I will thank you not to torment me in that missish way you affect!' he snapped. 'I am not glowering, as you so ill put it, nor am I sorry we came. I just—oh, it matters not a whit what I think!'

'And I will thank you not to speak to me in so peremptory a manner,' Celia flashed back. 'For I am not one of your little sisters to be put down in so rude a manner!'

'Oh, I am sorry,' he said after a moment and now he sounded very weary. 'But I am so *beset*. Your Mama—she promised me that we should talk of my drama. She *promised* me—indeed she has been promising me these past five weeks, but still I cannot get her to listen to a line of it——'

'Of course you cannot,' Celia said calmly. 'For she has no intention ever of doing such a thing. No, do not look so at me! You still are little more than a child, after all, Jonah Lackland, if after all these weeks in my Mama's house you have not seen the truth for yourself. She is of no patience at all in what does not directly concern her! I told you when you started that if you wished to write a play for Mama to take a close interest in, it must have a part for her that quite outshines all others. It is of little use giving her a great rodomontade of a thing in which the biggest part is for a man! She will not play that milk-and-water heroine you wrote, you know, nor will she listen to you read the play now she knows that you have not centred the action on the female in it—and if you cannot recognize that you are a greater fool than I took you for——'

Jonah said nothing. There was little more he could say, for this conversation seemed to have happened so many times since Christmas that he felt sometimes like a bird in a cage, going round and round the same narrow bars, fluttering and rapping at the stops in its way.

'That man she skates with,' he said abruptly, 'who is he? I did not see him before tonight.'

Celia shrugged, unconcernedly. 'I know not, and care less. He is no doubt one of the bucks of the Town who has recognized her and she is content enough to play a game of pretence with him. He is an indifferent skater, and she will soon tire of him, so do not fear your nose will be put quite out of joint! Tonight she is being the Good Mama taking the children on a jaunt. You too! You are one of the children in her eyes, not the buck you think yourself at all!'

'Oh, damn you, Celia! Will you leave me alone!' he flared, and turned his head to stare at her in the darkness with miserable eyes. 'Between you and your Mama, I know not whether I stand upon head or heels! One minute you treat me like a friend, the next you rail at me like some fishwife, or behave as if you were a nursery chit playing idiotish childish games! Your Mama is as bad for I never know where I stand with her, either! I tell you I have had enough. I care not for her, nor for you, nor for—oh, to perdition with everything!'

And he stood up and lunged towards the rickety steps set in the side of the tree to go plunging to ground level, leaving Celia staring down at him with her eyes hooded by the brim of her bonnet.

It seemed to him that he walked about in the Gardens for a very long time, his boots crunching in the ice crusted snow beneath them, his footsteps sometimes creaking as he turned corners, feeling the weight of the snow-laden branches above his head and the deadness of the cold earth beneath. Celia was right; he *had* greeted Lilith's suggestion of 'a small family visit' to the ice-skating pond at Cremorne with pleasure, for he had cast himself immediately in the role of her escort, had imagined himself walking arm in arm with her, telling her of his play, so agonizingly finished, so agonizingly awaiting her stamp of approval in order that it might be presented upon the Haymarket stage, had visualized her children skipping about before them.

Well, had visualized Ben and Lyddy, to be sure. In his imaginings he had left Celia out, for she was not one who would ever fit easily into his schemes. She had an uneasy way even in his thoughts and projections

148

into future happenings of going her own wilful way, quite ignoring any desire of Jonah's. It was not, after all, surprising that this should be so. Ever since that afternoon in the white-and-gold drawing-room at North Audley Street when he and she had talked properly for the first time, there had inevitably been a difficulty in their intercourse.

To be sure, sometimes Celia was all delight, a warm and good friend, someone who would sit on the floor before the leaping flames of the small sitting-room fire, her arms hugged about her knees and her eyes fixed on his face as he read aloud to her his poems and essays, and, latterly, the five acts of his great Play. Then the memory of that embrace they had shared was warm and right, even exciting in a curious way.

But other times she was sheer hell, all snappings and sharp edges, looking at him with her eyes glittering with a cold scorn that made him feel uneasy and in some way wanting, and she would lash him with a tongue as sharp as any needle about his affection for her Mama. He hated her when she was in these humours, for her aim was unerring and over and over again she would make some cutting remark that would go right through his carapace of adult calm (a pose which he knew, uncomfortably, did not impress her in the least, for he was, after all, only a year or so her senior) to the tender skin beneath.

That she was jealous of her sparkling, successful, altogether captivating mother was something he realized perfectly well, and indeed he would have been surprised had she not been so, for Lilith was—Lilith. No woman, not even her own daughter, could but fail to fade into insignificance beside her, and know of it. But he could not understand why Celia should display such anger towards himself, for did he not suffer as much as she from Lilith's caprices, her sharp storms of temper, her attacks of ugly swearing shouting rage? Of course he did!

Had he been less involved with his own new emotions engendered by Lilith, had he been less occupied in trying to keep at bay his un-expected pangs of homesickness for Gower Street and his sense of guilt about his refusal to tell his Mama of his whereabouts Jonah would perhaps have had the wit to see why it was that Celia behaved so to him. He would have seen that her attacks of anger and her most cruel taunts followed hard on the heels of one of Lilith's softer moods, when he would enjoy basking in her approval and would relax and soften under the warmth of her attentions.

But he did not see that, did not recognize the angry desperate need for his affection that filled Celia and which governed her every reaction to him. But then, how could he? Himself ensnared in a woman's enchantment for the first time in his young life, he had neither energy nor time left to perceive that Celia was in much the same case regarding himself.

He thought hard as he walked about the gardens, planned conversations with Lilith, and then abandoned them, saw himself sweeping her away masterfully and forcing her to sit and listen to his play, and then, as the absurdity of his imaginings came home to him, felt himself filled with a thick and heavy depression, so deep as to be like a solid thing in which he was wrapped. He could see no way forwards or sideways in his present situation. The only way, he told himself, with sudden honesty and a depth of misery he would not have thought possible in himself, was backwards.

He would have to return to his father's house, to accept his plans for his future, and be articled apprentice to the apothecary's and surgeon's trade. Hateful though such a prospect was it was not as impossible as going on longer as he was, living in Lilith Lucas's home as neither family nor guest, neither child nor adult.

His high hopes were dashed. The shining future that had opened before him the night he had fled to the theatre to pour into Lilith's ears his miseries, all of it was no more real nor lasting than the crystals of ice that sparkled on the edges of the branches that dipped and swayed in the bitter night breezes above his head. One hot breath of reality, and it was all gone.

He turned then to make his way back towards the distant twinkle of lights and the sound of the music which came from the direction of the skaters' pond, and now he walked with his head up and with a sharper more purposeful step. He was not happy in his situation, knew that the decision he had reached was one of defeat, but at least he had made it. The time had come to thank Lilith for her hospitality, and to leave her to find another moth to dance in her flame.

And even in his dejection, he liked the simile that had come so easily into his mind, and stored it away to be used in a poem sometime. Perhaps to continue that one he had started yesterday, standing there in the wings of the Haymarket and watching Lilith kill herself, in her role as Isabella in *The Fateful Marriage*. 'Dear Heart of All That Lives and

Breathes, The Light of Life and Joy Itself, the Flame Round Which a Yearning Soul, Shall Dance as in a——'

'So there you are, you foolish boy!' Her voice came sparkling at him out of the darkness, and he stopped and blinked and tried to penetrate the dimness with his gaze, but all he could see was a faint glimmer beneath the trees. 'I thought you had froze to death, alone here in the grottoes! Ah, you poets! Were you composing an ode for me, dear Jonah?'

'No, ma'am,' he said stiffly, and moved forwards a little awkwardly, for he could still not see her clearly. 'No, I was not. Well, not precisely,' he amended for he took pride in his veracity. 'I was making decisions, ma'am, about my future.'

'La, sir, you sound very serious, of a sudden!'

She moved then and came to stand close beside him to look up into his face, and he could smell the delicate scent she was wont to put on her skin.

'It is not kind in you to be serious when I had planned this evening to be a jolly expedition for us all. I have had to send the children home, all alone, and come to seek you myself! It is not *kind* in you—and it is not kind to call me "ma'am" in that fashion! I have told you so before. You are no schoolboy to behave so punctilious, and certainly not with me——' and she made her last words sound like a caress, so that he felt the familiar sense of enchantment rise in him again. But he had made a decision and he would be strong in it.

'You will forgive me, ma'am, if I am punctilious, but it is necessary I be so. I have enjoyed your hospitality these many weeks—no, let us be clear in our accounting and say months. I did not wish to become a—a sponger. It was never my intention that I should permit you to carry responsibility for me. I wish to work my way in the world, Mistress Lucas, indeed I *must*. You told me that you would set me to work as a playwright, and I have worked hard and long on my play. But despite my telling you a little of its contents, you will not let me read all of it to you! And how can you have your management set it into rehearsal if you do not know the play well? Forgive me, ma'am, but it is now clear to me that you have been but—kind, and humoured me a little, but do not wish to set my work upon your stage. So, I will take myself and my play away, and try its fortunes where I can. I am grateful to you for your many kindnesses to me, but I cannot go on longer in this way. I will, with your leave, take myself away tomorrow——'

'Ah, no,' she breathed softly, and quite suddenly he found she was so close to him that she needs must lay against his chest, and he needs must put his arms around her, and she seemed to him to fit in them as though she had grown there. She had her arms up, and with one soft hand caressed his cold cheek, and he felt the swan's-down muff tickle his face on the other side.

'You are sad! I know the ailment, dear boy, for you are a poet, and they always suffer so! You wish to make the clock run mad, and see your play upon the stage hot from your pen. I understand this, dear boy, but you must understand the workings of the theatre! These things take much time, indeed they do! But you show a nice concern for the proprieties, and I understand as no woman other than I could how sore it makes you feel not to be making your way in the world. And I have a plan, I have such a plan! You will be sure to like it, dear boy, and indeed, it will be an excellent thing for you as playwright, for it will teach you much matter that you need to know.'

'I have made a decision, ma'am, indeed I have,' he said uncertainly, and knew how young he must sound, and was angry with himself for it. 'It is clear to me that I am a burden to you and——'

'Never let it be said!' she murmured softly, and her hand moved from his cheek to press his lips and almost without his own volition he parted them and felt her fingertips move inside and touch the tip of his tongue, and was amazed at the sudden access of feeling that moved through him, making his belly quake in a quite extraordinary fashion. 'You are my friend, and could never be a burden! I have neglected you sorely, I see that now, and exposed you too much to the importunities of the children. They are good enough children, to be sure, but you should not have to tolerate the childishness and spite of a silly girl, as Celia can be when she chooses, and I believe she has been tormenting you, has she not? No, dear boy, do not answer——' again her fingertips tasting faintly and somehow very excitingly of salt and scent moved over his lips, 'for you are a good and honourable person and would not say aught of anyone if it could not be good. So, I shall protect you from the children's importunities by—can you guess my plan?'

'No, ma'am—Lilith,' he said and his voice sounded very husky in his own ears.

'Why, you shall work, dear boy, work! At the theatre. I am to rehearse soon for my benefit night next month, and you shall have a part. Not a big part, you understand, but enough to give you a taste of the business of acting. There! Are you not happy now?'

He tried to pull back a little, but although she did not move nor seem to hold him tighter it was somehow not possible for him to break the closeness between them, and he stopped trying, for it was an agreeable situation to be in, to be sure. 'I—it is kind in you, ma'am, to take such concern with me—but it is not an actor I wish to be but a playwright, and I was of the understanding that you were interested in these matters and would help me. But I would not put you to any inconvenience, and if it is not easy for you to let me read my play to you, or to read it yourself, why then I shall take it away and——'

'So determined a boy as it is!' she said, and there was a sharp undertow to her voice now. 'Of course your precious play shall be read! But you must not be tiresome about it. We shall give it to Mr Castleton to read, for he is the one who must say ultimately what we shall do, and if he thinks fit, it shall go to the Lord Chamberlain for a licence. There! You cannot ask for more than that, can you? And shortly we shall start you rehearsing with me, and that you will enjoy. Now do come home to supper, for these gardens grow outrageous cold.'

And she slipped from his arms as suddenly and as easily as she had moved into them, and tucked her hand into the crook of his elbow to hurry him, bemused and more confused about his intentions than ever, out into the streets of Chelsea to seek a hack to carry them back to North Audley Street.

16

He found it quite humiliatingly bewildering. It was like being a child again, at school for the very first day and not knowing anything, not even where the privy might be found, or who were all the obviously important people milling about, or how to address them——

This was worse, though, than school had been, for then at least he had been one of many new people. There had been other shrinking boys to whom he could attach himself, but here that was not possible for he was, as far as he could tell, the only person in this tumbling noisy chattering mob who did not know anyone. Apart from Lilith, of course.

Not that she was of any use to him, in that respect. She sat at the far side of the vast stage, on an armchair plumped with cushions which had been especially brought for her by a shambling panting old man in a dirty baize apron, surrounded by a number of people who clearly were ready to do anything she asked. They stood there, half a dozen men in fashionable clothes, their backs bent in obsequious positions as they listened to her and watched her, and she sat turning her head from side to side as they spoke, clearly preening in their attentions.

Behind her stood Hawks, grim and uncompromising in her heavy black dress, her hair scraped unfashionably back from her face, and her eyes never leaving her mistress except to throw gimlet glares of disapproval at any of the courtiers who moved in too close.

Depressed by the sight of her so distant from him in so many ways Jonah pulled his gaze away to stare around. The stage, lit only by a few hissing gas jets, turned low to conserve the precious fuel (and to be a little safer too; there had been that explosion at Covent Garden Theatre last November which had near ruined the place, and led to its being closed so that oil and wax lighting might be restored) was yet bright enough because of the illumination thrown in bars of dusty daylight from the wide-open scene dock doors at the side of the stage.

The light displayed a motley collection of people; actors and stage hands and musicians and hangers-on of all sorts. He had thought the crowds which hung about the greenroom exotic enough, in their high fashion clothes, so many of them famous or men of title and position in Government; last week he had seen Lord Brougham and Sir Robert Peel and Charles Lamb as well as Mr Coleridge there—and how he had longed to be one of the group of people around these men of letters, and how he had shrunk from so putting himself forward!—as well as several aristocratic ladies. But these—these were exotic in a different way. Their clothes were that much brighter, that much looser or tighter or shorter or longer than other people's, their voices that much louder, their gestures that much more expansive. It was as though, he thought, they were half as large again as ordinary people, while miraculously maintaining the illusion of being the same size.

That there was one man in charge of all that was happening was not at first apparent, but he realized gradually that the knots of activity happening about the stage were in fact under the direction of one Mr Castleton, who by turns cajoled and ordered and shouted and pleaded at actors and seamstresses, carpenters and painters, all of whom were busy in their different ways.

As the afternoon wore on, with the activity becoming ever more frenzied, yet to Jonah still as incomprehensible as it had been when first he arrived, he became more and more absorbed in watching, so much that it came almost as a shock to realize his name was being shouted.

'Lackland! Lackland! Where is the damned idiotish creature? He *is* to play Leontes, is he not?' and someone else took up the call, and then another until it seemed to him that half the people in the place were crying for him, their voices filled with a note of mockery.

He got to his feet with a rush, red with embarrassment, and moved so fast that he tangled his shoe in one leg of the stool upon which he had been sitting, and went sprawling, and at once a roar of laughter went up, and someone cried in a mocking falsetto, 'Oh, tumbler, tumbler! Do it again, tumbler! Please to give us a show, tumbler!'

He scrambled up again, wincing a little, for he had caught his ankle a shrewd blow, and brushed his clothes down, trying to look as insouciant as he could under the circumstances.

'I am Lackland,' he said. 'I am sorry—I did not hear you call at first.'

'Well, you had better hear better in the future,' Castleton growled, and thrust at him a sheaf of very dirty tattered paper. 'Look through these now, and seek the part of Leontes. It is no more than three lines in all, so do not imagine you are playing the comedian to go falling about the place. We shall leave that to Mr Garnery, since he is employed for that purpose, and his name appears on the playbills besides——'

'*And* he gets his work for merit and not for his pretty eyes——' someone murmured in the crowd, but not so soft that Jonah could not hear.

He looked through the papers as best he could, and a poor best he made of it, for few of the pages seemed to run concurrently. What he could read seemed to him to be poor ranting stuff, and his heart sank a little when at last he found the lines marked 'Leontes'.

'My Lady fair, thou art to me the apogee of glory, and naught of pestilence shall I, your swain, allow to touch the hem of thy gown': to which there was an answer so garbled in its way of setting on the page that he could make no sense of it, and then the stage direction, 'Leontes Stabs Himself and cries "Ah, woe is me". He dies'.

Jonah looked at this and then uncertainly raised his head to seek Lilith, for he felt, quite suddenly, afraid. To say lines on the stage and take a small part had seemed an easy enough task, even an agreeable one, when Lilith had first broached the idea, but now seeing these words actually set down, and that terrifying stage direction, he felt a sudden wave of cold fear rise in him.

He could not do this, could not strut as these people here strutted, could not shout these words so that they could be heard on the other side of the stage, let alone by people occupying the seats in the pit and beyond; and looking sideways at those seats the sense of horrified nausea rose higher and, almost in a panic now, he hurried across the stage, caring not at all whom he pushed aside, to thrust the sheaf of papers at Lilith.

Only three men were standing beside her now, and one was telling some involved tale when Jonah pushed through the little group.

'If you please Lilith—ma'am—I cannot possibly——'

'And who might this young cockerel be?' drawled the man who had been interrupted in his story, and with an apparently effortless movement he put out his stick and tangled it between Jonah's legs in such a way that he stumbled and almost fell, only just maintaining his balance. Once again he heard that titter of laughter ripple across the stage, and felt his anxiety rise with it.

'Dear Jonah!' Lilith said, and smiled warmly at him. 'What is the matter? You look as put about as a child told to learn his catechism! Come now, it is not so vast a part, is it? I believe Mr Castleton has put you to Leontes?'

'Aye, Leontes, but it is not that the part is—is too big, precisely, just that—I do not think, Lilith, that I can do it——'

One of the other men laughed. 'Leaned against the scenery has he, Lil, and caught the actor's plague? But now wishing he had never left his Mama's side? Let the creature go, dear lady, let him go! I see no young Kemble or Kean in the making here!'

'Hush, my Lord!' Lilith said, and put out her hand to close it warmly about Jonah's.

'Now, Jonah, do not distress yourself, for the part you have is small, and of no great moment. There is no need for you to rehearse at all just yet, for once you have committed the lines to your memory, all you will need to do in the performance is follow my lead. I am the centre of this play——'

'You are the centre of each and any play you adorn——' one of the men said, and Lilith flashed a glance at him and retorted, 'Aye, sir, and I make it my rule to choose to appear only in plays in which that will be the case!' at which all three men laughed uproariously, each trying to outdo the other in their appreciation of Lilith's sally.

Under cover of their noise she looked up at Jonah and clasping his hand even more tightly said swiftly, 'Never fear, Jonah! We shall contrive well enough without a fuss! Do not let yourself be alarmed by Mr Castleton, either. Go now and tell him he need not rehearse you yet, but to leave your schooling to me, and that I said so. Oh, and speak to him of your costume too. Now, my Lord,' and she returned her attention to the three men, 'if you have aught more of interest to say to me you had best say it speedily, for I must about my work, and I take that seriously, you know, and will not be distracted from it——'

Slowly Jonah went back across the stage to seek out Mr Castleton, and as he went several of the actors fell back before him with mock courtesy and then turned their backs on him with an obvious sneer, and again he felt the ready hot colour rise in his face.

He was no fool; he realized quite well that as a known protégé of Lilith's and a regular visitor to the greenroom he was to many of the actors an interloper upon the stage; they did what they did for a livelihood, and precarious enough a living did it provide. To see a new actor arrive, unschooled and untried and with no more qualification than his friendship with the imperious Mrs Lucas could not but make him the object of great dislike among the company.

Mr Castleton, too, looked at him with scant favour when he appeared at his side and delivered Lilith's message. But he grunted acquiescence and then turned away, and Jonah took his sleeve quickly and said, 'Li— Mistress Lucas said I was to speak to you about my costume.'

'Costume? Oh, to be sure, aught that is reasonable will do! 'Tis a medieval piece, and you need do little more than buy yourself hose and shirt and so forth. The character is no more than a hanger-on at court, and——'

'A wondrous strange piece of casting, to be sure!' a voice said softly near Jonah's left ear, and he whirled to see who it was, but the people around him were studiously engaged in conversation with each other and seemed oblivious of him and his anger.

He turned back to Castleton with what dignity he could muster. 'These items of clothing, sir, from whom do I obtain them? There is a wardrobe master, I suppose?'

'Wardrobe master?' Castleton looked at him with his eyebrows up. 'The costumes in our wardrobe are for the permanent company, Master Lackland. It is customary for tyros joining us to expect to make some stir upon their own behalf, and that means they provide their own necessaries. Shirts and hose are provided by the actors and only special garments drawn from our stock. Of course, if you wish to be *provided* with such items gratis, you must speak with— someone other than I. I have no deep purse in which to dip for such matters.'

The laughter which came from behind him now was quite clear, but with rigid self-control he did not turn his head. He would not have thought it could have hurt so much to be taunted for not having money in his own pocket; he had accepted Lilith's care of him, the provision of board and lodging at her expense with little discomfort for he was, in all conscience, unused to concerning himself in such matters. He had been kept by his father, fed in his house as a matter of course, had been equally treated in Mr Loudoun's house when he was at school, and in a curious way had felt no shame in being fed and sheltered by Lilith, for she was clearly not in any way deficient in money or any of the necessaries of life. But now, surrounded by people who had to earn every mouthful of bread, for whom the cost of a pair of hose or a stage shirt was a matter of great moment, he realized, for the first time, how much a parasite he had been, and he was ashamed. He would have his shirt and hose and other things besides—but he would provide them himself.

For the rest of that day and the next as rehearsals dragged on he fretted over the problem, for he had no money of his own, nor ever had had aught but the allowance his father had sent him. And at last, unwillingly, he decided he must borrow. Ever since his first letter to Abby he had used Hawks as his messenger and she had gone every Friday morning before nine to the Gower Street house to take a letter to his sister (and via her, to his mother) and to bring back her answers. He had chosen that time and day carefully, for he knew that his father left the house very early on a Friday for his regular weekly visit to the City counting-house, and his deliberations with Hunnisett, and also knew that his mother was never out of her chamber and about the house until after ten.

But this was only Tuesday, and he could not wait until Friday, he decided. Besides, if Abby was to obtain money for him, she might need some time. So he asked Hawks to go to Gower Street that afternoon at about three. His mother, he recalled, would normally be at a meeting of the London Ladies on this day, and Abby would not make calls without her, for he remembered how heartily bored she had been by such social intercourse; furthermore, his father would still be at Tavistock Street, for he did not generally return home until gone eight o'clock at night. Altogether, then, this would be a propitious enough time.

Hawks, not without some muttering and complaining, took his hastily scrawled letter and went off to Gower Street on foot, and he settled himself to wait for her return as best he could. He had asked

Abby to send him five pounds in silver if she were possibly able, assuring her he would repay it as soon as he were in a position to do so and begging her forbearance in this matter; his only fear was not that she would refuse him from any motive of parsimony, but that she would not be able to find the money. For, as he now realized, he did not know at all how his sister managed her financial needs, or even if she had an allowance as he himself had been used to do. He could only hope.

Dorothea was standing in her morning room at the front of the house waiting for the coachman to come round, and smoothing her gloves on to her cold hands. Today, perhaps, she told herself, as she did every day, today perhaps I shall see him. He must surely visit her soon, and I shall be most watchful, most alert, and this time I shall not miss him, as I must have done these many times since.

She heard the summons to the door, heard the measured sound of Jeffcoate's feet as he crossed the black-and-white tiled hall, and shrank back a little into the curtains beside the window. She had told the staff to deny her to callers, but she was a bad liar, and if this were a caller who happened to observe her through the open door of the morning room she would be hard put to it to refuse to be sociable. And then what would happen to her afternoon of vigilance in Piccadilly?

At first she did not hear any words, simply the sound of a voice, deep and rather coarse, and she relaxed as she realized that this was no lady calling in the usual social way, for Jeffcoate's voice had sharpened as it always did when he spoke to those he regarded as his social inferiors.

Again she heard the sound of steps in the hall, and the door close, and wondered idly for a moment how it was that Jeffcoate had not sent this patently kitchen visitor to the area door below, and then her neck stiffened as for the first time she caught the gist of their conversation.

'—you comes of a Friday mornin' as a rule, an' I got Miss Abby's instructions as 'ow I'm to let you in and set you down while she reads 'er letter and gets 'er answer done for you to carry back. And so I does, though it goes against the grain to 'ave the likes o' *you* clutterin' up my clean 'all. An' what you're doin' 'ere of a Tuesday afternoon is beyond me——'

'I told yer!' the harsh voice of the woman jarred on Dorothea's ears. ''E says as it's important, and I'm to give 'er this letter today, no matter what. So don't you go comin' the 'eavy 'anded lord o' the manor wi' me, on account it won't get yer nowhere at all. You'd best be sharp about yer business, and tell 'er——'

For Dorothea it was as though quite suddenly the grey winter sky outside, heavy and lowering with the threat of yet more snow, had rolled back like a blind to reveal the brilliance of a June day. This was how Abby had obtained the letters from Jonah which she had brought her each week! She had brought them on different days, so that she, Dorothea, should not know that her beloved Jonah's messenger came on Friday mornings. Oh, the perfidy of the girl, Dorothea thought, and felt a rare sensation rise in her. Cold anger——

'Well, I can't do nothin' about it, on account she ain't 'ere,' Jeffcoate was saying now, and again Dorothea listened with her ears feeling as though they were stretching themselves towards the sound. 'She goes off to 'er father's shop, like some cheap apprentice boy—and fair disgustin' I calls it, too—each day, so you'll 'ave to cool your 'eels, won't yer?'

The altercation between them went on, and then at last he weakened, and Dorothea sighed a deep relieved breath when she heard him telling the woman where the shop was.

'Go there and be damned to yer, *and* to yer blasted letters,' he said, and stamped to the door to let the woman out. 'An' yer can tell Miss Abby from me that I want no goin's over for a'tellin' you where she is, on account I got better things to do than stand 'ere arguin' with the likes o' you——'

Dorothea watched the woman from the window, a nondescript shape in a black gown and bonnet walking through the bitter cold and with her head down and her cloak pulled tight across her narrow shoulders, towards the Piccadilly end of the street.

'Now,' thought Dorothea with vast satisfaction. 'Now I shall discover him. For when she has been to Abby at the shop she will return to him. And I will be waiting to follow her. I shall see my boy again before the day is out——'

And with a calmness that quite belied her churning inner feelings she walked out of the room to the door as her carriage came clattering up to the steps with the horses steaming and stamping and snorting in the cold afternoon air.

17

In a curious way Abel knew he was performing for his sparse audience. Generally he gave not a damn for the admiration of others when he was working, unlike his old surgery teacher, Astley Cooper, who loved nothing better than a large and admiring congregation before whom he could display his speed, his elegance and his altogether beautiful surgical technique. That had never been Abel's way; if it had been he would have applied for a surgical post at one of the big hospitals, and built up his own school of students, as did so many others. No, for him, the work alone had been enough, always, the work and the patients. He wanted no glory, none of the reassurance of others' approval. He had wanted no more than Nancy or one like her beside him to help him with instruments, bandages and charpie.

But today it was different. Today he felt the weight of Gandy Deering's eyes on him, was as aware of the little man's scrutiny as if it had been a palpable thing, and he reacted for all the world like a prima donna, watching his own hands with positive pleasure, and devoting a part of his mind to assessing the effect the actions of those hands might be having on Deering.

They had arranged this afternoon's meeting in order to go together to Endell Street where, Deering had assured Abel, there were premises suited to his needs. All Abel had to do, Deering had told him jovially, was make his selection, for he could be offered a choice.

'None of your beggarly take-it-or-leave-it when you deal with Gandy Deering, Mr Lackland,' he had said, turning his wrist neatly as he inhaled a large dose of snuff. 'Warm a man as you are, my dear sir, I think I can say that when it comes to property, Deering is a warmer one! I had earmarked these two properties for other purposes, but there —my heart is set on building my new Hall, and yours is set on having your precious hospital, so what am I to do? I must change my plans!' and he had beamed confidently at Abel and arranged to meet him at Tavistock Street at two o'clock on the next afternoon to take him to display the possibilities of the Endell Street houses.

And Abel had been ready to go, putting on his heavy coat there in the hallway, Deering standing ready beside him, when the man had arrived. There had been a kicking at the front door that was so ferocious it had bade fair to stove in its timbers, and Abel had cursed and pushed Nancy aside in order to open the door himself.

But his anger had dissipated immediately at what he saw there. A big man, clutching the figure of a child, a child who lay back across those restraining arms with a rigid back and a taut neck and a blue-tinged face. As Abel pulled the door open, the man had lifted his foot to kick again, and at the sight of Abel his face, ravaged with terror and with the eyes staring almost as much as those of the child in his arms, lightened and he said hoarsely, 'Where shall I put 'er?'

'What's amiss?' Abel said quickly, and stood back to let the man come into the house and the big figure pushed past the three people in the hall and turned in the narrow passageway and said again urgently, 'Where'll I put 'er? You'll 'ave to work fast, I tell yer——'

'In here,' Abel said shortly, and hurried to open the door of the big room where he treated his street patients and the man carried in his burden and Nancy and Abel followed close behind.

At a jerk of Abel's head the man set the still figure down on the couch, and began to pull at the shawl in which it was wrapped, but without force yet with a calm acceptance of authority Nancy pushed him away and with swift fingers began to undo the layers of clothing in which the child was cocooned, while Abel pulled off his coat and hurried to the instruments lying in their neat rows on the bench at the side of the room.

The big man who had brought the child suddenly seemed to become aware of himself and where he was and pulled from his head the battered old brown beaver which had adorned it and moved awkwardly to stand with his back against the wall, turning the brim nervously between his huge fingers and never taking his eyes from the face of the child, now revealed to be a girl of about ten, lying on the table.

Deering stood beside him, his head on one side and his face filled with a lively curiosity, and Abel, catching a momentary sight of him as he turned to the couch to look at the child thought fleetingly, 'He behaves for all the world like a schoolboy at a raree show——'

But then for a while he quite forgot Deering as he examined the child. Her face was a much bluer shade now, and she seemed to be hardly breathing at all, though her lips were pulled back tautly from her clenched teeth, and her nostrils were widely flared in a clear indication of a desperate hunger for air. Abel bent his head and set his ear to her chest, and after a second grunted, and taking one of his lancets in his hand turned it so that he could thrust the handle between those tightly clenched teeth. He pushed and then twisted, grunting a little with the effort, and then the teeth gave under his pressure, and the mouth opened and the girl gave a great heaving gasp that seemed to half lift her frail body from the couch, and her eyes stared wider than ever, if that were possible, and her face became even more suffused.

Abel thrust one finger into her mouth, still holding the teeth apart with the turned scalpel handle, and then nodded, and said sharply to Nancy, 'A quinsy big as an egg. I shall have to cut a way if she's to breathe again——'

'What is it that ails her?' Deering said, and at the sound of his high light voice Abel remembered him, and with him the reason for his presence.

'What is it?' he said, as he turned back to his instruments and began to select what he should need. 'Why, she has an affliction of the throat so putrid that it leaves no space for the air to pass into her lungs. I must open a way in her windpipe. It may not serve, but leave her thus for many minutes longer and she's graveyard meat anyway——'

'No!' The big man almost shrieked it. 'No! She's to live, you 'ear me? If aught 'appens to 'er, I'll set about you and break every stinkin' bone in yer lousy body, you——'

'Hold your tongue,' Abel said calmly. 'I'm no God, man, and I can but do my best. She's fit to die if I do not set my knife to her, so there's all about it. She's fit to die if I do, but 'tis better than standing here and watching her choke to death in the midst of air. What's it to be?'

He was standing now with his knife poised above the girl's throat, which Nancy had revealed by setting a cushion beneath her shoulders and pulling back the head so that the chin pointed up at the ceiling and the glaring blue eyes stared sightlessly at the broad expanse of Nancy's calico apron. 'Either I cut a way, or you take her to another surgeon, for there's naught else to be done,' Abel said and looked at the man with his eyebrows raised. The child on the couch heaved again, her narrow chest curving creakingly, painfully inwards as she strove to breathe and there was a moment's silence as the big man stood rigid against the wall, staring at the child with his face working and grimacing for all the world like an organ-grinder's monkey. And then Deering said cheerfully, 'Oh, set about it, man! If the girl's fit to die if you don't, then you might as well, and I'd be most interested to see your skills at work. No need to be squeamish, Lackland, because I am here——'

'I do not give a damn for you, Deering, nor ever shall,' Abel said flatly but did not look at him, still keeping his eyes fixed on the big man. 'Well, shall I cut or shall I not, man? I tell you again, I'll not be held to the consequences whether she lives or dies if I do. I can tell you she will die if I don't——' Now he dropped his eyes briefly to the child's face. 'And she will at any second, the way she is.'

'Oh, Jesus, Jesus, Jesus!' The big man began to whimper, tears falling down his face in a ludicrous fashion. 'Jesus, Jesus, Jesus——'

'He'll be little enough help to you here, man, without my aid,' Abel said coolly and bent his head and set the point of his knife to the taut blue-tinged skin of the throat and as casually and as easily as if he were cutting a chicken sliced across it.

It was at this point that he realized that he was performing for Deering, as he thrust a finger into the opening he had made, and cleaned away the little blood that had appeared with a scrap of greyish charpie which Nancy thrust at him with her spare hand. He set his forceps to the hole, and twisted his wrist neatly, saw the hole widen and moved his gaze to the girl's face, still feeling Deering's bright and birdlike observation of his every movement.

The girl's face changed as her chest heaved and air began to move into her starved lungs. The blueness began to fade, and the desperate half blind glare became a piteous rolling of the eyes, and tears began to flow, running awkwardly down the sides of the narrow cheeks.

She grimaced, as though she were about to shout, and opened her mouth, but no sound came out, and Abel said almost conversationally, 'She can make no sound, since the air does not pass the larynx, you understand!'

'How is that?' Deering said immediately, and he moved closer to the couch to peer with great interest at the hole in the girl's throat. 'Damn me, but I've not been so interested in I cannot say how many years! I always had a taste for matters scientific, but this——'

'I did not arrange this for your delectation, Deering!' Abel said, but there was a warmer note in his voice than he had previously displayed to this bouncing little man. 'But because needs must when the devil drives. Now get you back, for I need space for this next operation, and it will be a deal more disagreeable than aught you have seen so far.'

Unwillingly Deering fell back a little, but kept his eyes eagerly on all that Abel did, taking a hefty pinch of snuff at the same time; and no one paid any attention at all to the man beside the wall, still turning his hat mechanically in his fingers, but now standing with his eyes tight closed and murmuring monotonously under his breath in a soft half-keening whisper.

Abel jerked his head at Nancy, and at once she moved so that she came round behind him, still holding the girl's chin firmly, and smoothly Abel changed places with her, and relinquished to her hand his grip of the forceps that were holding open the hole at the base of the throat.

Then, standing behind her, he made a sharp movement and forced the girl's mouth wider still, and stuffed into it a wad of charpie, and the girl's eyes rolled for a moment and then turned back, so that only the lower rim of the whites showed. Abel nodded sharply in approval. An unconscious patient was infinitely preferable to a sentient one when such work as he had to do was to be put in hand.

He picked up a lancet, and with one hand set firmly to the girl's mouth, guided it in and down, and Deering stood on tiptoe in an effort to see and, disappointed, subsided, for there was no way to observe the site of the operation, what with the charpie and Abel's long probing fingers.

'I have it——' Abel said suddenly. 'There it goes—faugh, such a stench as it is——' and the room filled with the heavy sweetness of pus as Abel moved swiftly, mopping and cleaning away deep in the throat gaping before him.

He seemed to go on in the same way for a long time, and then Abel nodded again and said to Nancy, 'You can ease the forceps now—gently, gently—aye, that's it——'

There was a silence broken only by the continuous breathy noises the big man was making and then Abel said with an enormous satisfaction, 'Well, then. I think she will do for the present. Aye, that she will——' for the girl had started to make hoarse gasping noises and Nancy grinned widely at the sound.

'Well, what has happened?' Deering demanded a little fretfully. ' 'Tis no use being given the chance to see such surgical matters if I am given no explanation of what befalls!'

Abel smiled at that and said willingly enough, 'I have opened the great abscess that was blocking her throat. The matter has been discharged and I have removed all of it I could. Now the air passes across her larynx as before, and she is sure of breathing. I can close the hole I made in her throat, and hope that she will survive.'

'Well, I must say it sounds simple enough!' Deering said, and again took snuff. 'M'father's brother died of a quinsy, now I recall. Would such a performance as this have saved his life, as you have saved this girl?'

Abel was tying a ligature to the wound he had made in the girl's throat, and did not look up.

'Who says she is saved?' he grunted. 'I have done this operation three or four times before for such a condition, and on each occasion the patient died. The matter from the throat enters the lungs in these cases and they die of a swift and putrid pneumonia.'

Deering frowned at that, and said loudly (for the girl had started to wail, thickly and hoarsely, and the noise was considerable in the crowded room). 'Then why do the operation if it is not to save life?'

Abel lifted his head and stared at the little man, and then he leaned forwards on the couch, his hands balled into fists on which he rested his full weight.

'Why?' he said deliberately, 'Why, in the hope that survival *will* be possible. You see, Mr Deering, an operation is not enough to cure a patient's afflictions. It is the care that comes after that is important.

The bed in a hospital where there are nurses such as our Nancy here who can look after them and feed them and soothe them back to health. Surgeons without hospitals, sir, are soldiers without muskets, and if I may suggest it, architects without bricks. I did not set this operation to hand for your benefit, Mr Deering, but by God, I am grateful to a watchful Providence that arranged matters so that you should see it. For now you perhaps see why it is I do not willingly give up this house. For depend upon it, Mr Deering, if I do not like the house you offer me in Endell Street, I shall not take it! I find this house insufficient to my needs as it is—this child I must send away to recover from her affliction as best she might in whatever hovel it is she comes from, for I lack the space in which to put her for the nursing she needs. And my recall of the properties of Endell Street does not fill me with the conviction that I shall find aught there that will fill me with the desire to abandon Tavistock Street! But, we shall see, we shall see——'

He straightened his back and smiled at Deering, a wide and warm smile of such sweetness that the little man blinked and stepped back, for this was the first time he had seen Abel Lackland do anything but hold himself in rigid control. And Abel, noting his reaction, smiled wider than ever, and turned his attention to the big man beside the wall.

'She may do, man, she may do well enough,' he said, and his voice was softer now. 'I did not mean to be so harsh with you before, for I know how it is to suffer the fear of death, but it was necessary, do you see, for us to set about our business quickly, and I could not have you procrastinating. But we have wrought as well as we can, and now must hope. She may remain here with Nancy till evening, and then you must take her away for I have no room here for her. Nancy will give you some laudanum to relieve her pain, for she will have much of it, and I hope that it will bring a sleep to her, for she is exhausted with her inflammation as well as her operation. You understand me? She is not fit to die just yet, but I cannot make promises that she will not. She will need devoted care for some time yet while we hope that she will not contract the pneumonia——'

'She's all I 'ave,' the big man said, suddenly, staring at Abel very fixedly. 'You 'ear me? Seven 'er mother 'ad, and none but this'n left, and 'er mother died of the flux last summer—she's all I 'ave——'

'Then you must take all care of her that you might,' Abel said crisply but not unkindly. 'I shall be here tomorrow. Come then and tell me how she fares. Nancy, you know what now to do for her? Aye. Well, Mr Deering, I shall wash my hands, and then we must be about our business. We shall see what you have to offer in Endell Street that might interest me.'

18

It amused Dorothea to sit back in her carriage and go clattering past the black-shawled figure hurrying through the snow-encrusted streets towards Piccadilly. She would be there before her, waiting purposefully this time, and she felt the warmth of the knowledge that soon she would see her Jonah fill her whole frame with pleasure. The weeks and weeks of waiting and worrying were coming to an end; her patience had been rewarded, she told herself.

Not for a moment did she feel any anger at all against Jonah. That he had treated her unkindly in refusing to come to her since leaving the Gower Street house; that he had treated her even more unkindly in refusing to communicate with her except secretly through his sister, she knew; but she held no blame attached to him for that. He had not been able to behave otherwise, after all. It was Abel who had caused the fracture in the family in the first place, and poor Jonah, Dorothea told herself, had suffered as much as she because of it.

Nor, curiously, did she attach any blame to Abel, even though she knew he lay at the heart of her misery. Abel was Abel, and had always done as he had to. She had accepted him for what he was from the moment she had first set eyes on him, a bedraggled dirty guttersnipe brought to her mother's drawing-room by a triumphant Jesse Constam (and was it so many years ago? In some ways it seemed to have happened but a handful of weeks since). He was driven—had been driven all his life—by some power she did not understand, but she respected it. He had tried to love her, and the knowledge of that warmed her, and she had always pitied him deeply for his unhappiness. She had been happy enough, for did she not love him, and care for him, and have the joy of being his wife? But what had he, poor Abel? Nothing but a dead love for a woman who did not love him. Poor, poor Abel, she thought. Poor Abel.

But at least he had his work, and that was something to be grateful for. It assuaged her own guilt a little, for that was the emotion that most plagued Dorothea now when she thought of her husband. She felt guilt, and always would, for separating him from his Lilith as she had with her long-ago whispers into the drunken Jesse's ear. But it was a guilt she could bear, for had she not done so, she reminded herself often enough, there would have been no Jonah. And a world without Jonah was inconceivable.

So she sat back in her carriage, hurrying ahead of Hawks to the Piccadilly shop, concealing her complex bewildering emotions under one great umbrella thought; she would soon see Jonah again.

Sitting in the back room of the shop in the dwindling light of the winter afternoon Abby watched him lying there on the horsehair sofa with his legs wrapped in her shawl and his shoulders draped with his own topcoat, and she felt a sudden cold fear move in her belly, for his face had a sharp look about it that she had not seen before, a translucency of the temples and the cheekbones which was strangely alarming. She did not know why she was alarmed, could not have explained to herself what thoughts came into her deepest mind, and in a manner quite foreign to her usual good sense, she did not wish to.

There was a faint sound from beyond the closed door of the office, and she raised her head and listened for a moment, and then, moving purposefully but very quietly, she got up and gently moved the shawl so that it covered him even more warmly, and stood poised for a second as he moved and sighed. But he sank back into his deep sleep and silently she slipped from the room, closing the door behind her.

She found Peter out in the shop coping well enough with the merchant's wife who had come in to purchase a complexion wash, and stood waiting impatiently in the shadows of the tall japanned boxes on the shelf at the back, willing the woman to hurry about her foolish business and be off before someone else came in.

At last the woman went, and as Peter closed the door behind her Abby hurried towards him and said quickly, 'Please to put up the shutters, Peter! Aye, I know it is early yet, but that is my wish. Mr

Caspar is not well, and I would not have him disturbed. He shall rest this afternoon, and he cannot do so if there is a bustle of customers——'

'Yes, Miss Abby,' Peter said, and went eagerly to do her bidding. 'I thought he looked bad when he come in, Miss, that I did. He gets these turns, o' course, don't 'e, from time to time?'

Abby frowned sharply at that, looking up from the cash box to which she had gone to collect the day's takings. 'What's that?' she said. 'He has been ill before?'

'Oh, yes, Miss!' Peter said cheerfully. 'His turns, he calls 'em. Gets tired like, and pale, and feels all any'ow. Or so I understand it. I dare say he's hid it from you, Miss, seeing as how—well, he wouldn't want to fret *you*, would 'e?' and he leered at her, looking sideways through his lashes with all a schoolboy's lasciviousness.

'That will be enough from you!' Abby said sharply. 'Do your work and be quick about it. If you make any noise, I shall have the hide off your back, and don't believe I cannot, female though I am.'

Obediently Peter scurried away, and as they went together through the ritual of closing the shop, Abby fought back the sick anxiety which was growing ever more swiftly in her. She had never seen James ill before. Oh, she knew he became tired, because he worked so hard. There had been days when he had not returned to the shop before she had to leave it, sending only a note by the hand of a messenger telling her he was too busy to return just yet. Had they been but excuses, she now wondered? Had he been ill, and wanting to hide the intelligence of it from her?

She cast her mind back, almost feverishly, trying to see if there had been signs of sickness that she had ignored. Had he been flushed often, or too bright-eyed, or had a cough that she had not noted? She would not let the word consumption move into her thoughts, but it lay there heavy and ugly beneath the surface. In her joy at their shared love, at their mutual expression of it, had she neglected the health of her beloved James?

But with a return of her good sense she knew she was wrong in her unspoken fear. He had occasionally displayed pallor, not the hectic flush of disease, a pallor that surely was part of his colouring, for people of his reddish tint often had pallid skins. He had displayed fatigue too, of course , but after all he was working very hard these days, with so much to be done at Wapping in the new manufactory——

When at last she closed the front door behind a jubilant Peter who was more than content to enjoy an unexpected half-day holiday, she leaned against it with her eyes closed and tried to see again how it had been.

She had been sitting at the desk over the books and not really concentrating on them at all, thinking instead of ways she might employ to persuade her father to let her and James be wed, for though she had thought she would be content enough to be near him, as this apprenticeship arrangement made it possible to be, she had to admit that still her heart clamoured for more. For his body as well as his mind, a part of her had whispered, and she had blushed a little, even in her solitude, at the way her thoughts so often bent themselves. It was not seemly, she would tell herself sternly, that a well-bred young woman should think the things that came into her mind, should look at a man and feel the bodily sensations she did, should feel such an extraordinary fire crawling in her when she was touched, or even thought of being touched——

The door had opened and she had looked up, startled, and seen him standing there white and drooping, and he had said in a voice quite unlike his usual tone, 'I had such a need of you, Abby——' and then, to her horror, he had pitched forward on his face at her feet.

She would never know how it was she had got him to the sofa without assistance, for Peter was out of the shop for his midday meal at the time, but manage she did, and then he had come to his senses and lay there looking up at her and clutching her hand with his own damp and cold one.

'I am sorry,' he had said. 'Forgive me, my dear love, but of a sudden I could not bear it. I felt so ill, so lackadaisical, and I wanted to see you so much——' he had turned his head restlessly on the pillow she had put beneath it and she had leaned forwards and stroked his cheek and crooned softly to him and he had settled more, and then fallen asleep. And she had sat and watched him and wondered and felt the fear rising in her like a slow oozing tide——

She snapped her eyes open and hurried across the shop, now almost dark behind its shutters, and went softly into the office, and he was sitting up and staring about him with a puzzled look on his face, and she went at once to his side, and pushed him firmly but gently back against the pillow.

'Abby?' he said, and his voice held its more normal everyday tone.

'Whatever—I cannot imagine what has befallen—what am I doing lying here?'

'You do not remember, my love?' she said, and could not help letting a frown of anxiety fill her face as she sat down on the sofa beside him. 'You came suddenly back from the manufactory, and told me you were taken ill and wanted me—do you not remember?'

He leaned back and closed his eyes, his forehead creased a little, and then he opened them and nodded slowly.

'Yes—yes, of course. I remember. Oh, God damn it, God damn it, God damn it!' and she shrank back a little at the suppressed violence in his voice, and he saw and at once looked contrite.

'Forgive me, my love, my little love, forgive me——' He put out his arms and she moved into them immediately and held tightly to him. 'I am angry with myself. I had no right to alarm you. I did not wish you to know. I did not wish you ever to know——'

'Know what?' She said it sharply, pulling away from him and looking up into his face, and all her earlier anxiety climbed up into her throat and made her voice shrill and he took her face between his hands and tried to soothe her, but she pulled his hands away and held them tightly and said again, 'Know *what*? If you have aught that worries you, you must tell me! I am—I am the other part of you, and you have no right, no right at all, to keep from me any intelligence about yourself! Tell me at once what it is that——'

He sighed, and nodded and said heavily, 'I do not know. Indeed I do not. I wondered if it were the phthisis and went to see Mr Charles Bell at Windmill Street, but he told me there was naught consumptive in my lungs. And besides, it behaves so strange——'

'What does? Oh, James, if you do not explain it at once I shall run mad——' and she felt tears clustering in her chest in a manner that she had not known since she was in the nursery. Weeping had never been Abby's way, and the strangeness of the reaction sharpened her fear and she took hold of his hands even more tightly and shook them. 'What ails you? Please, James, what *ails* you?'

He shook his head, and said simply, 'I told you, I do not know, nor yet do the surgeons to whom I have talked. I can only suppose it is some affliction of the system that it is not possible to recognize. Mr Bell told me of one thing only—he said I was never to let any physician bleed me, for it was his belief that my disorder was of the blood, that it was thin and weak and that there was no question of there being any plethoric tendency. All I can do when a fit takes me is to rest. I go faint and qualmish, do you see, my love. I feel such a languor creep over me as I cannot know what it is to move a muscle, and I wish only to rest and sleep. And then, do you know, I feel better again, though there is a lingering weakness in me. I do not understand it. And I did not wish you to know, for I did not want to fret you——'

She shook her head, dumbly, her tongue held hard between her teeth so that it hurt, and tried to calm herself. She felt within her a sudden sureness, as sure as if he had sat there with his life blood drain-away before her eyes, that he was very ill, and the fear boiled in her chest, pushing at the tears which, needlesharp, pressed against her throat, and she could hold it no longer, and the drops began to run down her face, carving its young roundness into ugly crevasses, and at once his own face creased in matching distress and he pulled her close to him in an embrace that was meant to express all the feeling he had in him, and she responded with an eagerness that was sharpened by her terror.

In later years she was always to remember that afternoon in the dim light of the office behind her father's shop. They had clung together like terrified children, holding each other, kissing, weeping together and kissing again, and then it was as though there were two quite different people. He was pulling at her clothes, and she at his, and his hands were caressing her body with an urgency that made her muscles strain towards him as though they were individually as deep in love with him as was the whole of her; and her hands seemed to behave of their own volition, moving over his body, across his sweating belly and flanks, exploring ever further. And when at last and inevitably they were together, joined as deep as two people could be there was, for her, no pain but only an enormous desperate need that rose and rose in agonizing intensity and at last disappeared in a great wave of sensation that she had never known before and would not have believed herself capable of knowing at all. And she looked up at him, at the face so near hers, so tense and eager with his head thrown back so that the tendons in his throat were as taut as ropes, and saw the expressions of need and then agony and finally ecstasy follow each other across it and loved him so totally and completely that it was as though she were no longer herself but part of one person, a person who was Abbyjames, or Jamesabby; and her fear at least receded completely, leaving her stranded and breathless on the shores of her own sensations.

They must have slept, she thought confusedly, staring up at the ceiling. She could hear the sound of thumping and calling coming from somewhere, but all she could see was the dim shadow of the ceiling, all she could feel was the sandiness in her eyes, and a languorous comfort in all her limbs. And then he moved, and she remembered in a great wash of pleasure, and turned her head in the dimness to smile at him. But the thumping started again, and she moved, unwillingly but swiftly, and pulled her clothes to rights and tugged at her tumbled hair, and went out of the office and across the shop, almost totally dark now, for the last light of the winter afternoon was fast fading, to open the shop door and blink at the figure standing there holding out a letter to her, feeling bewildered and quite extraordinary.

'Miss Abby?' said the woman outside. 'I was to deliver this to yer, most particular, and wait for the answer on account of 'e's in a right takin' about it. 'E says to tell yer it's very important, and not to fail 'im, no matter what——'

19

'I will tell you what I shall do, Deering,' Abel said. 'And I can tell you now you won't like it above half. But if you want your site cleared for your precious classical Hall, then you will see that there is naught for it but to do as I wish.' And he laughed , and tucked his chin into the collar of his heavy coat and looked sideways at the man standing beside him.

They were standing in the freezing grey mud of the gutter on the eastern side of Endell Street, with the bulk of the old Wren church looming up behind them, and staring at the row of dilapidated houses opposite. They might have been elegant houses once, when they had been built back in the 1770s, but now they were peeling and inordinately dirty, and the once beautiful iron work of the railings and balconies was rusted and twisting in the sulphurous London air.

'Well?' Gandy Deering said, and grinned at him, and took another pinch of his eternal snuff.

Abel was feeling well pleased with himself; had he not been so the outrageousness of the suggestion he was about to make would not have entered his head, but there it was. Deering's admiring reaction to his work had gone to his head like laudanum. In all the years of his working with the benighted human trash of these evil streets and alleys he had quite lost sight of the warm pleasure there was to be found in the approbation of an equal. His private patients, while treating him in a civilized enough manner, were deeply aware of the fact that they paid for his care, and this had a subtle effect on the relationship between themselves and their medical man. Skilled he may be, life-saver he may be, but paid attendant he undoubtedly also was, and neither he nor they could ever forget it.

But Deering's reaction to the operation he had performed on the choking child in Tavistock Street had wakened in Abel a whole new set of conflicting emotions. To be admired, to be liked—it was heady stuff. He would have to take care not to learn to like it too well, he thought fleetingly, and had a sudden vision of Jonah and Dorothea and wondered what it would be like to see them look at him with warm affection instead of the wary nervousness they usually displayed in his presence; but he snapped his mind away from that. Not to be thought of, not now when there were bigger matters afoot.

Again he smiled, more to himself than to his companion, and lifted his chin and said coolly, 'Well, Deering, I will propound. The hospital in Tavistock Street is too small for my purposes. I have needed bigger these many years gone. You come to me and say you want my house, and will exchange it for another. But, you know, these Endell Street houses are much of a piece with the one I already have. Indeed, they may even be a smidgeon smaller! So, I ask, why should I put myself out to transport my patients and all my medicines and my assistants from Tavistock Street to here? If I do that, none but you is better off, is it not so? And excellent a personage though you may be, I do not conceive it to be any duty of mine to make *your* path any smoother. So, to my plan. I will let you have Tavistock Street in exchange for premises here in Endell Street—but I shall take *both* your houses, not choose one. What is more, my friend, I shall——'

'You will what?' Deering had whirled on his heel and was standing gazing at him with his eyes so widely staring that the white could be seen above the iris, making him look for all the world like a frightened horse. 'You will—did I hear you aright?'

Abel threw back his head and laughed aloud with a huge pleasure. 'Aye, man, you heard aright! And you did not hear all, either! For that is not enough for me. I want *three* houses—so I'll take both of yours—*and* the one in the middle of 'em besides! I dare say you know who holds the property and can put yourself in the way of acquiring it!'

'You are run complete out of your mind, sir!' Deering said flatly, and turned away to stare again at the houses opposite.

'Oh, I think not, sir, I think not!' Abel said, now enjoying himself vastly. 'You want my house, you must have it, and there is no other way you will get it, so you may as well bite on the bullet! That is the way it is to be.'

There was a short silence, and then Abel went on musingly, 'Of course, if you say me nay, I can collect together my resources and buy new property myself. I dare say I can twist the arms of my trustees! Say the house adjoining mine in Tavistock Street. You may have had the promise of it from the Widow Willans, but you know, I believe if I went to her and told her I wanted her property she'd as lief sell to me as to you, for I treated her for a wen these ten years ago and she has good cause to be content with the cure of it I gave her——'

'I tell you, you are out of your mind, Mr Lackland! The work you do, while no doubt estimable in some eyes, does not give you leave to treat an honest architect who has no greater desire than to improve the lot of all the inhabitants of the city in so cavalier a fashion! I tell you, I could not agree to such a matter. Besides——'

He grunted and subsided and, shrewdly, Abel said nothing. He had recognized the note of resignation in the other man's voice and thought it best to let the yeast work its way unhindered.

The pause lengthened, and then Deering said abruptly, 'Besides, the landlord of the centre house is not an amenable individual. I have tried to buy from her many times, for I too can think of uses for three houses together that could not be obtained in two separated as these are, but she asks no more of her property than it should bring her a good rental, as indeed that house does, for it is, from all accounts, used as a bagnio and certainly is inhabited by any number of Covent Garden drabs. No, sir, I do not think that you will be able to force her to such a decision however much you may be able to bring your pressures to bear on such as I!'

'Oh?' Abel said easily, and smiled into his collar again. 'Well, that is no matter to me. It is you who will have to deal with the landlord, whoever it may be, for my mind is made up. The more I think on it, the more sensible a proposition does it sound to me to buy more property and extend my hospital in that manner. We can raise the finance in some manner or other, for our credit is good, and our cause a sound one. I can think of any number of rich cits who might enjoy to feel they have bought their place in eternal heaven for the price of contributing to my new hospital. I am grateful to you, sir!' He turned to Deering and uncharacteristically gave him a jovial thump on the shoulder. 'Had you not come to me with your plan to take Tavistock

Street from me, I believe I should not have seen so excellent a way to getting what it is I need!'

'Oh, I am not put out at your request from the point of view of money, sir, and do not think it! I am as charitably disposed as the next, I hope, and I am not diminishing my goodheartedness in any way if I tell you I paid little enough for these houses in all conscience, and the giving of the two of them to you would be a fair enough price for the property I need in Tavistock Street.'

Deering sniffed then, and turned on Abel a mournful gaze which sat ill on his round jowly visage.

'It is this demand that I try to buy the other house for you that I find I cannot meet. Now, sir, let me put it to you—if I agree to contribute, say, half the cost of the property, whatsoever it will be, and leave it to you to deal with the landlord, what say we clap hands on a bargain? I will give you these two houses, half the cost of the centre one and——'

'The whole cost,' Abel said implacably, and set his head on one side and grinned so that his green eyes sparkled in his long white face, and he suddenly looked very young and mischievous, and almost unwillingly Deering smiled back, a watery smile, but there none the less.

'Oh, be damned to you, sir! For an altruistic surgeon you carry in your veins some damned shrewd blood! I'd as lief deal with some riverside Lascar as you, any day! All right, you bloodsucker—for you are truly a leech in more ways than one!—so be it. On the understanding that you make your own shift to obtain the property, for I'll not face that hellcat again in search of a business arrangement, no, not for anything!'

'It's a bargain!' said Abel with huge delight and pulled off his glove and thrust out his hand. 'Shall we shake hands on it? I buy the house, and you pay for it! Indeed, sir, what better bargain could there be?'

Deering nodded resignedly and shook hands, and together they turned and started to pick their way through the mud past the huddles of children playing lackadaisically in the gutters, towards the purlieus of St Martin's Lane, in search of a chophouse and a hot fire at which to warm their chilled bones.

It was as they were crossing Broad Street, dodging the drays and shouting cart drivers, that Abel said, 'You did not say—who is this landlord with whom I am to deal?'

'Who? Oh, I thought I had—why, Mistress Lucas. Of the Haymarket Theatre, to be sure. You'll know the lady's name, I have no doubt?'

Dorothea stood in the shadow of the stage door, and felt her knees tremble beneath her. To follow Hawks from the shop, after she had seen her re-emerge from her half-hour sojourn inside (and Dorothea had been puzzled to see the shutters of the shop were up so early in the day, but in her usual way dismissed the matter since it did not directly concern her) and to trail her, in the carriage, from Piccadilly to the Haymarket had been so easy. But now what was she to do? The woman had disappeared inside, and eager as she was to see her Jonah, certain as she was that he was within that vast and terrifying building, still she could not quite bring herself to cross its threshold.

She turned her head and could see her carriage across on the other side of the street, with the coachman sitting stiff and disapproving on the box staring ahead and trying to pretend he was not there at all.

Dorothea knew she had shocked him to the core in demanding she be brought to such a place as this notorious street, with its bath houses and garish drinking shops and unashamed brothels. He had been at first mystified and then amused when she had told him to follow the black-shawled woman, and had quite enjoyed, she suspected, the slow progression through the town. Until, that is, they had reached the Haymarket, and she had felt her own heart sink when she had realized where she was. No lady of any respectability would come to such a place alone, and even if she came to the theatre, would always come with an escort.

She brightened as that thought entered her mind, and with a swish of her skirts turned and made her way back across the frozen cobbles towards the carriage. She *would* go inside the building, and she *would* find her Jonah, but in such a way that no one could think ill of her behaviour.

The coachman took her back to Gower Street at a rattling pace, and she leaned back against the squabs, her head back and her eyes staring sightlessly out at the crowds filling the early evening streets, thinking and planning, her mind going round in circles.

There must be some way in which to get Jonah back from whatever situation he was in. The fact that he had apparently gone to ground in so unsavoury an area did not surprise her unduly; protected rich wife of a respected surgeon and apothecary she may be, but she was no fool. Her dealings with the London Ladies' Committee for the Rescue of the Children of the Profligate Poor had taught her much of the evil ways of a city, and of the appetites of men and how ungovernable they were. So, it did not perturb her to think of her Jonah in a wicked part of the town, for was he not a young man and as such entitled to what pleasures he desired, and, also as a man well able to take care of himself? It was not for fear of his welfare that she wanted to get him away from these new surroundings of his, but because she wanted to have him to herself.

Bad enough had been the long years when he had been away at school, and she had had to content herself with contact with him during his vacations; but at least then she had known him to be well and happy in his absences. Now she had no such assurances, and until she could have him under her roof again, she would not enjoy true peace of mind.

So she tried to imagine schemes for getting him home without Abel's knowledge. Would it be possible, she wondered, to have him at home and to guard his comings in and goings out in such a way that Abel would never know he was there? Would she be able to get enough money, from Abby at the shop, to keep her darling provided for? There was much to try to plan, and her mind twisted and turned like a mouse in a maze as she pondered.

At home she sent immediately for her maid, and instructed her to go at once to the Haymarket Theatre to bespeak seats for the night's performance. The girl gaped at her, for it was well known in the household that no member of the family ever went to such entertainments, and Dorothea snapped at her, which made the girl gape even more—for Dorothea never snapped as others employers did—and go scurrying off to do as she was bid.

Dorothea dressed with the aid of the second parlour-maid, and was so deeply abstracted that she hardly noticed the girl's inept ways with her hair and her gown, but sent her away as soon as she was decently garbed, and hurried down to the drawing-room, there to send for Abby.

She stood there beside the fire warming her hands at the blaze, and when Abby came in, a little breathlessly for she had returned late from her momentous afternoon at the shop and had been hard put to it to dress in time for dinner, she stopped at the door for a moment to stare at her mother.

Was it because, since this afternoon, everything looked different to her that her mother looked so changed? She had a rather high colour, and her normally pale cheeks were lit with a soft rosiness that became her very well, and the inept attempts of the second maid to arrange her hair had resulted in a soft curliness of those faded fair locks that was much more attractive than the stiff shapes and ringlets into which it was usually pulled by the more expert fingers of her own maid. And she smiled differently, too, Abby thought, as she advanced across the room towards her mother . She looked positively *happy*. Abby was deeply puzzled.

'Well, Abby!' Dorothea said, and her voice held a note of raillery. 'The secret is out! There is no need for you to hide things any longer, for the matter is quite clear to me now, and I know all!'

Abby felt her face flame and then go a chalky white, and for one sick moment she felt the room revolve around her. She saw herself on that sofa in the office with James, saw her body in its crumpled gown, her own hands caressing his body, and tried to see how her mother could have been there, could have seen——

'My dear child, I had not thought to so distress you!' Her mother's voice came from a long way away, and then there was the sharp tang of vinegar in her nose, and Abby turned her head and found she was half sitting and half lying on the chair beside the fire with her mother kneeling beside her and holding a vinaigrette to her nostrils.

'I—what—I—do not understand you, Mama!' she said, trying as best she could to bring her thoughts into some sort of order. How was she ever to persuade her mother not to tell her father of what had happened? And if it did so reach Abel's ears, how was he to be persuaded that it was she who had seduced James as much as the other way about? How was a confrontation between the two men to be avoided? She closed her eyes for a sick moment, and could have groaned aloud.

'Indeed, dear Abby, do not take it so ill!' Dorothea said. 'I do not hold any ill will to you for concealing the matter! You have behaved only as a devoted sister should, and I am glad, indeed I am, that Jonah has enjoyed your care and protection as he has. I would not have quizzed you for the world, for apart from it being a waste of time'— and the note of practicality in Dorothea's voice was slightly absurd— 'I would do nothing to prejudice the safety of his line of communication with us. His letters were so very precious. But you see, I was here today when the woman came and I heard and had but to follow her, and now I know for myself where he is——'

Abby had been staring at her mother, relief flooding her, and she laughed now, almost wildly. 'It is of Jonah—oh, Mama, forgive me! I had not meant to——'

'Well, of course I forgive you, now I know that he is there! I quite understand why you could not tell me. But we must get him home again, somehow, Abby my dearest, and I have given much thought to the ways we must contrive! But I shall tell you on the way there of my ideas, and you shall say your opinion of them, for I value your good sense so highly. You are a *dear* daughter!' and she kissed Abby's cheek and then stood up and went back to the fire, leaving Abby staring at her and trying to comprehend all that her mother had said.

'On the way where, Mama?' she said carefully, and Dorothea turned and looked at her with a glance so full of pleasure it was as though she were another person altogether, and not at all the mother with whom she had lived all her sixteen years of life.

'I have sent Forder there, to bespeak two seats, my love,' she said. 'And I do pray that your Papa will choose not to come home tonight for dinner, but will eat a chop somewhere else, for I could not bear not to go and discover the full truth of my Jonah's situation. Do you suppose—oh, Abby, *do* you suppose they are doing a play he wrote? For he read his work to me, you know, his poems and his many writings and I know them to be of excellent taste and quality, and it would be a great thing—would it not?—for one of his creations to be upon the Haymarket stage, for all I know that your Papa so hates it. But we shall discover when we go, for there will be some intimation, I am sure, of the piece that is to be played and who wrote it, and much else besides. I went to the theatre some five or six times in my youth, you know, so I do have a small knowledge of these things——'

The tide of prattle went on, and Abby did her best to collect her thoughts. That her mother had followed the woman who had borne Jonah's letter to her from Gower Street to Piccadilly and thence to Jonah himself was apparent, and she marvelled a little at her mother's determination. She would never have thought her capable of so strong-willed an action.

To discover Jonah had gone to a theatre surprised her considerably. She had always known, of course, of her brother's poetical pretensions, but she had not imagined he saw himself as a playwright; indeed her lips curled a little at that thought; for she had read some of Jonah's work and thought it turgid enough stuff in all conscience. But then, as Jonah had pointed out to her with some acerbity, she had too practical a turn of mind altogether to be able to enjoy the subtle sensibilities of his vision.

And now her mother was planning to go to the theatre to seek more information about her son! Abby quailed a little at that thought. Life was complex enough for her as far as her father was concerned. To risk bringing down his wrath on her head by going to a theatre against which her father had so strong an antipathy (and she realized suddenly that she did not know why he should be so angered by them, for there was nothing of the religious evangelical about him, after all) would be foolhardy in the extreme. After this afternoon's experience—and she glowed a little within as the memory came rushing back to her—it was imperative that a wedding be arranged as soon as possible. Quite apart from any matters of practical need, she knew as sure as she knew she breathed that after one such sharing of body and heart and mind life would be barely tolerable until it could happen again, and again.

She raised her head to look at her mother, and opened her mouth to refuse, to tell her she would not go to the theatre with her, that she would keep her tongue between her teeth and not tell Abel aught of it, but go herself she would not.

But then she saw the look on her mother's face, and remembered how ill and distressed she had looked these many weeks past, ever since Jonah's departure, saw the hope and happiness that filled it now and she could not do it.

'Well, Mama, if you have decided it, so you have. But if you will allow me to suggest it, we shall not take the carriage there, but find our way in a hackney, and I shall take it upon myself to bribe your maid to say nothing to Papa of our errand tonight—for I promise you, his anger would be quite volcanic if he were to discover our jaunt. So, please, Mama, try to be circumspect about it all, I do beg you.'

20

'You'll 'ave to make a choice, my boy. That's all there is to it, an' it's no use you goin' on makin' such a pother about it. Either you gets what you wants in the way o' property by doin' the way I say or you goes without. Cut it 'ow yer likes, that's the way of it.'

Lucy was sitting bolt upright on the sofa in her yellow satin salon with a glass of hot negus in one hand and a chicken-skin fan, which she vigorously applied to the air before her red and streaming face, in the other, watching Abel prowling about the overheated and overscented room. The half-dozen of her girls who were lounging about in their diaphanous muslins, dampened in order to make them cling the more seductively to their ample curves, watched him too and whispered together as they did so. It had never ceased to amaze them that this very personable man (any one of them would have entertained him gladly without a hint of any other reward than the experience itself) should come so often to the house but evince interest in none but raddled old Lucy. Not that any of them would have dared to say such a thing aloud, for warm and generous a woman though Lucy was, she could be a veritable harridan if aroused.

'It is intolerable!' Abel burst out, 'Quite intolerable! I have kept my mind and—and feelings free of her these seventeen years, and now—pah! It sickens me, you hear me? I——'

'Aye,' Lucy said calmly. 'So you've told me these dozen times this past half hour. Come, Abel, lad, save your breath to cool your porridge! The situation is not to be changed by you stampin' around like some wild animal! You mun set yer mind to what it is you 'ave to do, not to complaints. 'Tisn't like you to be so lackin' in good sense——'

He stopped at that, and then came and sat down beside her and nodded heavily.

'Aye, you are in the right, as always. But I was so put about by the discovery that—oh, Lucy, I would not have thought the sound of her name could arouse such—such anger in me after all these years. Am I not the man I thought I was, Lucy? Have I been deceiving myself all this time? I thought myself strong, and able to control the way the lines of my life should fall, and yet in such a situation as this I find myself so upset that I cannot think clearly at all. Am I no more than a fool, Lucy? You will tell me the truth, will you not?' And he looked at her with his face creased into almost ludicrous lines of distress, his green eyes dark with anxiety, and she put out one huge heavily ringed hand and rested it gently on his knee, and looked up into his face with such a deal of love that even in his unhappiness he could not fail to be warmed by it.

'Oh, my dear lad, never think you are anything but a man of parts! When I recall the way you was when first I saw you, an' 'ow you made your life bend to your ways, 'ow you made a career of yer own choosin' out of so unpromising a beginning—why, my darlin' boy, even those that don't love you as I do must fall into an admiration! No, you're man enough, and more besides. It'd be a source o' worry to me if you *didn't* feel so strong about the Lucas woman, on account she treated you so very cruel, all those years ago. She was a fool, every kind of a fool, not to love you as you did her, but there it is—there's naught to be got out o' lookin' backwards. What you 'ave to do now is face up to it, the way my likely lad always faced up to 'is problems, and go and see 'er and——'

'No!' He said it almost violently, and she shook her head and took her hand from his knee and leaned back on her sofa with a creaking of her stays.

'So be it, then,' she said shortly. 'You asked me for my view o' the situation, and there it is. If you don't fancy it, then that's your 'ard luck. But don't go on askin' me to say different on account of I don't go cuttin' my cloth to any man's coat, not even yours. I've told you what I think—what you does now is your affair. Now, are you stayin' or goin'? I got business to concern myself with, for the men'll be comin' in at any moment now. The 'Ouse must a' risen by now, for not even those stinkin' politicians will talk the 'ole night away——'

He sat there in silence, ignoring her question, staring at the toes of his out-thrust boots and trying to set his mind to some sort of order.

Ever since Gandy Deering had thrown Lilith Lucas's name so casually at him he had been in a state of utter confusion. He had eaten a chop and drunk his pint of porter with Deering, letting the man chatter on about his plans for his precious Hall, and trying to decide what to do. But that had got him nowhere, and he interrupted Deering's flow of talk when they reached the stage of taking a piece of Stilton cheese with a glass of heavy old port to ask how it was that an actress should be the owner of a house such as that in Endell Street.

'Why shouldn't she be?' Deering had said indistinctly, for his mouth was full. 'I'm told she makes plenty of good cash from her play-acting. Why, on a good benefit night, they say she can take home close on six hundred pounds——'

'Six hundred? Good God!' Abel had stared blankly at him. 'It cannot be so much! Why, that's enough to buy any house in the whole of the district!'

'Aye. 'Tis so!' Deering said. 'For the town is full of fools and fops who have naught better to do than hang about the greenrooms and pay good cash to watch the mopping and mowing of mountebanks. It makes big values of theatre properties, I'll say that for it. Why, d'you know, sir, when Garrick sold half a share in Drury Lane to old Sheridan he made him pay full thirty-five thousand pounds? Aye! Thirty-five thousand pounds! And that was close on, well—it must be years ago now! What I could do with such moneys now in the building of my new Hall and the Strand improvements—why, it makes me positively slaver at the thought! And as well as making so much money at her trade, I'm told the lady is not averse to making more at other trades. I believe she's a warm woman—very warm, with pockets of good house property spread over half the town.'

He had cut himself another slab of the cheese and looked shrewdly at Abel over his high collar points. 'You seem mighty interested in the lady, Mr Lackland! I did not take you for a theatre-goer——'

'I am not,' Abel said shortly. 'I have not set foot in one for more years than I can recall.' But he did not say how much he had loved the theatre once, how much enchantment he had found in those painted people on their painted stages, in the smell of glue-size and lime, dust and grease-paint that filled those cavernous spaces behind the footlights.

It seemed strange to him now, remembering those years long ago when he had been the apothecary that the actors sent for whenever they were ill, to realize how little he knew of the current facts of theatre life.

Despite his rigid refusal to have her name mentioned, and his attempts to deny that such a woman had ever existed, and despite his flat refusal to let any of his family set foot in a theatre, he knew, of course, that Lilith had been reigning queen of the Haymarket these past seventeen years, long ago having toppled the great Sarah Siddons from her pinnacle.

He would have had to be blind and deaf not to know, for she was the subject of much general gossip in the town, and her name often appeared in newspaper columns; besides which the streets were too often plastered with playbills for him to be able completely to ignore them. So he knew of her position at the height of her profession; but that such a position should have made her so rich came as a surprise to him.

Had he thought about it at all, he would have assumed that she lived as had the actors he had once known; precariously eking out a difficult living on the ha'pence thrown to them by the controlling managements.

He said carefully now. 'You said you would not willingly deal with her in the matter of this house—no, do not look at me so! I am not going to back down on our bargain! You provide the wherewithal and I shall do the negotiating. But I wish to know why it is you are so adamant in this matter.'

Deering laughed at that. 'Why, sir, because she drives so hard a bargain! She knows to a penny the value of her holding and knows too well who people are in this town! If I go to her in search of an honest purchase of a piece of property she puts her prices up at once to the most absurd of levels, for she knows that such buying and selling is necessary to an architect with the desire to build a better town than the one in which he finds himself. I ask you to deal with her not in any spirit of meanness, I promise you, but on a purely practical ground. She will charge you a lesser price than she will me! It is as simple as that, my dear Mr Lackland. And who knows? You may find that beneath that money-minded surface of hers there beats a charitable heart! When you go to her, you with your leech's face and your good surgeon's soul, she may be prevailed upon to treat you with generosity and make her own contribution to your hospital. That way *you* get your hospital, and *I* am not forced to dip too deep into my pocket to complete my share of our bargain.'

He had laughed again, fatly. 'You must remember, Mr Lackland, that artist though I may be I am also a man of business, and there is no charity in business, or should not be. It is right and proper that I should save as much as I can of my money, as right and proper as that you should seek to build your hospital in the way you wish to build it. Which is why I made the bargain I did. Come, Mr Lackland! You cannot feel I am in the wrong! You will have what you want, I will have what I want, and all will be happy! *You* will not find it too irksome, I believe, to deal with Mrs Lucas. I will tell you this much—she is an enchanting pretty woman! I am as hardheaded as any man of the City, but I was hard put to it, the times I dealt with her, not to succumb to her wiles, for wiles they are. I find it almost in my heart to envy you, Lackland, for you will gain some pleasure, I'll be bound, in treating with her. Or could, I've no doubt, for you are a personable enough man, and they tell me she's as insatiable as any Paphian.'

And he had laughed with much lewdness (for the port was low in the bottle by now) and had fallen to talking again, interminably, about his plans for the Strand.

Now, sitting beside Lucy, Abel stirred himself and said abruptly, 'Very well. I shall deal with her.'

Lucy looked up at that, and grinned hugely. 'Now, there's my lad, again——' she began, but Abel interrupted her.

'But not directly, you understand. It is in no way my intention that she should know it is I who wish to buy her house, for I believe that if she knows this she will drive a wicked bargain. I am unwilling to face her not because of—because of any past acquaintance between us, but because I wish to make as good a shift for my hospital as I can. I believe I have a better chance of doing this if I deal with her through an agent.'

'You lie in your teeth,' Lucy said calmly. 'For you are still heartsore over her, and——'

'That's as may be, but I'll not discuss that—will you *listen* to me, Lucy! I talk now of business, not other matters. And what I have to say, you will see, makes excellent sense. If you will go to her and ask her——'

'I?' Lucy sat even more bolt upright with a ferocious squealing of the whalebone that encompassed her straining flesh. 'I? Be damned to you, you whorehound! Why should I do any——'

'Ah, Lucy, do listen,' Abel said, and put out his hand and took hold of one of hers. 'I had not realized it before, but you will see it is the best plan—indeed, the only plan! Deering tells me that the house is used by Covent Garden tails. Now, come, Lucy! Just think a little! You are known as the richest and most successful woman in your trade in all the Haymarket! You hold properties of your own, and——'

'That's none of your affair!' Lucy said snappily. 'None at all! And——'

'I know that! All I am saying is that it would not be thought at all amiss if you sought to buy such a house as this one in Endell Street, for do you not own a good house of your own in this trade?'

She sat and stared at him for a long moment and then let out a great cackle of laughter. 'Oh, Abel, you wicked lad! You have a tongue so honeyed would charm a donkey out of a thistle patch! Aye, I see what it is you mean. It would not seem all that strange were I to seek such a property, at that——'

'And you will do more than keep me from—an encounter I would be happy to avoid if you do act for me in this matter, dear Lucy,' Abel said, and his voice was gathering conviction now as the good sense of his plan began to impress itself more and more upon his mind. 'For I believe you will obtain the property for me at a good price, and though I hold no brief for Deering, it is surely incumbent upon me to make his purchase as easy as possible.'

She was thinking quickly as she looked at him and listened to his words. She was painfully aware of the fact that she had hidden from him the knowledge that his son was now living with Lilith Lucas; if she agreed to act as his agent in the matter of this house, it would be possible, she realized, to keep the intelligence from him even longer. She was no fool given to fantasies, and knew perfectly well that a day of reckoning would come when Abel would discover the facts of the matter, would realize she had lied to him. She did not at all relish the thought of that day coming, for she valued his affection too highly to gladly envisage any anger on his part that might set itself between them. Now, if she were to deal with Lilith for him, it would certainly put off that difficult day even longer.

And, she suddenly thought, perhaps for always. For if I go to the house to see her is it not possible that I will get a glimpse of the boy, and find the chance to talk to him, and persuade him to leave this wretched female's protection? Her heart warmed at that thought, and she beamed at Abel now, and threw her arms about his broad shoulders and kissed him heartily.

'Well, you insolent boy—for so you are to me, and always will be, however great a man you may seem, or may ever become—I shall do as you ask. I shall go to this fancy actress madam and relieve her of her house so fast she will not know what it is that has happened to her! And you shall have your hospital, and be able to get on with the business of your life with no more ado with La Lucas! Never let it be said that Lucy cannot make life easier for her likely lad!'

And he returned her hug and kiss gladly and went away to consider his plans for his three times enlarged hospital in a fully contented mood. She would get her way with the house, of that he was sure. And he also felt sure that despite his temporary aberration of the afternoon—for that was how he now saw his mood of confusion and distress—he *was* in control of the way in which his lines fell.

He smiled wryly to himself in the foggy darkness as he made his striding way back through the alleyways to Gower Street. Deerings and Lucases and trustees notwithstanding, his hospital should grow and be what a hospital should be. Might even, he thought daringly, one day come to rival the old establishments like Guy's and St Thomas's. Now, there was a thought to warm the heart of a surgeon on a cold winter's night in Seven Dials!

21

At least he had his costume, and had paid for it decently from his own pocket. He hugged that knowledge close to himself and found it absurd that it should give him such comfort.

Hawks had come back and thrust the bulky envelope from his sister into his hands, with much muttering and complaining about the mad dance she had been led all over town to obtain it, but he had found that easy to put up with, for he was getting used to Hawks's blustering and bad temper.

What he found much harder to get used to was the way Lilith was now behaving to him at the theatre.

During the weeks he had spent living in her house he had been but little at the theatre during the day. The evenings spent in the greenroom with the others of her adoring followers had been difficult, to be sure, but he had not blamed her for that; he had seen that it was the importunities of those overpainted and overscented men who hung about her that were to blame for his sense of being an outsider, and a childish and rather unwanted one to boot. But that had been compensated for by his days, which had been agreeable in the extreme, for he had spent hour after hour in her white-and-gold drawing-room, sitting at the little escritoire in the corner and writing and writing and writing until his head became hot and throbbing and his feet icy cold, sensations which he much enjoyed for they were, in a most curious way, a part of the effort of creation.

His play, which was an ambitious one indeed and heavily based on one of the more obscure of the Greek legends he had learned from Mr Loudoun, had grown most satisfyingly, and he had spent a full week in a state of bemused delight after he had finished, using his time to polish it, rewriting occasional pages for the sheer pleasure of it and generally poring over it in possessive joy. But then had come the weeks of waiting and hoping when he had tried, over and over again, to pin down her butterfly temperament long enough to hear his great rolling passages of blank verse, and had failed miserably.

But disagreeable though that had been, it had not been nearly as disagreeable as these days spent in rehearsal at the Haymarket were proving to be.

No matter what he did, no matter how hard he tried she behaved as though he were of no more import to her than one of the theatre cats, kindly but definitely shooing him away when he attempted to speak to her and virtually looking through him when he tried to catch her eye. All she seemed interested in was her work, and conversation with the privileged half-dozen men friends who were allowed to attend rehearsals.

As day followed day, and the play (which he was coming to hate most heartily, having no taste at all for its mock antiquities and its absurd—to him—over-melodramatic posturings in medieval dress) took shape, he felt more and more useless and bereft.

If only, he thought now, sitting hunched up on a stool in the corner of the busy, noisy, bitterly cold stage, if only I had had the courage to hold to my word that night in Cremorne, and had gone! Bad enough as it would be to go home to his father's house, surely it could not be as miserable as remaining here in so ambiguous a position as the one he now occupied. And even facing his father would be possible, he told himself, for was there not his mother to protect him in some small measure? Not that she could protect him much, he told himself mournfully, for she was often as frightened of his father as he was himself.

He had a sudden vision of his mother's face, with its drawn pallor and the fine lines between the pale brows and he felt an uprush of aching need rise in him that quite startled him with its strength, and he closed his eyes against the pain of it. Celia, watching him from the other side of the stage (for she could not bear to be away from a sight of him for longer than an hour together, and had therefore taken to attending each day's rehearsals, though keeping as much out of her mother's view as she could) saw the misery in his face, and bit her lip hard. She wanted more than anything else in the world to go to him and put her arms about him, and cradle his head and tell him of her love. But how could she? He was still, she told herself bitterly, in a state of adoration for her hellcat mother, and what eyes would he have for anyone else while that was the case?

But then she looked at him again, at the way his shoulders, those square strong shoulders that she so loved, were hunched in misery, at the way his face looked so pale and unhappy, and in her impetuous way went slipping through the knots of people at the back of the stage to reach his side.

He was still sitting with his eyes closed and all the speeches she had rehearsed in her head while watching him shrivelled and died, and she felt her belly lurch with pity and love. She knew too well how he was feeling, and she slid one warm and rather dirty hand into his and said softly, 'Oh, my dear Jonah, I am so sorry'.

His hand closed convulsively on hers and his eyes snapped open, and he found himself looking down into her wide grey ones, and saw such a warmth and approval there that almost involuntarily he smiled.

'Why, my dear Celia, what have you done?'

She smiled too at that, and turned her head and looked at her mother, who was now in the centre of the stage and declaiming a most passionate speech with much power, and his gaze followed hers and his face sobered.

'I was not apologizing, dear Jonah,' she murmured, and shot a swift glance at him. 'I was—commiserating. I know how you suffer, you see. I, too, know of the feelings you are experiencing.'

He managed a wry twist of his mouth at that. 'Do you?' he said shortly. 'Then indeed I pity you, for I am in sore case! I think you cannot know what it is I feel, but I thank you for your concern.'

She tightened her hold on his hand, and looked up at him with such intensity that he had perforce to look at her. 'I do know!' She still spoke in a whisper, for both knew better than to make any unnecessary sound when Lilith was rehearsing, for she could raise a storm of temper at anything that interrupted her concentration that would make the very roof tremble. 'I know because I have such feelings too.'

He looked down at her and smiled very warmly, but she could see the thought that lay behind his eyes, the thought that she was too young and raw to know of the power of emotion that filled him, and she felt the all to familiar anger rise in her, and almost snatched her hand away. But he was holding it tightly now and she looked at him again, and this time saw that the hint of condescension she thought she had seen was not there after all; only loneliness and hurt and young sadness.

'Oh, Jonah, my dear Jonah, I do love you so!' She blurted it out in the same soft whisper and then felt a wave of coldness rise in her that quite numbed her, and she sat and stared at him in consternation with her heart beating so loud she felt as though it would quite escape the confines of her chest.

He had been about to turn his head away, to look again at Lilith, but as the import of her words registered in his mind he snapped his head back and looked at her, and saw that little white face with its huge darkly lashed grey eyes and the soft mouth trembling a little now at the enormity of what she had said, at the stain of colour that had risen in her white cheeks, and remembered with a vividness so great that it was almost as though it had happened again the way he had kissed her that snowy afternoon in her mother's drawing-room. And almost without thinking he bent his head and let his lips brush hers.

At once she moved, sliding back into the shadows of the side of the stage, away from the sight of the rehearsing actors and their hangers-on, and he perforce went with her for her hand was still tightly clamped over his, and together they went stumbling through the dimness; until she stopped quite suddenly and he found that they were tucked into a corner of the wings, flanked on both sides by stacks of scenery unwanted for this production.

'You are not angry with me for saying that?' Her voice came out of the darkness as an urgent whisper, and he felt her hands on his cheeks, and he put up his own to cover them, straining his eyes to see. As they became accustomed to the darkness and he could see her, he felt that same warmth that had filled him enough to make him want to kiss her before come bubbling back, and again he bent his head towards her, but this time it was a gentle and deeply affectionate embrace, partaking of none of the passion that had so startled them both the first time.

But her response was just as urgent, and she clung to him desperately, murmuring and trembling in his arms, and it alarmed him a little, and as gently as he could he moved away from her and looked at her uncertainly in the dimness.

'Celia?' he said and knew his voice sounded young and doubtful. 'Celia? I do not think I quite understand——'

'No, I don't think you do—' She said it fondly, and it seemed to him suddenly that she was infinitely older and infinitely wiser than he, but the knowledge of this did not hurt him, as it hurt when Lilith made him feel so. It was as though they were truly equals, he and Celia, but that she just happened to have some information that he had not yet acquired, but that was available to him, and would one day undoubtedly be his.

'—Dearest Jonah,' she was saying, as he stood there with his arms about her and she warm and breathing and comfortable within their circle. 'There is so much you do not understand, and I have wanted to tell you these many weeks, though I could not, but I feel now that I can, and indeed I must if I am not to burst! I have loved you, it seems to me, all my life, but indeed, I believe it is from the very first time I saw you, and I am not ashamed to tell you so for although I am not a street creature as was my mother once, I *am* of the theatre and I care not for the conventions of drawing-rooms! I know only that I love you and I always will, and it hurts me cruelly to see you suffer so at my mother's hands, for I know her, and I know how she will make your life a pain to you if you cannot rid yourself of this mad fascination——'

He stood there in the darkness and tried to think and could not. That he was fascinated with Lilith he could not deny. To take his eyes from her when she was in a room was almost an impossibility, but then so it was for other people. He knew that well enough; even Celia was hard put to it not to pay her that special attention she demanded.

But at the same time there was another feeling battling in him, and he knew now what it was. He cared for this girl who lay now against his chest in the dusty cold darkness of the stacked scenery. Not with the painful intensity that he felt when Lilith came into view, but with a warm and comfortable sureness that was the most agreeable sensation he could remember knowing. It was as though she could blunt the edge of the gnawing pain her mother could inflict, and could make his life comfortable again to him. And he hugged her close, feeling the warmth rising in him, and said, almost in surprise but with a curious elation, 'I think I care for you, too, my dear Celia. I did not know it, but I think I do. You are indeed, so—so——'

But he could say no more, for again her lips were on his and now it was his turn to respond to her passion, and he did so with a delight that moved in his loins quite startlingly.

They stayed there together in the darkness for what seemed an age, talking and murmuring and kissing again, and he became more and more responsive as time went on, until it was he who rained kisses on her upturned face as much as she who strained towards him.

It came almost as a shock to remember where he was when suddenly he heard his name being called, and repeated over and over again, and they broke apart and Celia cursed softly under her breath.

'Please to go first, my darling,' she whispered. 'If they see us both come out together they will torment us unmercifully. And my mother —oh, just say you were in the privy or some such——' and she giggled breathlessly and seemed to melt away from him into the darkness, and he went stumbling out into the arena of the stage to stand blinking in the brightness as his eyes accustomed themselves to the light.

They wanted him to walk through his meagre lines, and he went across the stage as quickly as he could, and knew he stumbled a little, for he was bitter cold; he had not realized how the chill had entered his bones there in the dark with Celia, and he looked up and saw Lilith's eyes on him and smiled at her, and knew it to be a sheepish smile.

She looked at him very sharply, and then a faint line appeared between her brows and she looked quickly round, and swept the crowded stage with her glance.

Celia emerged from the other side of the stage, her face smooth and her eyes filled with an expression that was demure and virtuous, all that a young girl's should be, and she put up her hand to smooth her hair and let her glance drift across the stage and light on Jonah in what was meant to be the most casual of manners.

But Lilith saw the way her face softened, and she looked sharply again at Jonah and saw the expression on his face as he looked away from her and caught Celia's glance, and at once her own face hardened and her eyes narrowed, though neither of the young people saw, for they were quite taken up with looking at each other and then as casually as they might looking away again.

'Come, my dear Leontes!' Lilith cried, and her voice had a high hard edge on it. 'We seek for you everywhere, do you know, that we might continue the rehearsal! Were you set in a dream of a poem, there in the bowels of the theatre? My dear boy, this is no time for dreaming of poesy, for you are to be an actor, are you not?'

'I'm sorry,' he mumbled and essayed a smile at her. 'You must forgive me, but you call me so rarely for any rehearsal that I thought you would have no need of me, and went in search of some warmer spot ——' He smiled then, a quick and rather wicked smile, for he had not expected so smooth a lie to rise so easily to his lips, and almost without knowing he did it he slid his eyes away to catch Celia's gaze in a conspiratorial way, and she smiled too and turned away so that her face was hidden in the shadows.

And Lilith saw it all and wondered, and thought, and watched them both for the rest of the short afternoon.

22

Dorothea was feeling very cast down. All the sparkle that had invested her face and figure at the beginning of the evening was quite gone, and now she sat in the little red plush chair with its gilt back with her head bent as she dispiritedly watched her own fingers twisting and turning her fan upon her lap.

Abby in her turn sat and watched her, and tried again to search her mind for some words she could say to comfort her Mama, but quite failed. Apart from anything else, she was feeling extraordinarily fatigued, fully drained of any vitality, for with the strange entertainment of the evening following so hard upon the momentous events of the afternoon her mind seemed to be filled with wool. Whenever she tried to concentrate on the matter in hand, she would find her thoughts had slid away to a memory of the afternoon, a memory so vivid that it was almost strong enough to repeat the sensations she had known, so that she blushed at the images that came into her mind and found her tongue faltering; or else as she remembered James's illness she felt a sudden wave of fear which made her cheeks whiten, and again made her words slide away from her.

Dorothea, for her part, was far too preoccupied with her own thoughts to notice her daughter's recurrent attacks of discomfiture. She had entered the theatre with her head well down, half paralysed with fear at the enormity of her action, her cloak held close about her and the hood up to hide her face. No one had paid any attention to the two women and their maid, however, as they made their way through the fashionable chattering crowds thronging the passageways and crushes of the Haymarket to the box that had been bespoken for them, and gratefully Dorothea had set a chair into the shadows in such a way that she could see the stage without herself being observed by any members of the audience.

'We must take such care, Abby, my love,' she had twittered to her daughter, fussily making sure that her chair too was hidden in the shadows of the curtained box. 'For we have no way of knowing but that some of Papa's acquaintance may be here, and might inform him of having seen us, and that would be, I am sure you will agree, quite disastrous——'

The play had at first quite enchanted her. She had joined in the delighted applause that had greeted the actors, and been a little surprised at the volume of sound that greeted one of them, a spirited, elegant woman with dark curls and a wickedly beautiful face, dressed all in pale blue, but had joined in none the less, wondering aloud to Abby who she might be, and why she should be so rapturously received.

But that had been before the first interval, when they had sent the maid to purchase a playbill. After that Dorothea had changed.

There had been no sight at all of Jonah anywhere on the stage, either during the burletta that was set as the curtain-raiser, nor in the first act of the piece, although the stage was crowded with supers throughout for it was *A Midsummer Night's Dream* that was being performed and the production was lavish with 'attending lords and ladies'.

Dorothea had read every word of the playbill with ever-increasing urgency but had seen no mention of the name of her son, and her spirits had sunk deep at that omission; she had been so sure she would find some mention of him on that blurred and inky piece of paper.

But worse still, her heart had seemed to shrivel and die a little at what she *did* find there. She had sat and stared at the name that shouted up at her from the page in such heavy, large print, and the weight of the memory that it brought flooding back had been enough almost to rob her of her senses.

She remembered Abel's face as it had been on that far distant day when he had told her he was going into Kent 'to look for Lil', remembered his face as it had been on that more dreadful day he had come and told her that they could not be wed because he loved his Lil more than he loved her. And above all she remembered what had happened when she and her stepfather together had told him that he could not wed Lil, and why——

But that was a memory that could not be allowed any rein at all. Now, all these years later, she sat in a box at the Haymarket Theatre and saw the name of Lilith Lucas on the playbill, and it was as though a hand had moved into her chest and taken her lungs in its impersonal icy grasp and had started to squeeze and squeeze them——

They sat there as the people left the theatre at the end of the performance, dully watching the liveried footmen go about the vast auditorium below them with their long and rather battered poles, lazily extinguishing the myriad hissing gas jets that illuminated the house; saw the rows of seats plunged into dimness; and still they sat there, and Abby stopped trying to discover why it was her mother was so distressed, and why it was that she would not speak; she simply sat and watched her through a haze of weariness.

It was not until one of the theatre servants came blundering into their box to put out the light that Dorothea came out of the half-comatose state into which she had been sunk and stood up, and even then she did so heavily and slowly. Together the three women went silently down the steps to the foyer and Dorothea and Abby stood there, still without exchanging a word, while the maid went in search of a hack.

It was as they were climbing in that Dorothea got back her animation. She had clearly been sunk deep in contemplation, and as the theatre doorman held open the door of the battered carriage she stepped back and insisted that Abby enter before her, and that the maid should follow.

'I am going somewhere, Abby. Please to go home. No, my mind is quite made up. I shall return in due course in a hackney myself, so you need not fret yourself. I shall discover him, no matter if she—well, let be. I shall be safe enough. Now go home, and if you see Papa you must tell him I am gone to bed early—tell him anything you wish except that we have been here——' and with unusual despatch in one of so tentative a nature she smartly closed the door of the carriage upon her startled daughter, and disappeared into the shadows.

The greenroom was nearly empty of people by the time she found her way to it. She had asked the doorman if all the actors had gone from the theatre and he had grinned at her simplicity but told her good-naturedly enough that most of 'em were probably still drinking and eating in the greenroom, and that she'd be able to see whoever it was she fancied words with there if she would but take herself around the corner to the stage door in Suffolk Street.

She had gone there quaking, but shored up with the stubbornness born of her weakness. She had set her heart on seeing her Jonah tonight, and no matter what she would not rest until she had, she told herself.

She hovered in the doorway of the greenroom, blinking a little at the brightness and almost afraid to look about her at the people there, but she need not have feared. There were in fact only two people left in the room, the pretty woman, now wearing a frilled white peignoir, and a much older woman with a sour visage and her hair tightly pinned upon her head over her uncompromisingly black gown.

It was a moment or two before Dorothea recognized her as the woman she had followed through the streets, but when she did her courage, which had been fast ebbing, came back with a rush. Her Jonah *was* here, he had to be, and she, his mother, would not depart until she had some contact with him, or at least real news of him.

'Mrs Lucas,' she said flatly, and there was no question in her voice, for she knew perfectly well who was the pretty woman in the peignoir, although this was the first time she had ever set eyes upon her. It was strange, she thought fleetingly, that someone who had figured so large in her life should be so very much a stranger; odd to see her only now, after all these long years.

The woman in the peignoir looked up, and her brows creased at the sight of the slight cloaked figure at the door, and she dismissed her with a glance. Lilith Lucas had never been one to bother herself much about the impression she made on women and she was certainly not going to start doing so now, at the end of a long day filled both with rehearsals for her big benefit night and a performance. She did not even deign to open her lips but jerked her head at Hawks to indicate that she should send the interloper away.

Hawks moved towards the door, but Dorothea ignored her, watching the woman sitting at the dressing-table and wiping paint from her face. She's tired, she thought, almost wonderingly. Tired and not so young. Like me. Poor thing——

As Hawks reached her side, and took the door-knob in one hand preparatory to closing it in her face Dorothea spoke again in the same flat and almost conversational tone. 'I am Mrs Lackland. Abel's wife. Jonah's mother.'

Lilith's head jerked up at that, and she stared at Dorothea through her mirror, and Hawks seemed to be aware of her scrutiny and turned her head to look, still holding the door but no longer attempting to push Dorothea to the other side of it.

There was a pause, and then Lilith shifted her gaze and returned to the methodical cleaning of her face with the white towel in her hand. 'You may go about your business, Hawks,' she said easily. 'I will come home after you. Do not forget to take the tarlatan gown. I shall need it clean for Saturday. Good evening to you, Mrs Lackland. I trust you are in good health.'

Hawks, shrugging, crossed the room and picked up the drift of blue that was lying on the floor at Lilith's side, and went silently away, closing the door behind her and leaving Dorothea leaning on its scratched panels.

There was another silence, while Lilith went on with her absorption in her face and Dorothea stood and stared at her; and eventually it was Dorothea who moved to come across the room and sit down on the old horse-hair sofa against the wall, dropping the hood from her head to her shoulders, and leaning back wearily.

'I am well enough, thank you, Mrs Lucas,' she said. 'Well enough.'

'I am glad to hear it,' Lilith said pleasantly and began to rub an unguent into her face, running her fingers caressingly over her cheeks and under her eyes, lovingly smoothing the skin beneath her chin and across her throat, her eyes never leaving her mirror image.

Dorothea said nothing, watching the other woman with an almost mesmerized fascination, and after a while Lilith shot a sideways glance at her and spoke with a sharp edge to her voice.

'I collect you have come to talk to me of some matter of importance? I have not seen you here ever before, and I am told—I understand that your family does not, as a rule, attend theatrical performances.'

'It is important to me,' Dorothea said, and now she seemed to be speaking with an extreme effort, and indeed she was feeling very strange. The weeks of anxiety leading up to the hopefulness of this day, the courage she had displayed in coming here at all, the bitter disappointment of not seeing Jonah and the shock of seeing this woman instead, all had combined to numb her in a curious sort of way, and for one alarming moment she wondered if she was about to swoon, and reached towards her reticule for her vinaigrette. But then she saw

Lilith's cool and slightly mocking gaze on her and her strength came oozing back a little as she folded her hands on her lap. This woman could tell her where her Jonah was, and this was not the time to indulge her weakness, she thought in some confusion, and lifted her chin.

'It is important to me,' she said again. 'I believe you are acquainted with my son, Jonah.'

'Am I?' Lilith raised her eyebrows a little wickedly. 'If you say so, my dear Mrs Lackland, if you say so! You must understand that I am acquainted with a great many people. Indeed, as better than I have said, more people know Tom Fool than Tom Fool knows——'

'Oh, if you please, Mrs Lucas, let us not play these games of words!' Dorothea snapped and was surprised at her own sharpness. 'I know he is here somewhere for I followed your woman when she came to my house with a message from him for his sister. I did not come to upbraid you in any way or——'

'Upbraid me?' Lilith turned in her chair at that to stare directly at Dorothea and the cool mockery she had been displaying disappeared in a flare of anger. 'Upbraid me? It would take more than you, ma'am, to upbraid me! If you were to try to show me aught but the most respectful of——'

'Oh, I am sorry!' Dorothea said quickly, and closed her eyes wearily for a moment. 'I do not wish to offend you in any way. Indeed, I do not! I served you ill once, long ago, and I know it, but all I want now is to have some speech with my boy. He is so good a boy, and so very dear to me and——'

Lilith had set her head on one side and was staring at Dorothea with her eyes very bright, her snap of anger quite gone.

'You served me ill? How is that? This is the first I have heard of any disservice you ever rendered me! No one serves me ill, ma'am, without paying the full price for it! I am intrigued, Mrs Lackland, indeed I am. Do please to tell me of the *disservice* you rendered me!'

Dorothea swallowed. 'I came only to speak of Jonah——' she said piteously, but Lilith made an impatient gesture with her hand, as though she were brushing away a fly.

'We will speak of him later,' she said. 'Tell me now of this disservice of which you spoke. I am all eagerness to hear of it! You have quite captured my attention, dear Mrs Lackland, indeed you have! What could you ever have done to discommode me?'

Dorothea's face reddened. Even in her fatigue and distress she could recognize a sneer when she heard it, and she lifted her chin with a rare pride for one of her self-effacing disposition.

'I know I am not in any way as—as fascinating a person as yourself, Mrs Lucas,' she said, pulling the shreds of her dignity about her. 'But I am not completely contemptible, I believe. I am, after all, the wife of Abel. And you are not!'

Lilith raised her eyebrows at her again, and laughed, a soft and amused laugh with no hint of mockery in it.

'Is this the way in which you supposed yourself to have served me ill? My dear Mrs Lackland, I cannot imagine where came you by such a notion! I had no wish to be wed to your precious Abel, nor ever had!'

'So you say!' Dorothea heard the words flash back from her own lips in some surprise. She could never have imagined herself being so positive in conversation with anyone, let alone this sparkling creature. 'So you say, ma'am, but you must know that I am aware of the true facts, and no dissimulation by you can alter my memories of what transpired. Abel was set to wed you, until he—until he found—found there was a block in the way and——'

Lilith stared for a moment and then laughed even more loudly, throwing back her head and opening her mouth widely so that her cat-sharp tongue showed pinkly between her little white teeth. 'I know not what he told *you*, Mrs Lackland,' she said, when she had her breath back, 'but it is clear indeed it was a sad distortion of truth!'

There was an edge on her voice now, a malice in her expression that had not been there before.

'It was I who spurned his suit, I promise you, and not the other way about. And certainly not because I believed that great farrago of nonsense your stepfather had poured into his ears. Indeed, I had then, as now, a shrewd notion of its origins! Such a rubbishy tale! He was sorely bammed by it, indeed, but I was not, nor was I in the least persuaded by it to change my views of him. I can tell you that if you have been persuading yourself all these years that he chose you for your superior charms, then you have been sorely at sea! I told him straightly I was not intending to throw myself away on such a sawbones as he, and bitter indeed was his anger. Never think, Madam Lackland, that you have all these years been nurturing the love that I desired, and that you snatched your man from the great Lilith Lucas! It is quite other, I do assure you. *You* have been consoling yourself as best you may with my leavings, ma'am, and much joy you have probably had of 'em! I never yet heard of any man who found pleasure in any other woman's arms after he has known me, and it is not likely, is it, that such a one as Abel should actually prefer *you* to me? You try my intelligence and insult your own if you think otherwise!'

There was a long silence and Dorothea sat and stared at the mocking face before her, seeing it all too hatefully clearly, seeing the heart-breakingly lovely curve of the cheek and chin, the vividness of the colouring of those green eyes with their heavy black lashes and also seeing as clearly as though she looked in a mirror the pallor of her own thin cheeks, the washed out colour of her own faded blue eyes and lank hair; and she remembered with such reality that it made her skin creep beneath her gown the way Abel had been on those occasions when he had been to her as a husband should; remembered the almost despairing violence of his embraces, the roughness with which he had used her shrinking yearning body, and knew all too certainly that on every one of these occasions, few as they had been from her wedding night onwards, it was this woman's body he had wanted, this woman's soft curves and glowing skin he had ached for; and she closed her eyes in misery and pain and let Lilith's laughter, now rising triumphantly in her ears, flow over her.

But she managed to regain her voice at last and said as calmly as she could, 'Whatever may have transpired in the past, ma'am, it is of small moment now. I care not what you may think of me as—as Abel's wife, but ask only that you consider me as Jonah's mother. I do not know if you have children of your own, but I do beg you to consider, if you can, the anguish in a mother's heart!'

Lilith was leaning back in her chair now, with her hands linked behind her head in such a way that her peignoir fell open a little to display the curving swell of her breasts, and she stared at Dorothea with a look of such triumphant mockery on her face that it brought the ready colour back to Dorothea's pale cheeks.

'A mother, Mrs Lackland? Aye, I am a mother. Is that a matter upon which a woman must compliment herself? For my part, I consider it no greater an achievement than that of any cow in a field! I care more for the skill of my art than for any skill in dropping brats into the world!'

'No doubt, ma'am,' Dorothea said, and her colour deepened even more. 'I see it different, no doubt, having no such art with which to warm my self-esteem. I care for my children—for Jonah. And I ask you only to tell me of his direction, and whether he is well and—and indeed, ma'am, I have been so distressed this many weeks, not knowing of his whereabouts, and I would deem it a kindness in you if you were to put my mind at rest!'

Lilith sat and looked at her for a long moment, and then a smile curved her lips deliciously and she nodded her head slowly. 'Why to be sure, Mrs Lackland, if it means so much to you, of course I shall be of help to you! Never let it be said that Lilith Lucas is aught but kind! I can arrange for you to see your son, and will do so gladly.'

Dorothea felt a rush of relief come up in her so strongly that it was almost as though she had been put in a bath of warm water, and she leaned forwards eagerly.

'Oh, Mrs Lucas, I do thank you! He is well, I trust? He is not in any——'

'Oh, do not plague me with questions about his welfare, ma'am, I do beseech you!' Lilith turned back to her mirror and started to peer closely at her image. 'I know little enough about the ills and aches of my own brats, I assure you, without concerning myself with those of others! No, you shall see for yourself. I shall send a message to you when it is convenient for you to come to see him and——'

The relief gave way to the chill of bitter disappointment and Dorothea's face crumpled a little. 'But I would wish to see him now, and——'

'Oh, no doubt, ma'am, no doubt, but it is not convenient for me— nor perhaps for him! He has a right, after all, to decide whether or not he wishes to see you, whatever *your* wishes may be concerning him! So, I shall send you a message when it is suitable for you to pay a call——'

She yawned suddenly, wide and lazy and making no effort to hide the gape behind her hand, and stood up.

'So I will bid you goodnight, Mrs Lackland, for the present. I am tired now, and disinclined to further conversation,' and without another look at Dorothea she went across the room to disappear behind the screen in the corner; and after standing hesitantly in the middle of the room for a moment, Dorothea turned and went.

There was nothing else she could do, and at least, she told herself, as she went swaying home in the rattling old hackney-carriage the stage doorman had obtained for her, at least I know my boy is well enough. And I shall see him soon, I shall. Even if I do have to face that dreadful woman again. . . .

23

Lucy had thought carefully about how she should handle her meeting with Lilith, and decided that the best mode of approach was by surprise. To attempt to make any sort of assignation might give Mrs Lucas time to discover some facts about her would-be caller, and Lucy was well aware of the possibility that Lilith would discover the link between herself and Abel. Just as it was possible for Lucy to know of all that went on in the Town so was it possible for Lilith, for many of the same people who frequented Lucy's house frequented Lilith's Haymarket greenroom.

So, on the next morning she presented herself at the house in North Audley Street (for discovering where Lilith lived had been a simple enough matter) at the unconscionably early hour of eleven. Lucy knew that no actress was likely to set foot out of her bedchamber before the noon hour at the earliest, for rehearsals did not commence until two in the afternoon, but a healthy young man, argued Lucy to herself, was unlikely to be still keeping to his bedcurtains so late in the morning. And she had determined that he must be talked to before she confronted Mrs Lucas.

Hawks looked at her suspiciously when she came to answer the door to her summons, but let her in grudgingly enough when she demanded an audience of Mr Lackland. Indeed she had been virtually forced to do so, for as soon as the door opened Lucy had come sweeping past her into the elegant black-and-white hallway, for all the world like a lady of fashion with a right to be there.

Not that Hawks was at all bamboozled by Lucy's outfit of close-fitting blue merino cloth covered by a sober fur-trimmed pelisse. However ladylike she might dress it took more than fancy clothes to hide her origins from as knowing a Londoner as Hawks. But she had grunted a sulky acquiescence to Lucy's firm demand for audience of the young Mr Lackland, and left her standing in the hall while she went toiling up the stairs to call him.

But she stopped at Lilith's bedchamber on her way to Jonah's room, thinking it worth risking Lilith's rage (for nothing made her so irascible as being called too early from her sleep) to acquaint her of her protégé's visitor; and she had been right to do so, for Lilith, although she had started by cursing her for the disturbance finished by nodding sharply and thanking her for the knowledge and telling her to show the woman into the small drawing-room. And satisfied, Hawks continued on up the stairs to summon Jonah to his caller.

He was lying on the bed in his room, fully dressed but disinclined to leave its privacy, for he had much to think of. Ever since that magical hour spent with Celia in the stacked scenery his mind had been in a turmoil. When he had been with her he had not doubted for one moment that he cared more for her than for her mother, but now they were apart it was Lilith's face and figure that occupied his mind's eye, and Lilith's voice that filled his inner ear. Celia was there in his imaginings in her childish white gown and with her hair tumbling undressed about her shoulders, looking at him gravely with her wide eyes, but in the background it was Lilith who glittered most in the centre of his private stage; yet when he made the effort to think of Celia, remembered the way she had felt in his arms there in the cold darkness, he was filled with such a warmth, such a sense of comfort that it wrapped itself about his soul like a woollen blanket.

Oh, if only, if *only* he had never clapped eyes on Lilith Lucas, he thought petulantly, throwing himself from the bed to stamp across the room to the window, there to stare moodily out at the eternal greyish slush that filled the street below; if only! But then, his secret voice whispered in his ear, then you would not have seen Celia either, and it is Celia who loves you so dear, and who makes you feel so important, so valuable, so *manlike*.

In the midst of all this thinking and confusion it was a relief to see Hawks's sour face at his door, and the message, delivered in her usual terse and insolent manner, that there was a visitor awaiting him in the small drawing-room intrigued him most agreeably.

He, to have a visitor here? Who could it possibly be? For one mad moment he wondered if it were Mr Castleton come to call in a lather of excitement about his play, to tell him it was a work of genius and was to be set to rehearsal forthwith; but even his hopeful and romantic soul could not long sustain so large a fantasy, and more practically he opened his mouth to ask Hawks who it might be.

But she had gone stamping away, and he could only take himself down the stairs, his mood temporarily banished by his conjecturing. Could it be Abby, perhaps, who had managed to find out his direction, and who had come with some urgent message from home?

Conjecture sharpened into anxiety and he hurried his steps to go rushing impetuously into the small drawing-room, and stopped sharply at the door, his brows creased with puzzlement at the sight of the large woman who awaited him there, sitting stiffly in one of the small gilt chairs the room contained, and bidding fair to either overflow it or cause it to collapse under her vast bulk.

She, for her part, looked up at his tempestuous entrance and at once her face softened. It was as though her very own likely lad were standing there, she thought fondly, looking at that tall, spare, yet muscular frame and the long white face with the narrow green eyes under the dark curly hair; it was as though a score or so of years had been peeled away from her life to bring back those happy uncomplicated days when Abel had been a contented medical student always running to her to tell her in great excitement of his prowess in the operating theatre, of his successes in the wards. And almost without thinking she creaked to her feet and went across the room to take the startled young man beside the door in her great arms and hug him till his very ribs cracked.

He pulled himself away from her in enraged surprise, his face scarlet with mortification.

'Good God, ma'am, you forget yourself! Who—how—I—dammit, ma'am, I do not know you!'

She laughed at that, a thick gurgling laugh that bubbled in her throat.

'Well, mayhap you don't, or think you don't, an' you must forgive an old woman for bein' so free in 'er ways! Lucy was never one to mind 'er manners, an' I knows *you*, even if you don't remember the fact. And you've such a look of your Pa as made me forget meself for the moment——'

His brows snapped together at that, and he turned towards the door as though to go, but immediately she put a heavy hand on his arm and pulled him back.

'Oh, for Gawd's sake, lad, don't go gettin' yerself into a state of excitement just because I mentioned yer Pa! 'E don't know you're 'ere, nor shall if I 'ave aught to do with it. I told you, I——'

He had turned his head to look at her, and now memory was stirring in him. 'Did you say—what did you say your name was?'

She grinned comfortably at him, displaying her rotting teeth with great equanimity. 'Beginnin' to come to an understandin', are you? Lucy, my boy, that's 'oo I am. Lucy. Now don't tell me you ain't 'eard of me on account of I know better——'

'Aye, I've heard of you,' he said slowly, and now his curiosity overtook him and he moved into the room after her, as she made her way back to her chair. 'Nancy told me of you. But why do you come to see me here? And how did you know I was here and not at Gower Street, and why——'

'Nay, lad, save yer questions!' She lowered herself, grunting, into the chair, and disposed herself as comfortably as she could. 'My Gawd, but you lives miserably uncomfortable 'ere, if this is the best you got in chairs to rest yer weary visitor's bones! Still, what do you expect of such as 'er——'

Jonah frowned at that. 'If you speak so of my—my benefactress and hostess, ma'am, I must ask you to——'

'Lawks a'mussy me!' she said, and threw her head back and laughed hugely. 'Such a punctilious lad as my Abel 'as managed to rear, an' no error! All right, lad, not a word more about 'er furniture.' She sobered suddenly, and put out her hand and grasped his wrist tightly, so that he almost winced. 'But there's some things as 'ave got to be said, and you'll 'ear 'em, be you displeased with what I got to say or not, do you understand me? I'm 'ere on account I loves yer Pa, and 'as for a long time, and I loves 'im too well to start meddlin' in any troubles between the two of you in any way that'll make those troubles worser. But if I can see a way to 'elp you, then 'elp you I will, on account of you're the spittin' image o' my Abel, and on account of—well, on account of that's 'ow Lucy is. Now, is there any can 'ear us and what we're saying? Because what I got to say is for your ears, and none other. I'm takin' one 'ell of a chance as it is in talkin' to you, for there's no guarantee you won't go rushin' off to tell Madam up there all I says. But I'm 'opin', when you've 'eard me out, you'll have more sense nor that. Now, are you sure we're private in 'ere? Is there any in the next room?' and she jerked her head towards the half-opened double door that led to the large drawing-room beyond.

He shook his head, completely mystified. 'There are none abroad at this hour of the morning, for this is a house of theatre people, and they keep different hours to those of most others. I wish you will come to a point, ma'am, for I am——'

'Oh, I'll come to a point,' Lucy said grimly. 'Get yerself a chair and come and sit close where you can 'ear without me 'avin' to shout like the town-crier——'

Bemused and obedient he did so; and in the large drawing-room Lilith breathed softly and came back from the doorway to the hall towards which she had fled when she heard Lucy's question about being overheard, and came quietly back to her place behind the panels of the linking doors. From this vantage-point she could see as well as hear them through the narrow crack by the jamb.

Lucy was staring at the boy who was sitting stiffly embarrassed in a chair beside her, and after a moment she sighed gustily.

'Oh, but you're that like 'im!' she said. ' 'Tis no wonder you two's been at daggers drawn so long! It's my bet you're like 'im in more than just the cut of yer jib, an' that's why you don't get on——'

'If you mean my father, ma'am,' Jonah said stiffly, 'I must tell you that any likeness in our physiognomy is not matched by any likeness of —of character. I am a—I would wish to be a poet, and write for my bread, while my father is set on quite different lines. I would not have you think that I chose to relinquish my family ties for any foolish reason, such as childish disagreements with my father. Our—our quarrel was based on matters of real importance, and——'

'Oh, I know that!' Lucy said comfortably. 'Wanted you to be a surgeon like 'im, and you wouldn't 'ave none of it. But that's what I mean, lad! You're cut out of the same cloth, you an' yer Pa, for didn't Jesse Constam want to make a spice man of 'im, and didn't 'e fight and argue and get 'is own way to make himself the surgeon 'e is? It's like I said. Peas from the same pod, the pair of yer. You'll be a poet and writer or whatever it is you fancy, just as 'e ran his life 'is way, an' always will. Never fear that——'

He felt the warmth of her encompassing him, felt the sense of approval with which she looked at him, and relaxed a little, and she grinned her great affectionate toothless grin at him again, and he could not help but smile back.

'I'm glad you think so,' he said. 'For I often wonder, myself, if I will ever have the chance to do as I wish and——'

'Well, that's why I'm 'ere.' She was brisk suddenly, and leaned forwards heavily, dropping her voice a little. 'On account I think you're in a very likely way to scupper yerself for good an' all, if you don't get out of this 'ere 'ouse and away from that madam as you calls your *benefactress* and *'ostess.'*

At once he was all stiffness and suspicion again, and she shook her head impatiently at the way his shoulders came up and his face hardened. 'No!' she said sharply. 'Don't you go lookin' at me so affronted, not till you 'ear what I got to say to you. This woman, this Lilith Lucas you're so set on regardin' as one as cares for your good, is one as cares for naught but 'erself. I knows that for a fact, boy, and you're all kinds of a fool if you don't take the evidence as is offered to you!'

'What evidence?' he snapped. 'It will take much to convince me she's anything but kind and good, for she gave me shelter when I most needed it, and is to see my work set upon the stage as soon as maybe ——'

But he had to stifle his sudden sharp awareness of the weeks of frustration that lay behind him, of the way Lilith's caprices so often set him from the heights of delight one moment to the depths of the most abject misery the next, had to push away his recollections of Celia's impassioned anger towards her mother; and some of this must have shown upon his face, for at once Lucy said triumphantly, 'Ah! Then you ain't so sure as you was! You've seen 'ow she picks up people an' sucks 'em dry and chucks 'em over 'er shoulder like a lump of orange peel! Are you set to be another piece of 'er rubbish?'

'You spoke of evidence,' he said shortly. 'What evidence?'

She shrugged, for she was improvising now, casting around in her mind for whatever she could think of that would loosen the boy from Lilith's side. 'Why, the evidence of all that I've 'eard said of 'er these past seventeen years or more—the whole of your lifetime, my lad, and then some! She's clawed 'er way from nowhere, riding up to the top of 'er tree on other people's backs—aye, and by lyin' flat on her own.'

She laughed raucously, then, making Jonah wince a little.

'She's the sort as looks very disdainful on such as my girls, callin' them tails and cheap whores, but I'll tell you this much—my girls take no more from a man than 'is money and they gives 'im real kindness in return as well as a little simple pleasure. But this one— why, she's not above takin' their money, but takes their souls besides, *and* lets 'em think she loves 'em and regards 'em 'igh, and altogether robs the best of 'em of all their wits! She's not fit for the name of honest whore, for girls like mine are warm with the goodness of their 'earts, and gives more the world than ever they takes from it, and Christ, but who should know that better'n me! But this one does nothing but destroy——' Her face had darkened, and Jonah, looking at her, felt some of his initial revulsion at her words give way to a very real curiosity.

'How, destroy?' he said. 'What is it makes you so sore against her?'

She lifted her eyebrows a little, and said shortly, 'She destroys men's 'appiness. She sets about to beguile 'em, and enslave 'em, and that's all very well upon a stage, for that is what a stage is for, but she takes it off the stage and sets 'er cap at any man she feels like spoilin', and makes 'im so beset that 'e don't know if 'e's on 'is 'ead or 'is 'eels. When I remember 'ow your Pa was in the days before she came back into 'is life, and 'ow he's bin ever since——'

He drew a sharp breath at that, and she stopped and looked at him anxiously. Had she gone too far? She had not meant to say so much but a sudden vision of Abel's face, as it had been yesterday, of the misery on it as sharp and new as it had been back in the days when this woman had first found a way to hurt him, had risen in her mind's eye, and her anger had moved hotly within her, and made the words spill out.

'My father knows—has been close acquainted with Mrs Lucas?'

'Aye, lad,' she said simply, ''e's known 'er longer'n you've bin on this earth.'

There was a silence and then when he did speak again his voice was thin and tight and very controlled.

'How close acquainted were they? And was it before—before or since he and my Mama—I mean——' he faltered. 'She said he had been surgeon to the theatre once but I thought she must have been in error.'

She shrugged at that. 'That was true enough. As of 'ow close acquainted they was—well, 'e knew her well enough to make 'im fair beside 'imself when—oh, it's not seemly that you should know all of 'is affairs nor that I should speak so to you of your Mama and 'im! Let be, let be, lad. Take my word for it that Lilith Lucas is a bad woman, a cruel woman, and means you no good. It's my guess 'er interest in you is as much a part of whatever it was 'appened all those years ago, and—well, all I can say is that if you let 'er go on twistin' you around her finger the way she so plainly is you're playin' a game to please 'er an' doin' yerself no good at all. Take Lucy's word for it, young Jonah, will yer? Can you see me as your friend, and believe me when I tells you you'll save yourself and your family much misery if you walks out of this 'ouse this very day?'

She was leaning forwards now and entreating him with great earnestness in her eyes. 'You can come to me, if so be you can't bring yerself to go back to yer own 'ome, and I dare say we can arrange matters there to please all you prideful Lacklands well enough. Just leave 'ere, my boy, will yer? Don't go digging around in ancient history, but take old Lucy's word for it, and go——'

He shook his head stiffly, still sitting there upright and rather absurd in the little gilt chair.

'I think, ma'am, that I must make my own decisions about the matter you have brought to my attention here today,' he said very carefully. 'You will forgive me now, I trust, if I ask you to take your leave, for I must——'

She shook her head at that. 'No, lad, for I 'ave further business in this 'ouse. I 'ave to talk to Madam 'erself—no, don't fly up into your 'igh trees, for Gawd's sake!' for he had jumped to his feet and was frowning at her with great ferocity. 'The business I 'ave to settle with 'er 'as naught to do wi' you at all, except inasmuch as it affects yer Pa.'

Jonah was still looking very black, and she shook her head irritably. 'Oh, you're a disbelievin' young devil! I tell you, I'm on an errand for yer Pa to do with property for 'is 'ospital! There's 'ouses to be bought and sold and—well, enough. It's naught to do wi' you, and the less anyone knows the better. All I ask of you now, boy, is to believe I spoke to you out o' nothin' but true affection for you. I saw you first when you was but a baby, and a lovely little creature you was, to be sure! I reckon I could be as stupid fond of you as I've been of yer Pa all these dunnamany years, given 'alf the chance. Just believe me, boy, ask no more questions, and get away! You can come to me at Panton Street—next to Tom Cribb's, I am—at any time, and be welcome too, and not a word would I say to yer Pa if you didn't want it. I'll say no more! I've said more'n enough already, I reckon, so set I am on gettin' you away from 'ere, but I won't insult you by askin' you to 'old your tongue about aught I've said. Whatever grudge you may 'old against your Pa there's no call for you to go blabbin' and damaging any business affairs 'im an' me might be involved in, and I'm sure you knows it. So, boy!' She grinned up at him, her head on one side and her face filled with a warmth that was hard to resist. 'We'll say good-bye for the present, eh? I've done all I can for you, and must speak to your what-yer-call-it—benefactress and 'ostess. If you'll be so good as to tell 'er she's got a visitor, I'd be grateful. Don't want that frosty-chopped old bitch as opened the door to me tellin' 'er as 'ow I spoke to you first, do we? No——'

In the large drawing-room Lilith moved softly, closing the door to the hallway behind her very carefully and reaching the staircase to run swiftly to her room before Jonah had even reached the hall door of the small drawing-room. When he arrived in her boudoir with the message that there was a visitor for her in the small drawing-room, she was sitting up on her chaise-longue, looking as serene and rested as though she had not moved from it for the past hour.

24

She had come straight back to North Audley Street after the performance, refusing to see any of her followers in the greenroom—much to their chagrin—and now she was sitting beside the fire in her boudoir, a tray of her favourite bread and butter and hot chocolate beside her, staring at the leaping licking flames and thinking.

She was hard put to it to explain to herself why she felt as she did. That she, the great Lilith Lucas, could be as put out of countenance by a man as she had been by Abel Lackland amazed her. In all the years since she had left infancy behind she had used her charm and her beauty and her wit to bend people to her will. From Fitch and French John and Barliman onwards (and her lips curved as she remembered them, and the times she had gone with them to midnight graveyards in search of surgeon's fodder) men had been her creatures to be used as was needful and all of them had been more than willing to be so used; so she had never had to feel any concern for what happened to them afterwards.

Celia's father had not been the only one to have died for love of her, but whenever she had heard of such an outcome to the life of one of her lovers she had shrugged and murmured polite condolences, but felt nothing more than impatience. If men were fools enough to hang about her gawping like great mooncalves and then to perish of their affliction, that was their affair, she would tell herself.

But Abel was different. Sitting there on that winter night in North Audley Street she cast her mind back to the time when she had first met him, there in the stews of Seven Dials, recalled the nights they had spent cosy and contented in her little cellar room in Old Compton Street, and marvelled at the way the memory of him was so fresh in her mind, even though she had not set eyes on him these seventeen years. Not since the day, in fact, when he had come to her with that mad tale he had been fed by Jesse Constam and Dorothea, and she had scoffed, but still had offered him her friendship, and he had—but she pulled her mind away from that. She had offered him so much and he had had the temerity to refuse it, because it was not enough, and the memory of that insult still rankled too much to be willingly paraded again before her mind's eye.

She felt the old sharp-edged anger burn in her again, and let it happen, relishing it. It was interesting to experience such a sensation, she thought, for in all conscience she felt little enough these days. There was the high pleasure of money, still, of course; she could glow most agreeably as yet another set of deeds were stored away in her escritoire, and prolong the glow for many days at a time. There was also the pleasure of seeing yet another man fall prey to her eyes and her body and her wicked sideways smile, but that was a very transient satisfaction, after all, and soon gave way to ennui and irritation, both of which were sensations she abhorred and which were altogether too like the emotions aroused in her by her children. This anger she felt now, however, was interesting, and she sat there in the firelight and fed it with consideration of Abel as he had been—and Jonah as he was now.

And at that thought she gave herself a saucy smile and stretched a little. It may have started as little more than another foolish conquest, with the small added piquancy of the boy having been so obviously Abel's get; but it was fast becoming much more amusing. Not only was Celia besotted by him (and at the thought of Celia she felt again that stab of irritation that so filled her whenever she saw her daughter, with her insolent face and her breasts straining against the muslin of her gowns; she had no *right* to be so) but the boy was mightily attractive. Those lean shanks of his and the tight buttocks in the fashionably cut trousers could move her in a way that was all too rare, for although there were many men who could—and indeed did—melt for want of her, there were few indeed, over the years, who had been able to do as much for her bored flesh.

And now, as things were falling out, the situation promised more, much more. Jonah's arrival at the Haymarket may have been merely fortuitous but what had happened since and was going to happen in the future was in her control, and would remain so. She smiled again as she contemplated matters as they now stood, and relishing the dramatic potential of it all fell to planning how she would further exploit it.

It was an hour later, when she had come to her decision and had set matters in train, that she stood up and stretched and laughed aloud, softly, before going to her dressing-table to scent herself, to brush her hair to a gentle softness, and to pinch extra rosiness into her cheeks with a practised twist of thumb and forefinger.

She had written two letters. The first, to Dorothea, had been easy to compose and well to the point. She had bade her come to North Audley Street on the following Friday afternoon, at half an hour past four o'clock, when she, Mrs Lucas, would be happy to give Mrs Lackland news of the Person in whom she was interested, and on whose Behalf she had come to the theatre so recently.

The second letter had not been quite so easy, but after some struggles and false starts she completed a missive that pleased her well enough to be sanded dry and folded and sealed.

'Dear Abel,' she had written. 'I trust you will forgive so Informal a manner of address from One with whom you have had no intercourse for Many Years. I use it since it would Fall Ill from my pen to address you in any other way, for I bear Tender Memories of our Old Friendship, and could not be Formal with one whom I have known since my Earliest Childhood, and who is indeed my Oldest Friend, despite the Regrettable Lapse in our communication with each other. I write to you now to Chide you a little, for it is a matter of Some Pain to me that you found it in your Heart to be Devious with so Old a Friend. To send to me your Messenger with some foolish tale about wishing to Buy my Property in Endell Street for herself is not kind in you, when in truth it is *You* that require the house for Purposes of your own connected with your Hospital (you see that I have much Information about your Doings!). In Short, Dear Abel, despite the woman's Loud Protestations and most Skilful Prevarications I am perfectly convinced that the Property in Question that she was so eager to purchase is one that is required by *You*. This being so, I must tell you I deal only with Principals, and refuse quite purposefully to sell to your Messenger. However, I would not wish it thought that I would stand in the way of any Honest Business, and will gladly treat with You in the matter of this Property. If so be I am Right—and I have every

Reason to suppose that I am—and you are Enamoured of this House and wishful to buy it, you will come to me at my house in North Audley Street, the afternoon of Friday at four o'clock to discuss the matter. You will not find me Difficult, I promise you, for even though in Matters of Business I am most efficient and indeed Manlike, in matters of Friendship I am all Malleability. It would give me much Pleasure, I do assure you, to sell you this House as an Earnest of my Never Ending Interest in you and your Wellbeing.'

Standing now before her mirror and looking at herself in the soft candlelight, she imagined how it would be the next morning when Hawks delivered both her letters to the same house, and hugged herself with pleasure. Would they tell each other? Of course they would not! They would make their several ways to her, and she would play her game with Abel, and then they would see each other and it would be all most amusing and delightful. But now there was more to be considered. 'Much more,' she whispered to her reflection in the mirror and then picked up a candle in a crystal stick, and went softly across her room to open the door and go out into the hallway.

Hawks had doused all the other lights in the house when she had gone to bed a couple of hours earlier and the house lay heavy and silent in a darkness broken only by the pale light of her single candle, and she stood still for a moment with her head up, listening.

It was as though she could hear the house itself breathing all around her, and she let her pleasure in her ownership of the bricks and mortar, the slates and wooden beams, the glass and metal and upholstery that made up the house and its contents wash over her. All this was the very core of her life, more important than the children she had borne, all of whom were also breathing somewhere in this dark silence, more important even than the theatre; for although night after night and performance after performance she made that triumphantly her own, could bring a whole audience to its feet with applause and approbation, she did not own the theatre nor the people in it the way she owned this house, and others like it. Oh, it was good to be Lilith Lucas, she thought, taking a deep breath of sheer pleasure, better than being anyone else!

She moved wraithlike along the Turkey carpet of the hall, letting her fingers stroke the white panelling as she went, moved on past the door behind which small Ben slept the damp helplessly deep sleep of the very young, and Hawks the thin, watchful sleep of the middle-aged, and then past Lyddy and Celia's room.

She paused there for a moment, and looked at the door and thought of Celia lying in the darkness beyond, her hair thrown in a tangle in the pillow as it always was, and remembered the times when Celia had been a charming plump baby and she had crept in to stand beside her bed and marvel at the prettiness of her; but that had been long ago, before she had become so changed, so sly, with her tallness and her slenderness and her—Lilith hardened her mouth and moved away, leaving the darkness to wash over the door behind her as she made her still silent way to the stairs that led to the floor above.

Jonah had been lying awake for a long time, it seemed to him. The whole household had gone early to bed, picking up from Lilith her mood of preoccupation; Hawks glad enough to have the chance, for with her responsibilities for Lilith's household and Lilith's capricious hours she was chronically short of sleep, and Jonah because he had needed to be alone; Celia, disconsolately aware that something was amiss with Jonah, but unable to get him alone at any point at which to ask him what was disturbing him, had miserably followed suit and was also lying in bed on the floor below, listening to Lyddy's easy breathing beside her and worrying and wondering about her Jonah.

But Jonah was not thinking about Celia, nor, for once, of himself. He had been more shaken than he would have thought possible by the revelation that his father and Lilith had been close acquainted. He had long since forgotten the fact that Lilith had seemed to know his father the first time he had spoken to her, but Lucy's embarrassment and anxiety had communicated much to him, much more than her actual words, and now he was bewildered.

He tried to imagine it, tried to see his father in love, as besotted with Lilith as he himself had been, tried to imagine them in conversation, tried to see his father with a smiling face, animated by affection, tried to see them in embrace——

He turned over in bed again, restlessly, the sheets tangling themselves about his legs, and his nightshirt rucking up around his waist, and tried to force his thoughts to a new mould. He would plan a new play. No, a poem. A poem about the theatre—Fair Portals of Terpsichore's Muse, Where All Who Would the Dance Adore, Where Joy Shall be As——

Again he turned in his bed and swore softly under his breath. It could not be as Lucy had said! Could it? His father who, for all his life that he could remember, had been a dour man interested only in his work, in his hospital, and occasionally in Abby for whom alone he had been known to smile, his father who so filled him with fear and despair that—such a man, in love? It was unthinkable.

He tried then to see how his father might have been before, when he was young himself. He had not always been the responsible father of a large family, after all, Jonah told himself reasonably. Once he had been a boy, had been a pupil at the same school as Jonah himself. Had been a student. Had been *young*.

But it was no use. All Jonah could see in his imagination was a smaller version of his father; smaller, but not in any real way any younger. It was impossible to see him ever yearning for anything. Or any-body——

Again Jonah turned restlessly in his bed, thumping the pillow beneath his head, and then he stiffened and remained very still, staring at the door. He had caught a momentary glimpse of light beneath it, and puzzled, he sat up and called softly, 'Is anyone there?'

In a corner of his mind a small voice whispered 'Celia?' and he felt his heart lift at that. Indeed, it would be good to talk to Celia of what had happened with Lucy that morning, good to ask her if she thought it at all possible that Abel and Lilith had ever been intimately acquainted. And he quite forgot that Lilith was Celia's mother, and that Celia might therefore be as perturbed as he by talking of the matter, and slid out of his bed, feeling his feet curl against the rough coldness of the floor, to go padding over to the door to open it, expecting to see Celia outside with a candle in her hand——

'Dear Jonah!' Lilith breathed, and slipped past him to put her candlestick down on the walnut bureau against the wall, and he turned and stared at her, his mouth half-open.

'Please to shut the door, my dear boy,' she murmured, and smiled, and obediently he pushed the door behind him so that it clicked and closed, and then stood there with his back to the panels, suddenly very aware of his rumpled hair and startled expression and above all of his nightshirt and bare legs and feet.

She sat herself down on his bed and laughed up at him, her mouth dimpling.

'Don't look so alarmed, my dear Jonah! Did I awaken you? No, to be sure I did not! I know the look of one who has lain awake for a long time. Poor Jonah! Is something concerning you, and fretting you? You must not let it, not when you have me for a friend! Come and sit down and tell me what it is that is filling your mind with such anxiety that it shows upon your face so clearly!'

For one mad moment he felt he wanted to do more than that, wanted to throw himself at her feet, and set his hands over hers in her lap and pour out all that was worrying him, for who else could tell him better than she if it were true, if his own father had——

But he did not do so. He moved instead to come and sit down on the bed beside her, but with a gingerly care in his movements, and with a controlled air about him that made her eyes glitter momentarily.

'You do not *have* to speak to me of your worries, Jonah!' she said lightly. 'I offer you merely the ear of friendship should you need it. I came, indeed, to speak to you not of whatever it is that might be worrying you, but of a concern of my own—the play, and of your part in it——' and she lifted limpid eyes to his face, and set one hand on his lap and he was uncomfortable suddenly for he had not realized he had sat down so close beside her. He thought to move away, but it was difficult, and besides the enchantment that she could so easily weave began to steal over him. She was so very soft, even to look at, and smelled so delicious that it made him think she would be as good to taste, and how agreeable it would be to take that soft hand in his and sink his teeth into the pink roundness of that part just below the wrist.

He swallowed, and looked away from those gleaming green eyes and said awkwardly, 'I hope you do not regret giving me the role, ma'am. For my part, I think myself uncommon clumsy in the playing of it and——'

'You must not call me ma'am, Jonah!' she said softly, 'But Lilith! I told you we are friends, did I not? And friends should not be so formal with each other, but be close and affectionate——' and she moved quite deliberately now and sat so close that her hair was against his cheek, and her face so near to his that he could feel the warmth from her skin enveloping him, and she pouted a little, and he found his gaze had dropped to her mouth, and he could not take it away, for she was holding it half-open with her tongue caught between her teeth and pointing at him from one corner, and he felt his own teeth clench a little as sensation began to move across his belly and the small of his back.

He moved quite suddenly, almost hurling himself away from her and holding his nightshirt absurdly to his sides, and she leaned back and laughed at him, her eyes twinkling and merry in the candlelight.

'Oh, my dear Jonah!' she said, and laughed again. 'Do not stand so! You look for all the world like an old man who fears his pockets are about to be picked! It is not your pockets I am interested in, nor indeed in any of your garments——' and then she had moved and was standing next to him, close in front of him, her hands on his face as they had been that night in Cremorne Gardens; and her touch had the same effect on him, making his whole body move and flex and tighten itself under his thin nightshirt, and he felt his face flame with the shame of it as he realized that under the thin frilled white wrapper she was wearing she was as naked as he was, for he could feel her body against his, and what was more alarming to him, could feel his own body moving against hers with an urgency he would not have thought possible.

And in his bewilderment and young ignorance he tried to move back, putting his arms about her at the same time in an effort to hold away from his own body her infinitely disturbing shape, but that only had the effect of pushing him into an embrace with her that made their bodies fit together like spoons in a drawer. Her mouth was very near his, now, and he could feel her breath on his lips, and altogether he did not know quite whether he stood upon his feet or upon the back of his neck; and they swayed and moved together towards the bed, as she seemed to fall backwards upon it.

Behind them the door moved and creaked and he tried to turn his head to see what was happening but somehow he could not, for Lilith had her arms about his neck in such a way that the only thing he could do was kiss her. And he did, with a sort of helpless, self-hating yet hungry eagerness that filled him with such confusion that it was as though he was himself and his father too and she was herself and also Celia.

Celia had heard the first creaking sound some five or ten minutes earlier and had lifted her head to listen and then sat bolt upright and listened again. Once more she heard it; footsteps and the faint creaks of floorboards above her. Her spirits lifted suddenly. He was as awake

228

as she, and miserable too, for he was walking about his room restless and unable to sleep. Which was absurd while she lay here below in so much the same case!

She would go to him, and they would sit and talk and hold each other as they had that afternoon and be happy together. Eagerly she had gone speeding barefooted up the stairs, wearing only her bedgown and not bothering to light a candle, for she could see well enough in the dim starlight from the landing window, and anyway lighting a candle might throw too much illumination and waken her Mama, and that was the last thing she wished to have happen.

She had actually said aloud, 'Jonah! I heard you, my love, and I cannot sleep either!' after she had pushed open his door and seen them wrapped tightly in each other's arms, for it took an appreciable time for her to actually encompass what was happening before her eyes. She saw her mother with her wrapper half off her shoulders, and her breasts rising and falling heavily in the candlelight, saw his long legs bare beneath his rumpled nightshirt, and said again, stupidly, 'I cannot sleep either.'

And then he moved, scrambling awkwardly to his feet, but her mother only lay there against the crumpled sheets and laughed and laughed and laughed.

25

Abby sat in the office at the back of the shop, biting her thumb and staring unwinkingly at the wall before her. The ledgers lay on the desk in front of her, but it was no use; she would not be able to concentrate on them until she had seen James, and had been able to talk to him and make some sort of a plan. So, as always when she had the opportunity now, she remembered that time they had spent in each other's arms on the sofa behind her, and smiled secretly at the thoughts and sensations that moved in her.

He came to the door so quietly that she did not hear him and he could stand there looking at her, taking in the sight of her as though it were in some way as sustaining as food and drink, filling his whole being with her. He could not have said what it was about her that was so satisfying to him, for love her though he did, he could not call her beautiful, not in the way that many of the fashionable women who came into the shop were beautiful. Her face was too round, her figure too sensible, her features too ordinary for her to be regarded thus; and yet in his eyes she was breathtaking in her loveliness, and the sight of her sitting there with her elbow set on the desk and her thumb so childishly set between her teeth made him ache with pleasure.

She sensed him there, even though he made no movement, and turned her head slowly and her eyes filled with a tenderness that washed over his tired bones like a blessing, and he smiled.

'My love,' she said, 'I was waiting for you.' And had she poured out a million words of passionate sensuality, had she hurled herself at his feet in a paroxysm of desire she could not have displayed her love for him more clearly, and he breathed deeply and contentedly and came in, dropping his coat on the chair beside the door.

'I came as soon as may be,' he said, and now it was her turn to find his commonplace words filled with messages of love and need and satisfaction, and she put out her hand and touched his softly, and he sat down beside her and for a little while they remained there, silent and content.

But she moved at last and said, 'I think we must make some sort of arrangement, must we not, James? We must consider every eventuality, and besides——' she smiled then and touched his hand again. 'I *wish* to make a plan for us.'

He nodded. 'I have thought with great care, of course, Abby. I do not think you have been out of my mind for two minutes together since—since last we were here. Are you well, my dearest one? Are you happy?'

She took a deep breath and lifted her chin and sat so for a moment with her eyes closed, and her head tipped back, and then looked at him and nodded. 'I am very happy, and very well,' she said deliberately. 'And, oh, so glad! I was afraid you might be castigating yourself, and be having some foolish regrets and I could not bear it if——'

He shook his head at that. 'I have none. Oh, indeed, I have been feeling much repentance and anxiety ever since, but—no, my own, hear me out—but not because of what happened. Because I was so *glad* it had happened, do you see, because I knew it in my heart to be all as it should be and yet knew with my mind and reason that I ought to be filled with remorse for having damaged you and hurt you——'

'But you did not damage or hurt me,' she said. 'How could you? There could be nothing but—but true virtue in our encounter, just as there always will be——'

'Oh, I know this, as well as you do, my love, but you and I do not make the whole world. There will be those who will censure us greatly if—who would consider me a most wicked man, and you a—oh my love, I have been thinking myself to a standstill! A plan we *must* decide upon and that soon, for I would not have aught occur to cause you the slightest uneasiness, or to allow any future—any slur upon your good name'

She laughed softly. 'You must not fret yourself so, James! I have thought too, and it is clear to me that we must take ourselves away and be wed in the first possible place where it is permitted. I do not know much of these matters, but I believe that we can be tied over the anvil at Gretna Green, if we can but get there and——'

He laughed fondly at that. 'Have you been reading popular romances, my love, to think of that? I thought you scorned them.'

She reddened a little. 'Indeed, I do scorn them, but it is not from such a source I obtained this information. I—I told Miss Ingoldsby this morning a Banbury tale about a customer that came to the shop enquiring about such matters and asked her to discover the law for me.'

She blushed even more. 'I told Miss Ingoldsby that the lady who asked was very young, and—and was in a delicate condition, although unwed, and Miss Ingoldsby was seized of compassion, as I knew she would be, and engaged to discover for my mythical customer what she should do. She said she believed the answer that would serve best was Gretna Green, but she would, she was sure, know for me by tomorrow.'

He put an arm about her shoulders and hugged her briefly. 'It was well thought of, but not necessary, I believe. I have been most busy, I promise you! To commence, I have been considering the matter of our—of making a living. You must understand, Abby, that I have no fortune, and only my trade to——'

'Hush!' She set her finger upon his lips, and smiled. 'If I had been the sort of female to care about such matters as competences and marriage portions, I assure you we should not find ourselves in this situation now. I would have set my cap at some moneyed citizen long since, had I been such a one!'

'I know,' he said. 'But matters of economy *are* to be thought of, and we cannot live on air! It is not enough to arrange a wedding. We must think beyond that.'

She nodded soberly. 'That is true, and I must confess I have few ideas on the matter, apart from throwing ourselves upon the goodwill of my father. And that——'

'—is not to be thought of.' James said firmly. 'Not for any reason of pride, which would be foolishness, but because it would be a waste of effort. He would not for one moment countenance such a match, and would assuredly do all he could to actively oppose it, and well we both know it.'

She nodded and looked at him with an uncharacteristic timidity. 'Dear James, what are we to do? I—generally, you know, I contrive to find an answer to all the problems that beset members of my family. I have long enjoyed a reputation for practicality and good sense, but in this situation of my own I must confess myself quite at a standstill. I have great need of you, James, to decide what we should do. Can you contrive, my love?'

'Indeed, I can, and it is right and proper that it should not be a matter upon which you need distress yourself,' he said, and it was as though he drew strength from the words, for he straightened his shoulders and his thin face took on a better colour than its usual muddy pallor. 'Now, I will tell you what I have done, and I trust you will find it to your taste.'

He hesitated then. 'I must tell you that it—well, not to put too fine a point upon it, it is against your father's interests. But I thought in the situation as it is that your interests—and with it mine, together with those of—of any progeny we may have—were paramount, and the shop is not after all your father's prime concern. So I hope you will not be too put out by what I have done.'

'I doubt I will be,' she said calmly. 'I have a great affection for my father, James, as well you know, and if I am permitted so to do will always display to him my regard and daughterly interest. But I am a different person now. No longer Abigail the daughter of Abel, but Abigail the wife of James.'

'As soon as may be——' he said with a tightening of his voice and took her hand in his and kissed it with great fervour, and she smiled down at his bent head and said, 'But I already am, James, anm't I? I regard myself so. Any ceremony is to me now a mere irrelevance, only needful for the opinion of other people. In our own eyes we are more than handfast—we are soulfast, and I ask no more. If you told me we could not be properly wed but must live together as we are, I would be content to do so. I need no other sacrament than the one we have already celebrated.'

'You are a brave and good girl, my love,' he said. 'But I must take more consideration than this. So, to what I have done——'

He hesitated, and then stood up and began to move about the room, not looking at her. 'I know my health to be in some way precarious. No, I wish we would not talk about it in any detail. Suffice it to say that for some time now I have had these symptoms, and since none can put a name to the condition from which they arise, I must assume I will have them always, for however long always may be. So, it is incumbent upon me to make such arrangements as are needed not only for—for the present, but for all future eventualities. So——' He looked at her now, his face very serious. 'I have told you but little of the history of this plan upon which I have been working for your father these many months. The manufactory for medicines. Has your father told you aught of it?'

She frowned. 'We have not spoken much of it, except that your preoccupation with it all was to make Jonah's presence here necessary—which is, after all, why I am here.' She smiled suddenly, a brilliant smile of pure happiness. 'We have much to be grateful for in the existence of the manufactory, have we not, James? For without it, we would not have been able to spend so much happy time together——'

'We will have more to be grateful for than even that,' he said, and came to sit close beside her again. 'The machinery in the manufactory at Wapping—you must know that the designs for it are mine, that the original ideas for the making of medicines in large quantities as we do there were mine—in short, although it is your father who put the matter in hand, I am the originator of much of it.'

She said nothing, looking gravely at him, but her face was puzzled.

He went on with some uneasiness. 'When the matter was first broached at your father's house, I asked that the patents for the design of the machinery be my own property, and your father agreed this readily enough, on the understanding he would pay me no more money for the extra work I had to do.'

'Why do you tell me all this, James? I cannot see precisely what it can matter to our situation. Unless——'

'I would not wish you to think me dishonourable, Abby. I have much to be grateful to your father for, for he taught me my trade, after Josiah Witney's death, and has treated me well enough in all the years I have worked for him. And I am now to take from him property he agreed is mine—and yet I feel uneasy about it. I need, perhaps to explain as much to myself as to you——'

He stood up, to resume his restless prowling about the room. 'Perhaps I am more hurt in my conscience that I am taking you from him than for taking what is my rightful property.' He stopped and stood still, almost visibly struggling to be honest. 'No, it is not entirely that. It is also that I know he did not see the value of the patents he so casually threw back at me. He is a man of much wisdom and foresight, but he lacks a certain—oh, I do not know what it is, precisely—a sort of vision if you will. He can see the effects of only those matters which directly concern him and his interests. Any others he dismisses out of hand.'

He sighed sharply. 'Well, there it is, my love. I am trying to tell you that I have as of a right the designs of the machinery I have been building at Wapping for your father. I have decided to cease working those designs, and have this very day removed all the information and drawings to my own possession. None but I know what is to be done, so the machinery he has there is now little more than a useless hulk.'

There was a long silence and then she nodded very slowly, never taking her eyes from his face.

'You will use the patents to build the machinery yourself,' she said flatly. 'For your own uses.'

'For our uses,' he said.

There was another silence, and then she nodded soberly. 'I see. I quite understand why you were so—well, I can see it had to be done. Our only fortune and our future lie in the skills of your brain and hands, and it is justifiable that we should take all necessary steps to make the best use of those skills. You did—well—what had to be done.'

He came and sat beside her again and took one of her hands in both of his and held it tightly.

'I have also gone to the Society of Apothecaries and looked at the registers of businesses, and I find that there is in the village of Paddington only one apothecary, and he of doubtful value——'

'Paddington?' she said, and frowned a little. 'To the west of the Park?'

'Aye,' he said eagerly. 'It is not so far away as it might be from the middle of the Town, and to tell the truth, my love, I could never find the money to start any nearer and——'

She sat up very straight and stared at him. 'You mean you are intending to—oh, James, I had not thought of that! A shop of your own! But that requires capital expenditure, does it not? And I have none but the small amount of pin-money my Papa gives me, and such little as I had saved from that I sent to Jonah when——'

He shook his head. 'Please to hear me out, Abby. It is indeed my intention to have a shop of my own—not a large and elegant one such as this, for that cannot be—but one of manageable size near enough to London to make regular visits in to the town a practicability. You see, it is my plan to lease a small cottage there, and set myself up in business with the local people and hope that will bring in enough to pay the rent and perhaps feed us a little, but to really make our fortune, I will set up my own machinery there, and then sell my pills to whomsoever in the metropolis will buy them. Do you see? I will come into the town each week and visit the shops of those men in the trade that I know and——'

'You will have to work so hard!' she said, and put up her hands to his face. 'And you are not well, my love, and must conserve your strength, not burn it out on such a plan——'

'Can you think of any better?' he said, and there was a long silence as they sat and looked at each other. And then she stirred and said flatly, 'No, I cannot. And you will not be alone, after all. I can work too——'

He grinned crookedly at that. 'I had counted on your care of the work of the counting house, my love, I must confess! More than that, of course, you shall not do! I will not have you handling machinery or——'

'That is as it may be,' she said and her voice was still flat and very practical. 'I am not stupid, I believe, and it should not be beyond my wits to encompass some of the work that must be done!'

She sat still, brooding over all he had said and he sat and watched her, saying nothing. He had too great a respect for her to try to push her towards any decision, and besides that he had a great need of her full and willing approbation of his scheme.

She nodded at last with great decisiveness. 'It is in many ways an excellent plan, James. I have no doubt that any cottage you find in which to start the shop will provide some living accommodation for us, and that is important. There is one point that concerns me however, and that you have not talked of, and that is where you are to obtain the necessary capital for the start. And what of machinery? Patents alone are not enough—you must buy the metal and so on for building it, surely?'

'I have thought of that too,' he said. 'I have enough friends in the trade to stand me surety, I believe. I shall go to Lombard Street and see what the Jews can do. I have, indeed, some small acquaintance with one such. Nahum Henriques—my father before his death did some business with him——'

Abby set her head on one side. 'That is the first time you have said aught about any of your own connections, James,' she said. 'I had not thought of it before——'

He smiled at that. 'We have had little enough time to talk but of our own affairs, my love. I was my father's only son, and he outlived my mother barely five years. I have been my own man this—oh, it is close on eighteen years now! This is why I grew so close to your father's business, you see. I had only my work here after my father died, and ——' He shrugged. 'Well, that is all spent water now. Enough I have you. I can brave your father's wrath at what has befallen.' But he looked bleak for a moment and she went to him to hold him close.

'Well, so we have a plan for our future!' she said then. 'What is at least as much to the point, James, is how we contrive to be wed. In my heart I would wish to go to my father and tell him straight and honest, for it will hurt him deeply if I do not—and yet——'

'And yet it will hurt him as much if you do, will it not?'

She nodded soberly. 'Oh, James, I wish it would be all easy and smooth for us! I would so like him to be as happy in my love for you as I am! I wish that——'

'Wishing is of little sense, Abby,' he said gently, 'and I see no other course but to mislead your father and present him with our marriage as a *fait accompli*. I did consider, however, that we might approach your Mama. I can post the banns for us, but it would be easier to arrange this if your Mama shares the secret.'

Abby shook her head. 'She will never go against Papa on my behalf,' she said. 'And even if she would, I could not ask her. He would make her so very unhappy afterwards, not because he wished to be cruel, you understand me, but because he would not be able to do otherwise. My Mama might suffer this and more for Jonah, but I cannot expect her to do so for me. I am my father's favourite, you see.'

'Yes,' he said and again they remained silent for a while, each occupied with their own but parallel thoughts.

It was James who stirred at last and he stood up and went to pick up his coat from the chair beside the door. 'Well, I must be about matters,' he said. 'I do not know how long it will take for us to—to arrange all, but I think we can imagine ourselves in some sort of place of our own within the month. It should not take so long to find a suitable property and settle on rents with a landlord, and I believe Mr Henriques will oblige me fast enough. He was a good man as I recall him. I can rebuild my own set of machinery fast enough once I have that to hand. The matter of a wedding—well, I must talk of the banns for one who is under age, as you are, with the parish clerk. We shall, I have no doubt, make some sort of shift——'

He stopped then and looked at her, his face very solemn. 'It is a strange thought, Abby, is it not? That we shall be full man and wife? You—you are sure about it? I have taken it much for granted that——'

She smiled at him, a smile as full of warmth and reassurance as she could make it.

'A strange thought but a most agreeable one, James,' she said. 'And as for asking whether or not I am sure—my dear, what sort of question is that, to me? You know the answer.'

'Yes,' he said. 'I know the answer,' and kissed her cheek and went away to seek a hack to carry him to Nahum Henriques's counting house on the corner of Lombard Street and Nicholas Street in the City.

He was weary, bone-weary, with his body feeling as though its strength were evaporating away through his skin. 'If only,' he thought, leaning back in the hack and closing his eyes against the glare of the thin winter sun on the dirty snow on the pavements they passed. 'If only I were in full possession of my physical self, how contented I should be at this moment!' Life had never had more to offer him than it had now, and he knew it; and somewhere deep in his being he knew with equal certainty that he had all too little time in which to enjoy it.

As the hack rattled on its way tears squeezed themselves through the tight-closed sandy lashes to move down his white cheeks, but he made no move to brush them away.

26

Abel took himself to Rule's in Maiden Lane to eat his noonday meal. All morning, throughout the long hours spent with the outdoor patients who had come in an ever-increasing flood to Tavistock Street, the letter had lain against his chest like a lead weight; he could feel it in his pocket now as he bent his head beneath the chophouse's doorway to step on to the sawdust-covered floor of the noisy steam-filled room.

He stood there for a second or two, breathing deeply, trying to find the sense of well-being he usually experienced here. Long ago, when he had been a dirty street urchin, Jesse Constam had brought him to this convivial warm place, with its blazing oil lights and lavish wax candles, its all-pervading smell of roast beef and meat pudding, pease porridge and hot yeasty bread soaked in clove-scented gravy, and the then owner Thomas Rule had sneered at him, and wished to turn him out of doors.

Well, that had been then; nowadays he was a valued and respected customer of Thomas's son Benjamin and he could always feel a certain sense of pride, a stirring of his self-esteem, when he came here and compared the respectful greetings he got with the attitude that had been displayed towards him on his very first visit.

But today there was no comfort to be found in memories of the past; far from it. It was as though the past, which he had long ago buried under the weight of work and work and more work, had reared up from the ashes of his dead young self to gibber and jeer at him, so intensely aware had he been all morning of his memories. Lilith as a child, capering in the light of her flickering fire, dressed in Dorothea's hand-me-downs and trying to ape the lady; Lilith in a pretty gewgaw-filled sitting-room in Edenbridge in Kent, looking at him with delight and throwing open her arms to greet him; Lilith in a white nightdress, tearstained and staring mournfully at him over a candle beside his curtained bed in Mr Lucas's house; above all Lilith standing still and amazed as he ripped her single flimsy garment from her shoulders and staring at him as the emotion built in him and—and at this point he closed his eyes and wrenched his mind back to the present and the dilemma presented to him by that damned letter.

So had it been all morning, with his thoughts swinging from past to present and back again, and now as he threw himself on to one of the wooden benches beside the whitewashed wall and signalled at the waiter, he felt his anger simmering ever more hotly. How dared she do so; after all these years during which he had managed to banish her and all thoughts of her from his life, how dared she come back into it in this insolent manner?

Raging within he thought of Gandy Deering, and had that rotund little man been there, Abel would gladly have rent him limb from limb; for if he had not had such lunatic notions about building his stupid great Hall in the Strand, he would never have come to Tavistock Street and——

'Bring me a plate of roast mutton and a pot of ale,' he growled at the waiter who, wrapped in a heavy calico apron and with his shirt sleeves thrust up above his elbows, had come to take his orders, and the man went scurrying away to tell the kitchen that Master Surgeon was in a fine old wax and would have all their guts hauled out of 'em were he to be kept waiting above the minimum, while Abel sat with his chin on his chest, pondering.

Should he ignore her letter altogether, he was asking himself, and tell Deering he wanted only the two houses in Endell Street, and would ignore the existence of the other between them? Perhaps, he thought, with a sudden spurt of hope, he could devise some link between the two, building a roofway that would span the intervening one.

But he dismissed that almost as soon as it came to him, for it was obviously not feasible. She would never give him a right of way over her property, not without demanding a confrontation again, just as she had now. She had him over a barrel and he knew it and worse still, knew she must be as aware of her power as was he.

The alternative, then, was to run the hospital in two separate buildings, with no link but the street between them. That this would be difficult was undoubted, but it could be done, he mused. And deliberately he pushed from his mind the splendidly grandiose plans he had made for knocking down the walls between the three houses and creating vast rooms where forty or more patients could be bedded at a time, and given lots of light and air and space, where he could have an operating theatre big enough not only to undertake some of the more heroic surgery after which his professional heart hankered, and which had made so resplendent a reputation for his old mentor Astley Cooper, but which would also accommodate students.

For days now, he had been in such a dream of his new hospital, had seen it filled not only with patients, but with so many students paying their way that the place would run if not at a profit, at least within its means, instead of being forever gnawed by debts as was now the case. He had, in fact, dreamed that almost overnight he could create here in Seven Dials almost as large and effective an establishment as those that were enjoyed by the patients of Guy's and St Thomas's. He had thought of the child with the quinsy, of the way his surgical skill had been wasted (for her father had come weeping to him the day after the operation to report her death; and Abel had known, as sure as he breathed, that she had died for want of hospital care, for want of the nursing his Nancy could have provided) and had swallowed his rage and disappointment as best he could. There would be no more such wasted operations when he had his splendid new hospital, he had promised himself. The people of the Dials *would* have good care.

And now, with one letter, delivered to his hand as he took his breakfast this morning, the whole vision had been shattered to fall in shards about him. He almost stamped his foot in his rage sitting there at his solitary table in Rule's.

And not the least of his rage, a secret little voice whispered to him, was due to the fact that he knew full well how easy it would be to do as Lilith demanded, to go to her house, hat in hand, to deal with her. He knew she wanted only to show off to him, to display herself in all her splendour and riches, knew it as sure as he knew he sat there and chewed his mutton, for she was Lilith, and despite the seventeen barren years during which he had refused to so much as think of her, he had not forgotten. Her need to parade herself for approval, her appetite for adulation was something that could never fade, not if she lived to be ninety.

So why could he not let her do her harmless prinking—for that would be all it was, he was sure—and tolerate it, and go away with the promise of the house in his pocket? It was little enough to do, in all conscience, to get so worthwhile a plum. A hospital near half as big as Guy's, here in Seven Dials.

Was it pride? He sat and stared sightlessly at the crowded eating-house before him, and tried painfully to assess his own motives; and knew he could acquit himself of that. Pride of the sort that made it impossible for a man to ask, to bend his head and even beg, was not important to him. How could it be, he who had grown from a gutter pickpocket and graveyard thief to be what he was?

So what was it? He bent his head again to his food, and tried to hide the knowledge from his conscious mind, but quite failed.

The reason was shouting itself at him. *He was afraid.* He had spent all those years spinning a shell about his feelings, protecting that agonized boy he had once been who had loved so completely and so helplessly, had learned to make a life for himself in which Lilith had no part and this letter, this single sheet of pale thick paper with its scented pink wax seal, had struck a blow on that carapace that had damaged it severely. Not completely to break it, but to threaten it enough so that it would take very little more for it to shatter completely and leave him shivering and exposed to his own feelings. It was that and only that that lay between him and his dream of his hospital, and the knowledge of so paltry an emotion deepened his anger to a self-hate that was very painful to him.

So deep was he in his thoughts that young Rule had spoken to him twice before he became aware of him, and he raised his head and said shortly, 'Aye? What is it?' when the man at last put a timid hand on his sleeve.

'Mr Lackland, I'd be glad of a private word with you,' Rule said, and his voice was so low and the surrounding hubbub so great that Abel had to strain to hear him.

'What's that?' he said irritably, and put his hand in his pocket to seek the wherewithal to pay for his meal. 'I must be away to my patients, and have no time for——'

'It is a matter of some importance,' Rule said and his expression was strained and his jaw moved a little as he tensed and relaxed the muscles of his face; it was clear that he was labouring under some strong emotion, and Abel, at last pulled out of his deep reverie, peered more closely at him and said, 'What ails you, man?'

'Not I, Mr Lackland, naught ails me,' Rule said earnestly. 'Never you think it! I'm as fit a man as any you've seen this se'nnight and——'

'So, well and good!' Abel stared at the man's working face. 'No need to get in such a pother then! If you are well and——'

'It is another about whom I am concerned, sir,' Rule said in a low voice, putting his head close to Abel's so that he could be quite sure not to be overheard by the people sitting nearby, who were showing an undoubted interest in the colloquy. 'I'd take it kindly, Mr Lackland, sir, if you would come to the kitchens and see to one of my men. But— if it please you, not to make a matter of it, but to be most casual and ordinary in your manner, for I would not any—any anxiety be caused, not for the world.'

Abel frowned. 'If anyone is behaving in a particular manner, Mr Rule, it is not I, by any means! You whisper and mutter like some Cato Street conspirator! Your customers will be sending for the Runners if you go on in this fashion!'

'Well, I have cause, Mr Lackland, I have cause, as I believe you will agree!' Rule's whisper sharpened a little. 'If as I ask you, sir, you will come to the kitchen. But please to come in an ordinary sort of manner. I will go ahead—I think it best—and will you follow me in due course? I do assure you, it is a matter of some moment.'

'Oh, well enough!' Abel growled, bored by the man's fussing. 'If it is as essential as you say. But I will be sore put about if it be for no more than a kitchen maid's vapours——' and immediately Rule bobbed his head and went hurrying away, weaving his way through the close-packed scrubbed wooden tables, and nodding and becking at his customers as he went.

Abel followed him as soon as he had paid his score, shrugging on his heavy coat and then picking his way through the sawdust to the narrow door at the rear of the room which led to the kitchen premises.

Here was noise and steam and smells multiplied by ten, compared with the eating-rooms, and he stood still for a moment blinking around at his surroundings. The fire burned vast and red across one wall, with a huge spit above it on which half an ox, it seemed to Abel's practised eye, was being turned by a sweating scrawny child wearing no more than a dirty grey rag about his buttocks. Beside him stood a taller boy, just as dirty and as greasily soot-streaked, who was basting the smoking reeking meat with a long spoon, and swearing monotonously at the child who was not working fast enough at the turning for his taste; beside them, on the top of the metal slab above the ovens that flanked the fire stood the great iron cauldrons in which the puddings were boiled, steaming and hissing and bubbling. Other men were working at the huge central table, one opening oysters from a great salt-encrusted barrel with practised twists of his bony wrists and another ripping the guts from the drooping carcases of capons and floppy-necked ducks and flinging them into a blood-streaked bucket on the floor at his feet.

Already Abel was feeling the heat as the sweat started out on his skin under his heavy street clothes and he swore softly, and turned to go, but then Rule appeared out of the murk at the rear of the big clattering stone-floored room, and came bustling across to take him by the arm and lead him towards the door from which he had emerged.

'I would not have anyone know at all that this has occurred, not till you have seen him and told me that—well, what I would wish to be told though I fear that—oh, it is a matter of great fortuitousness that you should come in today, Mr Lackland, when I had so great a need of you! When my waiter said as you were out there, I could have wept with gratitude to a munificent God, indeed I could—in here, if you please——'

Again Abel had to duck his head, for the lintel was low, and he found himself in a small dark room which was heavy and oppressive to his nose, but at least had the virtue of being cooler than the kitchen he had just left.

It took a few moments for his eyes to become accustomed to the darkness, and then he saw he was in a store-room, for the ceiling was hung with flitches of bacon and huge greenish hams, with bunches of dried herbs hanging beside them, and the floor was littered with sacks and boxes from which onions and turnips and huge purple cabbages spilled out to make any passageway across the room a perilous business.

'Over here——' Rule's voice came from the shadows and he turned his head and looked, and saw that Rule was fiddling with a lantern and a tinder, and after a second the light flared and then settled as the shutter was pulled across.

Abel could see clearly now. In the corner huddled up against the dripping raw brick wall was a pile of old sacks, and on it lay a man. He was gaunt, painfully thin, and almost like a dead skeleton for his ribs described a series of deep ridges on his hollow chest that were made even more ugly by the shadows thrown by the lantern, and his temples were dark hollows above which his cheekbones described great promontories. He lay with his head back and his eyes half-closed, although the lower part of the whites could still be seen, and his mouth was half-open too as he struggled to breathe and his chest heaved painfully with every inspiration.

Abel stood and looked, making no move to touch him for the moment, and Rule babbled, 'Came to me for work two days ago, and asked no more than his food and a place to sleep, and I thought him fit enough to be a kitchen hand, and who can blame me, for times are hard and the wages of these lazy good-for-nothing creatures as are out in the kitchen there are an exorbitant drain on an honest businessman! Though I knew no more of him but what he said, I took him, for—well, he said he had come but recently from India or some such outlandish parts, on one of the big merchantmen, and had lost all his money on the dockside, and down Ratcliffe, and it was no more than Christian charity to set him to work as would give him his vittles and no questions asked and——'

'When did this start?' Abel said harshly, still staring at the pathetic heap of bones and fine drawn skin that lay there on the old sacks.

'Yesterday,' Rule said wretchedly. 'Yestereven it was. I came out to see why he was not at his work, and he was lying here and groaning and moaning and burning with a fever—and he had been purging and vomiting, and I threw out his bedding and set these clean sacks to him and——'

'And when did this occur? Come, man, don't stare so! You know what I mean—the marks—when did these occur?' And Abel bent and pulled the man's filthy shirt away from his belly so that the rosy dusky rash could be clearly seen staining the skin of the distended belly as well as the narrow heaving chest.

'You know what it means, man,' he said again, 'so answer me!'

'This morning,' Rule whispered. 'I saw it this morning, and I have been so beset! I did all I could for him, indeed I did, Mr Lackland, for you know full well there's many a man faced with this as would throw the poor creature out of doors into the gutters, as far away as was possible, and give no thought at all to his needs. But I did all I could, and gave him clean bedding and wine and water for his raging thirst and——'

He stopped and turned a piteous countenance to Abel. 'Indeed, Mr Lackland, until this eruption this morning, I thought it no more than a fever, a congestion of the lungs perhaps, or some such. But now—what am I to do? I am a businessman! I have an eating-house! If they out there——' and he jerked his head, 'if it were known I had this here, can you not see what would happen?'

'Aye, I know,' Abel said more gently and knelt down beside the man, thrusting aside the cabbages and onions to do so, and bending his head to listen to the man's heart with his ear pressed hard against his chest.

After a long moment, while Rule crouched beside him with the lantern held high and throwing weird long shadows across them, and the only sounds to be heard were the man's harsh uneven breathing and the distant murmur of voices from the kitchen beyond the heavy door, he grunted softly and stood up, and carefully and tenderly pulled the man's inadequate shirt back across his chest and then covered him with one of the sacks.

'Well, I cannot blame you for your anxiety, Rule,' he said. 'It is as you feared, of course. He has the typhus——'

Rule moaned softly and the light jerked and danced, throwing even longer and stronger shadows as he crossed himself.

'What am I to do? Oh, Mr Lackland, what *am* I to do? There's Hannah—my wife—due to be brought to bed of our first child in no more than a week or two and—once such a piece of news as this is out, no one of the men will work for me, for they would as lief starve as be near this fever and who would come to eat here? Would you?'

'Oh, for my part, I am not concerned,' Abel said roughly. 'I am near so many different ills a hundred times a day, and I escape contagion. But I have the surgeon's special health—I know you are right to be so fearful.'

He stood brooding for a moment, while Rule stood and watched him with an expression of hope upon his smooth young face that was ludicrous in its intensity.

That the man on the sacking bed was in desperate ill health was not the least of the problem. The disease he suffered, and which he had no doubt brought with him from the rat-infested ships which plied the Eastern routes, could go through these filthy gutters and hovels like a river in full flood, carrying men and women and children helplessly before it. The houses and streets could within a few days be littered with dead and dying bodies and cause such a further contagion as could spread out of the Dials to the richer streets beyond Oxford Street, even to the splendid purlieus of St James's and the comfortable dwellings that lay around Gower Street and Bedford Square. The man must be put somewhere to be kept safe and cared for until such time as he recovered—and looking at that livid face again Abel thought that a forlorn hope—or died of his affliction.

But where—where in all these teeming stinking streets was there a place to put him? If only he had his hospital, his great new hospital where there would be a room where such a one as this could be set to be alone, where Nancy who shared his 'surgeon's health' and did not succumb to such ills as afflicted other people, could care for him and wash the encrusted mess from that stretched skin, and wet those parched and cracked lips with comforting fluids.

But he had no such place, for the two wards he had in Tavistock Street were chockfull with sick and immovable people; put this man in a corner of one of those rooms, and by the week's end he would have death stalking even more rapidly from bed to bed——

Again he swore, but this time with a sort of hopeless anger, rather than the mechanical irritation that had plagued him earlier, and bit his lip, and Rule said timidly, 'You will not broadcast it abroad, Mr Lackland, that I have the fever here? I will do all I can to contain the disease, once you have got him away from here—I will burn pastilles all night, in the kitchen and the rooms beyond and——'

'Oh, burn the whole place, for my part,' Abel said savagely. 'What good your pastilles will do I know not—I hold no faith in such tricks! It is clean air and light that you need here—and people about you who are fed sufficient good food and live snug and warm enough to escape disease when it comes to them! What matters now is to get this man to some place where he will be safe and where his contagion can be stopped from spreading itself. And God damn it all to hell and back, I know not where to send him! My hospital is so full it promises fair to burst its walls and—oh, there is no help for it! Have you a cart, man? I can think of only one chance. I will send him across the river. They will not thank me there at Guy's but they have the space and the people, and will not turn a sick man away, I am persuaded, even one that bears the typhus——'

Rule nodded eagerly. 'Oh, a cart, Mr Lackland, that is the easiest thing i' the world! I have those I use to bear produce from the markets— there's one I use for Spitalfields which will serve us better than that from Billingsgate, for that stinks so fishlike that it will——'

'Then be about it, and no more chattering,' Abel said. 'You have a door to the back here? Or must we bear him through the kitchen? If we do, your care and secrecy is a full waste of time, for you and I are not the only ones to know the significance of those spots upon his skin——'

'I can haul him to the upper door, and lower him then to the cart——' Rule jerked his head and held up his lantern, and Abel could see the door set high in the wall through which the loads of supplies were sent to the store-room and nodded.

'Well, then, set about it. I will go back to Tavistock Street now, and send to you one of my people to aid you. She's a good soul and will treat the poor wretch kindly.'

He looked again at the sick man beside him, and reached in his pocket to take out his handkerchief and wiped from the narrow fore-head the beads of greasy sweat that lay there, and then bent down to hold to the dry lips the cup of watered wine that lay beside him.

The man turned his head fretfully and opened his eyes momentarily, and looked at Abel with the deep shadowed stare of pain. Abel murmured softly, almost crooningly, and his face was absorbed and showed a tenderness that almost startled the watching Rule; and as though he were a child the man sipped, and convulsively swallowed, and then his eyes glazed a little and half-closed, and he rolled his head once more and produced the same husky moan. Abel sighed sharply and stood up.

'I will be away at once, then. Nancy will bring with her a letter for you to give the surgeons at Guy's. Be firm when you get there, now. Tell 'em there's no other place for him, and that he has neither kith nor kin, and they will take him. They'll be unwilling but they will take him——'

He strode back to Tavistock Street through the narrow alleys with his head up and his jaws set. Before he had eaten his meal he had been confused, and ill at ease in his confusion, knowing not at all what to do about Lilith's letter. Now, he knew. His own fear of what might transpire between them on any personal level was a paltry one, as insignificant as the streaks of grey cloud that moved sluggishly across the thin icy blue of the winter sky above his head. He *had* to have his hospital, his great big new hospital, and no woman in this world could stop him from getting it. At four o'clock on Friday afternoon she would find him in her drawing-room.

But for just long enough to settle the affair and no longer. That much he could promise himself.

27

When Dorothea appeared at the door of the office behind the shop and stood there looking anxiously at her, Abby felt a wave of surprise so great that it transmitted itself to her stomach, and for a moment she feared that illness was about to overtake her, and she would cast up her accounts at her mother's feet.

But the qualmish moment passed, and she stood up and said as easily as she could, 'Why, Mama! What do you here? You have never come before to see me thus since I have been spending my days here ——'

Still her mother stood there and looked anxiously at her without speaking and Abby felt a matching anxiety rising momentarily in her, and said a little sharply, 'Is something amiss, Mama? Is that why you are here?'

'Oh no, my dear Abby!' Dorothea said at last, and came timidly a little further into the room. 'I was a trifle alarmed, I must confess, that you might be annoyed with me and I could not at the moment bear to be greeted with any irritation, for I am so confused in my mind as to burst into childish tears, I vow, if one cross word be spoken to me!'

Abby bit her lip in compunction, and hurried forwards to take her mother's elbow and lead her to the old sofa.

'Oh, Mama, I hope I am not so alarming a person that you must needs fear my temper! Indeed I have always thought myself a creature of some equanimity!'

Dorothea looked up at her and spoke with great warmth. 'Oh, indeed, dear child, you are and have always been such a strength to me! I know you understand and—and forgive my great partiality for your brother—I cannot help my feelings, after all!—and I would not wish you to doubt the love I bear you! It is a measure of my affection that I come to you now—and as for my finding you alarming—well,' she hesitated, and then smiled one of her tremulous smiles, 'I must confess to sometimes finding you a *little* formidable, for you are, after all, very much like your Papa, are you not?'

'Am I, Mama? I had not thought of it too much, but I suppose it may be said that there is a likeness in our temperaments.'

'Oh, indeed there is, my dear child,' Dorothea said earnestly. 'Though you are kinder, I think, and——'

'Oh, Mama, he does not mean to be unkind, you know!' Abby said quickly, leaping as ever to soothe her mother's feelings. 'It is just that he has not much patience, you understand, for his life is so full of work and—and——' she faltered. She and her James were going to step between Abel and that work, and for the first time as she tried to imagine her father's reaction she felt a thrill of real fear.

But Dorothea seemed not to have noticed her hesitation, and said quickly, 'Oh, yes, indeed, my love, of course I know that! But it is difficult for one such as I when observing such—such dedication—not to feel a little chilled, you know, and . . . and as though one's own concerns were of small import! Even when those concerns are for one's children's well-being——' and now it was her turn to falter and stop, and for a long moment the two women were silent, sitting side by side on the old sofa and each occupied with her own thoughts.

It was Abby who spoke first, and she said abruptly, 'Mama, may I ask of you some small opinion? I—it is difficult for me to frame the words, but I would indeed be glad to know—tell me, Mama,' and she stopped and thought for a moment before going on, picking her words with great care, 'tell me, Mama, what is right. I do not mean right in the way Mr Spenser speaks of right in his sermons, for to tell the truth, Mama, I have little use for his milk-and-water morality. Religion is a matter of importance, I know, but for my part——' she shrugged. 'Well let be. What I would wish to ask you, as—as my Mama, and as a woman of this world who has a deep understanding of—of people, for you cannot fail to know more than I do, is to tell me what is right in the question of one's dealings with the people one loves.'

She turned her head and looked at her mother very searchingly. 'You will find this a strange conversation, perhaps, Mama, but I was so exercised in my mind with such thoughts before you came that I cannot completely rid myself of my preoccupations with them.

Perhaps, though, it would be better that you tell me why you came to see me, first, for——'

Dorothea shook her head. 'That can wait for the moment, my dear,' she said, and it seemed to Abby that her voice had a strength it did not usually display, and she realized suddenly that it was because the timidity had gone from it, and she bit her lip in some shame; clearly she had been less than kind to her mother, she thought, since leaving the schoolroom, for a lack of timidity to be so noticeable.

'What is it you wish to know, Abby?' Dorothea said, and put out her hand to rest it on her daughter's.

'Oh, it is difficult, Mama, to explain, but I find I must consider who —well, not who matters most precisely, but whose welfare I should consider first. There are people one loves dearly, but differently, you understand, and sometimes one is faced with a dilemma in which one must select to do as one of the beloveds wish at the expense of the good of the other. Do you follow me, Mama? How do I choose which of the people whom I love matters most?'

She raised her eyes and looked at her mother with great appeal in them, and immediately Dorothea's hand closed more tightly on hers.

'The dear child!' Dorothea was thinking. 'Torn between her brother and her father—and me. It cannot be anything but painful for her——'

'You choose the one who seems to have greatest need, Abby,' she said after a moment. 'This is not a Christian answer, I know, for Mr Spenser is always preaching to us of the absoluteness of right and wrong, but for my part I cannot but advise you thus. In any dealings with people, you will find there are some who are strong and some who are weak, and it seems to me—it has always seemed to me—that it is just and indeed necessary to protect the weak even at the expense of the strong.'

She paused then and said painfully, 'I have wished many times these past years, my dear Abby, that your Papa could love Jonah as I do, and could see in him the . . . the gentleness as well as—and I cannot deny it— the weakness of him. But your Papa is *so* strong, and for all his compassion for the sick and halt that he cares for in his work, he has small understanding of what weakness may be. So, you see, although I love your Papa as dearly as ever I did—and I must tell you I was quite hopelessly adoring of him from the moment I first knew him—' and she reddened and looked suddenly very young, and now it was Abby who pressed her mother's hand in a sudden access of fellow feeling—'I still found I must take the part of Jonah, even though it has caused some friction between your Papa and I.'

She stopped again, and then went on with a painful honesty, 'Although it cannot be denied that there have been other causes of difficulty between us. But that was long ago and cannot be of concern to you.'

She paused then and looked again at her daughter with some return of her old timidity. 'Does that answer your question, Abby? Do you see why it is necessary that Jonah be protected and helped to the best of our ability, even if it does anger Papa? For Papa is so strong, and Jonah so . . . so not weak, precisely, but . . . *ordinary*, you understand. He has not his Papa's power, for he did not suffer his Papa's distresses in his infancy, and it is suffering that hardens the soul and the character . . .' and she sighed a gusty little sigh and let go of Abby's hand.

And Abby, thinking of James, seeing his pale face and the shadows beneath his eyes and in the hollows of his cheeks, nodded heavily. Poor Papa. He would suffer much hurt at what they were planning to do, but Mama was quite right; Papa was so strong. The strongest of them all, indeed.

And I am like him, she told herself with a spark of her usual self-assurance. All are agreed that I am like him, and I too am strong in that case, and must be strong for James as well as myself. I pray it will not be too painful for all of us, but strong I must be. . . .

'Mama,' she said again, a little abruptly, 'as we are speaking on—on such matters of behaviour, might I ask of you another thing? I am not a child any more, and I must one day think of—of marriage.'

'Oh dear,' Dorothea said and looked a little helplessly at her daughter. 'Indeed, I suppose you must, and I have made no push to take you out in society and arrange for you to meet such young men as might be suitable. But I have been so beset since Jonah——'

Abby waved that away a little impatiently. 'Oh, I am not concerned with *that*,' she said. 'Indeed I can think of nothing I would despise more than being taken about in society for such a purpose! I have no doubt that when the time comes I will—I will contrive to find a man that is suitable for me without such——' and she went a little pink. But Dorothea was fiddling with her reticule and did not see it. 'I wish to ask you, Mama, how important it might be to love the man to whom one is married. I know that many young females—and their Mamas—concern themselves only with such things as marriage portions, and prospects, and where a newly-wed couple shall live and——'

At once Dorothea was all attention, and she turned her body on the sofa and took hold of Abby's shoulders in both her mittened hands, and looked at her face with great earnestness, her cheeks a little tinged with the power of the feeling she had in her.

'Oh, my dear child,' she said, and her voice was very clear. 'My dear Abby, you must love the man you wed! It is of all things the most important! All my married life I have been glad, so glad, that I could wed where my heart lay. It has not been easy, as you are of an age to understand, but I have never regretted it! I loved your Papa dearly from the start, and always have, and life with any other would have been insupportable, I know! It was because I knew this from the beginning that I made such a push to engage his attentions, for I cannot deny—but that is by the way. It has—I cannot pretend that your Papa has always returned my regard, not in the same way that—that I have felt it—but that is not to my mind of—oh, it saddens me a little, of course. But the *important* thing is that he lives with me, and is my husband, and I would not have it otherwise. When it is time for you to choose to wed, remember this, please, my love, and follow your heart as I did, at whatever cost to yourself and others, for whatever people might say, and however your lines fall thereafter, it is all a woman can ask of life. To get love is good, but to give it is much greater!'

Again there was a silence, and then Abby said wonderingly, 'Mama, why did you never speak so to me before? And have you ever spoken so to Papa? I cannot think so, for he does not know, I am sure, of the power of the love you bear him! I mean——' and again she bit her lip in some embarrassment. 'I would not have you think we talk of you, when we are alone, but I believe I understand him very well, and'— she raised her eyes—'I am sure he does not understand. I did not before now.'

Dorothea had turned again in her place and was sitting fussing with her mittens and the ribbon on her reticule, her head bent, and now she spoke again in her usual colourless way.

'No one asked me to offer an opinion on the matter before, my dear

Abby. I expect that is why I seem to you so—so animated now. But so it is, as I have told you. I believe it is important that one loves well, and yet be able to cross the will of one's beloved if it is necessary for another's well-being. There are many kinds of love, Abby. You will learn.'

And she looked up at her daughter and smiled and Abby nodded. She would not have thought she could have found so great a comfort in her mother's words, for in the hours since James had gone away to the City, she had been sitting and pondering, torn in both directions as she thought of her father and then of her husband-to-be. Now she said impulsively, 'I am so glad you came today, Mama. It was very good to be given the opportunity to speak to you. At home there never seems to be—well, it is difficult—is it not?—to talk there, when there is the business of the household going forward——'

She stood up and went to the desk and sat down in her chair and then turned and smiled at her mother. 'But I am very thoughtless. I have not asked you to explain what it is that brought you here! Or did you come merely for an afternoon's excursion, as I used to do before I came here every day?'

Dorothea sat up very straight on the sofa, and her eyes were very bright. 'I have had a letter, Abby,' she said, 'about Jonah!'

'Oh?' Abby sat up straighter too. 'He wrote to you?'

'No.' Dorothea's lips twisted a little. 'This was not a letter borne from Jonah by that messenger woman, the one who brought his letters to you, but one from the—the woman whose protection he sought when leaving his own home.'

Abby frowned sharply. 'Woman? I do not understand.'

'It is a little difficult for me to understand fully, too,' Dorothea said. 'But so it is. He went to the house of an actress—one Mrs Lucas. She plays at the Haymarket Theatre. You will remember her. She was the one in the blue dress who acted the person called Titania in the play——'

Abby nodded. 'I remember her. A pretty creature.'

'Pretty indeed,' Dorothea said a little dryly, and then hurried on. 'When I went back to the theatre after the performance and sent you home, Abby, I found that—well, Jonah is living in her house and——'

'Oh, Mama.' Abby said gently, and with great compassion in her voice. 'Oh, Mama, I am so sorry! But you must understand that a young man is—well, he must live his life as a man must, and you must not be too distressed! It bespeaks no evil in him that he should choose to——'

Dorothea, to Abby's great surprise, laughed a little at that. 'Oh, I do not fear he is in some carnal situation, my love!' she said, almost merrily. 'That is the last of my concerns, for I understand the needs of gentlemen, I am sure!' She sobered then. 'No, there are other reasons for his presence in her house, I believe. However——' and she reached purposefully in her reticule instead of fiddling with it as she had been continuously doing, and pulled out of it a letter, written on thick pale paper and with the shreds of a broken pink seal on it. She gave it to Abby, and nodded at the girl's raised eyebrows, and obediently Abby bent her head and read it.

'Will you come with me, please, Abby?' Dorothea asked simply. 'For I must tell you that I am much alarmed to go alone—but go I must. I would be so glad of your strength at my side, my dear child.'

And Abby smiled at her mother and said at once, 'Of course, Mama! I will gladly come! Indeed I would be more than happy myself to hear good news of Jonah, for it is so worrying to think of him in his present situation.'

Dorothea nodded happily. 'And by Friday evening, perhaps, we shall have him home again with us, shall we not? For I am determined, Abby, to persuade him to come to Gower Street again, and I will protect him against his Papa's wrath as best I can. And if you will help me it will be better still, for your Papa listens so to you, does he not? And you asked me where your duty lay, my love, and it does clearly lay with the weak one, do you not agree?'

And Abby looked at her mother's face, and saw James's, and nodded gravely and said, 'Yes, Mama.'

28

Jonah stood beside the window in the white-and-gold drawing-room staring down into North Audley Street, his hands behind his back under his coat tails and his face quite expressionless.

The street below looked strangely naked to his eyes; for the first time since last November the cobbles and paving slabs were not covered in hardpacked snow, and the brownish grey of the naked stones at last revealed by the long-awaited thaw looked unfamiliar and a little threatening in consequence. It was almost as though, he thought, the street had run its life parallel to his own in this house; all through these past months it had been shrouded in a blinding whiteness, a whiteness too easily and too swiftly sullied with the filth brought by the feet of men and horses, then purified again with a new fall of snow as the wind went screaming furiously around the high roofs of the houses, only to be dirtied yet again by casual passers-by. And now all the disguise of that wintry covering was gone, the pure tinselly white and the dirty slushy mudbath both quite, quite gone, leaving only the reality to be faced——

He sighed at the elegance of his simile and turned away from the window to look lugubriously about the room, and to try, yet again, to reach some sort of decision.

His feelings when Celia had come upon him tumbling among the sheets with Lilith had been very confused. First he had been enormously, heartburstingly grateful; it had all been getting to be more than he wanted, more than he felt he could cope with, and Celia's blessed appearance at his door holding her bedgown clutched to her chest had been like the answer to an unspoken prayer. But then he had felt that first sensation quite swept away in a wash of shame, a shame so hot and so huge that it had made his skin positively tingle, but as he had

257

scrambled to his feet, absurdly trying to hold his own nightshirt in such a way that it would cover his bareness this feeling too had given way to another, and one that bewildered him at first—a sense of furious disappointment.

Whatever had been about to happen might have been alarming, might have been something he could not easily handle, might have been completely beyond his control, in fact, but it had promised to be at the very least interesting. And Celia's appearance had put paid to that, for Lilith had laughed and laughed and then quite composedly got to her feet and rearranged her nightgown and smiled sweetly upon them and said lightly, 'No doubt you have matters to discuss, my dears!' and with enormous aplomb and one last wicked glance over her shoulder at Jonah had gone away down the stairs, bearing her candle with her and leaving the two of them behind her speechlessly staring at each other in the dimness.

And at that point his feelings had settled into the deep dull ache of anger, an ache which had been with him ever since. The expression of pain on Celia's expressive face, the darkness of her eyes as she had stared at him in disbelief had hurt and enraged him; his deep awareness of the insultingly easy way in which Lilith had been manipulating him had shamed and infuriated him, and his total inability to say anything to Celia that would set matters right between them had been the hardest of all to stomach.

Oh, he had tried. He moved across the room now in a series of short sharp lunges as he remembered how he had tried. He had put out his hand to Celia and said simply, 'She came to me. It was none of my——' but Celia had said nothing, had just stood and stared at him, and he had said again, 'She came to me——'

He moved about the drawing-room now even more restlessly, touching tables as he passed them, kicking the slender gilded chair legs, and glowering. The harder he had tried to explain his own innocence in the scene she had witnessed the more enraged he had become, for he had sounded lame, foolish, a stupid half-boy, half-child, one open to the simplest of seductive wiles, and that was not a vision of himself that he had at all enjoyed.

And as well as this painful blow to his self-esteem, to his own view of himself as a man of the town, capable of taking excellent care of himself, there was the pain of seeing how Celia was suffering. He had known he cared for this girl in a warm and comfortable sort of way, and had known that she cared for him—indeed that knowledge had been a large part of his own feeling; nothing was easier than to love a person who made it so patently clear that she held one in high esteem. But he had not realized until that moment when she stood and stared her pain at him how very deep her feelings were; and this new awareness frightened him. It was as though she had put a burden upon his back that he was not fully able to carry.

At last he had stopped trying to explain, and had just stood and looked back at her with the same helpless dumb misery that she was displaying, and after a while she had seemed to dissolve a little and her face had changed, losing its rigid stillness and settling into a new mould, and one that he did not recognize. She had looked older suddenly, and infinitely wise, and very, very tired.

'We shall talk another time,' was all she had said, and then she had turned and gone, leaving him to the darkness of his room as he watched her silhouette go dwindling away as she bore herself away down the stairs. He had stood there in the dark for a long time, and then gone to bed and thrown himself upon it in a sudden sharpening of his anger; and been surprised to wake chilled and blinking to the thin early light some eight hours later, having slept the deep sleep of exhaustion all night.

Curiously enough, it had all seemed easy then. He had washed and shaved himself in the cold water in his jug and dressed with great speed and not a hint of his usual concern for the niceties of his appearance; and had immediately set to work to pack into his portmanteau the few items of clothing he had. He had been sure then, sure that there was only one course of action open to him.

The fat old woman who had nodded and becked so earnestly at him had been right; Lilith *was* a bad woman, a cruel woman, one who hurt people. He remembered momentarily Lucy's dark comment about the effect she had once had on his father, but he could not cope with that thought, and pushed it away. It was enough for him to have to think of his own situation, and he had positively decided. He would do as Lucy advised him, not because he had fully evaluated her evidence but because of his own experience at Lilith's hands.

He must leave this house, and leave it forthwith. Lilith must become a creature of his past, a person to be pushed to the back of his mind, and quite forgotten; or at most, only to be remembered in tranquillity some time in the remote future.

He had liked that idea; to have such a woman as Lilith Lucas as part of a person's past would be to lend that past considerable splendour; no one could regard him as an innocent, a half-child, half-boy, in such a case. And as he closed his bag the previous night's scene was already undergoing a sea-change, taking on new meanings and new patterns as his dramatist's eye relimned the strokes that went to make up the picture.

It was at this point that he realized that he could not do as he had planned, and write a letter and simply walk out of the house (where he had been about to go he was not yet sure; the important thing was to *go*) for his most precious possession was not in his portmanteau.

His Play. Lilith had taken it from him, had said she was to give it to Castleton for his consideration, but he could not be sure that she had done that. And if she had it still in her possession and he did not get it from her now, before he left her house, he knew as certainly as he knew he stood in this chilly bedchamber that he would never get it back. And much as he longed to turn his back and go, to run away from this house and never come back, to leave his Play behind would be unthinkable.

So he had gone downstairs, holding his head high with an imitation of much greater courage than he actually felt (and who he dreaded to see most, Lilith or Celia, he could not for the life of him decide) to await with what patience he could Lilith's awakening time so that he could persuade Hawks to go and ask her for his precious manuscript.

It had been this delay that had been his downfall. During the long hours spent in the drawing-room, after breaking his fast with the sketchiest of meals, he had been swept from side to side by his emotions, his fears, his pride, by a whole range of feelings he had hardly known he had. He had thought of going back to his father's house, and admitting his fault and agreeing to become his father's creature; and remembered that morning at Tavistock Street and had been nauseated again. He had thought of Celia and her love for him, and had softened almost to tears at the thought of the pain it would inflict upon her if he were to reject her. And he had thought of the theatre, of Lilith turning and twisting on that brilliantly lit square of stage, of the scenery towering high and with such fragile strength above her, and imagined her saying words he had written, imagined seeing his characters living there with her, through her, beside her—and his resolution had shivered and fled from him.

Altogether, Jonah was not a happy young man on that cold March morning. Nor was he any happier when at last the time arrived when Lilith could be expected to be awake, and he sent in his message via a grumbling Hawks. For all that Hawks would say when she came back was that her mistress would see him that afternoon, at some time around four of the clock and he could obtain his play from her then.

'Though she says she don't know why you should want it so bad, for to be sure you've writ quite enough for all necessary purposes,' she had thrown back at him over her shoulder as she had gone stumping away down to the kitchen to prepare a nuncheon for young Ben and Lyddy. And he had bitten his lip and wondered bleakly whether Lilith had meant it was too good to need any extra work, or so bad that no amount of extra work would help it——

As Jonah prowled unhappily about the drawing-room, filling in the hours as best he could and searching ever more miserably and confusedly through his own feelings, Lilith sat on her blue chaise-longue in her boudoir in a high good humour. That her previous evening's ploy had not fallen out precisely as she had intended did not matter a whit; in many ways, she thought comfortably, it was more amusing as it was. She knew, better than any, that in matters of passion intention and desire could be as important as actual experience, could leave much the same memories and sensations behind; and remembering the look on Celia's face as she had seen it last night she laughed softly, and drank from her cup of thick dark chocolate with a sensuous relish.

And even when her door opened and Celia came in to stand there with her head held high and a look of stubborn disobedience on her face she was not angered, although she would have been at any other time for Celia was defiantly wearing one of her mother's discarded dresses in her favourite shade of blue and cut low and tight to show the young breasts and narrow waist, and her hair was piled on her head in a creditable attempt at a modern Grecian mode.

Lilith leaned back against her cushions and smiled and put down her chocolate cup. 'Well, my dear, and how are you this morning? Better than you look, I trust, for that gown ill becomes you——'

'You say that of any gown that is suited to my age rather than to that of a nursery chit,' Celia said, and her voice was high and thin. 'And I must tell you that I will no longer wear such clothes, nor will I any longer ape the schoolroom miss to please *you*—I shall look the woman I am, and not let you seek to make a baby of me any longer——'

Lilith raised her eyebrows at that, and smiled again, even more lazily. 'Hoity toity miss! Is it rebelling against its betters, then?'

'Against its elders, perhaps,' Celia said spitefully, and Lilith's smile lost some of its good humour and her eyes narrowed.

'So? Are we to have another series of your foolish tempers and tantrums? We have had some peace here these past weeks—I had thought you had grown some sense if not beauty——'

Celia nodded slowly, never taking her eyes from her mother's face, still standing with her back to the door, and her arms set against the panels with her fingers spread wide; it was as though she could only maintain this conversation while she had some bulwark against which to support herself.

'I have grown sense,' she said softly, 'more than you think. I have all these years—indeed, as long as I can recall, I have thought you one to—to love and hope to be loved by. I thought you no more than cruelly indulged by other people, and one made careless of others' feelings because of the manner in which you were so shocking spoiled by the attentions of fools and fobs. But after last night I know better——'

Lilith was sitting up now, with her arms about her knees in a pose that made her look as young as Celia herself, and staring at her daughter with her eyes very wide and bright.

'What do you know better after last night?' she said softly. 'Do you know better that I am ten times—*twenty* times—the woman you will ever be? That I can have any thing and any person I want, that you are a stupid birdbrained piece of rubbish if you think you can ever emulate me in gifts or——'

Celia shook her head, almost sadly, looking at her mother with her eyes shadowed and dark. 'I know you are spiteful,' she said. 'I know you are made of malice, and will do what you will and when you will with never a thought of any other person's needs but your own. I saw you there last night, with Jonah, and I knew then what I should have known long since—indeed, I think perhaps I did know it, but had not yet come to find the words to give it substance—but last night I saw

262

you for the creature you are, I really *saw* you, and I do not know whether I should hate you or pity you——'

'Pity me? You pity me? You lump of gutter-meat, you pity me? You think to——' Celia still stood quite unmoving, her face equally unchanged, only raising her voice to overtop her mother's shriller tones.

'Aye, pity you! For you are not only malicious and cruel by choice, but you are jealous! Are you not, my *dear* Mama?'

And now her voice could drop again, for Lilith was silent, staring at her with a look of quite genuine puzzlement on her face.

'You are jealous of *me*. Of Jonah and me. I did not know it, I did not see that you behaved as you did for such a reason, but I saw it last night, and——' she laughed softly, 'I have not felt so happy for a long time! That you should be so jealous of me, so frightened of me, as to seek to use Jonah as you did last night—it is a pitiful thought, is it not? I believe I am enough your daughter to find great satisfaction in such a spectacle——' and she laughed again even more softly, and still Lilith sat with her arms about her knees and never took her eyes from her daughter's face.

'And you failed, did you not?' Celia's voice was rising now with a sort of triumph in it. 'You did not get your poxy way with him, did you? You failed! He is not one of your creatures, for all your wiles and——'

She stopped suddenly and looked uncertainly at her mother, for Lilith had started to smile, a long slow and very satisfied smile, and the thin shell of courage in which Celia had wrapped herself began to tremble, and she pushed her hands harder against the comforting solidity of the wooden door.

'You failed!' she said again, and now her voice was shriller, young again, and at the sound of it Lilith laughed aloud and leaned back into her chaise-longue with a comfortable wriggle, like a cat settling itself on a pile of feathers.

'Failed, did I?' she said. 'I think not, you know! I did not perhaps—shall we say *complete* my visit quite as I had expected, but bless your little heart, had you come but five minutes later you would have been in at the finish! A fair sight would have met your eyes, indeed it would! The sight of your pretty boy's arse cantering its way home, that's what you would have seen—and an edifying spectacle that would have been for such a *woman* as you! Your chosen jockey riding his first filly in the best stakes of all! Oh, a pretty sight!'

'You failed——' Celia said again. 'I know you did. It was you who went to him, who sought to use him, and it was in no way any desire of his! He told me so! He had no wish for you——'

'Told you so, did he? *Told* you so? And did he tell you all?' Lilith linked her hands behind her head. 'Did he tell you how hot he was for me? Did he tell you how near he came to ramming home? A woman can cry seduction and rape, and who can disprove her word? None but she can know how her desires really were at that time—but not so a man! You who are such a *woman*, so ready to set yourself in my shoes and ape my clothes and style, you should know that in such situations a man bears hard and obvious evidence of *his* feelings! And I tell you that your precious Jonah, your pretty little sweetheart was so ready for an encounter he was fit to burst his skin! Never think that you saved your boy from the arms of one he did not desire, for you could not be more wrong! You kept him from what he wanted more than he had wanted anything in all his life, by your arrival! And if he denies it——' and she laughed again. 'If he denies it, I could not blame him, nor would anyone. But I tell you he will be hard put to it ever to be so ready for an encounter with *you* as he was ready for me last night!'

Celia shook her head in almost violent denial, but could say nothing. She had been so sure, after her long night of thinking, her morning of scheming, that she was right. She had planned this confrontation with her mother with such care; she had expected anger, had been prepared for fury and been sure she could face that. But this—this amused reaction, this sureness on Lilith's part, this she had not expected.

For she knew with a sudden certainty that what Lilith had said was true. Despite those long hours during which she had assured herself over and over again with a positively feverish intensity that it was she whom Jonah loved, and not Lilith; despite the fact that she had been quite convinced when she had come to her mother's room to confront her, now she knew that she had deceived herself. Jonah indeed might have affection for her, but it was an affection that had none of the intensity of her own feeling. His passion, his deepest emotion, he had given to Lilith. And Celia closed her eyes for a moment, shutting out the sight of her mother's laughing face so that she could absorb this knowledge and somehow come to terms with it.

There was a long pause, and then Lilith said lightly, 'You need not look like that! I do not wish to steal your precious Jonah from you! You may have him for my part.'

Celia opened her eyes then, and Lilith set her head to one side and added perkily—'For what good he may do you! I can tell you, poor thing, that he will never forget me, nor what happened last night.' She giggled then. 'Or rather what should have happened but didn't—and nor will you. For I promise you, whenever he embraces you, it will be me he thinks of, and you will always know it, and will always see me there, no matter what happens——'

'Why do you hate me so?' Celia said it almost wonderingly. 'What did I ever do to you that you should treat me so? I am your daughter, am I not? You should have a care for me—not treat me so——'

Lilith shrugged. 'Oh, as for mothers and daughters—pooh to that! I managed well enough from my earliest childhood without a mother, and you are so set to be a woman grown that you amaze me to care so much! I live my life as I will, and give my affections where I will, and you have no greater demand upon me than any other—and you have become very boring of latter years! I cared well enough for you when you were small and biddable, but you have become so sullen and so set upon your own ways that I have lost all patience with you——'

'And all interest too,' Celia said flatly.

'Aye, I dare say. And you are boring me now—so go away and leave me in peace——' Lilith swung her legs over the side of her chaise-longue and stood up and stretched, yawning widely. 'I have had enough of all your whinings and complainings. Be about your business——'

'I shall go away from here. Today,' Celia said.

'Shall you? Indeed? And where shall you go, tell me? To your Jonah's people? Much good that will do you——' Lilith smiled widely suddenly. 'As you would see if you but tried! They'll have you as fast as he will—which is not at all——'

Celia shook her head. 'There are theatres I can work in. I have seen enough of the stage to——'

'The theatre? Pah! You have no talent!'

'Perhaps not,' Celia said heavily. 'But I know enough of the tricks——'

She opened the door then, and stood hesitantly on the threshold. 'I shall not see you again,' she said, and looked very directly at her mother, but Lilith turned her back, and said easily, 'Shall you not? Well, we shall see——'

Quietly Celia closed the door, and stood outside in the hall, and after a moment she said softly to the blank panels. 'I shall not see you again. And nor shall he——' And she turned and ran softly along the passageway towards the stairs and Jonah's room.

29

It was not until she saw his portmanteau sitting in the shade of the hatstand near the front door that her alarm subsided. She had seen in one glance at his room that he had quitted it for good, for he had left the wardrobe door gaping wide upon its own emptiness, and she had turned and gone hurtling downstairs to seek Hawks and ask her if she knew what had happened. And seen his bag, and felt a great wash of relief flow d through her.

But she stood there in the hall hesitating before setting out on a search of the house for him, trying to analyse her feelings. That she could no longer stay here, could not bear to be near her mother for any longer than was necessary to organize her departure, was sure; but what of Jonah? This morning she had been able to convince herself she was loved by him, had felt secure in her knowledge of his affection. But now, with her mother's sneers and laughter and crude words still echoing in her inner ears, she could not be so certain. This morning her plan had been easy. She would persuade Jonah to go away with her, to join one of the many provincial travelling theatre companies—and with all the arrogant optimism of the very young she never doubted that many such companies would welcome her—and they would earn their own way. She had not given any thought to anything more definite than that.

But now—she was filled with the most agonizing of doubts. Would Jonah wish to go with her? The sense of security born in that whispered colloquy between the dark and dusty flats beside the Haymarket stage had quite gone now—perhaps, she thought miserably, he will want to stay here, with *her*. After last night——

And even if he doesn't, a secret voice whispered deep within her mind, even if he doesn't, do you still want to take him away with you?

She has damaged him, has spoiled him, has stolen him away; do you want the leavings she so contemptuously threw to you? Will it not always be as she said it would—*her* shadow lying between you, whatever you do and wherever you go? Is that what you want? the little voice whispered.

And standing there in a patch of dull sunlight in her mother's hallway, staring sightlessly at the pattern of the black-and-white marble tiles she knew that the answer had to be yes, she wanted him, knew that she would have to take the chance of life with him, no matter what shadow might lie over such a life; better to be with him in a shadow than without him in the blaze of midday light.

So she went in search of him, and found him in the drawing-room still staring moodily out of the window at the street below, at gutters now running with icy black water, and horses slipping on the muddy cobbles. He looked up dully at the sound of the door, but at the sight of her his face flamed a sudden crimson, and he leapt to his feet.

'There is no need to look so alarmed,' she said, and closed the door behind her. 'I do not come to rant at you——'

He looked at her for a long moment, and then came across the room towards her, a little nervously at first, and then, as he saw the calmness of her expression, with a little more confidence.

'I thought you would not wish—wish to see me again,' he said. 'Last night you were so very——'

'That was last night,' she said collectedly. 'I have thought much since then.'

'I too,' he said heavily, and turned away from her to go back across the room, but she put out a hand and touched him and said softly, 'Please to stand still. I must talk with you, Jo.'

He stopped at once and turned to look at her with a wariness in his mien that did not escape her, but she lifted her chin and said as bravely as she could, 'I wish to talk with you of—of future plans.'

'I have made mine,' he said, 'as best I can.'

'Do they include me, these plans?'

He blinked at her directness. 'I—how can they? After last night, it is a matter of—of no little surprise to me that you wish to speak to me at all, for I failed signally, did I not, to convince you that the—the en- counter that—that what you saw—that it was—Oh, devil take it, Celia, you know what I mean!'

'You did convince me,' she said calmly. 'I thought much last night after I left you, and I weighed what I knew of you, and what I knew of —of her' (and suddenly she could not bring herself to say her name) '—and I decided you spoke only the truth, and that she did indeed press her unwanted attentions upon you.'

He moved eagerly towards her, but she stepped back and shook her head slightly.

'But that was before I conversed with her this morning.'

He stopped and looked at her, puzzled, his head on one side. 'You spoke to—to your Mama this morning? About what happened last night?'

'Yes,' she said, and now she moved away to stand beside the window looking out, so that she presented her back to him. 'And she told me that I was wrong in my belief. That her attentions were far from un-welcome to you, and that—that had I come to your door but a few moments later, all would have been different.'

She swallowed hard to clear the lump that had risen in her throat, and turned and stared at him with her chin held very high. 'Is that true, Jonah? I would wish that you would tell me, for it—it matters to me.'

'I—I tell you, she came to me. I thought, indeed, that it was you at the door, come to talk to me, and—and when I saw it was her, I was indeed startled, and——'

'You do not answer my question, Jonah.' Suddenly all her careful calm shattered, and she stamped her foot and almost shouted it. 'Did you want her, did you? She says you were as lecherous for her body as —as any man could be, that—I must know! I told you that I love you and so I do, and I must know, it is my *right* to know, where I stand in your regard! If you cannot love me, then better I know now than——'

'Oh, what is love, what in the name of God is love, and what is lechery? You ask *me*? I don't know, Celia, I do not know! I am as sore perplexed as you!' He was shaking now, his hands clenched tight at his side, and his neck trembling a little. 'Do you not think I have driven myself mad all these long hours, asking myself the same questions as you ask me? I thought I loved you, indeed I still believe I do, but she— she has but to look at a man, to touch me, and such things happen as cannot be explained! She has some—some power in her that——' He turned away sharply, and shook his head and went again on his little rushing walks about the room, his fists still balled at his sides, and she watched him, both hands held to her mouth, her eyes wide and staring above them. 'It is better I go away from here, and never see you or she again,' he said. 'I had so decided anyway.'

'Then why did you not go? Why are you still here so late in the day?' she asked softly, her calm quite recovered. At the sight of his distress she had felt the same surge of relief she had felt when she had seen his portmanteau by the door; a sudden sense that all was not yet lost, as she had so feared. 'You could have been gone any time this past three hours and seen neither one nor other of us.'

He turned and looked at her miserably. 'She has my Play,' he said piteously. And she stared at him for a long moment and then threw back her head and began to laugh, a high giggling infinitely girlish laugh, filled with real amusement, and he looked at her and then frowned and then looked sulky, and at last she stopped and spluttered, 'Oh, forgive me, my dear Jonah, please to forgive me, but you looked so—so like Ben when you said that, I could not help but be amused——'

'I am glad to please you so easily,' he said stiffly.

'Forgive me, Jonah,' she said again and moved swiftly across the room to his side. 'I—it was not so very funny, to be sure, but I have been so sore distressed, you know, that I think I *needed* to laugh so. But I was not laughing at you, indeed I was not.' She stopped for a moment, and then said a little awkwardly. 'I too have been thinking, and making plans, Jo. Mine include you.'

He looked sharply at her and opened his mouth to speak but she shook her head and hurried on.

'I am leaving this house, for always. Just as you ran away from your father's house, so am I running away from *her* house. The only difference is that I have told her so, and she doesn't care a whit——'

'Running away? Where to? And how can that——'

'As to where,' she said impatiently. 'I am not perfectly sure yet. I shall seek out a provincial theatre and work there. Wherever the next stage is going when I reach the Golden Ball at Charing Cross will serve well enough.'

'You said I have a place in this plan?' Jonah said a little cautiously, and she nodded and went on in a rush of words, not looking at him now.

'I know that it is with her that all—all your passions lie, while all of mine are with you, but that is my misfortune, and one that must be borne as best it can for as long as it must be, but I believe that you have

—that you do bear affection for me, and I believe that if once I get you away from this house, and from *her*, it will be possible for you to forget her, and to turn your love to me, as it should be turned, and then we will be happy together, for I for my part ask no more of life now or at any other time than to be in your company, and with your concerns always at the forefront of my mind and—and'—she took a deep breath—'and so it is my plan that you too should leave this house with me, and start a life for just the two of us where she cannot come to hurt us. And soon, with me to teach you, you will forget her, and—and forget last night and—'

But even as she spoke, she knew she lied, knew that for her the memory of what she had seen last night would always be with her.

'But we would not be wedded,' he said a little stupidly after a moment. 'How could we go in such a manner as——'

'Oh, pooh to that!' Celia said with a sudden airiness. '*She* never was wed, not to any one of the men she has known, so why should I care for that! And if I do not care, why should you, for it is only to females that things matter, after all——'

He shook his head in slight bewilderment. 'You are too—too rapid for me, Celia! I had not thought of such things as—I do not feel able to make such sweeping plans! I ask little enough of life, in all conscience! I want only to write, to make my life with words, and to be happy and——'

She smiled at him with an infinite tenderness and put her hands out to take his face between them. 'And so you shall, dear Jonah, so you shall, for I will make you happy, I *will* make you forget her'—and she pushed down her own clamouring doubts—'and you will write and I will act and we will not think of London or the Haymarket or North Audley Street ever again, but be happy, and be together——' and she lifted her face and kissed him and almost bemused, he returned her kiss though with a somewhat abstracted air; but she was content enough and beamed up at him as they separated and said, 'Your bag, I know, is packed, and I shall be ready in—oh, half an hour, no more——'

He shook his head slightly and said again, 'You go so *fast*, Celia,' but she sparkled up at him and went hurrying across the room to the door.

'We can never leave here too fast,' she said. 'For we are going to be happy, and never again be plagued by—by *anybody*! You shall see, my love——'

She stopped at the door and said with a sudden wickedness, 'You say she has your play? It will be in her escritoire then, and I have my own manner of seeking a way into that——' She giggled suddenly, 'And there is more I need from there as well as your manuscript. In half an hour, no more, my love! I shall be ready, and we shall *go*!' And she left in a swish of blue skirts leaving him blinking a little in the coldness of the gold-and-white room.

Standing there in the hall, with his coat still on and his hat in his hand—for he had curtly refused to allow Hawks to take them from him, having no intention of appearing to Lilith as anything but the most transient and hasty of callers—he found himself remembering with painful clarity the time he had stood in a similar hall, in a house in Clarges Street, waiting to see this same woman. But that had been so many years ago, and he had been young then, and unsure and deeply troubled in his mind. . . .

Now I am a man of power, he told himself, as he allowed Hawks to lead the way to the drawing-room upstairs, one with matters of business with which to concern myself and not a green boy to be twisted into the vapours by some whorish actress—but he had to keep his mind firmly to that thought, for behind the façade he was erecting he knew that green boy existed still, could feel the flutterings of the belly that had afflicted him all those years ago in Clarges Street. And the control he was exercising, and the strength of his decision was so intense that it transmitted itself in some way to Hawks, who, for the first time that she could remember, was in awe of one of the men who visited her mistress.

She bobbed nervously at the door of the drawing-room, pushing it open with all the timidity of a kitchen maid unused to the goings-on above stairs, and dodged back as Abel went moving resolutely forwards, and said breathlessly, 'I'll tell ma'am as you're 'ere, sir—yer 'Onour—if you please, sir——' and went scuttling away to Lilith's boudoir, leaving Abel to make his own way in to the drawing-room.

And so it was that he saw his son again for the first time since the boy had gone lurching out of the house into Tavistock Street to vomit his horror of his father's trade into the gutter outside. And which of the two men was the more horrified at the sight of the other, which of them was the more confused, and which the most anguished at the implications of their meeting in Lilith Lucas's house it would have been impossible to say, as the two of them, so very much alike to look at, stood staring blankly at each other amid the fripperies and elegancies of the white-and-gold drawing-room.

30

It was, in a curious way, a source of intense relief to both of them when Lilith came into the room, through the double doors that led from the small drawing-room, and together they turned to look at her with an almost eager movement. The silence between them though it had lasted but a matter of a minute or two had become almost intolerable, almost physically palpable in the way it had pressed down on them. Individually, they had been dreading this moment of confrontation, Jonah with the agonized memory of the previous night's encounter so clear in his mind, and Abel with his equally vivid memory of a similar occasion long ago; yet now, because they were together and thrown into such emotional disarray by their meeting they became in some sort allies. In that one brief moment they were as close in sympathy and mutual need as both had so often longed to be, but never had achieved.

But the moment passed almost as it arrived, for she looked from one to the other with her eyes sparkling with all the innocent charm of a child being shown a pile of sugar-plums, and clapped her hands and laughed softly and said, 'Oh, how delightful! You have both saved me so much trouble in meeting thus, for I would have had to tell you severally, would I not, that I was acquainted with both of you! Dear Abel, how well you look! Quite as handsome, I vow, as ever you were when you were a stripling!'

She moved across the room in a swish of blue frills, her hand held out towards Abel, but he stood there, foursquare and very still, his hat held in both his hands before him, his body in its caped overcoat bulking large against the now dwindling light of the winter afternoon coming through the long windows, and made no move to accept her proffered hand. And with consummate skill she turned her wrist slightly so that by the time she reached his side it was clear to any observer that she had intended only to touch his sleeve in passing, and had not for one moment expected him to respond to her; and moved on to stand at Jonah's side, and linked her arm in one of his rigidly held ones and said lightly, 'So, Abel! Does not your young hopeful look to be in fine fettle? Have I not taken excellent care of him?'

Jonah stood there woodenly, too overset in his mind to respond at all to what was happening. The sight of his father here, looking grimmer than even Jonah could ever remember him had so powerfully proved the truth of the suspicions fed to him by Lucy that he could not cope with the new knowledge at all. This man, this terrifying figure of authority for whom he had felt little but awe tinged with frank fear for all his life, to be so long known to Lilith—it was unbearable. Unbearable because he realized in the deepest recesses of his mind that any man who knew Lilith at all inevitably must know her in the biblical sense as well. His own experience last night proved that to him. And recalling now the way his body had responded to the touch of her hand on his skin, the way her naked flesh had felt beneath his amid those tangled bedclothes, the sense of sick abandonment that had filled him when Celia had appeared at the door, he closed his eyes in misery. His mind raced in circles, trying to dodge the all too vivid pictures that were being conjured up, of himself in Lilith's arms, and then his father in the same situation, and, absurdly, himself in Mr Loudoun's classroom listening to the tale of the wickedness of Ham, who had so disgraced his father Noah in looking on his nakedness——

He opened his eyes wide and tried to speak, seeking desperately within himself for some inconsequential remark that would somehow reduce this dreadful tension to a semblance of social normality, but caught Lilith's eye, for she was looking up at him with her head turned quizzically on one side, and this so unnerved him that he closed his lips again.

She laughed her soft little laugh. 'Indeed, Abel, he will tell you, no doubt, at some time when you two are together again in true familial amity, that I have taken more than care of him, for I have been at some push to enlarge his education. Have I not, Jonah?' and she put her hand up to his cheek and stroked it, letting her touch linger as she drew her fingers across his lips, and he stared at his father over them. 'Hmm, my little one?' and again she laughed that throaty little laugh, and moved

275

coolly away from his side to settle herself in a chair beside the newly lit flames in the tall grate.

'So, my dears! *A nos moutons, oui?* Pleasant though it would undoubtedly be to settle to a cosy little prose, and speak of the dear dead days of the past, we must not so indulge ourselves, for you have come for other purposes, have you not, Abel? Dear Jonah, I am sure you will forgive us if we discuss these business matters in your presence? No doubt it will be a source of great ennui to you, but——'

'I am going now.' Jonah's voice sounded cracked and thick in his own ears, and he coughed, and moved towards the door, only to turn and stand there awkwardly for a moment before letting the words burst from him in a high flat tone that bespoke a strong attempt at control. 'It is, ma'am, my intention to leave this house today, and not return. I—I believe I must be at some pains to thank you for—for your kind hospitality at a time when—when I was much in need of succour. But as I am sure you will quite understand, it is no longer—no longer possible for me to remain here.'

He lifted his head a little higher and spoke more surely now, steadfastly not looking in his father's direction.

'Permit me to assure you, ma'am, that—that this decision has not been in any way—uh—precipitated by this meeting here this afternoon. I had decided quite independently that I could no longer trespass on your generosity——'

He turned and set his hand to the door-knob, and then, after a moment's pause turned back and blurted, 'Celia is going too. She says you know.'

Lilith had not moved, but was sitting looking at him with one eyebrow slightly raised, and after a second she shrugged and said lightly, 'As to Celia, my dear boy, her comings and goings must be her own affair. For my part I am heartily bored by her mooning foolish ways—but there is no need for *you* to go, no need at all! Your—Papa——' and she slid her eyes sideways to look at the still unmoving Abel—'your Papa shall not force you to leave me, I promise you for——'

'It is nothing to do with—with anyone but myself!' Jonah said swiftly. 'I do as *I* choose, will run my life as *I* see fit——' and then as he suddenly remembered Celia's eager chattering scheming and the way she had rushed him into her plan not half an hour since, he faltered for a moment; but then his voice tightened as he saw the faint look of amusement on Lilith's face. 'And it is my wish that I leave this house now. Your pardon, ma'am——' and he sketched a bow and again set his hand to the door-knob.

She moved then, and came rustling across the room to set her hand on his arm and look appealingly up into his face.

'I would wish you to stay a little longer, Jonah,' she said, 'for I——'

He shook his head roughly, and pulled his arm away from her grip. 'If you please, ma'am, my mind is quite made up. I have had my bag ready since early morning, and await only Celia. And such waiting as is necessary I will pass in the hall. Good day to you, ma'am, and again my grateful thanks—and—and—I am sorry about the benefit. I cannot play Leontes after all——' and almost wrenching the door open he went, leaving her staring at the blank panels with her face twisted with a sudden access of fury.

But then almost at once her expression cleared, and she made a very faint shrug and went back to her chair.

'The foolish child!' she said lightly, arranging her skirts around her with an air of great concentration on the delicate movements of her hands. 'He is, I know, labouring under much distress——' She looked up at Abel with her eyes wide and limpid with mock innocence. 'The poor young wretch set his cap at me, you must know, child though he might appear in your eyes, and last night——' she shrugged again, and hooded her eyes only to peep up at him immediately through the fringe of heavy lashes and went on softly, 'You will know how it is when one is young and hot with love for a woman, eh, my dear Abel? You will not have forgotten that night we spent in Edenbridge—was it so long ago? I am sure that you have not——'

And she laughed again, that throaty bubbly laugh that he remembered so well and went on, 'Ah, well, poor Jonah! He will recover in time, no doubt. And he will have his memories now, as every man should have his memories, should he not, dear Abel?' And now she was leaning back and frankly jeering at him, and still he did not move, never taking his eyes from her face.

'It is a pity the poor boy felt he could not remain a little longer for in——' she looked up at the little gilded French clock on the mantel— 'oh, in a very little while, we shall have other callers, no doubt, who would much have enjoyed conversation with him——'

She smiled widely at him, and settled her hands upon her lap, and looked at him with her brows slightly raised in interrogation. 'But now, you shall break that mulish silence of yours perhaps, to tell me for what purpose it is you have come to me this afternoon?'

His voice was harsh but quite expressionless. 'You know perfectly, ma'am, that it is at your express command that I attend here this afternoon. It is my wish to purchase the property you hold in Endell Street, and you have refused to deal with my agent in this matter. Hence, my presence here.'

'Ah, yes,' she murmured. 'I had quite forgot! You must forgive me, dear Abel, for in my pleasure at seeing you again, I——'

'I am here solely to discuss the matter of the house in Endell Street, ma'am. It is in no wise my intention to discuss any other matters whatsoever with you——'

She set her head on one side again. 'What, not even the welfare of your dear son? Why, Abel, you surprise me! I had thought you a man of deep feeling, one who would care much for the affairs of his family! That is how I remember you, after all—as one of great sensibility much given to talk of family life, and home and children——' she giggled then. 'Who would have thought that I too would have children, dear Abel? Is it not an absurdity? But there, one must pay the costs of one's pleasure, must one not? Imagine, if you and I had——'

His face was almost grey now, so tensely were his muscles set, and his lips were equally as devoid of colour for he was holding himself on the tightest of reins. 'I will not discuss aught but the purchase of the Endell Street house,' he said again, and now his voice was louder and so hard that for a moment she felt a faint thrill of fear; and liked it and relaxed in her chair to gaze up at him.

'So strong a man, so hot of temper, so violent as I recall! Did *she* ever arouse you enough to strike her, Abel? Did *she* ever light so strong a fire within you that——'

For the first time he moved and turned towards the door, setting his hat on his head, and at once she jumped to her feet, glancing swiftly at the little clock, and said quickly, 'But to be sure—the house. You wish to buy it from me——'

He stopped and turned his head to look at her, but made no move to doff his hat, and she nodded and said in a voice that was quite different, crisp and businesslike and quite bereft of any of the liquid beguiling softness that had characterized it hitherto, 'I will require the full market value. There is no sentiment in me when it comes to matters of business.'

'That is the price that will be paid,' he said harshly.

'Five hundred pounds.'

He shook his head. 'The market value is no more than four hundred. I hold the deeds of contract on similar properties in the same thorough-fare with which to prove the point.'

'The market price is what the market will bear. You want it, so——'

'I will pay no more than four hundred and twenty-five pounds. This allows much leeway, and is an earnest of my wish to possess the property.'

'Four hundred and fifty.'

'I am adamant.'

There was a pause.

'And suppose I were to be adamant, also? Suppose I were to say that I shall not sell the house to you?' Her tone was still businesslike, but beneath it lay a faint hint of the provocativeness that was so much a part of her. 'What then?'

'Such intransigence would serve you ill, for I already hold the deeds of the flanking properties. It is my intention to start a hospital in them, and if you do not allow me the purchase of the house I want, I can assure you your tenants will find me to be an ill neighbour. There are ways in which a hospital can be made to fit peaceably enough into a busy thoroughfare—but also ways in which peace can be neglected.'

Her lips curved gently. 'You are more of a businessman in your own right than I took you for, Abel. Well, now, I must consider. Will you be a more tedious neighbour to my tenants than my tenants will be to you? That is the question!'

Again she threw a swift glance at the clock, and nodded softly as she saw the hands point so closely to the half hour after four. 'You must realize, my dear Abel, that I have but small control over the—activities of those who rent my house from me, and I am told by my rent collector that this Endell Street house may on occasion appear to be a—place of assignation. It is a busy place, certainly——'

Somewhere in the house a door slammed, and she lifted her head at the distance-muffled sound and then said quickly, 'But there—I will for once in my life allow the ties of long-held friendship to tangle themselves in my business dealings. You shall have the house for four hundred and thirty pounds. You cannot refuse me that.'

There was a silence, broken only by the faint sounds of activity from beyond the drawing-room doors, and then Abel nodded.

'Four hundred and thirty pounds. For the freehold. I shall give you my note of hand upon it.'

'And I my signature. My man of law will complete the transaction soon enough, and you will hold the deeds as soon as may be.'

She was all swiftness now, and moved across the room to a table in the corner, to seat herself and seize a piece of paper and the pen which stood near it. 'I will at this time write no more than a cursory document,' she said, and wrote swiftly, signing with a flourishing hand, sanding the sheet with an abandon that spread the sand liberally across the carpet at her feet. 'It will suffice——'

She rose, and held out to him the piece of paper and he bent his head sharply, and put his hand to his pocket to remove a sheet of paper in his turn, and she smiled at him and stood back to leave him a way to the table and the pen; but not so far back that he did not feel her skirts brush his legs as he passed her, nor fail to smell the scent of musk that clung about her.

He seated himself, and with a swiftness that matched her own set his signature to the promissory note, and she leaned across him, although he stiffened his back in rejection of her closeness. He felt her breath warm on his neck and ignored it, setting his jaw hard as he wrote.

He had just sanded the paper when the door opened behind him, and he turned his head and made to stand up, but she was so close beside him, with her hand set upon his shoulder with what appeared to be the lightest of touches but which was in fact a strong grip, that he could not move. And when he saw who it was who followed Hawks into the room, he could not have moved anyway.

For the second time within half an hour he found himself staring at members of his own family, feeling the shock moving coldly within him as he looked at Dorothea and Abby. And as they stared back in equal amazement he heard Lilith above him laughing and laughing and laughing, as though she would never stop.

31

It was Dorothea who spoke first. First she had looked at her husband
with an expression of complete disbelief upon her face, peering at him
as though he were a total stranger who happened to bear an incredible
likeness to someone she knew, and then with confusion, and finally
with a dawning delight that lifted her pale cheeks to a soft rosiness and
brightened her eyes quite remarkably.

'My dear Abel,' she said breathlessly, and hurried across the room
towards him. 'You sought and found him too? Oh, my dear husband,
I am so glad! I have hoped and longed and prayed that you would lose
your animosity towards him, and would accept him home again
without recrimination, and that we should all be content and easy
again——'

'I do not know of what you speak, ma'am!' he said loudly and stood
up as at last Lilith took her hand from his shoulder, and went drifting
away to stand beside her fireplace and watch the two of them with her
face filled with an expression of huge glee. 'I came to this house in
order to purchase a parcel of property I require.'

She stood uncertainly before him, peering up into his face. 'But
Jonah? Did you not come to seek Jonah?'

She turned and spoke urgently to Abby, standing in a still silence
just inside the drawing-room door. 'Abby! Did you not think Papa
was here to seek Jonah, as are we?'

She turned back to Abel and put one hand timidly upon his coat
sleeve. 'Why else, Abel, should I expect to see you here in this house,
if not to——'

She stopped, quite suddenly, and turned her head to look over her
other shoulder, and stared at Lilith, who was sitting now on her

favourite long chair, leaning back with her hands linked behind her head so that the sleeves of her gown fell back to reveal her white arms, and smiling lazily at them. She raised her eyebrows gently at Dorothea's regard, and Dorothea, after one frozen moment, dropped her hand from Abel's sleeve, and took a step back.

'You must excuse me, Abel,' she said dully, bending her head to look at her reticule which she was gripping now in both hands. 'I was a little startled to see you here.'

'I came to buy property,' he said again, and then with a sort of controlled violence in his voice that made her shrink back slightly— a movement which Lilith clearly saw, and which made her smile even more widely—'How came *you* here, ma'am, is a question much more to the point!'

'To seek Jonah, Papa,' Abby came further into the room, moving with a cool certainty that masked her inner turmoil. Her confusion on seeing Abel had been quite as great as her mother's, and she had looked from Lilith—somewhat stunned by the beauty of her, for she seemed to look even lovelier than she had upon the stage that night—to Abel in great bewilderment. Some awareness of the possibilities revealed by her father's presence here struggled in her mind for her attention, but she pushed that away. There would be time enough to consider such implications when the present situation was under control.

'You might as well know now as later, Papa, that I have been in constant correspondence with my brother ever since he left your house. I have been somewhat mendacious with you on this score, perhaps, but it was not reasonable in you to suppose I could abandon my sisterly affection quite so easily. It was because of this correspondence between us that Mama discovered that Jonah—that he was in some wise connected with this lady.'

'Well, he is not here,' Abel said flatly, 'so there is no need for you to remain. You will oblige me by returning home immediately and——'

'Not here?' Dorothea cried sharply and jerked up her head to stare at Abel. 'He is here—of course he is here! The letter said he was here, and that if I came at half past four I would——'

'Oh, no, ma'am, it did not!' Lilith said in a comfortable conversational sort of tone, as though she were discussing the inclemencies of the weather. 'It said, as I recall—and I wrote it after all—that there

282

would be news for you of a certain person—no more——' She laughed then, 'And of course news you have had, for Abel—forgive me, *Mr Lackland*—has told you with admirable precision the information I had for you. The person is not here.'

'You said he was here, and that I should—I should—Abby, did not the letter say he was here? Did you not read it so?' and Dorothea turned her head to stare at Abby with her eyes very wide in her pinched face.

'As to the content of the letter, Mama, it does not matter,' Abby said, almost impatiently, and turned to her father. 'Where is he, Papa? How is this lady connected with him? I do not understand, and I would wish to be told. He is my brother, after all, and I have surely a right—as has Mama——'

'I do not know!' Abel almost shouted it, and thrust back the chair beside him with such force that it fell over, but he ignored that and went moving across the room to the door. 'I do not know, nor do I care! I long since washed my hands of him and——'

'Well, that is most unkind in you, Abel!' Lilith said softly. 'I knew you always to be a hard man—for you must know, Miss Lackland, that your Papa and I have been acquainted—oh, these many years!— but I did not think your life as it has been since we shared so much in our youth had so hardened you as to treat a charming boy like Jonah in so peremptory a manner. Indeed, Mrs Lackland, if this has happened to him, I find myself perforce wondering what you have done to him, for I believe that wives can have a considerable influence upon a man!' She laughed again. 'Although I cannot pretend to a great knowledge of wifely matters, since I have never found myself drawn to the life of a woman who can be content with the—*attentions*—of but one gentleman!'

And still she had not moved, sitting there with her head resting on the hands linked behind her head, and the firelight dancing prettily on her slender white arms.

Abby was quite suddenly deeply tired, filled with a sense of sick ennui that threatened almost to overwhelm her. Standing here in this vulgar, over-decorated room, with her father standing glowering on one side, and her mother drooping piteously on the other and this incredible and beautiful woman dominating them all—it was as disr agreeable an experience as any she had ever known. And behind he awareness of what was happening here, other matters jostled in her mind for her attention; her own concerns, her anxiety about James, her worrying about the plans he was making for them both, and her distaste for it all became, quite suddenly, an enormous irritation, and she burst out, 'You will not speak so to my mother, Madam! I know nothing of you, nor of your history, and I have no wish to know. My Mama came here today at your express bidding for one purpose only—to seek news of my brother. If you have any information about him, you will oblige me and give it to us immediately. If you have not, then say so, and we will remove ourselves. But do not, for God's sake, waste our time with your silly posturings, for such is what you appear to me to be doing, for whatever reason! And I for one am heartily bored by such behaviour!'

'Bored?' Lilith sat up now, and folded her hands upon her lap, staring at Abby with her brows raised. 'Bored, Miss Lackland? I am sorry indeed to hear that! I would have thought you would be quite agog to know why your father is so angered by the way your poor brother came here to me in his extremis! I would have thought it a matter of great interest to you, having your dear Mama's welfare at heart, as you so clearly have, to know of the past connection between your Papa and myself! Indeed, I believe you should know, *boring* though the matter may be to your young ears, for——'

'Be quiet!' The words came from Abel very softly, but with so much venom in the tone of his voice that even Abby shrank a little at the sound, but Lilith showed no alarm at all, and indeed seemed to develop a brighter sparkle, for she turned her gaze upon him and went on as though he had not spoken.

'You must know, Miss Lackland, that there was a time, some years ago, when your Papa—who was a pretty lad in all conscience, prettier even than your delightful brother—when he was, I think I can say in all modesty, quite moonstruck with me! Indeed, he was perfectly heartset on making a wife of me!'

She laughed a tinkling little laugh, and her gaze never left Abel's face. Abby could see the direction of her eyes, but could not for the life of her have turned her own gaze in the same direction; it would have been as shaming to observe her father's reaction to this woman's words as to observe him in his bath or in the privy—and as for looking at her mother—that was equally unthinkable, although she could feel the stillness of her presence there just outside the line of her vision. And so the three of them stood there, quite still, and Lilith's soft voice went on unhindered.

'But your Mama, Miss Lackland, was heartset upon him! There! Is that not a romantical story? She and he and I—I caring not a whit for either of them——' and now her voice sharpened—'not a whit, Miss Lackland, not a whit! I would wish you to know that! And your Mama in her need told your Papa some Banbury tale that made him believe that it would be in some sort sinful to wed me—although, you know, I had no notion of wedding him—and took him away to church with her, so that she should have him!' Again that hateful bubbly little laugh. 'Though I had had him first, for there had been a night in Edenbridge, in Mr Lucas's house—your Papa I dare say recalls it——'

She stood up now, and came slowly across the room to stand in front of Abel and peer up at him. 'And not hide nor hair have we seen of each other these many years—until your brother happened to see me upon the stage, and showed his inheritance in all truth, for did he not become so enamoured of me that—well, it would be immodest and *boring* of me, Miss Lackland, to tell you more. Suffice it to say that the father and the son are much alike—much alike——' and she stood suddenly on tiptoe, and moving as lithely as a cat slid her arms about Abel's neck, knocking his hat to the ground, and fastened her lips upon his.

And now Abby had to turn her head to look at them, and it all seemed to happen so slowly that she felt quite relaxed, almost as if she were half asleep, watching her father's rigid shoulders soften and make an involuntary forward movement, as though he would lift his arms to set them around the slender blue shape in front of him; and she was aware of the sense of passion that moved in him, as certainly as if it had been moving within herself, and she thought confusedly of James, of that dark afternoon on the sofa in the back room of the shop and the way her own limbs had seemed to melt and then reform in newer, more sensate shapes; and closed her eyes against not only what she saw, but what she felt. The link between herself and her father was more than that of mere affection; they shared in some sort the same physical attributes. Her passion for James, his for this woman; it tied them so close that it made her feel her breath was being squeezed out of her body, for was she not even now waiting for James to come to her with news of how he planned to separate them, to take from Abel not only her own person, but other things as well——

But then her feelings were fragmented by the sound. It all seemed to happen at once; her mother's scream, Lilith's sickening choking cry, and a curious growling sound that emanated from her father, and she snapped open her eyes to see that he had both hands about Lilith's throat and was shaking her and shaking her, so that her head banged helplessly against her shoulder and her face was suffused and her eyes staring wetly.

Abby stared in blank horror for one brief moment, aware of rather than seeing her mother's shrinking frame cowering against the door, and then she moved with a speed of which she hardly realized herself capable, and was beside that struggling pair, and reached up and put her hands over Abel's shoulders and seized whatever she could to pull him away from the woman; and by some vast good fortune her hands had closed about his jaw and her pulling made his head come back, and he almost choked in his turn at the pressure of it.

It seemed as though this brought him abruptly to an awareness of what he was doing, for he immediately stopped the shaking movement, and then very slowly unclawed his hands and dropped them to his sides; Lilith stood in front of him with both her own hands held to her where already the weals and bruises he had inflicted were beginning to show, and looked at him with her eyes glittering with a most curious expression in them. To Abby, giving her one revolted glance, it seemed as though she were pleased, was finding some deep and curious pleasure in what had happened, and Abby, sickened, pulled her eyes away and as gently as she could put her arm about her father's broad shoulders and moved him away, and led him to a chair, forcing him to sit down upon it.

There was a short heavy silence, and then Lilith made a curious sound, half cough, half little moan and then took her hands from her throat and raised them to her hair, and patted it, almost absentmindedly, as though all that mattered was the disarray into which her Grecian curls had been thrown.

'You are—still—the Abel I—knew,' she said, and her voice was deep and cracked, and she coughed, painfully, and then tried again. 'Still the man I knew—loving me yet——'

'I hate you—I have always hated you——' He almost wailed it, in a voice so unlike his usual sure note that Abby sank to her knees beside him, and put her hands over his on his lap and looked anxiously up into his face. 'Papa?' she said urgently, 'Papa—are you all right?——'

'All right?' Lilith said, and though her voice was still hoarse, it came more easily now. 'He is as right as ever he can hope to be, for he loves me still, and always will, the foolish, stupid great lump of a half-witted sawbones that he is——' She began to laugh, but now it had a cracked note. 'As stupid as his son, who loves me too, and always will——'

'No. No, no, no——'

It was Dorothea, and her voice made them all turn to look at her in vague surprise for they had for the moment quite forgotten she was there, pressed hard against the door as though she would melt into it and through it if she but could, and she stood there staring at the three of them, with her face white and stricken. 'No, not Jonah. Not Jonah ——' she said, and looked at Lilith. 'It is not so——'

'What? That he loves me?' Lilith seemed to have quite recovered herself now, though her voice remained husky, and she moved easily away and back to her chair beside the fire. 'Of course he does! He has been mooning about after me these past I don't know how many weeks, as boring as a baby! He is as besotted with me as ever his father was—and still is——' and she shot a look of delighted malice at Abel still sitting heavily in his chair with Abby at his side. 'She may have taken him away with her, and think she has him, but she will discover just as you did—she will discover the truth of it——' and she settled herself in her chair and with one gentle forefinger touched her bruised throat.

'She?' Abby said. 'Who is she? Where has he gone?' It was now a matter of supreme importance to Abby that she should get from this woman all the information she could about Jonah's whereabouts, so that she could gather her parents about her and bear them away from this dreadful room with its gilt fripperies reflecting the dancing mocking firelight. She felt as though it were she who was the parent, and Abel and Dorothea who were the helpless ones, the ones who needed care and protection. 'Where is Jonah?'

'Gone away,' Lilith said, almost absently, leaning back and gazing at Abel with a considering look on her face. 'With Celia. I do not know where they have gone, nor anything else. They have gone—that is enough——'

'No—no——' Dorothea said again, and then she turned and scrabbled at the door, dropping her reticule, and still moaning, 'No—no—no,' with a monotonous keening sound she managed to pull it open, and went plunging through into the hallway beyond.

'Mama——' Abby scrambled to her feet, almost falling over as one shoe caught in the hem of her gown.

'Oh, let her go,' Lilith said lazily. 'She was always a fool——'

And Abby shot one look of sheer hate at her, and hesitated for the moment, wanting to say something, anything that would shake that hateful beauty into the ugliness of the reality of what was happening; it was as though she was on a stage playing before a vast audience instead of just the three of them, she thought confusedly, and I want her to know what it is she is doing, I want her to know—but almost immediately she turned and followed her mother, hurrying across the room and through the door and down the staircase.

But not immediately enough, for even as she reached the top of the flight, she saw her mother in the hallway below pull open the front door and go hurtling through, out to the cold street outside. She followed, holding her gown almost knee-high so that she could speed the more easily after her, and reached the doorstep as her mother's figure went on across the pavement and straight out into the traffic-busy cobbles of the roadway, with never a look to either side.

It was almost absurd in its inevitability, almost funny to see the way the horse pulling the fashionable carriage reared at the urgent tug at the reins given by the white-faced jarvey above, almost comic to see the way its rear hooves slithered on the icy cobbles so that it went agonizingly screaming on to its back, its great yellow teeth gleaming in the twilight and its eyes glaring whitely above its flaring nostrils; and most ridiculous of all to see the way one of its forelegs swung out in a glancing blow to hit the side of Dorothea's head and send her sprawling ludicrously into the mud of the gutter.

32

The room was very bright though the bustling woman he had hired to help with the nursing had tried her best to fill it with traditional sickroom gloom by drawing the heavy curtains close; but Abel had been adamant. The late April sunshine must be allowed in, and even more revolutionary, so must the April air. The windows were to be set open to the sun all day, and the fire kept banked high to warm it, he had instructed. He had with his own hands brought bowls of daffodils and narcissi and tiny purple grape hyacinths to strew about the little tables and these too added to the curious appearance of half-hearted gaiety the chamber presented to visitors. Even Charles Bell had remarked on it when he had come at Abel's request from his home in Soho Square to see Dorothea, standing at the door and looking about him with his brows slightly raised.

'Indeed,' he had said in his deep soft drawl—not quite as Scottish as it had been in those long-ago days when he had been Abel's tutor at Great Windmill Street, but still carrying some of the sounds of his northern childhood in its burring notes—''tis more the chamber of a bride than of a poor sick lady. But ye do well to nurse her so; I would I could have every sickroom as light and airy. Well, my dear man, I am sorry to see you thus! A great lady, your good wife, for I recall how well she wrought when your patron died and you were so sore distressed by it——'

He moved across the room to stand beside the big bed, with its heavy green curtains pulled well back and looped to the bedhead, to stare down at the figure that lay so still and so tidy in the middle of it. ''Tis indeed a tragedy to see her in such a case——'

She was lying with her head supported on a flat pillow, and her thin fair hair had been pinned on top by the nurse in a way that made her look very young, like a baby prepared for the bath. Beneath that childish topknot the face looked flat and smooth, the faint lines that had been used to run from nose to mouth and between the thin fair brows quite rubbed out. The mouth was slightly open, and dragging a little to one side, and the eyes too had a lopsided look, for while one lid was neatly closed the other was only partially over the eye, leaving a line of white clearly to be seen. Her hands lay quietly on each side of the small hump that was her body, and the sheet was folded across her breast so neatly and moved so very slightly with the faintness of her breathing that it could almost have been carved of wood instead of being made of fabric.

Bell had spent a lot of time in his examination and Abel had watched him closely, for there was no man in all England—or Europe come to that—who knew more about the passage or the behaviour of the nerves of the body than did Bell. Abel had been at the meeting of the Royal College of Physicians at which Bell had first discussed his great discovery of the two kinds of nerves the human frame included, and had marvelled at the delicacy of his techniques. Now, watching him use those same techniques in his examination of Dorothea as he drew wisps of charpie across the sagging side of her face, watching closely for some activity in twitching muscles, and moved her hands and fingers in a vain attempt to elicit some response, he marvelled again. And then felt the weight of the knowledge that nothing could be done for her sink deeper still into his consciousness.

Bell had confirmed that knowledge in his no-nonsense, direct way, but with a warmth in his voice and with a touch of one shapely hand upon Abel's shoulder that did much to express his sympathy.

'She has brain damage of an order that I doubt can be regenerated, Lackland. Had she rallied in her consciousness at all since the injury, I would have had some hope that a degree of will could return to her, but after four weeks——' He had shaken his head and pursed his lips. 'Well, you know as well as I. There's naught we can do.'

'I thought of trephining,' Abel had said heavily. 'Once her fever had subsided a little and the first fears we had for her life had been resolved.'

Bell shook his head again. 'Come, man, ye must know as well as any that the time has passed for that! Besides, she has no bony injury of the skull, has she? No pieces of bone are driven into the brain tissue, so the most we could have expected to do was remove such blood clot as might have formed. And after all this time—no. The nerves are damaged beyond repair, I do assure you. 'Tis an interesting case. The damage seems to have produced some of the effects of an apoplectic fit, did you observe? Aye, no doubt ye did, no doubt ye did, for you are a considerable clinician, and—well, let be. I can offer naught to her and to you but my regrets. I'll come again if you feel the need of me, for friendship's sake—but there's naught I can do for her, no more than any other physician.'

And Bell had gone away and left her to him, and Abel had sent the nurse off to gossip in the kitchen, and sat down, as he always did now, in the chair that was on the right of the bed, between the window and that silent blankfaced figure, to look at her and brood and watch and brood again.

Abby had tried at first to persuade him not to do so, for she had realized very soon that as her mother was now, so would she be for the rest of her life, however long or short that might be. She had wept on James's shoulder, pouring out her anger at Lilith who had made it happen, her deep remorse because she had been too slow to catch her mother, her anguish at the state into which her father had been thrown, and then had wiped her face and breathed deep and set about making what repairs she could to the life of the household at Gower Street.

Her attempt to stop Abel from passing what little time he spent in Gower Street at Dorothea's side failed totally. He had sat and stared, his chin on his chest and his hands thrust into his trouser pockets, never taking his eyes from Dorothea's face while Abby had spoken to him softly, and then more loudly, moving from wheedling to crisp common sense to peremptory commands to quit the bedchamber, but he had only sat and ignored her, until the time when, driven beyond all patience, she had suddenly wept (and that day she had been feeling somewhat queasy anyway, and been unable to eat her food for the qualmishness of her stomach, and that too had contributed to her loss of self-control); and then he had turned on her almost viciously and cried out, 'It is all I can do for her! It is all I could ever do! Hold your tongue and leave me to what I must do!'

The despair in his voice had brought her more of those rare and therefore painful tears and she had crept away to seek out James (who now came to the house in Gower Street more often than he had ever dared to do in the past, for Abel was quite oblivious of anything beyond Dorothea's bedchamber) to creep gratefully into his arms.

He had held her close, and told her that he knew how distressed she was, and that he wished nothing but what was best for her, for he loved her above anything in the world, and that was why they must talk of their own plans.

'For, my beloved,' he had said softly, 'we have so little time—so little time. I would not have any harm come to you for want of a little haste—unseemly as it may seem to you in your present state——'

And she had nodded, and scrubbed at her red eyes with her wisp of cambric handkerchief and listened gravely as he told her what must be done to set their affairs in order, and tried not to think of her father's silent figure above stairs, or of her mother's still and shrunken shape in the great bed.

And remembering the way she and her mother had talked that afternoon in the shop (and could it have been the same day as the one on which they had gone to North Audley Street and the horror had happened? Surely not! The two events seemed in her memory to be set apart by aeons of time!) she accepted all that James said to her with a nod of her head, and her agreement that she would do as he bade her.

'For he is strong, is he not, James? Papa is strong?' she had said with a sudden urgency and James had looked at her, puzzled for a moment, and then bent his head and kissed her. It was no wonder to him that she was sometimes a little bewildered, in a way that she had never been before, with so much happening to her and around her, he told himself. She needed much assurance that all would be well in the future——

'Aye, my little love,' he had murmured soothingly, 'your Papa is very strong——'

And so it had gone on, weeks passing with painful slowness during which Dorothea lay silent and helpless in the bed upstairs, fed pap through a baby's feeding cup by the bustling nurse, and being washed and cleaned and handled as though she were an idiot child, incapable of feeling or knowledge or anything but the most basic of animal functions. She breathed and swallowed and evacuated and that was all.

Each day Abel spent long hours out of Gower Street talking with the trustees and supervising at the hospital the renovations being made to the buildings in Endell Street, but as soon as he returned to the house, he went to Dorothea's room to eat his frugal dinner at her side and to sleep on a truckle bed at her feet, always silent.

To Abby it was as though her mother had in truth died that cold afternoon beneath the horse's hooves in North Audley Street, and she set about organizing the household as though in fact there had been a funeral, and she must take charge. She arranged for Barty to go to school at Mr Loudoun's immediately, not waiting for the commencement of the academic year, and he had gone gladly, hating the heavy atmosphere of the house where he was hissed at and frowned at if he so much as raised his voice; home was no pleasure at all to him now, little as it had been before.

She talked, too, to Miss Ingoldsby at some length, extracting from her a promise to remain with Mary and Martha no matter what should befall.

'For I cannot hide from you, dear Miss Ingoldsby, that we are sorely set about, and I—I do not know what may happen in the future. My—my father is so bereft that I cannot talk to him of any domestic matters and I cannot be certain I will always be here, can I?' Abby had said earnestly. And Miss Ingoldsby, who had observed James's comings and goings with her shrewd and not too romantic eye had promised gladly enough, for she had much affection for her charges. And had promised too, to keep an eye to the care of little Gussy if Abby were not about, by any chance, to oversee the nurse. All of which had comforted Abby a great deal, for as well as the sense of responsibility she had, she was carrying a great burden of guilt with her which sharpened her usually round face to a new ascetic look and smudged purple shadows beneath her eyes.

She had also made some efforts to seek out Jonah, enquiring after him in various places, and even writing a stiff little letter to Lilith on the subject. But Lilith had ignored it, and curiously Abby had been glad of that. It would gain nothing for her mother if Jonah did know of her pitiable state, and in a rather muddled way Abby felt that Dorothea herself would not wish her dearly beloved Jonah to see her thus.

'Let him be happy,' Abby had whispered to her mother's silent figure one afternoon when she had gone to her chamber to look at her and check that the nurse was doing all as she should. 'Let him be happy. That would please you most of all.' And then, embarrassed by what seemed to her to be mawkish sentiment, she had upbraided the nurse for an untidiness detected on the table which bore her mother's feeding cup and dish of arrowroot and gone rustling away.

Slowly the house moved into a rhythm of life, not particularly different from that which it had followed in the days when Dorothea had moved about the rooms and given her orders. It was as though the house and its routine had swallowed her up and made a space within itself for her, and then forgotten her.

But Abby and Abel did not forget her; or rather, Abby could not remove from her mind her concern for Abel's incredibly changed behaviour.

Always he had been a dour man, but to her at least, always reasonably accessible. As long as she could remember she had known she could coax him out of his megrims, that she above all others could help him to relax and be comfortable. Now she no longer could and the mystery was that he had become as abstracted as he was, so far removed from her, because of Dorothea. Knowing as she did how little overt affection he had ever shown Dorothea, knowing how often he had been irritated to the point of fury by her it puzzled Abby vastly to see him thus.

Had she not attempted to reassure her mother, over and over again, that Abel cared for her—while believing in fact that he did not? Had she not tried to smooth the way between them ever since she had been old enough to comprehend the situation? Yet now Abel was behaving like the most bereaved of men, like one who had lost the person he loved most dearly in all the world.

She turned, of course, to James with her dilemma. In these past weeks the bond between them, powerful as it had been before, had become extraordinarily close, draining both of them in equal measure to the way it fortified them. To Abby it was as though the knowledge of her own powers that she had always had, the awareness of her own capabilities and good sense, had been thinned in some way by the existence of James; she was at depth the same person perhaps, but in a much altered way. With James's approval, James to talk to about her ideas and feelings she was twice the person she had been; but without him, when he was not there to be consulted on whatever it was that concerned her, be it trivial or important, she was in some way attenuated. She felt sometimes as though he were actually physically attached to her, and when he was absent from her side she was flayed, exposed, and shivered a little in the knowledge of her own vulnerability. To be so deep in love, so dependent, so greatly in need of another person was bliss, was hell, was all there was of comfort, and all the agony of fear, all at once; and sometimes when the memory of his attacks of illness came struggling to the surface of her mind she felt physically sick, as a tide of cold terror rose in her.

But that fear was not to be entertained, could not be looked at, and in her worry about her father she turned gratefully to James.

They were sitting one afternoon in early May in the back room of the shop, for now the household was running smoothly there was no need for Abby to be in Gower Street all the time, and she needed to escape to the comfort of her ledgers and the work of the apothecary's establishment. James had been telling her of the final arrangements he had made to lease the little house in Paddington Green upon which his eye had lighted, and haltingly, had gone on to explain to her how it could be arranged that they be wed even without Abel's deliberate consent.

'If we have the banns called by Mr Spenser—for that is your parish church, is it not?' She had nodded. 'And if none object at any of the three times they are called, then we may legally be wed, even though you be under age.' He looked at her anxiously. 'You have not changed your mind in any way?'

She gave him a swift smile, strained but full of warm affection. 'About wedding you? I never could, my love. But I am—most anxious about Papa——'

He nodded, but said nothing, keeping his eyes on her face.

'He behaves so strange——' she said, and frowned, and shook her head a little as though to clear it. 'I thought I knew him, but I do not understand him at all! In all the years I can remember he was short of patience with her, and was so often driven to great irritation by her, and spent little enough time in her company, yet now—he sits and looks at her and cares for her, does things for her that—that are more the province of the nurse—why, she told me he even changes the bedding when—when—oh, I do not *understand* it! Why should he show such—such tenderness to her now, when she cannot know of it?' Her eyes suffused suddenly, although she did not cry. 'It would have given her such pleasure——'

He came across the room to sit beside her, and she moved on her chair to make space for him, and rested her head on the comfort of his shoulder.

'For all your wisdom, you do not really know your father as well as you think,' he said. 'I have worked with him these many years. I told you, did I not, that I once idolized him? And then—then learned to be angry with him, for it cannot be denied he is a hard man, with little concern for others—except for *some* others—and it is this that you do not realize, my love.'

She looked up at him, and frowned. 'He has always had concern for me,' she said.

James shook his head. 'Interest, perhaps—but not *concern*. That tenderness you now perceive in him, this care he shows your poor Mama—he never showed you this.'

She narrowed her eyes, trying to remember, and then nodded slowly. 'Aye, I see your point. But you say he has concern for *some*? How do you mean?'

He put her away from him gently and stood up and began to move around the room, finding it easier to talk when he could use his hands and body to express his ideas, and she watched him with a sense of deep pleasure underlying her interest in what he was saying.

'Your father is a man who was, I believe, born to the business of the surgeon. I know it was almost accidental that he entered the world of the apothecary and then trained for surgery, but he was born for it, of this I am certain. You see, Abby, there is a part of him that I know and you do not—I have seen him when he is with patients, with ill people. He is very different then——'

'Different?'

'Aye.' He stood still, and looked at her, but his eyes were a little glazed, as though he were seeing a scene enacted before his eyes. 'I recall once going with him to Tavistock Street to oversee some matters of medicines, and spending time watching him with those people who came to him—such dreadful people, such diseased and rotting carcases of people as—oh, you must never see such sights yourself, for they are the most sickening and—and degrading possible—but with those people, your Papa——' he blinked and his blank gaze focused on her again. 'He seemed to speak the same, to be as curt and harsh as he ever is with any of us, but with them he was *different*. I cannot give it words to describe it other than that. But this tenderness, this concern for your

296

Mama that you now discern in him, and that you feel was absent when she was well and in full command of her senses— I can comprehend it It is because she is not whole, you see——'

There was a long silence, and then Abby said almost timidly, 'Do you mean, James, that he now has an affection for Mama that he never had before?'

'I cannot say that! I know little of his feelings for your Mama, although affection must have existed in some sort, for he has been wed to her close on a score of years, has he not, and they had many children ——' He reddened a little. 'I cannot say that he had no affection for her in the past, though you, I know, believe he lacked it. But I am as sure as I stand here that he feels great concern for her now and concern can be a form of affection, can it not?'

'I would wish to believe you,' she said abruptly, 'for although we are set to wed, I cannot hide from you my—my feeling of wickedness. To leave her now, in such a state—to leave *him* in such a state—it seems——'

'I know,' he said. 'And I am not, I promise you, trying to tell you tales to persuade you to complete our plan, for you must be as eager for it as I, if it is to be right. I do most truly believe that your Mama has all the attention she can ever need from your father, because he is the man he is. And he—I cannot say what his needs are. He has always been too silent a man for me to know aught of him.'

'And he is strong,' Abby said, but she said it so softly that he did not hear her.

'So, dearest Abby, shall we set about the banns? For I am afraid— so afraid, for you. It has been—some weeks since—I am so anxious for you——'

She smiled up at him. 'But pleased as well?'

'Pleased? There is no word to express——' He shook his head, and said with an oddly stubborn look on his face. 'We must tell him. If you are ready.'

'Yes,' she said. 'We must tell him—but not quite yet—'

33

She could feel the hum of the place even before her carriage finally came to a stop at the stage-door. For a moment she leaned back against the blue velvet squabs so that her face was hidden by the curtain and looked out at the mob of people hanging about, leaning against the theatre walls, and eagerly grabbing at the playbills which were being hawked by an enterprising boy in a tattered but still glittering old stage costume.

Above them the lights smoking heavily against the greasy stone walls guttered and flared, lifting the muddy street below to occasional brilliance, and in the gutters hurdy-gurdy men, sellers of hot pies and oysters, and hawkers of gallows ballads jostled for the crowd's attention, while pickpockets and sauntering bright-eyed prostitutes slid among them on their business affairs; altogether it was the warm familiar scene she knew so well, and loved so dearly, and she sighed in contentment. Whatever happened, this never changed. Always there were *her* people waiting for her at *her* theatre, always the lights and the smell and the excitement. No matter what stupid people like the wretched Celia and the even more wretched Jonah might do—above all, whatever the hateful Abel might do, she still had this. And tonight was her Benefit and proved likely to be even more glorious and glittering than ever it had been in previous years.

She moved then, and at once Hawks opened the door of the carriage and jumped awkwardly down, and the handsome footman (and she had picked him solely for his good looks and well-rounded calves, caring not a whit that the man was well known from Seven Dials to Marble Arch to be a thief and blackguard) leaped down to set the steps for her, and she came out of the carriage to stand poised at the top of them, wrapped in her swan's-down pelisse and peeping out prettily from beneath her feathered bonnet.

As though she had jerked a piece of string held between her white fingers, string which at the other end was attached to the heads of the mob, they turned, and a soft cry went up, a sort of combined sigh and shout of welcome, and she dimpled and lifted her head, and stepped with great daintiness down the steps to go sailing towards the stage-door. And even though she appeared to be laughingly holding them off, with every gesture and every sound she made she in fact invited them closer until she was quite surrounded by adoring eager faces and was carried to the stage-door being held open for her in a wave of noise and affection with Hawks, cursing and shoving, plodding along behind her.

If he could see *this*, she thought viciously, he'd be sorry. He'd know better than to look at her as he had that afternoon, crouched above the crumpled figure of Dorothea in the gutter, and looking up at her window with an expression of such loathing, such disgust on his face that even she had shrunk back, and dropped the curtain. It had not been *her* fault the stupid woman had seen fit to throw herself under a horse! The world was full of idiots, and well rid of those who were more idiotish than most, and he should, in some sense, have been grateful to her. . . .

She set the dressing-room into a vast bustle, sending servants to fetch bottles of wine and plates of beef for she was, she announced charmingly to the collection of lounging gentlemen who had enough money to bribe the stage doorman into letting them within to wait for her away from the stink of the cheap mob, quite famished! And there had been jokes about her looking as though she dined on nectar and ambrosia only, and extravagant compliments about her being so ethereal that she surely needed no food at all, before she sent them packing with a wave of her hand so that she could settle to the important business of preparing for the performance.

First she ate ravenously, for she was in truth very hungry, although she sent the wine away to be prepared for her after the play, for she was too much the professional in every way to dull the edge of her awareness with alcohol before an appearance. She owed it to herself to be in perfect form when she stepped on to that stage, and for such perfection

Lilith Lucas had no need of the artificial stimulants upon which other, lesser lights depended; she carried within herself all the bubble and sparkle that anyone could possibly want.

While Hawks, grim-faced and muttering as ever, prepared her dressing-table with its clean hares' foot brushes and pots of paint and set her costumes ready, she went, wrapped in a dark shawl, along the narrow corridors to the stage. She enjoyed this little journey, one she made each night before a performance. It took her along the narrow walkways behind the scenery which hung from the creaking swaying struts high above in the shadows and which were held to the stage level by ropes and braces, through the heavy reek of fish-glue size and lime and gas (for however carefully the lights were handled, there was always a small leak of the stuff to thicken the air) and the undertow of rotten wood and damp cloth, finally to deliver her at the prompt side of the great shadowy stage.

The scene-shifters, sitting over their jugs of porter and packs of greasy cards, shuffled to their feet and bobbed their heads as she passed them, but she ignored them and went directly to the great wall of fabric that was the front curtain. There was the peephole that Castleton had arranged at her command long ago; a tiny hole, backed by gauze and flapped over to hide it when not needed, it gave a clear view of the whole auditorium.

Each night she would go to look and with her swift eye and even swifter brain estimate the size of the house and the resultant value to her in hard cash. It would be a brave management that dared to try any tricks with its mathematics and underpay Lilith Lucas any of her share of the takings. She knew to the last penny what was due to her, and all from that one swift scrutiny of the house.

Tonight she was most particularly concerned to know how business was (not that she doubted for a moment that it would be capacity and beyond with the rear of the auditorium swaying with those willing to pay to stand to see her) because tonight was her yearly Benefit. Much as she earned on every other night she appeared—for she was one of the rare London performers who could command a percentage of the takings, rather than a mere salary—on these nights she expected to earn more than simple cash. Every Benefit she had ever had had yielded her the thing she most enjoyed: possessing property. Before the week was out, after a Benefit, she always claimed her money from the management and exchanged it even more swiftly for a house upon which she had set her avaricious gaze.

She had bought the Endell Street house, she remembered suddenly now, with the Benefit of 1826; she must have been mad to sell it to him as she had, for barely sixty pounds more than she gave for it. Standing there before the curtain she felt her anger suddenly rise; she *must* have been clean out of her attic to relinquish a property for the mere pleasure of revenge, just to keep him there long enough to see his precious Dorothea arrive, and for her to see him in her house. Where was the dividend in revenge? Sheer lunacy it had been!

But then she breathed deep, and smiled as she recollected the look on his face when he had seen Dorothea arrive; it had in many ways been worth it, to see him look like that, and she could use the money obtained from him to buy elsewhere, after all. Not that he had paid in full yet for the way he had treated her over the years, neglecting and ignoring her—and then memory played her a most cruel trick, for she suddenly saw herself in that little basement room in Old Compton Street, crouching over her fire cooking bacon for him, while he knelt at her side looking at her with those green eyes of his lit with warmth, obviously liking her, and not merely wanting her, and making her feel as comfortable and as pleased with herself as she could ever remember being, before or since——

With a sudden sharp movement she lifted her hand to sweep aside the flap that covered her peephole, and with the movement swept away thoughts of Abel and everyone to do with him; she would not think of such matters! It was all dead and gone and what mattered now was the money that was in the house tonight, and nothing else; and she looked at the rows of seats in the galleries and the pit fast-filling with a pushing, sweating, shouting crowd of good-natured Londoners, and at the heavy velvet seats of the better sort bearing the markers to show they had been bespoken by the quality who would come later, and let contentment rise in her. If this house brought her less than five hundred pounds she'd be very surprised——

And as she applied her paint with swift experienced fingers, and swore at Hawks as she tweaked her hair into shape, and pulled herself into the stays she needed under the heavy medieval costume she let the sense of power and energy build in her, as it always did in a manner that was both familiar and yet new and exciting each time. The sense of hollowness in her belly; the faint tremor that was felt by her but was so deep within that it never transmitted itself to hands or head or legs as it did with less capable actors; the faint dryness of the mouth, the pounding in her ears—she loved the sensations, and revelled in them to the extent of deliberately imagining herself on stage so that they were all intensified to go sliding through her body like a tide; it was all deeply, completely enjoyable. And necessary, too, for without such feelings she would never give as good a performance as she was capable of giving, as well she knew.

They greeted her first entrance with a vast roar of approval, setting up a wall of sound against which she could almost lean, and wickedly she swept across stage and turned her back on them, immediately to look over her shoulder with a glance so delicious and so provocative that the sound became almost hysterical in its intensity; and then turned upstage again to see the face of her leading man, the feeble if beautiful Edwards, looking daggers at her. Again she threw her outrageous glance of complicity at the audience who knew precisely what she was about, and added delighted laughter to their noise.

Even after the audience had settled down to watch the play and she had slipped into the pattern of it, throwing her body and her passions about the huge light-bedazzled stage with apparent abandon, and yet with total control shrewdly judged and exercised to a hairsbreadth, the magic went on. She felt it herself, knew she was giving a superb performance, one of her best ever, and regretted for one brief instant that it was not a better play, but then went on to give each scene all she had, and more besides; loving her audience, herself, and everything that went to make up this glorious, joyous, perfect thing that was Lilith Lucas on her Benefit night.

There was only one moment during the play when her concentration faltered, and then so momentarily and so lightly that only she knew it; when Castleton came on, taking over the tiny role of Leontes. They went through the ritual, and then came the line, 'My Lady fair, thou art to me the apogee of glory, and naught of pestilence shall I, your swain, allow to touch the hem of thy gown——' and she looked at Castleton, at the lined and tired face under the heavy paint, and saw for one brief moment Jonah's face, a pale handsome face, long and narrow with a fine mouth and green eyes, so like his father at his age——

They came backstage afterwards in their hordes, so that the green-room was packed as tight as a drum and the noise of conversation and laughter could be heard clear out to the street, where still the mobs of ordinary people hung about, waiting for a glimpse of their angel, and fighting and chaffering among themselves long after most sober citizens of the town were abed, until indeed the hay wains came lumbering heavily into the street bearing the first of the Kentish making for the City's horses. She had removed her costume swiftly, and was cleaning her face of its heavy coating when Hawks set a small prick into her bubble of self-satisfaction.

'I could copy this sort o' sleeve, I reckon, in one o' yer day gowns ——' she said thoughtfully, holding up the heavy costume with its thickly embroidered front and trailing sleeves.

'Whatever for?' Lilith said, a little abstractedly, as she rubbed a little lanolin into her throat. ''Tis a pleasant enough mode, but of no special virtue——'

'It would 'ide yer arms a bit,' Hawks said, as she went across the room to hang the gown. 'Round the top, like. Gettin' a bit on the scraggy side, ain't they?'

Of course she had sworn at her, and fumed and raged, and Hawks had shrugged and gone away until her temper had subsided, but the damage had been done. She looked at her arms in the mirror, holding them above her head, and felt a sudden sense of deep depression as she noted the way the flesh was softer now from armpit to elbow than she had remembered. She was still rounded, still white-skinned and slender, but it was there, that faint movement of dependent flesh, and the sight of it quite spoiled her triumph, for the moment at any rate.

But she had put on her most pretty peignoir, the one with the drifts of frills that took Hawks hours and hours to iron, and went sweeping about the greenroom to greet her public, and further enrage her fellow actors (to whom no one paid any attention at all once Lilith Lucas appeared) and forget the cruelties of stupid maids and the passage of time.

And went home to North Audley Street at well after four o'clock, rattling in her carriage through deserted rain-washed streets where buildings leaned threateningly over the gutters to peer blindly down at her and her companion; for tonight she had felt the need of someone to share her bed, not so much because of any passion (for in fact Lilith had little interest in the pleasures of the bed, except inasmuch as they could provide her with the things she did care about) but because she was tired and a little lonely, not that she would have admitted it for the world.

Even to herself.

While Lilith in North Audley Street lay beside her handsome young captain of dragoons (who happened also to be the heir to an Earldom, a fact which had greatly enhanced his charm in Lilith's eyes), staring up at the muslin canopy above her head and thinking her own confused thoughts, her daughter Celia lay in a much less elegant bed—indeed, a most shabby and uncomfortable bed—in a smelly run-down inn in Portsmouth, curled up beside Jonah and sleeping very deeply indeed, while Jonah himself stared at the grey square that was the uncurtained window and tried to imagine what shape the company could possibly give to his play.

They were such poor performers, compared with those he had seen on the Haymarket stage so often, and had to work in so dingy and dismal a manner—he could not believe it possible that people would actually pay hard money to sit in so uncomfortable and crowded a place as the barn they called their theatre, to look at so tattered and ugly a stage and scenery—and were above all so under-rehearsed (for they had given no more than three days to the preparation of it) that nothing but disaster could possibly ensue.

He lay there and worried and chewed over in his mind the words he had written, trying to hear them as they would be spoken by this troupe of half-starved pathetic creatures who called themselves actors, and which had been the only company of the many they had approached (walking wearily from town to town in order to preserve as far as possible the dwindling store of money they had, for Celia had managed to extract very little from her mother's escritoire that day they had fled from North Audley Street) willing to accept them. And somewhere, at the very back of his mind he knew he worried about his play because it was less agonizing than worrying about their situation.

Celia was insouciant enough, could sleep peacefully at nights, convinced that all would be well for them in time, but he could not be so sanguine. When he allowed his mind to run that way, he was almost sick with fear as he imagined the sort of life that lay ahead of them, comparing himself as he was now with those worn and weary creatures with whom they now worked. To become like that—it would be unbearable.

He thought of his mother, suddenly, and how much he would like to return to Gower Street to be wrapped in the benison of her care and affection, and then, with a whispered 'Pah' turned on the lumpy mattress, and pulled Celia towards him, so that she stirred in her sleep, and then murmured contentedly and put her arms about his neck, nuzzling at his chest. For good or ill, he was a man now, and not a child. He would make his way in the world, somehow, and show them all. And he kissed Celia suddenly and very hard, so that she woke completely and blinked up at him in the darkness. But was very glad to be awake, she assured him in a whisper. Very glad——

And in some curious way Celia's warm whispering against his cheek, her eager responsiveness to his sometimes clumsy embraces (for the role of the lover was yet very new to him) fed him with a new optimism which carried him through the next day of final rehearsals on a tide of power. He seemed able to instil into the rabble of actors some of his own enormous enthusiasm for his play, so that by the time the curtain was about to rise they were on a knife edge of excitement, all of them, from the tired old manager, who had seen so many hopeful new plays thrown to an uncaring public, down to the most callow of supers who had little more to do than carry a lighted candle from one side of the stage to the other.

Jonah, peering round the side of the curtain at the rows of sailors and their girls, local tradesmen and their buxom wives and daughters, and the sprinkling of farmworkers seeking a Saturday night's entertainment found himself marvelling at the strange magic of the theatre, a magic that exerted as much of its effect in a shabby barn such as this as it did in the glories of the Haymarket. 'Do but fill a place with an eager audience,' he told himself, 'set lights and a curtained stage before them, offer some music, albeit as poor as it was here—a couple of fiddles and a pipe or two, and there is Metamorphosis. There is True Romance and True Poetry, and True——'

Celia, coming soft-footed behind him slipped her warm arm about his waist and rested her head on his back, and he turned his face to her so that she could nuzzle his cheek.

'I feel it in my bones, Jonah,' she said softly. 'I truly do. This may be but a poor place for you to see your play performed, and for me to make my stage début, but you will see—something will come of it, something good for us. I *know* it. You will be glad we did as we did and left what we did behind us. Tonight will be like dropping a stone in a pond. It will send ripples going out and out, and—oh, I am not sure what will happen, precisely, but *something* will!'

He turned to smile down at her, looking at her grey eyes fringed with not-too-expertly applied paint, at the eager lovingness that filled every plane of her face, and took each of her cheeks between his thumbs and forefingers in a gently mocking tweak.

'If you are so sure then so it will be,' he said. 'For I am learning much about you, Madam Celia. Such as that you have but to will a thing to make it happen. You have a remarkable power in that direction!'

'Have I?' she said, and smiled hugely at him. 'Have I so? Then I shall tell you something else I will. I will that you shall love me to distraction, and will wish to live your whole life with me, for ever and ever, and make us into the greatest and most famous people of the theatre in the whole of the Kingdom! What do you think of that for a will, my love?'

He laughed indulgently, feeling very adult, very strong and in control of all with which he came into contact, himself, the theatre, the world outside the theatre, everything. 'It is a splendid will! and I now will you to take yourself to the prompt side ready for your first entrance, for the curtain rises in a minute or less and you are on third. All good fortune, my love! All the good fortune in the world!'

'And you!' and with another of her swift kisses she was gone, slipping away through the narrow passageway behind the makeshift stage, and he settled himself to the painful joy of the next three hours during which his beloved play would come to life; and was startled to find that despite his preoccupation with being a playwright at his first First Night a part of his mind was thinking of the plans they would have to make to be wed, he and Celia. And he thought of her 'will' and smiled to himself in the exciting darkness in that last moment before the curtain rose. Had she willed such thoughts of marriage upon him? Well, perhaps—but it did not matter. Whatever the source of the thought, he liked it well enough.

And on that same spring evening, a wet and windy spring evening that bent the heads of the daffodils in gardens and whipped the branches of the trees into a hissing accusing crying, Abby too was thinking of the future, of plans of marriage and the effects those plans might have.

She was standing in the drawing-room at Gower Street, staring out into the street below as though she had never seen it before. The cobblestones of the roadway gleaming dully in the lights from windows and from the linkboys' smoking flares, the flat-fronted houses with their iron traceries of balconies, the caped and hatted passers-by, at all of it she stared with a sort of avidity as though she were trying to store in her memory every minute aspect of the scene. And indeed in some-wise she was. I have lived here all my life, she was thinking, all my life. I have seen this street a thousand thousand times and never looked at it. All my life——

'You are quite sure, Abby? Quite, quite certain that this is the way you want it?'

She turned from the window and smiled as reassuringly as she could at James, who was standing uncertainly beside the door with his hat held in one hand and his coat over his arm.

'You should not doubt me now, James. Have I ever swerved for one moment? I want to marry you. Tomorrow will be for me a day of——'

'Oh, I have no doubt of that!' he said swiftly. 'None at all. It was not that about which I spoke. But I still believe I should not leave you to speak to him alone. It goes against everything I feel, every care I have for you, to allow you to do so.'

'Dear James,' she said. 'You are in grave risk of making me very angry you know, persisting as you do in this argument! I have told you of all the many reasons why having you with me would be disastrous, for all of us.'

She crossed the room to take his coat from his arm, and held it out so that, willy-nilly, he had to put it on, and she straightened the fabric across his shoulders in the proprietorial way that he so loved.

'It would be cruel, too, you know,' she added in a low voice. 'He has a right, don't you think, to talk to me alone, to be treated as I always have treated him, as long as I can remember, with understanding of his nature? It is from that understanding that I tell you—again, my love, for I seem to have said it so often!—it would be quite out of place for you to be with me. Rest easy, and wait for tomorrow.'

He put his arms about her and hugged her close. 'I cannot quite believe it has come,' he said a little huskily. 'By this time tomorrow ——'

'We shall be in our own home in Paddington Green, and man and wife,' she finished with a prosaic note in her voice and kissed him, and then pushed him firmly away. 'Shall, that is, if you will be on your way now and leave me to do what must be done. I shall arrive at church tomorrow with Miss Ingoldsby at half past ten o'clock. Be sure you are on time.'

He laughed at that and hugged her again, briefly, and turned and went; she stood again at the window watching his figure dwindling away into the dusk. He knew she was doing so, for just before he crossed the corner into Bedford Square he turned and raised his hat, although of course he could not see her from so far away.

She lifted her own hand, momentarily, and then dropped the curtain to turn back to the room, and look once more about it before moving purposefully to the door. The time had come, and what must be done must be done *now*. And she smiled a little wryly, remembering long ago days reading Shakespeare in the schoolroom with Miss Ingoldsby. 'If it were done when 'tis done, then 'twere well it were done quickly ——'

Really, she told herself sternly, it is quite absurd the way my mind runs away with me these days, with memories of the past, nonsensical thoughts of the future.

It is because of your state of health, a tiny voice whispered to her somewhere in the recesses of her mind, and again she smiled, but this time with a soft pleasure. For all the difficulties she and her James were suffering now, for all the misery she expected from the coming interview, the state of her health promised so much for them all, so very much.

Abel was sitting at the desk that he had had set in the embrasure of the window in Dorothea's bedchamber, and Abby stood at the doorway for a moment looking at him. He was writing in one of his notebooks; his dark head, more plentifully sprinkled with grey than she had noticed before, outlined in a nimbus of light from the oil lamp at his side. Dorothea lay in shadow, as still and silent as ever between the curtains of her bed, and a scent of hyacinths drifted to Abby's nose from the blue Delft bowl at the bedside. He never fails, she thought inconsequently. Ever day he brings her fresh flowers. He never did when she lived.

'Papa,' she said softly, 'I must talk with you.'

He wrote on for a moment, and then carefully sanded the page and closed the book before lifting his head and looking at her, his face expressionless.

'Well?'

'It is a matter of some importance, and I would ask you to come to the drawing-room so that we might talk the easier.'

He sat and stared at her, his face a carved and wooden mask, and she felt a sudden twinge of fear. 'He knows,' she thought. 'He knows, and he is just waiting his time to treat me as I have seen him treat others, to explode into anger and to——' she felt the shrinking within her, and was angered at herself; to be so alarmed by him now, after all the years she had enjoyed his love and confidence. It was unjust and unkind in her to feel so!

'Will you come, Papa?'

'We can talk here as well as anywhere else,' he said harshly. 'We will cause no disturbance to any but ourselves.'

'I would prefer it,' she said.

'And I prefer not. What is this, Abby? You do not usually come to set me in a pother when I have work to do. If it is some domestic matter, then set about it yourself. I have neither interest nor time to deal with it.'

'It is domestic, in a sense,' she said, and came further into the room to sit composedly in a chair beside the hearth where the embers of the fire glowed sadly in the dimness. But for all that look of composed calmness as she folded her hands on her taffeta lap and crossed her ankles neatly, she was in a turmoil with her pulses beating thickly in her throat.

'I have to speak to you, Papa, about my plans for my future. They concern you in many ways, and you will, I fear, be angered by some matters of which I have to tell you. I ask you to hear me out, to try to understand that I do what I do because I am certain that I must, and that I would not hurt you in any way, in any way at all, where it is in my power to avoid it.'

She stopped and coughed a little, for her voice was husky, and then almost against her will burst out, 'Oh, Papa, please, please not to be hurt, not to be angry with me, for I do love you so, and I have been so wretched fretting about it all!'

'You speak in riddles,' he said after a moment. 'With none of your normal good sense. You had best explain yourself.'

He turned his head to look into the shadows at Dorothea, and Abby sat very still and felt the ache start in her, the ache that came from tears that wanted to be shed, from the yearning of a small child to throw herself at both her parents, and bid them to live and be happy and young and loving to each other and to herself, and she swallowed hard, and told herself confusedly, 'You are not a child now, no longer a child, but a woman grown——'

'Papa, I am to be married tomorrow morning,' she said, and her voice sounded so harsh and sharp in her own ears that she wanted suddenly to throw herself across the room at his feet and cry aloud, 'No, no—it is not true, I am but bamming you, it is only a game, of course I am not to be married, of course I shall not leave you, not ever!'

But she had said it, and his head snapped round and he stared at her with eyes so shadowed in the light of the oil lamp that she could not see any expression in them at all.

'What did you say?'

'I am to be married tomorrow morning. At Mr Spenser's church.' She knew her voice trembled now and could do nothing about it. 'The banns were called the necessary times, it is all quite proper. It cannot be stopped now without I wish it so. Or James does.'

The name fell into the space between them like a stone down a mountainside, leaving echoes of its passage behind it. James, James, James. She seemed to hear her own voice over and over again, but she showed no sign, still sitting quiet and erect.

'James,' he said flatly. There was no hint of question in his voice, no sound of surprise. Just a flat statement. 'James.'

'James Caspar,' she said. 'I am to marry him tomorrow.' She swallowed then, and lifted her chin and looked at him very directly. 'I am carrying his child, Papa.'

Quite what she had expected him to do she did not know. In all her anxious and often agonized wonderings of the past weeks, in all her imaginings of this scene she had never managed to go beyond the statement of her situation. She had rehearsed that in her mind, over and over again. but no more. So she did not know what to do now, for after one moment of staring at her he began to laugh, a thick throaty laugh that went on and on until she put up her hands to cover her ears against the sound of it, and shook her head violently, feeling tears running down her cheeks and not knowing when or how they had started.

He stopped as suddenly as he had begun, and shakily she uncovered her ears. She took her handkerchief from her sleeve and with trembling fingers scrubbed at her pale cheeks while he watched her, his face bearing a curiously sardonic cast to it.

'So,' he said at length. 'You are to be married to James Caspar! You will bear him a child! Such schemes and plans the two of you have been brewing, to be sure! Helped, I have no doubt, by the fact that your mother has not been to hand to make some shift to control you! Well, I knew you to be a clever creature, a person of great sharpness and wit, but I would not have thought you so clever as to deceive me so completely! To use your mother's state to——'

'No!' she almost shrieked it, and jumped to her feet. 'You are wicked, wicked to say such a thing! I—we—it was before Mama's accident! Our child is to be born in no more than five months' time, Papa! I cannot, I will not have you suggest so wicked a thing! I am heartbroken that Mama should not—will not ever know of my situation! How can you be so cruel, so unjust as to——'

'And what will you feed this child of yours on? You did not think, did you, you and your precious Caspar, that I would continue to employ him after such a state of affairs has been carried on under my nose? Did you? And are you fool enough to think he cares aught for you? He will sing a different song than a wedding one when you tell him—and tell him you shall!—that not a penny piece will he ever get of me! And when he leaves you—as he will!—will you go the way of the others of your ilk, the gutter creatures who couple where they will and when they will, like animals beneath a hedge? And feed your brat on what you get for it? Have I reared a Covent Garden whore?'

She stood there staring at him, her face drained of any colour, and shook her head unbelievingly. It could not be he who spoke so, it could not possibly be. For all his harshness, all his dourness, she had never known him to speak to anyone as cruelly as this. And some of her amazement seemed to communicate itself to him, for he stopped speaking, and sat there at his desk with his back rigid and his mouth clamped tightly shut.

There was a long silence, and then they both jumped when an ember in the grate settled with a sudden flicker of light as a flame rose and died in a wisp of smoke.

She took a deep breath then and put up her hands to smooth her hair, with an almost automatic movement.

'We are to start a—an enterprise of our own,' she said dully. 'It was James's wish that he come here himself to speak to you of our plans, but I forbade him, for I thought—I hoped we could make an amiable agreement, despite what I knew would be a matter—a matter of some surprise to you. I see that I was wrong. I wish I had let him come to speak to you.' She looked now at the silent Abel with her face twisted with hurt. 'He would never have let you speak so to me,' she said and there was a sudden dignity in her. 'Never.' And she turned to the door.

Her hand was on the knob when he said with a sharp urgency, 'Abby! Where are you going?'

She had recovered some of her original composure now, and turned back to look at him with her face quiet and expressionless again.

'I go now to my room,' she said. 'Tomorrow, as I told you, I shall be married, and we go to live and work together in Paddington Green. If you ever have need of us you will find us there. We will not fail to come should you ask us. Both of us.'

He said nothing, still sitting as he had when she first came into the room, and after a long moment she said softly, 'I love you very dearly, Papa. I always have. I understand you, and I pity you, and I love you. I had hoped you would find it in you to wish us happy, for all we have not behaved as proper as we should. What I did I did not do from any wish to be perverse or wilful. It just happened to me, Papa, and I thought you would in some measure understand, for you are a man of your own will, not one swept by the opinions of others. I came to you hoping for understanding and acceptance. What you have given me is——' she shook her head, unable to say more, and stood there staring at him; and he stared back, but still he said nothing.

There was another long silence, broken only by the occasional muffled sound of traffic from the street outside and the hiss of the dying coals, and then she sighed softly and turned to the door again.

'We shall be at church at half past ten o'clock tomorrow, Papa. I will hope to see you there, and find we can—we can be friends again. Goodnight, Papa.'

It was raining hard, great sheets of shining water sweeping across the street, when Abigail walked down the same aisle her mother had trodden almost eighteen years earlier, clasping her new husband's arm just as Dorothea had clasped Abel's. Dorothea on her wedding day had walked with her head turned towards her husband, looking up into her Abel's face adoringly, but Abby walked with her gaze set straight ahead of her, looking at the world that waited for her outside the church doors, not needing to seek any reassurance in her new husband's eyes. She could feel his love for her, his need for her, his great concern for her, coming through the tips of his fingers which were resting on her arm.

When they reached the church door there was a little flurry as Miss Ingoldsby ran forward with a cloak to protect Abigail from the rain, and James hurried her protectively towards the waiting carriage. So she did not see the bareheaded figure standing across the square and watching the little wedding party. But see him or not, she was thinking of him as she sat there beside her new husband in the carriage, one of her hands held tightly in both of his as they went rattling through the streaming streets westwards to Paddington Green.

'Dear Abby,' James said softly, and bent his head to kiss her. 'My dear wife. Are you happy?'

She smiled up at him, her face a little paler and more peaky than it had been used to be last autumn, and said softly, 'Indeed I am. Very happy, my love. We have much to worry about ahead of us, and much work to do, but we shall contrive, shall we not? We shall contrive.'

THE PERFORMERS
Book I
GOWER STREET

Claire Rayner

The streets of London in the 1880s are no place for a
respectable gentleman to take his evening stroll –
especially around the notorious Seven Dials.

But Jesse Constam is no ordinary man. Born a child of
the gutter, he was one of the lucky ones who has escaped
the squalor of the slums, and now he lives in fashionable
Gower Street. So when a young lad tries to pick his
pockets one evening, he makes no attempt to hand the
culprit over to the law – for how could he prosecute a
phantom from his own past?

And so the future of this child – called Abel Lackland –
is subject to the whim of Jesse Constam. But his plans for
Abel are to be thwarted by the 'adoption' of another
gutter child, the rebellious Lilith, by the eccentric spice
merchant of Gower Street . . .

0 7474 0740 1
GENERAL FICTION

THE PERFORMERS
Book III
<u>PADDINGTON GREEN</u>

Claire Rayner

Abel Lackland's children are grown up and making their way in the world, in the reign of young Queen Victoria.

William and Rupert have followed their father into the medical profession. Jonah, married to the daughter of the bewitching actress Lilith Lucas, is watching his early dreams of theatrical success dwindle in the face of having to provide for his wife and children. Abby, now widowed, is a successful businesswoman, running the medicine manufacturing firm set up by her husband.

Then suddenly into the lives of Abel and his family comes something that overshadows all their private crises – uniting them in common need, yet turning one against the other . . .

0 7474 0742 8
GENERAL FICTION

SCARLET
Jane Brindle

On a fateful winter's day in 1937 eighteen-year-old Cassie Thornton boarded the *Queen Mary* and set sail for England. Her mission: to find the mysterious Scarlet Pengally, the mother who abandoned her many years ago.

Her search leads her to the West Country, and to the dark, forbidding edifice of Greystone House, where Scarlet was born, home to generations of Pengallys. Yet it is also home to an unspoken dread, and the birthplace of a tale of haunting tragedy, desperate love and a dark vengeance that had plagued a family for generations.

The key to it all is Scarlet. And Cassie must find her: because now a family's curse is threatening her own young life . . .

0 7474 0763 0
GENERAL FICTION

THE SECRET TOWER
Mary Williams

When Olwen March comes to Llangarrack, it is as an
unwilling bride. The brooding, darkly handsome Owain
Geraint is a stranger, the marriage arranged, and Olwen,
loved by another man, feels trapped amidst the lonely
beauty of the Black Mountains.

Owain, Master of Llangarrack, is a man obsessed by the
desire to regain his family's fame and fortune – and by a
deep, dark mystery that will plague Olwen's life unless
she can solve it. It is a mystery that centres on the secret
tower, a sinister, haunting place that draws Olwen like a
compelling force . . .

0 7474 0599 9
HISTORICAL ROMANCE

FORSAKING ALL OTHERS
Victoria Petrie Hay

Caught up in a new life with his smart new Cambridge
friends, Gerry Beviss lets them believe that he is, like
them, a gentleman. But he most certainly is not; Gerry is
the son of a gypsy. Only one person knows the truth
about his background: Kate Erith, and she would never
betray him. She loves him. She is the best thing in
Gerry's life – and he betrays her.

It is an act that will cost him dearly. Unhappy, yet
desperate to maintain the façade he has built up, he
plunges into a loveless marriage while Kate, unable to
forget him, risks both her career and her reputation for
him. Throughout the stormy course of their lives – from
Cambridge to South America, from the City of London
to the horseracing world in Wiltshire – their illicit love
dominates: wayward, obsessive, undiminished . . .

0 7474 0379 1
GENERAL FICTION

SEASON'S END
Anna Dillon

Senga Lundy, on the brink of womanhood, has no reason to love her domineering mother. Yet Katherine's disappearance from glittering 1930s London plunges Senga reluctantly into her affairs – and into dangerous conflict with the law and ruthless villains alike – as the secrets of Katherine's past emerge to threaten Senga's life.

Frightened and confused, Senga flees to Montmartre and then to the uneasy dazzle of pre-war Berlin, her pursuers ever closer on her heels as she draws nearer to the very heart of the mystery. But which of her protectors – tough Scotswoman Billy, enigmatic policeman Colin Holdstock, adoring Rutgar von Mann, comfortable Aunt Tilly, or even her beloved brother Patrick and Katherine herself – can she truly trust?

0 7474 0658 8
GENERAL FICTION

All Sphere Books are available at your bookshop or newsagent, or can be ordered from the following address:

    Sphere Books,
    Cash Sales Department,
    P.O. Box 11,
    Falmouth,
    Cornwall TR10 9EN.

Alternatively you may fax your order to the above address. Fax No. 0326 76423.

Payments can be made as follows: Cheque, postal order (payable to Macdonald & Co (Publishers) Ltd) or by credit cards, Visa/Access. Do not send cash or currency. UK customers: please send a cheque or postal order (no currency) and allow 80p for postage and packing for the first book plus 20p for each additional book up to a maximum charge of £2.00.

B.F.P.O. customers please allow 80p for the first book plus 20p for each additional book.

Overseas customers including Ireland, please allow £1.50 for postage and packing for the first book, £1.00 for the second book, and 30p for each additional book.

NAME (Block Letters) ....

ADDRESS ....

....

☐ I enclose my remittance for _____

☐ I wish to pay by Access/Visa Card

Number ⊔⊔⊔⊔⊔⊔⊔⊔⊔⊔⊔⊔⊔⊔⊔⊔

Card Expiry Date ⊔⊔⊔⊔